MORE
SPORTS *Best*
SHORT STORIES

Edited by Paul D. Staudohar

CHICAGO
REVIEW
PRESS
CPL

Library of Congress Cataloging-in-Publication Data
Is available from the Library of Congress.

Published by Chicago Review Press, Incorporated
814 North Franklin Street
Chicago, Illinois 60610
ISBN 1-55652-504-4

Printed in the United States of America
5 4 3 2 1

CONTENTS

ACKNOWLEDGMENTS

It is always a pleasure to be able to thank the people whose time and effort bring a book to fruition. Publisher Linda Matthews, executive editor Cynthia Sherry, and managing editor Gerilee Hundt of Chicago Review Press were indispensable as they have been for the seven previous books in this series. Sharon Melnyk and Carol Vendrillo at the University of California, Berkeley, provided helpful insights. Thanks also to the librarians and archivists who were important contributors, including Christopher Shay, librarian at *The New Yorker;* Michael Salmon from the Amateur Athletic Foundation; and Lynne LeFleur, Kristin Ramsdell, Ilene Rockman, Doug Highsmith, Judith Faust, and Stephen Philibosian from California State University, Hayward. Also from Cal State, Linda Wickwire and Julie Macedone provided helpful secretarial assistance.

In 1996, writer W. P. Kinsella and I shared a book-signing table at the National Baseball Hall of Fame, where he was the keynote speaker at the annual Cooperstown Symposium on Baseball and American Culture. Kinsella asked me why I hadn't included one of his stories in my baseball collection, an omission also noted by a reviewer of that book. I'm glad to be able to remedy the oversight in this book. Thanks also to Faith Freeman Barbato, director of permissions at HarperCollins; Florence B. Eichin, editor at Penguin Putman; Edith Golub, editor at Simon and Schuster; and Robert Scheffler, research editor at *Esquire,* for their generous assistance.

Paul D. Staudohar

INTRODUCTION

The Best Short Stories series began with *Baseball's Best Short Stories* in 1995 and includes *Golf's Best Short Stories* (1997), *Football's Best Short Stories* (1998), *Boxing's Best Short Stories* (1999), *Fishing's Best Short Stories* (2000), and *Hunting's Best Short Stories* (2000). The first collection on a variety of sports, *Sports Best Short Stories,* came out in 2001. This is the second volume devoted to short stories on a variety of sports, and our objective in this book remains the same: to present the very best short fiction on sports.

Few sports fans confine their interest to a single sport—because variety is the spice of life, they follow different games depending on the time of year. Many fans enjoy baseball in the summer, football in the fall, and basketball and hockey during the winter. Active participants in sports also schedule their activities seasonally, as they golf, fish, or hunt at different intervals during the year. Part of the attraction of indoor sports like card games and chess is that they can be enjoyed at any time.

Most of the stories in this book are about games played in team or individual athletic competition, and the bulk of them deal with traditional sports, such as baseball, horse racing, boxing, and football. But readers will also be pleasantly surprised to find stories about chess, polo, cross-country, bullfighting, card playing, and table tennis. And, as usual in this series, all of the stories draw on the full range of human expression to portray themes of love, mystery, chicanery, courage, luck, perseverance, and a rich vein of humor.

Just as sports fans follow their favorite games, players, and teams, literary buffs have their favorites, too, and this book links a wide variety of sports with a widely admired group of authors. Not all of them are famous writers, but many prominent literary figures will be found here.

Most of the stories are by American authors. Ring Lardner and W. P. Kinsella's offerings on baseball are splendid. Jack London's story revolves around boxing, and Irwin Shaw's piece on tennis is the best ever written on the sport. The talented young writer Ethan Canin talks some basketball, while the inimitable Mark Twain's hilarious spoof about frog jumping had to be included. Damon Runyon's horse racing yarn shows off his customary sagacity and wit. Other heralded American authors such as Sherwood Anderson, Frank Harris, Paul Horgan, and Richard Ford contribute wonderful stories containing drama, suspense, and humor.

In addition to the American offerings, we have Sir Arthur Conan Doyle unleashing his ace detective Sherlock Holmes to solve a mystery involving a rugby player. Other legendary British writers such as Rudyard Kipling (polo), Agatha Christie (chess), and P. G. Wodehouse (golf) provide delightful stories. Guy de Maupassant, the distinguished French author, has a fascinating yarn on fishing. The classical Russian poet and author Alexander Pushkin spins an engaging tale based on the card game faro. These well-known European writers lend a glittering international presence to the book.

There are 25 selections in this book. Many were initially published in such popular literary outlets as *Esquire, The New Yorker, Redbook,* the *Saturday Evening Post,* and *Collier's.* Some have been included in *Best American Short Stories,* while others have won literary prizes like the O. Henry award. Rudyard Kipling was honored with the Nobel Prize for literature, Richard Ford won the Pulitzer Prize, and Paul Horgan won the Pulitzer twice. Great writers provide a realism and sense of anticipation that can make reading about sports as entertaining as the real thing. Let's begin with our first adventure, on baseball, by W. P. Kinsella.

W. P. Kinsella is best known for his novel Shoeless Joe *(1983), which was made into one of the most celebrated baseball movies of all time,* Field of Dreams. *The title of this short story is drawn from that same novel, in which Joe Jackson says, "I'd wake up in the night with the smell of the ballpark in my nose and the cool of the grass on my feet. The thrill of the grass." Kinsella's other books include* Dance Me Outside *(1977),* The Iowa Baseball Confederacy *(1986), and* The Dixon Cornbelt League and Other Baseball Stories *(1995). The following story depicts irate fans who take matters into their own hands during the 1981 baseball strike, which was the first lengthy and season-interrupting work stoppage in sports history.*

W. P. Kinsella

THE THRILL OF THE GRASS (1984)

1981: THE SUMMER THE BASEBALL PLAYERS went on strike. The dull weeks drag by, the summer deepens, the strike is nearly a month old. Outside the city the corn rustles and ripens in the sun. Summer without baseball: a disruption to the psyche. An unexplainable aimlessness engulfs me. I stay later and later each evening in the small office at the rear of my shop. Now, driving home after work, the worst of the rush hour traffic over, it is the time of evening I would normally be heading for the stadium.

I enjoy arriving an hour early, parking in a far corner of the lot, walking slowly toward the stadium, rays of sun dropping softly over my shoulders like tangerine ropes, my shadow gliding with me, black as an umbrella. I like to watch young families beside their campers, the mothers in shorts, grilling hamburgers, their men drinking beer. I enjoy seeing little boys dressed in the home team uniform, barely toddling, clutching hotdogs in upraised hands.

I am a failed shortstop. As a young man, I saw myself diving to my left, graceful as a toppling tree, fielding high grounders like a cat leaping for butterflies, bracing my right foot and tossing to first, the throw true as if a steel ribbon connected my hand and the first baseman's glove. I dreamed of leading the American League in hitting—being inducted into the Hall of Fame. I batted .217 in my senior year of high school and averaged 1.3 errors per nine innings.

I know the stadium will be deserted; nevertheless I wheel my car down off the freeway, park, and walk across the silent lot, my footsteps rasping and mournful. Strangle-grass and creeping charlie are already inching up through the gravel, surreptitious, surprised at their own ease. Faded bottle caps, rusted bits of chrome, an occasional paper clip, recede into the earth. I circle a ticket booth, sun-faded, empty, the door closed by an oversized padlock. I walk beside the tall, machinery-green, board fence. A half mile away a few cars hiss along the freeway; overhead a single-engine plane fizzes lazily. The whole place is silent as an empty classroom, like a house suddenly without children.

It is then that I spot the door-shape. I have to check twice to be sure it is there: a door cut in the deep green boards of the fence, more the promise of a door than the real thing, the kind of door, as children, we cut in the sides of cardboard boxes with our mothers' paring knives. As I move closer, a golden circle of lock, like an acrimonious eye, establishes its certainty.

I stand, my nose so close to the door I can smell the faint odor of paint, the golden eye of a lock inches from my own eyes. My desire to be inside the ballpark is so great that for the first time in my life I commit a criminal act. I have been a locksmith for over forty years. I take the small tools from the pocket of my jacket, and in less time than it would take a speedy runner to circle the bases I am inside the stadium. Though the ballpark is open-air, it smells of abandonment; the walkways and seating areas are cold as basements. I breathe the odors of rancid popcorn and wilted cardboard.

The maintenance staff were laid off when the strike began. Synthetic grass does not need to be cut or watered. I stare down at the ball diamond, where just to the right of the pitcher's mound, a single weed, perhaps two inches high, stands defiant in the rain-pocked dirt.

The field sits breathless in the orangy glow of the evening sun. I stare at the potato-colored earth of the infield, that wide, dun arc, surrounded by plastic grass. As I contemplate the prickly turf, which scorches the thighs and buttocks of a sliding player as if he were being seared by hot steel, it stares back in its uniform ugliness. The seams that send routinely hit ground balls veering at tortuous angles are vivid, gray as scars.

I remember the ballfields of my childhood, the outfields full of soft hummocks and brown-eyed gopher holes.

I stride down from the stands and walk out to the middle of the field. I touch the stubble that is called grass, take off my shoes, but find it is like walking on a row of toothbrushes. It was an evil day when they stripped the sod from this ballpark, cut it into yard-wide swathes, rolled it, memories and all, into great green-and-black cinnamonroll shapes, trucked it away. Nature temporarily defeated. But Nature is patient.

Over the next few days an idea forms within me, ripening, swelling, pushing everything else into a corner. It is like knowing a new, wonderful joke and not being able to share. I need an accomplice.

I go to see a man I don't know personally, though I have seen his face peering at me from the financial pages of the local newspaper, and the *Wall Street Journal,* and I have been watching his profile at the baseball stadium, two boxes to the right of me, for several years. He is a fan. Really a fan. When the weather is intemperate, or the game not close, the people around us disappear like flowers closing at sunset, but we are always there until the last pitch. I know he is a man who attends because of the beauty and mystery of the game, a man who can sit during the last of the ninth with the game decided innings ago, and draw joy from watching the first baseman adjust the angle of his glove as the pitcher goes into his windup.

He, like me, is a first-base-side fan. I've always watched baseball from behind first base. The positions fans choose at sporting events are like politics, religion, or philosophy: a view of the world, a way of seeing the universe. They make no sense to anyone, have no basis in anything but stubbornness.

I brought up my daughters to watch baseball from the first-base side. One lives in Japan and sends me box scores from Japanese newspapers, and Japanese baseball magazines with pictures of superstars politely bowing to one another. She has a season ticket in Yokohama; on the first-base side.

"Tell him a baseball fan is here to see him," is all I will say to his secretary. His office is in a skyscraper, from which he can look out over the city to where the prairie rolls green as mountain water to the limits of the eye. I wait all afternoon in the artificially cool, glassy reception area with its yellow and mauve chairs, chrome and glass coffee tables. Finally, in the late afternoon, my message is passed along.

"I've seen you at the baseball stadium," I say, not introducing myself.

"Yes," he says. "I recognize you. Three rows back, about eight seats to my left. You have a red scorebook and you often bring your daughter. . . ."

"Granddaughter. Yes, she goes to sleep in my lap in the late innings, but she knows how to calculate an ERA and she's only in Grade 2."

"One of my greatest regrets," says this tall man, whose mustache and carefully styled hair are polar-bear white, "is that my grandchildren all live over a thousand miles away. You're very lucky. Now, what can I do for you?"

"I have an idea," I say. "One that's been creeping toward me like a first baseman when the bunt sign is on. What do you think about artificial turf?"

"Hmmmf," he snorts, "that's what the strike should be about. Baseball is meant to be played on summer evenings and Sunday afternoons, on grass just cut by a horse-drawn mower," and we smile as our eyes meet.

"I've discovered the ballpark is open, to me anyway," I go on. "There's no one there while the strike is on. The wind blows through the high top of the grandstand, whining until the pigeons in the rafters flutter. It's lonely as a ghost town."

"And what is it you do there, alone with the pigeons?"

"I dream."

"And where do I come in?"

"You've always struck me as a man who dreams. I think we have things in common. I think you might like to come with me. I could show you what I dream, paint you pictures, suggest what might happen . . ."

He studies me carefully for a moment, like a pitcher trying to decide if he can trust the sign his catcher has just given him.

"Tonight?" he says. "Would tonight be too soon?"

"Park in the northwest corner of the lot about 1:00 A.M. There is a door about fifty yards to the right of the main gate. I'll open it when I hear you."

He nods.

I turn and leave.

The night is clear and cotton warm when he arrives. "Oh, my," he says, staring at the stadium turned chrome-blue by a full moon. "Oh, my," he says again, breathing in the faint odors of baseball, the reminder of fans and players not long gone.

"Let's go down to the field," I say. I am carrying a cardboard pizza box, holding it on the upturned palms of my hands, like an offering.

When we reach the field, he first stands on the mound, makes an awkward attempt at a windup, then does a little sprint from first to about halfway to second. "I think I know what you've brought," he says, gesturing toward the box, "but let me see anyway."

I open the box in which rests a square foot of sod, the grass smooth and pure, cool as a swatch of satin, fragile as baby's hair.

"Ohhh," the man says, reaching out a finger to test the moistness of it. "Oh, I see."

We walk across the field, the harsh, prickly turf making the bottoms of my feet tingle, to the left-field corner where, in the angle formed by the foul line and the warning track, I lay down the square foot of sod. "That's beautiful," my friend says, kneeling beside me, placing his hand, fingers spread wide, on the verdant square, leaving a print faint as a veronica.

I take from my belt a sickle-shaped blade, the kind used for cutting carpet. I measure along the edge of the sod, dig the point in, and pull carefully toward me. There is a ripping sound, like tearing an old bed sheet. I hold up the square of artificial turf like something freshly killed, while all the time digging the sharp point into the packed earth I have exposed. I replace the sod lovingly, covering the newly bared surface.

"A protest," I say.

"But it could be more," the man replies.

"I hoped you'd say that. It could be. If you'd like to come back . . ."

"Tomorrow night?"

"Tomorrow night would be fine. But there will be an admission charge . . ."

"A square of sod?"

"A square of sod two inches thick . . ."

"Of the same grass?"

"Of the same grass. But there's more."

"I suspected as much."

"You must have a friend . . ."

"Who would join us?"

"Yes."

"I have two. Would that be all right?"

"I trust your judgment."

"My father. He's over eighty," my friend says. "You might have seen him with me once or twice. He lives over fifty miles from here, but if I call him he'll come. And my friend . . ."

"If they pay their admission they'll be welcome . . ."

"And *they* may have friends . . ."

"Indeed they may. But what will we do with this?" I say, holding up the sticky-backed square of turf, which smells of glue and fabric.

"We could mail them anonymously to baseball executives, politicians, clergymen."

"Gentle reminders not to tamper with Nature."

We dance toward the exit, rampant with excitement.

"You will come back? You'll bring others?"

"Count on it," says my friend.

They do come, those trusted friends, and friends of friends, each making a live, green deposit. At first, a tiny row of sod squares begins to inch along toward left-center field. The next night even more people arrive, the following night more again, and the night after there is positively a crowd. Those who come once seem always to return accompanied by friends, occasionally a son or young brother, but mostly men my age or older, for we are the ones who remember the grass.

Night after night the pilgrimage continues. The first night I stand inside the deep green door, listening. I hear a vehicle stop; hear a car door close with a snug thud. I open the door when the sound of soft-soled shoes on gravel tells me it is time. The door swings silent as a snake. We nod curt greetings to each other. Two men pass me, each carrying a grasshopper-legged sprinkler. Later, each sprinkler will sizzle like frying onions as it wheels, a silver sparkler in the moonlight.

During the nights that follow, I stand sentinel-like at the top of the grandstand, watching as my cohorts arrive. Old men walking across a parking lot in a row, in the dark, carrying coiled hoses, looking like the many wheels of a locomotive, old men who have slipped away from their homes, skulked down their sturdy sidewalks, breathing the cool, grassy, after-midnight air. They have left behind their sleeping, gray-haired women, their immaculate bungalows, their manicured lawns. They continue to walk across the parking lot, while occasionally a soft wheeze, a nibbling, breathy sound like an old horse might make, divulges their humanity. They move methodically toward the baseball stadium which hulks against the moon-blue sky like a small mountain. Beneath the tint of starlight, the tall light standards which rise above the fences and grandstand glow purple, necks bent forward, like sunflowers heavy with seed.

My other daughter lives in this city, is married to a fan, but one who watches baseball from behind third base. And like marrying outside the faith, she has been converted to the third-base side. They have their own season tickets, twelve rows up just to the outfield side of third base. I love her, but I don't trust her enough to let her in on my secret.

I could trust my granddaughter, but she is too young. At her age she shouldn't have to face such responsibility. I remember my own daughter, the one who lives in Japan, remember her at nine, all knees, elbows, and missing teeth—remember peering in her room, seeing her asleep, a shower of well-thumbed baseball cards scattered over her chest and pillow.

I haven't been able to tell my wife—it is like my compatriots and I are involved in a ritual for true believers only. Maggie, who knew me when I still dreamed of playing professionally myself—Maggie, after over half a lifetime together, comes and sits in my lap in the comfortable easy chair which has adjusted through the years to my thickening shape, just as she has. I love to hold the lightness of her, her tongue exploring my mouth, gently as a baby's finger.

"Where do you go?" she asks sleepily when I crawl into bed at dawn.

I mumble a reply. I know she doesn't sleep well when I'm gone. I can feel her body rhythms change as I slip out of bed after midnight.

"Aren't you too old to be having a change of life," she says, placing her toast-warm hand on my cold thigh.

I am not the only one with this problem.

"I'm developing a reputation," whispers an affable man at the ballpark. "I imagine any number of private investigators following any number of cars across the city. I imagine them creeping about the parking lot, shining pen-lights on license plates, trying to guess what we're up to. Think of the reports they must prepare. I wonder if our wives are disappointed that we're not out discoing with frizzy-haired teenagers?"

Night after night, virtually no words are spoken. Each man seems to know his assignment. Not all bring sod. Some carry rakes, some hoes, some hoses, which, when joined together, snake across the infield and outfield, dispensing the blessing of water. Others cradle in their arms bags of earth for building up the infield to meet the thick, living sod.

I often remain high in the stadium, looking down on the men moving over the earth, dark as ants, each sodding, cutting, watering, shaping. Occasionally the moon finds a knife blade as it trims the sod or slices away a chunk of artificial turf, and tosses the reflection skyward like a bright ball. My body tingles. There should be symphony music playing. Everyone should be humming "America the Beautiful."

Toward dawn, I watch the men walking away in groups, like small patrols of soldiers, carrying, instead of arms, the tools and utensils which breathe life back into the arid ballfield.

Row by row, night by night, we lay the little squares of sod, moist as chocolate cake with green icing. Where did all the sod come from? I picture many men, in many parts of the city, surreptitiously cutting chunks out of their own lawns in the leafy midnight darkness, listening to the uncomprehending protests of their wives the next day—pretending to know nothing of it—pretending to have called the police to investigate.

When the strike is over I know we will all be here to watch the workouts, to hear the recalcitrant joints crackling like twigs after the forced inactivity. We will sit in our regular seats, scattered like popcorn throughout the stadium, and we'll nod as we pass on the way to the exits, exchange secret smiles, proud as new fathers.

For me, the best part of all will be the surprise. I feel like a magician who has gestured hypnotically and produced an elephant from thin air. I know I am not alone in my wonder. I know that rockets shoot off in half-a-hundred chests; the excitement of birthday mornings, Christmas eves, and hometown doubleheaders boils within each of my conspirators. Our secret rites have been performed with love, like delivering a valentine to a sweetheart's door in that blue-steel span of morning just before dawn.

Players and management are meeting round the clock. A settlement is imminent. I have watched the stadium covered square foot by square foot until it looks like green graph paper. I have stood and felt the cool odors of the grass rise up and touch my face. I have studied the lines between each small square, watched those lines fade until they were visible to my eyes alone, then not even to them.

What will the players think, as they straggle into the stadium and find the miracle we have created? The old-timers will raise their heads like ponies, as far away as the parking lot, when the thrill of the grass reaches their nostrils. And, as they dress, they'll recall sprawling in the lush outfields of childhood, the grass as cool as a mother's hand on a forehead.

"Goodbye, goodbye," we say at the gate, the smell of water, of sod, of sweat, small perfumes in the air. Our secrets are safe with each other. We go our separate ways.

Alone in the stadium in the last chill darkness before dawn, I drop to my hands and knees in the center of the outfield. My palms are sodden. Water touches the skin between my spread fingers. I lower my face to the silvered grass, which, wonder of wonders, already has the ephemeral odors of baseball about it.

Literature buffs know that Guy de Maupassant (1850–1893) wrote some of the finest short stories in the world. "The Necklace," "The Piece of String," and "The Wedding Night" are among his classic tales and are set in his native France. De Maupassant was fond of the outdoors and occasionally included hunting and fishing themes in his stories. The humorous yarn presented here describes the court trial of a man who resorts to murder when an intruder has the audacity to occupy his favorite fishing hole.

Guy de Maupassant

THE HOLE
(1884)

CUTS AND WOUNDS WHICH CAUSED DEATH

THAT WAS THE HEADING OF THE CHARGE that brought Leopold Renard, upholsterer, before the Assize Court.

Round him were the principal witnesses, Mme. Flamèche, widow of the victim, Louis Ladureau, cabinetmaker, and Jean Durdent, plumber.

Near the criminal was his wife, dressed in black, a little ugly woman who looked like a monkey dressed as a lady.

This is how Renard described the drama:

"Good heavens, it is a misfortune of which I am the first and last victim and with which my will has nothing to do. The facts are their own commentary, Monsieur le Président. I am an honest man, a hard-working man, an upholsterer in the same street for the last sixteen years, known, liked, respected, and esteemed by all, as my neighbors have testified, even the porter, who is not *folâtre* every day. I am fond of work, I am fond of saving, I like honest men and respectable pleasures. That is what has ruined me, so much the worse for me; but as my will had nothing to do with it, I continue to respect myself.

"Every Sunday for the last five years my wife and I have spent the day at Passy. We get fresh air, not to say that we are fond of fishing—as fond of it as we are of small onions. Mélie inspired me with that passion, the jade; she is more enthusiastic than I am, the scold, and all the mischief in this business is her fault, as you will see immediately.

"I am strong and mild-tempered, without a pennyworth of malice in me. But she, oh la la! She looks insignificant, she is short and thin, but she does more mischief than a weasel. I do not deny that she has some good qualities; she has some, and those very important to a man in business. But her character! Just ask about it in the neighborhood; even the porter's wife, who has just sent me about my business—she will tell you something about it.

"Every day she used to find fault with my mild temper: 'I would not put up with this! I would not put up with that.' If I had listened to her, Monsieur le Président, I should have had at least three bouts of fisticuffs a month."

Mme. Renard interrupted him: "And for good reasons too; they laugh best who laugh last."

He turned toward her frankly. "Oh! very well, I can blame you, since you were the cause of it."

Then, facing the president again, he said:

"I will continue. We used to go to Passy every Saturday evening, so as to be able to begin fishing at daybreak the next morning. It is a habit that has become second nature with us, as the saying is. Three years ago this summer I discovered a place, oh! such a spot! There, in the shade, were eight feet of water at least and perhaps ten, a hole with a *retour* under the bank, a regular retreat for fish and a paradise for any fisherman. I might look upon that hole as my property, Monsieur le Président, as I was its Christopher Columbus. Everybody in the neighborhood knew it, without making any opposition. They used to say: 'That is Renard's place'; and nobody would have gone to it, not even Monsieur Plumsay, who is renowned, be it said without any offense, for appropriating other people's places.

"Well, I went as usual to that place, of which I felt as certain as if I had owned it. I had scarcely got there on Saturday when I got into *Delila*, with my wife. *Delila* is my Norwegian boat which I had built by Fourmaise and which is light and safe. Well, as I said, we got into the boat and we were going to bait, and for baiting there is nobody to be compared with me, and they all know it. You want to know with what I bait? I cannot answer that question; it has nothing to do with the accident; I cannot answer, that is my secret. There are more than three hundred people who have asked me; I have been offered glasses of brandy and liquors, fried fish, matelots,[1] to make me tell! But just go and try whether the chub will come. Ah! they have patted my stomach to get at my secret, my recipe. Only my wife knows, and she will not tell it any more than I shall! Is not that so, Mélie?"

The president of the court interrupted him:

"Just get to the facts as soon as you can."

The accused continued: "I am getting to them; I am getting to them. Well, on Saturday, July eighth, we left by the five-twenty-five train, and before dinner we went to grind bait as usual. The weather promised to keep fine, and I said to Mélie: 'All right for tomorrow!' And she replied: 'It looks like it.' We never talk more than that together.

"And then we returned to dinner. I was happy and thirsty, and that was the cause of everything. I said to Mélie: 'Look here, Mélie, it is fine weather, so suppose I drink a bottle of *Casque à mèche*.' That is a little white wine we have christened so because if you drink too much of it it prevents you from sleeping and is the opposite of a nightcap. Do you understand me?

---

[1] A preparation of several kinds of fish with a sharp sauce.

"She replied: 'You can do as you please, but you will be ill again and will not be able to get up tomorrow.' That was true, sensible, prudent, and clear-sighted, I must confess. Nevertheless, I could not withstand it, and I drank my bottle. It all comes from that.

"Well, I could not sleep. By Jove! It kept me awake till two o'clock in the morning, and then I went to sleep so soundly that I should not have heard the angel shouting at the Last Judgment.

"In short, my wife woke me at six o'clock and I jumped out of bed, hastily put on my trousers and jersey, washed my face and jumped on board *Delila*. But it was too late, for when I arrived at my hole it was already taken! Such a thing had never happened to me in three years, and it made me feel as if I were being robbed under my own eyes. I said to myself, 'Confound it all! Confound it!' And then my wife began to nag at me. 'Eh! What about your *Casque à mèche!* Get along, you drunkard! Are you satisfied, you great fool?' I could say nothing, because it was all quite true, and so I landed all the same near the spot and tried to profit by what was left. Perhaps, after all, the fellow might catch nothing and go away.

"He was a little thin man in white linen coat and waistcoat and with a large straw hat, and his wife, a fat woman who was doing embroidery, was behind him.

"When she saw us take up our position close to their place she murmured: 'I suppose there are no other places on the river!' And my wife, who was furious, replied: 'People who know how to behave make inquiries about the habits of the neighborhood before occupying reserved spots.'

"As I did not want a fuss I said to her: 'Hold your tongue, Mélie. Let them go on, let them go on; we shall see.'

"Well, we had fastened *Delila* under the willow trees and had landed and were fishing side by side, Mélie and I, close to the two others; but here, monsieur, I must enter into details.

"We had only been there about five minutes when our male neighbor's float began to go down two or three times, and then he pulled out a chub as thick as my thigh, rather less, perhaps, but nearly as big! My heart beat and the perspiration stood on my forehead, and Mélie said to me: 'Well, you sot, did you see that?'

"Just then Monsieur Bru, the grocer of Poissy, who was fond of gudgeon fishing, passed in a boat and called out to me: 'So somebody has taken your usual place, Monsieur Renard?' And I replied: 'Yes, Monsieur Bru, there are some people in this world who do not know the usages of common politeness.'

"The little man in linen pretended not to hear, nor his fat lump of a wife, either."

Here the president interrupted him a second time: "Take care, you are insulting the widow, Madame Flamèche, who is present."

Renard made his excuses: "I beg your pardon, I beg your pardon; my anger carried me away. . . . Well, not a quarter of an hour had passed when the little man caught another chub and another almost immediately and another five minutes later.

"The tears were in my eyes, and then I knew that Madame Renard was boiling with rage, for she kept on nagging at me: 'Oh, how horrid! Don't you see that he is robbing you of your fish? Do you think that you will catch anything? Not even a frog, nothing whatever. Why, my hands are burning just to think of it.'

"But I said to myself: 'Let us wait until twelve o'clock. Then this poaching fellow will go to lunch, and I shall get my place again.' As for me, Monsieur le Président, I lunch on the spot every Sunday; we bring our provisions in *Delila*. But there! At twelve o'clock the wretch produced a fowl out of a newspaper, and while he was eating, actually he caught another chub!

"Mélie and I had a morsel also, just a mouthful, a mere nothing, for our heart was not in it.

"Then I took up my newspaper, to aid my digestion. Every Sunday I read the *Gil Blas* in the shade like that, by the side of the water. It is Columbine's day, you know, Columbine who writes the articles in the *Gil Blas*. I generally put Madame Renard into a passion by pretending to know this Columbine. It is not true, for I do not know her and have never seen her, but that does not matter; she writes very well, and then she says things straight out for a woman. She suits me, and there are not many of her sort.

"Well, I began to tease my wife, but she got angry immediately and very angry, and so I held my tongue. At that moment our two witnesses, who are present here, Monsieur Ladureau and Monsieur Durdent, appeared on the other side of the river. We knew each other by sight. The little man began to fish again, and he caught so many that I trembled with vexation, and his wife said: 'It is an uncommonly good spot, and we will come here always, Desiré.' As for me, a cold shiver ran down my back, and Madame Renard kept repeating: 'You are not a man, you have the blood of a chicken in your veins'; and suddenly I said to her: 'Look here, I would rather go away, or I shall only be doing something foolish.'

"And she whispered to me as if she had put a red-hot iron under my nose: 'You are not a man. Now you are going to run away and surrender your place. Off you go, Bazaine!'

"Well, I felt that, but yet I did not move while the other fellow pulled out a bream. Oh! I never saw such a large one before, never! And then my wife began to talk aloud, as if she were thinking, and you can see her trickery. She said: 'That is what one might call stolen fish, seeing that we baited the place ourselves. At any rate they ought to give us back the money we have spent on bait.'

"Then the fat woman in the cotton dress said in turn: 'Do you mean to call us thieves, madame?' And they began to explain, and then they came to words. Oh Lord! those creatures know some good ones. They shouted so loud that our two witnesses, who were on the other bank, began to call out by way of a joke: 'Less noise over there; you will prevent your husbands from fishing.'

"The fact is that neither of us moved any more than if we had been two tree stumps. We remained there, with our noses over the water, as if we had heard nothing; but, by Jove, we heard all the same. 'You are a mere liar.'

" 'You are nothing better than a streetwalker.'

" 'You are only a trollop.'

" 'You are a regular strumpet.'

"And so on and so on; a sailor could not have said more.

"Suddenly I heard a noise behind me and turned around. It was the other one, the fat woman, who had fallen on to my wife with her parasol. *Whack! whack!* Mélie got two of them, but she was furious, and she hits hard when she is in a rage, so she caught the fat woman by the hair and then, *thump, thump.* Slaps in the face rained down like ripe plums. I should have let them go on—women among themselves, men among themselves—it does not do to mix the blows, but the little man in the linen jacket jumped up like a devil and was going to rush at my wife. Ah! no, no, not that, my friend! I caught the gentleman with the end of my fist, *crash, crash,* one on the nose, the other in the stomach. He threw up his arms and legs and fell on his back into the river, just into the hole.

"I should have fished him out most certainly, Monsieur le Président, if I had had the time. But unfortunately the fat woman got the better of it, and she was drubbing Mélie terribly. I know that I ought not to have assisted her while the man was drinking his fill, but I never thought that he would drown and said to myself: 'Bah, it will cool him.'

"I therefore ran up to the women to separate them, and all I received was scratches and bites. Good Lord, what creatures! Well, it took me five minutes, and perhaps ten, to separate those two viragoes. When I turned around there was nothing to be seen, and the water was as smooth as a lake. The others yonder kept shouting: 'Fish him out!' It was all very well to say that, but I cannot swim and still less dive!

"At last the man from the dam came and two gentlemen with boat hooks, but it had taken over a quarter of an hour. He was found at the bottom of the hole in eight feet of water, as I have said, but he was dead, the poor little man in his linen suit! There are the facts, such as I have sworn to. I am innocent, on my honor."

The witnesses having deposed to the same effect, the accused was acquitted.

This delightful spoof features a beatiful lady who plays a superb game of chess. Author Jeffrey Archer has been called "one of the top ten storytellers in the world" by the Los Angeles Times, *and millions of copies of his books have been sold. Among his best-known novels are* Kane and Abel *(1980),* The Prodigal Daughter *(1982), and* First Among Equals *(1984). A former world-class sprinter from Oxford University, he entered politics at age twenty-nine as a member of the British Parliament. In 1985 he became Deputy Chairman of the Conservative Party and a close confidant of Prime Minister Margaret Thatcher. Archer was elevated to the House of Lords in 1992.*

Jeffrey Archer

CHECKMATE
(1998)

AS SHE ENTERED THE ROOM every eye turned toward her.

When admiring a girl some men start with her head and work down. I start with the ankles and work up.

She wore black high-heeled velvet shoes and a tight-fitting black dress that stopped high enough above the knees to reveal the most perfectly tapering legs. As my eyes continued their upward sweep they paused to take in her narrow waist and slim athletic figure. But it was the oval face that I found captivating, slightly pouting lips and the largest blue eyes I've ever seen, crowned with a head of thick, black, short-cut hair that literally

JEFFREY ARCHER

shone with luster. Her entrance was all the more breathtaking because of the surroundings she had chosen. Heads would have turned at a diplomatic reception, a society cocktail party, even a charity ball, but at a chess tournament . . .

I followed her every movement, patronizingly unable to accept that she could be a player. She walked slowly over to the club secretary's table and signed in to prove me wrong. She was handed a number to indicate her challenger for the opening match. Anyone who had not yet been allocated an opponent waited to see if she would take her place opposite their side of the board.

The player checked the number she had been given and made her way toward an elderly man who was seated in the far corner of the room, a former captain of the club now past his best.

As the club's new captain I had been responsible for instigating these round-robin matches. We meet on the last Friday of the month in a large clublike room on top of the Mason's Arms in the High Street. The landlord sees to it that thirty tables are set out for us and that food and drink are readily available. Three or four other clubs in the district send half a dozen opponents to play a couple of blitz games, giving us a chance to face rivals we would not normally play. The rules for the matches are simple enough—one minute on the clock is the maximum allowed for each move, so a game rarely lasts for more than an hour, and if a pawn hasn't been captured in thirty moves the game is automatically declared a draw. A short break for a drink between games, paid for by the loser, ensures that everyone has the chance to challenge two opponents during the evening.

A thin man wearing half-moon spectacles and a dark blue three-piece suit made his way over toward my board. We smiled and shook hands. My guess would have been a solicitor, but I was wrong as he turned out to be an accountant working for a stationery supplier in Woking.

I found it hard to concentrate on my opponent's well-rehearsed Moscow opening as my eyes kept leaving the board and wandering over to the girl in the black dress. On the one occasion our eyes did meet she gave me an enigmatic smile, but although I tried again I was unable to elicit the same response a second time. Despite being preoccupied I still managed to defeat the accountant, who seemed unaware that there were several ways out of a seven-pawn attack.

At the half-time break three other members of the club had offered her a drink before I even reached the bar. I knew I could not hope to play my second match against the girl as I would be expected to challenge one of the visiting team captains. In fact she ended up playing the accountant.

I defeated my new opponent in a little over forty minutes and, as a solicitous host, began to take an interest in the other matches that were still being played. I set out on a circuitous route that ensured I ended up at her table. I could see that the accountant already had the better of her, and within moments of my arrival she had lost both her queen and the game.

I introduced myself and found that just shaking hands with her was a sexual experience. Weaving our way through the tables we strolled over to the bar together. Her name, she told me, was Amanda Curzon. I ordered Amanda the glass of red wine she requested and a half-pint of beer for myself. I began by commiserating with her over the defeat.

"How did you get on against him?" she asked.

"Just managed to beat him," I said. "But it was very close. How did your first game with our old captain turn out?"

"Stalemate," said Amanda. "But I think he was just being courteous."

"Last time I played him it ended up in stalemate," I told her.

She smiled. "Perhaps we ought to have a game sometime?"

"I'll look forward to that," I said, as she finished her drink.

"Well, I must be off," she announced suddenly. "Have to catch the last train to Hounslow."

"Allow me to drive you," I said gallantly. "It's the least the host captain can be expected to do."

"But surely it's miles out of your way?"

"Not at all," I lied, Hounslow being about twenty minutes beyond my flat. I gulped down the last drop of my beer and helped Amanda on with her coat. Before leaving I thanked the pub owner for the efficient organization of the evening.

We then strolled into the parking lot. I opened the passenger door of my Scirocco to allow Amanda to climb in.

"A slight improvement on London Transport," she said as I slid into my side of the car. I smiled and headed out on the road northward. That black dress that I described earlier goes even higher up the legs when a girl sits back in a Scirocco. It didn't seem to embarrass her.

"It's still very early," I ventured after a few inconsequential remarks about the club evening. "Have you time to drop in for a drink?"

"It would have to be a quick one," she replied, looking at her watch. "I've a busy day ahead of me tomorrow."

"Of course," I said, chatting on, hoping she wouldn't notice a detour that could hardly be described as on the way to Hounslow.

"Do you work in town?" I asked.

"Yes. I'm a receptionist for a firm of estate agents in Berkeley Square."

"I'm surprised you're not a model."

"I used to be," she replied without further explanation. She seemed quite oblivious to the route I was taking as she chatted on about her vacation plans for Ibiza. Once we had arrived at my place I parked the car and led Amanda through my front gate and up to the flat. In the hall I helped her off with her coat before taking her through to the front room.

"What would you like to drink?" I asked.

"I'll stick to wine, if you've a bottle already open," she replied, as she walked slowly round, taking in the unusually tidy room. My mother must have dropped by during the morning, I thought gratefully.

"It's only a bachelor pad," I said, emphasizing the word "bachelor" before going into the kitchen. To my relief I found there was an unopened bottle of wine in the larder. I joined Amanda with the bottle and two glasses a few moments later, to find her studying my chess board and fingering the delicate ivory pieces that were set out for a game I was playing by mail.

"What a beautiful set," she volunteered as I handed her a glass of wine. "Where did you find it?"

"Mexico," I told her, not explaining that I had won it in a tournament while on vacation there. "I was only sorry we didn't have the chance to have a game ourselves."

She checked her watch. "Time for a quick one," she said, taking a seat behind the little white pieces.

I quickly took my place opposite her. She smiled, picked up a white and a black bishop and hid them behind her back. Her dress became even tighter and emphasized the shape of her breasts. She then placed both clenched fists in front of me. I touched her right hand and she turned it over and opened it to reveal a white bishop.

"Is there to be a wager of any kind?" I asked lightheartedly. She checked inside her evening bag.

"I only have a few pounds on me," she said.

"I'd be willing to play for lower stakes."

"What do you have in mind?" she asked.

"What can you offer?"

"What would you like?"

"Ten pounds if you win."

"And if I lose?"

"You take something off."

I regretted the words the moment I had said them and waited for her to slap my face and leave, but she said simply, "There's not much harm in that if we only play one game."

I nodded my agreement and stared down at the board.

She wasn't a bad player—what the pros call a *patzer*—though her Roux opening was somewhat orthodox. I managed to make the game last twenty minutes while sacrificing several pieces without making it look too obvious. When I said "Checkmate," she kicked off both her shoes and laughed.

"Care for another drink?" I asked, not feeling too hopeful. "After all, it's not yet eleven."

"All right. Just a small one, and then I must be off."

I went to the kitchen, returned a moment later clutching the bottle, and refilled her glass.

"I only wanted half a glass," she said, frowning.

"I was lucky to win," I said, ignoring her remark, "after your bishop captured my knight. Extremely close-run thing."

"Perhaps," she replied.

"Care for another game?" I ventured.

She hesitated.

"Double or quits?"

"What do you mean?"

"Twenty pounds or another garment?"

"Neither of us is going to lose much tonight, are we?"

She pulled up her chair as I turned the board around and we both began to put the ivory pieces back in place.

The second game took a little longer as I made a silly mistake early on, castling on my queen's side, and it took several moves to recover. However, I still managed to finish the game off in under thirty minutes and even found time to refill Amanda's glass when she wasn't looking.

She smiled at me as she hitched her dress up high enough to allow me to see the tops of her stockings. She undid the garters and slowly peeled the stockings off before dropping them on my side of the table.

"I nearly beat you that time," she said.

"Almost," I replied. "Want another chance to get even? Let's say fifty pounds this time," I suggested, trying to make the offer sound magnanimous.

"The stakes are getting higher for both of us," she replied as she reset the board. I began to wonder what might be going through her mind. Whatever it was, she foolishly sacrificed both her rooks early on, and the game was over in a matter of minutes.

Once again she lifted her dress but this time well above her waist. My eyes were glued to her thighs as she undid the black garter belt and held it high above my head before letting it drop and join her stockings on my side of the table.

"Once I had lost the second rook," she said, "I was never in with a chance."

"I agree. It would therefore only be fair to allow you one more chance," I said, quickly resetting the board. "After all," I added, "you could win one hundred pounds this time." She smiled.

"I really ought to be going home," she said as she moved her queen's pawn two squares forward. She smiled that enigmatic smile again as I countered with my bishop's pawn.

It was the best game she had played all evening, and her use of the Warsaw gambit kept me at the board for over thirty minutes. In fact I damn nearly lost early on because I found it hard to concentrate properly on her defense strategy. A couple of times Amanda chuckled when she thought she had got the better of me, but it became obvious she had not seen Karpov play the Sicilian defense and win from a seemingly impossible position.

"Checkmate," I finally declared.

"Damn," she said, and standing up turned her back on me. "You'll have to give me a hand." Trembling, I leaned over and slowly pulled the zip down until it reached the small her back. Once again I wanted to touch the smooth, creamy skin. She swung around to face me, shrugged gracefully, and the dress fell to the ground as if a statue were being unveiled. She leaned forward and brushed the side of my cheek with her hand, which had much the same effect as an electric shock. I emptied the last of the bottle of wine into her glass and left for the kitchen with the excuse of needing to refill my own. When I returned she hadn't moved. A gauzy black bra and pair of panties were now the only garments that I still hoped to see removed.

"I don't suppose you'd play one more game?" I asked, trying not to sound desperate.

"It's time you took me home," she said with a giggle.

I passed her another glass of wine. "Just one more," I begged. "But this time it must be for both garments."

She laughed. "Certainly not," she said. "I couldn't afford to lose."

"It would have to be the last game," I agreed. "But two hundred pounds this time and we play for both garments." I waited, hoping the size of the wager would tempt her. "The odds must surely be on your side. After all, you've nearly won three times."

She sipped her drink as if considering the proposition. "All right," she said. "One last fling."

Neither of us voiced our feeling as to what was certain to happen if she lost.

I could not stop myself trembling as I set the board up once again. I cleared my mind, hoping she hadn't noticed that I had drunk only one glass of wine all night. I was determined to finish this one off quickly.

I moved my queen's pawn one square forward. She retaliated, pushing her king's pawn up two squares. I knew exactly what my next move needed to be, and because of it the game only lasted eleven minutes.

I have never been so comprehensively beaten in my life. Amanda was in a totally different class from me. She anticipated my every move and had gambits I had never encountered or even read of before.

It was her turn to say "Checkmate," which she delivered with the same enigmatic smile as before, adding, "You did say the odds were on my side this time."

I lowered my head in disbelief. When I looked up again, she had already slipped that beautiful black dress back on and was stuffing her stockings and suspenders into her evening bag. A moment later she put on her shoes.

I took out my checkbook, filled in the name "Amanda Curzon" and added the figure "£200," the date, and my signature. While I was doing this she replaced the little ivory pieces on the exact squares on which they had been when she had first entered the room.

She bent over and kissed me gently on the cheek. "Thank you," she said as she placed the check in her handbag. "We must play again sometime." I was still staring at the reset board in disbelief when I heard the front door close behind her.

"Wait a minute," I said, rushing to the door. "How will you get home?"

I was just in time to see her running down the steps and toward the open door of a BMW. She climbed in, allowing me one more look at those long tapering legs. She smiled as the car door was closed behind her.

The accountant strolled around to the driver's side, got in, revved up the engine, and drove the champion home.

Next up is a sports whodunit, featuring homicide at an exclusive hunting lodge in the Adirondack Mountains. Colin Starr, a physician, is the sleuth trying to unravel a mystery involving several gun-toting suspects. Author Rufus King (1893–1966) wrote popular mystery novels, including Murder on the Yacht *(1932),* The Deadly Dove *(1945), and* Duenna to a Murder *(1951). This story originally appeared in* Redbook *magazine.*

Rufus King

THE SEVEN GOOD HUNTERS (1941)

THE LAKE HELD A HELIOTROPE FLUSH of dawn, and it was very cold, very still. Fragile ice rimmed its edges, tentatively seeking a glaze for the late fall's first imprisonment of the water.

The crack of a single rifleshot came clear, down from westward.

Gertrude Enford woke up. There was no blurred transition from slumber about it. She knew exactly where she was. She knew the day. She knew the time of day. She suspected that the source of her wakening had been a shot.

Gertrude was an odd woman, lean and stringy, tough in her fibers, and indefinably smart, no matter what she wore or how she put it on. There was a great assurance in all of her movements; and her voice (which she never bothered to lower) was decisive, final and clipped. Gertrude's age was forty-seven. Her hair, which she wore rather long, and arranged with an artful simplicity, still excitingly retained its natural deep-auburn tones. She was very rich.

You had to be rich to stay at the Lodge, for its tariff was stiff, and you either paid it and liked it, or else you stayed away. The Jenklins owned it, Jerry and Sara: a rambling estate in the heart of the Adirondack Mountains, having its own lake, four hundred acres, and the best hunting in the north country.

Gertrude never minced decisions. In spite of the earliness of the hour, she decided to get up. She had had enough sleep, and her nerves were in excellent condition. She dressed. She looked at herself critically in a mirror. Her face, she decided, was in shape: colorless, ageless, with interesting wide frank eyes and a mouth whose shading held a dash of fuchsia in its red.

She went through the living room of her suite and out into a central hallway, darkly paneled, dark with the obscurity of the day's pale dawn, and down stairs of waxed oak. Lighted candles were somber in the main hall (the Jenklins leaned heavily on atmosphere), and she saw the stranger vaguely, standing before a large open hearth where birch logs flamed.

She said: "I'm Gertrude Enford. When did you get in?"

"I came on the morning train. The one that dumps you out at half-past four. I'm Colin Starr."

"Oh, yes. They said you were coming—but they said next week."

"It's hard for me to arrange anything definitely."

"Yes, I suppose that would be so."

Gertrude stared at Starr openly, taking him all in, his compact tall vigor and brief ugliness of features which gave to his face a curious effect of charm. One of those healthy animals, she thought, who live in the eternal forties, with digestions like clockwork. A server, a good man. A keen, kind honest man and to hell with him. One who from birth would have lived on the proper emotional side of the tracks, in a lovely house of clear-white glass bricks secure on a foundation of ethics. She thought: "What I need is a couple of cups of strong black coffee."

Gertrude sketchily recalled Dr. Starr's dossier as she had obliquely learned it: his home was in Ohio, in one of those settled small towns which you sometimes see at fairs done in miniature, a well-cleaned, polished microcosm of all that was sturdiest and best in the nation. The name, if she remembered, was Laurel Falls. He was a doctor of considerable repute, a repute that reached beyond any local or state boundaries, a man of wealth, and a man with a strange aptitude for the medico-legal angles of his profession. This, in the sense of his having been instrumental in the unmasking of several apparently natural deaths and stamping them as murder.

"I understand you have been here before, Doctor."

"Yes, several times. Whenever I can arrange to, in fact. The Jenklins are old friends." Starr considered Gertrude's turnout, its severe smartness, the inappropriateness of her shoes. "You're not going out this morning?"

"I don't hunt. I'm here with Jack, my brother, and a friend of his—an intense young thing by the name of Mason Hallway, whose family is involved with soaps. Jack hopes to bag a twelve-point buck. I've no objection to this mounting the heads—we live on Long Island, a little town called Mealand, and his den is littered with antlers—but I do object to his making us eat up the rest of them. Jack thinks it's the only sporting thing to do. Would that be atavism or just a plain obsession, Doctor?"

"Perhaps just a healthy appetite?"

"Well, if it's healthy, it's the—"

The main door opened and Bill, one of the guides, came in: a hardened youngster, leathery, and with deep-blue, vital eyes. Hard running had left him breathless.

He said to Gertrude: "Where's Mr. Jenklin, Miss Enford? Mr. Singmen's been shot. He's bad."

Gertrude's pale long fingers clutched the back of a chair for support, and Starr observed her sudden convulsive trembling, and thought her about to faint.

She said: "Mr. Singmen—Mr. Singmen is dead?"

"No, he ain't dead, but he's near enough to make no difference. They're bringing him in. I got to find Mr. Jenklin. I got to find a doctor."

"I'm a doctor."

Bill looked relievedly at Starr.

"Maybe you can fix him up?"

"Maybe I can."

But he couldn't. Nothing could. Starr knew that when Singmen was brought in and carried up to a bed. Singmen was of medium build, a middle-aged man wearing corduroys, stout boots, a gray hunting jacket and a red cap. He had been shot through the back. There was not, on the gray hunting jacket, much blood, and Starr believed shortly that an internal hemorrhage would make death a matter of minutes or of an hour or so at most.

Singmen's eyes were cloudy and almost absurdly kind. They gave his pleasant face a stricken spaniel look. He said to Starr: "I should have worn my red hunting jacket after all, not that gray one. The red cap wasn't enough."

("There's no use," Starr thought, "in making him preserve his ebbing strength. He might as well talk, and keep his mind occupied. There's nothing at all I can do.")

"Who shot you, Mr. Singmen?"

"I don't know."

"Do you mean to say that whoever did it didn't come to your help?"

"Yes. Too frightened, I guess. A couple of the guides found me and brought me in." Singmen sighed gently and closed his cloudy eyes. "It's a funny thing how excited some men will get when they think they see a buck."

"Were you in brush or on a trail?"

"A trail, Doctor."

"Fairly straight?"

"Yes, right along there it was, for almost a hundred yards or so. But you know how it is with buck fever."

"Look here, Singmen, that shot went directly through your back in a straight line. Surely whoever fired must have seen you pretty clearly. Tell me this—"

"I'm very tired, Doctor."

"I know you are. But tell me, of the people who are up here, of the men out hunting this morning, has any one of them anything against you?"

"Me? Lord no, Doctor. I've always been my own worst enemy." Singmen smiled feebly at this feeble airing of the bromide. "Don't get any notion like that in your head."

"Was any one of them using the same trail you were on?"

"No. I did meet Mason Hallway for a minute at the fork, where there's a cross trail of sorts, but he hit on off to the left up toward the ridge. He's that young friend of Jack Enford. Enford has a nice sister, by the way. A very interesting woman. She's staying here. You'll meet her."

"I have. Was Mason Hallway the only man you saw?"

"That's right, Doctor. It couldn't have been he who caused this accident, because he knew the way I was heading. Just how bad am I, Doctor?"

"You are all right." And Singmen was. . . . He was dead.

Starr talked with Sara Jenklin while they were waiting for the sheriff. Gray peppered Sara's dark sleek hair, and her animated eyes were heavy with shock and worry.

Seven hunters (Sara said) were out that morning, including Singmen, who was dead. None of the others had as yet returned, including Mason Hallway, whom Singmen had met at the fork and who had branched off to hit it up for the ridge. No concerted drive had been set for the morning. Each man had started off on his own. The guides were out now, bringing them in.

"Tell me, Sara, something about Singmen."

"There isn't much, Colin. He was a widower. No children. His wife was Alice Dobbs. Alice and I went to school together, which is how Arthur started coming up here."

"What did he do?"

"Arthur? Nothing. He had a good income, and more or less budgeted it. He owned a co-operative apartment in New York, just a good, plain fine one with nothing bizarre about it—old stuff, old silver. He kept a place on the beach at Miami." Sara looked at Starr earnestly. "He couldn't have been a kinder man, or more harmless."

"You're puzzled, Sara, too?"

"Naturally I'm puzzled. I know the place in the trail where he was shot. There's a good clear view for quite a stretch back. Anyhow, every man who went out this morning is experienced. I just can't believe that any one of them would get buck fever."

"What of Mason Hallway, Sara?"

"I don't know, except that I like him. It's his first time here. He came with the Enfords. I've known them, of course, for several years. They met him sometime last spring, I understand, when both of them were applying for the Reserve Corps. Each was turned down for one reason or other, and it seemed, well, to form a bond. They become quite friendly."

"Did Hallway know Singmen?"

"Only in the sense of their having met two days ago."

Starr thought back upon Gertrude Enford's convulsive trembling, the sharp clutch of her fingers upon the chair when the guide had told them about Singmen having been shot. It had struck him as far too sharp a reaction at news concerning a stranger, no matter how shocking. There was a connection with Singmen, he felt, either through Hallway or through the Enfords themselves.

"Tell me about Jack Enford. I've met his sister."

Sara thought for a while, staring contemplatively at Starr with her blue-gray animated eyes.

"Jack's all right."

"That suggests reservations."

"Yes, I know it does. Jack's the type of man whom all sorts of things are said about. But nothing's ever proved. I feel sorry for him because I know how that sort of thing goes. How it spreads. He's a magnet for innuendoes."

"Unpleasant ones?"

"Some. Very."

"Moral? Ethical? Financial?"

"Oh, they run the whole list. His job's promoting things. Sometimes they come off; more frequently they don't–leaving a lot of bagholders."

"Including, perhaps, Singmen?"

"No; I'm sure about that. Jack and his sister only met Arthur two days ago, too."

"I've still a feeling that there's some connection. I gathered that from Miss Enford's reaction to the news."

Sara leaned forward and said earnestly: "Colin, Arthur Singmen never harmed anyone in his life. There's not even anyone I know of left who will gain by his death. He told me last season that he was leaving his money to charity. Now if it had been Jack–" She bit her lip, and stopped abruptly.

"Yes, Sara?"

"I'm doing exactly what I've just complained about in others. Going in for innuendoes. You see, with the exception of Arthur and Mason Hallway, Jack knows the other men who were out this morning fairly well. And I mean by that, of course, that they know him. Frankly, they don't like him. And to be still more frank about it, I think that each has been bitten by one or another of his promotion schemes."

"Deeply enough to want to take a pot-shot at him?"

Sara hesitated.

"Who can ever tell about that? But it wasn't Jack who was shot; it was Arthur."

"Did you see them when they left this morning, Sara?"

"Yes."

"What sort of hunting jacket was Jack Enford wearing?" Starr asked.

"His regular red one."

"Then that knocks out that thought. Singmen's was gray."

They were sitting in Sara's living room: a pleasant clear place of pickled pine, with casement windows having a magnificent view across a valley that was flooding with the rising sun. A maid came in without knocking. She said to Sara: "It's Miss Enford, ma'am. I think she's got hysterics. Anyhow, she's screeching awfully."

Gertrude had them, all right. Severely. And there was little that Starr could do but give her an opiate to knock her out. He observed the usual disjointed mélange of sense and nonsense to her ravings: a mélange of fears and remembrances, all uprooted from the sable caves of her sub-conscious mind, and brokenly shrieked out.

He felt strongly disturbed, more so even than was usual with him during such exhibitions. He thought: "She thinks that it was murder, all right. her brother's on her mind like an obsession. It must be that she thinks that the shot was meant for her brother—as Sara did."

Starr stood watching Gertrude quiet down; then a man stepped into the room very softly. His face was deadly pale, and stamped with a weak prettiness that contrasted oddly with his large, rangy build.

He said to Starr: "Oh, you're the doctor, aren't you?"

"Yes."

"I'm her brother. How is she?"

"She has had a bad shock, Mr. Enford."

"Yes, I know. Look here—nothing will happen to her, will it?"

"No, she'll get over it."

Jack felt sweat on his forehead. He found it distasteful, and wiped it away petulantly.

"Awful thing. Awful thing about Arthur Singmen."

"Very."

"You were with him, weren't you? I mean when he died."

"Yes."

"Well—did he say anything?"

"He did speak of having met your friend Mr. Hallway along the trail. He mentioned a fork."

"Yes? He didn't imply—I mean he didn't seem to feel that Mason was responsible, did he?"

"No, on the contrary. He felt strongly that Mr. Hallway could not have been."

"It's funny that whoever did fire the shot didn't come forward—right away—and help Singmen. I suppose it was panic at the accident."

"I suppose it was."

"It makes it awkward."

"Awkward, Mr. Enford?"

"Sure, for the rest of us."

"Your sister seemed to feel—I don't know exactly how to put this, but I got the impression that she, well, has her own rather strong ideas about this business."

"Yes?"

Both of them stared down at the bed, at Gertrude with her lips a little parted over sharp white teeth, with her breath coming through them in the first deep plunge into the opiate sleep.

"Your sister—I almost gathered that she was inclined to consider it murder, but that the bullet wasn't meant for Singmen."

"Gertrude? She said that?"

"Not in so many words. I felt it implied, rather, in her hysteria."

"Look, Doctor, that's all that it was. Just hysteria. I know Gertrude, and she gets that way. She's highly strung. She goes right off her bat sometimes just over trifles." Jack's hand was petulant again with sweat. "It isn't only Gertrude. Our family has always been that way. I am myself sometimes. High-strung."

"Was that why they rejected you for the Reserves last spring, Mr. Enford?"

"Well, not entirely." Jack smiled. There was some syrup on the smile's deprecatory sweetness. "I believe they just considered me as temperamentally unfit."

"I understand that Mr. Hallway was rejected at the same time, that that was how you met. Was he rejected on the same grounds?"

Jack suddenly stopped being pleasant.

"Why do you harp on him? Singmen gave him a clean slate, didn't he? Well, isn't that good enough for you?"

"Sorry, Mr. Enford."

"That's all right. So am I. I told you that I—that it ran in the family. Forget it, Doctor."

Four men stood in the main hall.

Welford, a banker from Boston, dominated the others in appearance: strikingly silver-haired, thin, and tall to the point of gauntness, with sharply chiseled ears and nose and lips. They gave him (as he very well knew) the patrician look. He also knew its value to him in business, even though it amused him considerably when he considered his private vices, which were pigs' knuckles, Western novels, and gin mixed with plain water and no ice.

He observed Jack Enford coming into the room with a stranger. He did not see the stranger very clearly, because his fine bold eyes were concentrating so sharply on Enford. Their expression was not pleasant. He thought: "You wait!"

Burkell stood beside Welford. Denwood Burkell was a novelist of a brief repute whose flair lay in calling soil *soil.* He was a little man, barely five feet two inches in his lifts, and still he publicized himself amazingly as a sportsman: big fish, big game. Secretly it bored him stiff, but his agent though it useful with his public and for his press. The hours were the things that "got his goat." It irked him constantly that no animal of the slightest publicity value could, apparently, be bagged at noon.

Haskell Fortescu was on Welford's other side. He was a corporation counsel for a general-utilities outfit in the South: a stout man, rotund all over, with limpid little eyes and a merry mouth. People thought him famously jolly. His reaction to Enford was a little smile.

The fourth man, Hallway, was very much the intense young thing that Gertrude had called him. You got that from the deep burning look in his dark eyes rather than from his build, which was medium and placid enough. But his eyes were extraordinary and Starr read in them, as he shook hands, a hint of emotionalism, the suggestion of the dreamer or the fanatic, say in the sense of a hero-worshiper who would let his god or enthusiasm of the hour go to good lengths before admitting even the possibility of any feet of clay.

Starr met them and noted that they wore, to a man, hunting jackets of assorted reds. He acknowledged the usual perfunctory generalities: "*Terrible.... Fine man, Singmen.... Can't understand it.... Happens every year— terrible.... You would think that by now ... Buck fever—you might expect it in a novice, but not one of us—terrible!*" Then he went into a small lounge room where he saw Jerry Jenklin.

Jerry, Sara's husband, seemed lethargic when you first met him, which wasn't so. He was like an animal that way, slipping from a lounge into the most fluid physical sort of activity without any consciousness on the part of anyone watching him of the transition. Everything about him looked sleepy and somewhat sultry and slow. You expected him to scratch himself and continuously yawn.

He said to Starr: "You've still got to meet McDuff."

"The seventh hunter?"

"Yes. He'll be along soon. Well?"

"Well?"

Jerry continued to slouch and look sleepy. He offered Starr a cigarette, lit one himself, and let it dangle.

"This is bad, Colin. It's murder. And there's one thing that makes it pretty convincing that Singmen was meant to be the victim. He's the only one of the lot who wore a gray hunting jacket. They all must have known that, because they started out together. Still, you've been talking with Sara. I can only emphasize what she told you, that there's no sane reason why anybody here or anywhere else would want to kill Singmen—but someone did. So that leaves us what?"

"It leaves us with Miss Enford in hysteria."

"Yes, Sara told me that, too. Jack's at the bottom of that. She's pretty blind about him, but she can't be so utterly blind as not to realize what a more rational victim he would have made than Singmen. Or than anybody else who's here."

"She seems quite a good deal older."

"She is. She's always dominated him. She brought him up."

"From childhood?"

"Nearly. He was eleven when their parents died. Gertrude was going on nineteen. She made a fine mess of it, if you ask me." Jerry leisurely turned his head. "That's McDuff now. Hey, McDuff!"

McDuff came in. He was a huge, raw-boned, beef-skinned, red-nosed man and, Starr realized, full of Scotch. He was dour. He walked with precise care. He shook hands with Starr, and lowered himself into a chair, and said: "I've been up all night." His eyes looked it. They were as red as his hunting jacket. "You're the doctor. Why couldn't you pull old Singmen through?"

"It was too late."

McDuff turned to Jerry.

"Who was the fool who got buck fever?"

"No one's saying."

"He will." McDuff stuck a bony finger out at Starr. "You know that, Doctor. No man can escape from a consciousness of guilt."

"I'm afraid they've been known to, Mr. McDuff. Sometimes it has to be smoked out."

Starr sent a wire. He sent it to the proper department of the Reserve Corps at which Enford and Hallway had applied. He wanted to know on what grounds the two men had been rejected. He wanted to know whether there was any record on the files about a man named Arthur Singmen. As a right to the courtesy of this information, he referred to himself as a friend of the Adjutant General.

It was, he felt, an arrow shot into the air but it was impossible to get rid of the belief that Jack Enford was a focal point in the case. It was impossible to forget that Jack's friend Mason Hallway had met and talked with Singmen just before the shot was fired. It seemed of pressing importance to get all of the information about Enford and Hallway and Singmen that he could.

The sheriff was starting to spread out his bag of tricks in the main hall. Starr jointed the group and was introduced. He liked the sheriff for his air of plain forthrightness, and the healthy color of his skin, and (in spite of the air of forthrightness) his political ability to skate with dexterity over these assembled surfaces of human importance and considerable wealth. He followed the sheriff's casual but pertinent questions carefully.

"Well, gentlemen," the sheriff said in conclusion, "I think it's murder, all right; and because of any seeming lack of motive, I think that Mr. Singmen was murdered by mistake. Now there's only one thing that made him look different from the rest of you at any distance away in the woods, and that was his gray jacket. All the rest of you had on some shade of red. The point as I see it is this: was that Mr. Singmen's jacket? Was it the one he wore habitually, or did he borrow it from somebody else?"

McDuff aroused.

"That gray jacket was mine. I was up all night and saw Singmen when he came down this morning. He had ripped the sleeve of his own jacket yesterday and was looking for one of the maids to sew it. I suggested he leave it and borrow that gray one of mine. Gentlemen—I sent that man to his death."

"No, I'd hardly say that, Mr. McDuff. The question seems to be, did you sometimes wear that gray jacket yourself?"

"Certainly. I wore it every day last week. I'd ordered a red one, but it only came through last night."

The sheriff was pleased.

"Well, now we seem to be getting some place."

McDuff, who was not so pleased, began to get the impact of the drift. "Me? That shot was meant for me?"

"After all, Mr. McDuff, it was aimed at the only gray jacket in camp."

Starr thought: "Wait—this is wrong; you've gone off the track somewhere. They all started all together this morning; they would have known that Singmen was wearing the gray jacket, not McDuff." Then he felt a presence behind him, and turned, and saw Gertrude Enford in the doorway. She was looking at the sheriff with her wide, frank eyes. Then she turned them on McDuff.

Then she started to laugh hysterically.

The answering wire came toward late afternoon.

No one by the name of Arthur Singmen, Starr read, was listed or known. Mason Hallway rejected under suspicion of an incipient psychopathological trend. Jack Enford rejected for deuteranopia, but recent experiments in the detection of camouflage made it desirable Enford apply again.

Starr thought carefully for a long while. So it was like that.

He folded the telegram and put it in his pocket. He looked up the sheriff. He looked up Bill, the guide who had found Singmen that morning. He asked Bill to take him over the trail which Singmen had followed. The sun was sinking below the top of the range. Pine and balsam needles offered a silent, pungent strip of carpeting for their steps, while Starr talked with the sheriff.

It was, Starr said to the sheriff, one of the oddest cases he had ever come upon. At least he thought so. He asked the sheriff to take the five protagonists; a kindly man who was dead; a local, easy-going character who had loaned the kindly man a gray hunting jacket; an idealist who touched on being a zealot and who was thought to have a psychopathological trend; a weakling, and a woman who feared desperately for this weakling whom she herself had brought up. The case should, he thought, be speedily cleared up. For he believed that there was danger still.

They came to the "cross trail of sorts" which Singmen had mentioned, and where there was a definite fork to the left. It was here that Singmen had met and spoken briefly with Hallway. They stood at the fork and Starr explained to the sheriff his theory of what could have occurred.

He suggested that they observe the trail along which they had just come: it was a winding one, and masked by a turn as closely as ten yards back.

They observed the "trail of sorts" which Hallway had used that morning. It too was tortuous, and from their viewpoint briefly obscured.

He indicated then the trail which forked to the left, the one which Hallway had taken after his chat with Singmen: he pointed out that you could not see any farther than several yards along it at the most.

On the other hand, the right fork, which Singmen had continued upon, held a straight and unobstructed stretch through the woods for possibly a hundred yards; and therein, Starr suggested to the sheriff, could lie the answer to the case.

He suggested that they return to the Lodge. He suggested that the sheriff put some pressure to bear upon young Hallway. . . . He suggested that they borrow seven coats.

Gertrude decided on a jade-green net. It offset her hair. She fixed her face carefully so the jade didn't also offset her skin. Pretty good. They'd have to get out of here on the morning train. Get right out and away from here, if that milk-fed sheriff didn't force them to stay. Nice guy, the sheriff. A he-man. With a whittler's delicate touch. And, no doubt, a rattler's fang. Tooth? No, fang. She felt that every hour they stayed there spelled, for Jack, the most desperate sort of danger. . . . Gertrude shuddered.

She'd been shuddering a lot all through the day, and even seven old-fashioneds hadn't soothed the jitters. She clasped an emerald necklace about her throat. What would an eighth old-fashioned do? Well, what would it do?

She went downstairs, a smart, flowing shaft of jade.

All right. Why not? If he wanted to sit beside her and watch her down her eighth, let him.

"Sit down, Doctor Starr. I'm thinking of a cocktail. I'm still on the first today—the first dozen.—Jane!"

"Miss?"

"An old-fashioned."

"Yes, miss. And you, sir?"

Starr would, he said, have an old-fashioned too.

"I missed you this afternoon, Doctor. I haven't thanked you yet for your kindness this morning."

"Not at all, Miss Enford. Any St. Bernard in a storm."

"I go off that way all the time. People get so they supply other house-guests with that stuff you stuff in your ears to keep out street noises."

"Haven't you ever done anything about it?"

"Of course I have. I've been to every psychiatrist in town. My major reaction was that most of the psychiatrists needed *me*. Honestly, Doctor, there was one man who had the infernal nerve to ask me how I would handle the situation if the *Normandie* started sailing up Broadway."

"Of course you told him?"

"Explicitly. After I got home, I sent him a bill for twenty-five dollars." (*"I wish that old-fashioned would come. I can't keep this up much longer. I'll start shuddering again."*) "Tell me—you've been talking with the sheriff; has he found anything out?"

"About Singmen?"

"About his murder."

Starr looked evasive.

"I'm afraid the case is in his hands."

"Oh—then there is a case?"

"He thinks so. He plans to conduct a little experiment."

"Really? Of what nature, Doctor?"

"I understand it has to do with the selection of a hunting jacket."

"Are you being serious?"

"Very serious, Miss Enford."

"That maid is taking a wretched time with those old-fashioneds."

Gertrude looked toward the door hopefully, on the last outpost of her nerves. There were people coming in, but there were no old-fashioneds, and there was no maid. The sheriff came first carrying, amazingly, some hunting jackets on his arm. The six men left from the morning hunt trailed him. They grouped, with awkward reticence, near the blazing hearth. The Jenklins, with odd formality, came in and sat on a settee near the doorway.

"It's like a tableau," Gertrude thought: "stilted. Jack looks terrible. I wish he'd look at me." She examined Hallway. "He's worse off than Jack," she decided. A chill ran through Gertrude and she thought, still covertly examining Hallway: "He's talked. He's spilled it." Then the future became a tunnel through which she was entering into bitter darkness.

The sheriff was folding the hunting jackets lengthwise and placing them side by side on a lounge. Odd—six of them were in different shades of red, ranging from maroon to vivid scarlet, but the seventh one was gray. The sheriff was speaking, and Gertrude listened with a feverish impatience to this prelude which, from the look on Mason Hallway's tortured face, she had already discounted.

"—defalcation," the sheriff was saying, "—outright theft of a good many thousands of dollars, nearly two hundred, to be exact—a swindle perpetrated by Mr. Enford and achieved partly through the influential and trusted position of his friend Mr. Hallway. There was no doubt but that Mr. Hallway had been completely deceived as to the transaction, but Mr. Hallway had ultimately discovered its criminal nature and had insisted that the miserable business be exposed, even though he himself would also be subject to prosecution and disgrace. Mr. Hallway was that kind of man—an idealist."

("Yes," Gertrude thought, "we know all that. Get on with it. Get *through* with it.")

There was, the sheriff said, a curious angle about the matter which gave it a classic touch: the strange power of domination which Miss Enford held over her young brother, who all of his life had been a moral weakling. It was a power, in Doctor Starr's opinion, analogous to that exercised over her husband by *Lady Macbeth*, in the sense that Miss Enford had planted in her brother's mind the seed of murder. A seed which she had then nurtured into fruition.

(Gertrude thought: "Give us your proof. It was still a hunting accident, and nothing can make it come out differently.")

Mr. Hallway had admitted to him, the sheriff said, that he had agreed to accompany Miss Enford and her brother on this hunting trip, so that they could all talk things over. Miss Enford had pleaded that her own disgrace at her brother's exposure would be as deep as theirs. She had begged Mr. Hallway not to force her into social ostracism. She had insisted that a reasoned discussion of the disgraceful affair would show them some honorable way out. That, of course, was nothing but a lure. Mr. Hallway had been deliberately brought up here to be "accidentally" shot and killed—to silence him and his zealous moral qualms. Mr. Singmen had unhappily been shot instead. Perhaps Doctor Starr would offer his conclusions about that?

Starr was nervously depressed. It affected him this way—the end of a chase, and any psychological trick devised to cause a suspect to crack. He sensed the virulence in Gertrude, her fierce mental intention to make her brother look at her so that she could control him. Starr spoke to her directly, forcing her to attend to him.

"Miss Enford, your brother followed Mr. Hallway this morning, staying at a careful distance behind. By the time your brother reached the fork, Mr. Hallway had completed his brief talk with Mr. Singmen and was already lost to view behind the first turning of the trail that leads up to the ridge. On the other hand, Mr. Singmen was still in view, say a hundred yards or more away, at the farther end of the clear stretch of the right-hand trail. Your brother took it for granted that Mr. Singmen was Mr. Hallway and followed him. He shot him. His mistake was a natural one, because of all the men who were out hunting this morning only Mr. Singmen and Mr. Hallway had similar builds."

Gertrude's head was shot with sharp pain. Her eyes, in memory, compared Singmen's body with Mason's. All right. That much was true. Both were of medium build, whereas the others grouped by the fire were a varied assortment of gaunt, of small, of large size, of fat. And still all right. She looked at Jack. That was true, too. He was a weakling, and a flash of honesty made Gertrude admit that perhaps it was she who had made him one. Then the hunting jackets neatly lined up on the lounge began to fascinate her.

She said desperately: "You're wrong, Doctor. Mason wore a red hunting jacket, whereas Mr. Singmen's jacket was gray. No matter what the distance, no matter what the similarity in their builds, Jack would have noticed that. He would have known by the jacket alone that Mr. Singmen couldn't have been Mason."

Starr crossed to the hearth.

He said: "Mr. Enford, there are six coats on that lounge of varying shades of red. There is one coat there that is gray. Will you indicate the gray one, please?"

Sweat was unpleasant on Jack's face. His lips felt abominably loose, and he was terrified at the thought that he was about to cry. One chance in seven. Like that ordeal-by-fire stuff, and other tests for guilt or innocence of the Middle Ages. It suddenly didn't matter—nothing. Singmen, he remembered absently, had given several convulsive twists before he had fallen. Even Gertrude seemed a long distance away.

He pointed to the end jacket on the left.

He said: "That's the gray one."

Gertrude looked at him for a breathless second; then she screamed.

"*No*, Jack—that one is red."

Starr held her firmly by the shoulders.

"Not to your brother, Miss Enford, I suppose his vanity prevented him from ever telling you. He's color-blind, you see. He *knows no red*."

In the early twentieth century, Jack London (1876–1916) became one of the most widely read authors in the world. Many of his books and short stories are considered classics today. Among London's best-known novels are The Call of the Wild *(1903),* The Sea Wolf *(1904), and* White Fang *(1906), which were also made into movies. Presented here is London's moving story about a Mexican youth who takes up boxing to support his revolutionary ideals.*

Jack London

THE MEXICAN
(1911)

NOBODY KNEW HIS HISTORY—they of the Junta least of all. He was their "little mystery," their "big patriot," and in his way he worked as hard for the coming Mexican Revolution as did they. They were tardy in recognizing this, for not one of the Junta liked him. The day he first drifted into their crowded, busy rooms they all suspected him of being a spy—one of the bought tools of the Diaz secret service. Too many of the comrades were in civil and military prisons scattered over the United States, and others of them, in irons, were even then being taken across the border to be lined up against adobe walls and shot.

At the first sight the boy did not impress them favorably. Boy he was, not more than eighteen and not overlarge for his years. He announced that he was Felipe Rivera, and that it was his wish to work for the revolution. That was all—not a wasted word, no further explanation. He stood waiting. There was no smile on his lips, no geniality in his eyes. Big, dashing Paulino Vera felt an inward shudder. Here was something forbidding, terrible, inscrutable. There was something venomous and snakelike in the boy's black eyes. They burned like cold fire, as with a vast, concentrated bitterness. He flashed them from the faces of the conspirators to the typewriter which little Mrs. Sethby was industriously operating. His eyes rested on hers but an instant—she had chanced to look up—and she, too, sensed the nameless something that made her pause. She was compelled to read back in order to regain the swing of the letter she was writing.

Paulino Vera looked questioningly at Arrellano and Ramos, and questioningly they looked back and to each other. The indecision of doubt brooded in their eyes. This slender boy was the Unknown, vested with all the menace of the Unknown. He was unrecognizable, something quite beyond the ken of honest, ordinary revolutionists whose fiercest hatred for Diaz and his tyranny after all was only that of honest and ordinary patriots. Here was something else, they knew not what. But Vera, always the most impulsive, the quickest to act, stepped into the breach.

"Very well," he said coldly. "You say you want to work for the revolution. Take off your coat. Hang it over there. I will show you—come—where are the buckets and cloths. The floor is dirty. You will begin by scrubbing it, and by scrubbing the floors of the other rooms. The spittoons need to be cleaned. Then there are the windows."

"Is it for the revolution?" the boy asked.

"It is for the revolution," Vera answered.

Rivera looked cold suspicion at all of them, then proceeded to take off his coat.

"It is well," he said.

And nothing more. Day after day he came to his work—sweeping, scrubbing, cleaning. He emptied the ashes from the stoves, brought up the coal and kindling, and lighted the fires before the most energetic one of them was at his desk.

"Can I sleep here?" he asked once.

Aha! So that was it—the hand of Diaz showing through! To sleep in the rooms of the Junta meant access to their secrets, to the lists of names, to the addresses of comrades down on Mexican soil. The request was denied, and Rivera never spoke of it again. He slept they knew not where, and ate they knew not where nor how. Once Arrellano offered him a couple of dollars. Rivera declined the money with a shake of the head. When Vera joined in and tried to press it upon him, he said:

"I am working for the revolution."

It takes money to raise a modern revolution, and always the Junta was pressed. The members starved and toiled, and the longest day was none too long, and yet there were times when it appeared as if the revolution stood or fell on no more than the matter of a few dollars. Once, the first time, when the rent of the house was two months behind and the landlord was threatening dispossession, it was Felipe Rivera, the scrub boy in the poor, cheap clothes, worn and threadbare, who laid sixty dollars in gold on May Sethby's desk. There were other times. Three hundred letters, clicked out on the busy typewriters (appeals for assistance, for sanctions from the organized labor groups, requests for square news deals to the editors of newspapers, protests against the highhanded treatment of revolutionists by the United States courts), lay unmailed, awaiting postage. Vera's watch had disappeared—the old-fashioned gold repeater that had been his father's. Likewise had gone the plain gold band from May Sethby's third finger. Things were desperate. Ramos and Arrellano pulled their long mustaches in despair. The letters must go off, and the post office allowed no credit to purchasers of stamps. Then it was that Rivera put on his hat and went out. When he came back he laid a thousand two-cent stamps on May Sethby's desk.

"I wonder if it is the cursed gold of Diaz?" said Vera to the comrades.

They elevated their brows and could not decide. And Felipe Rivera, the scrubber for the revolution, continued, as occasion arose, to lay down gold and silver for the Junta's use.

And still they could not bring themselves to like him. They did not know him. His ways were not theirs. He gave no confidences. He repelled all probing. Youth that he was, they could never nerve themselves to dare to question him.

"A great and lonely spirit, perhaps, I do not know, I do not know," Arrellano said helplessly.

"He is not human," said Ramos.

"His soul has been seared," said May Sethby. "Light and laughter have been burned out of him. He is like one dead, and yet he is fearfully alive."

"He has been through hell," said Vera. "No man could look like that who has not been through hell—and he is only a boy."

Yet they could not like him. He never talked, never inquired, never suggested. He would stand listening, expressionless, a thing dead, save for his eyes, coldly burning, while their talk of the revolution ran high and warm. From face to face and speaker to speaker his eyes would turn, boring like gimlets of incandescent ice, disconcerting and perturbing.

"He is no spy," Vera confided to May Sethby. "He is a patriot—mark me, the greatest patriot of us all. I know it, I feel it, here in my heart and head I feel it. But him I know not at all."

"He has a bad temper," said May Sethby.

"I know," said Vera with a shudder. "He has looked at me with those eyes of his. They do not love; they threaten; they are savage as a wild tiger's. I know, if I should prove unfaithful to the cause, that he would kill me. He has no heart. He is pitiless as steel, keen and cold as frost. He is like moonshine in a winter night when a man freezes to death on some lonely mountaintop. I am not afraid of Diaz and all his killers; but this boy, of him am I afraid. I tell you true. I am afraid. He is the breath of death."

Yet Vera it was who persuaded the others to give the first trust to Rivera. The line of communication between Los Angeles and Lower California had broken down. Three of the comrades had dug their own graves and been shot into them. Two more were United States prisoners in Los Angeles. Juan Alvarado, the federal commander, was a monster. All their plans did he checkmate. They could no longer gain access to the active revolutionists, and the incipient ones, in Lower California.

Young Rivera was given his instructions and dispatched south. When he returned, the line of communication was re-established, and Juan Alvarado was dead. He had been found in bed, a knife hilt-deep in his breast. This had exceeded Rivera's instructions, but they of the Junta knew the times of his movements. They did not ask him. He said nothing. But they looked at one another and conjectured.

"I have told you," said Vera. "Diaz has more to fear from this youth than from any man. He is implacable. He is the hand of God."

The bad temper, mentioned by May Sethby, and sensed by them all, was evidenced by physical proofs. Now he appeared with a cut lip, a blackened cheek, or a swollen ear. It was patent that he brawled, somewhere in that outside world where he ate and slept, gained money, and moved in ways unknown to them. As the time passed he had come to set type for the little revolutionary sheet they published weekly. There were occasions when he was unable to set type, when his knuckles were bruised and battered, when his thumbs were injured and helpless, when one arm or the other hung wearily at his side while his face was drawn with unspoken pain.

"A wastrel," said Arrellano.

"A frequenter of low places," said Ramos.

"But where does he get the money?" Vera demanded. "Only today, just now, have I learned that he paid the bill for white paper—one hundred and forty dollars."

"There are his absences," said May Sethby. "He never explains them."

"We should set a spy upon him," Ramos propounded.

"I should not care to be that spy," said Vera. "I fear you would never see me again, save to bury me. He has a terrible passion. Not even God would he permit to stand between him and the way of his passion."

"I feel like a child before him," Ramos confessed.

"To me he is power—he is the primitive, the wild wolf, the striking rattlesnake, the stinging centipede," said Arrellano.

"He is the revolution incarnate," said Vera. "He is the flame and the spirit of it, the insatiable cry for vengeance that makes no cry but that slays noiselessly. He is a destroying angel moving through the still watches of the night."

"I could weep over him," said May Sethby. "He knows nobody. He hates all people. Us he tolerates, for we are the way of his desire. He is alone . . . lonely." Her voice broke in a half sob and there was dimness in her eyes.

Rivera's ways and times were truly mysterious. There were periods when they did not see him for a week at a time. Once he was away a month. These occasions were always capped by his return, when, without advertisement or speech, he laid gold coins on May Sethby's desk. Again, for days and weeks, he spent all his time with the Junta. And yet again, for irregular periods, he would disappear through the heart of each day, from early morning until late afternoon. At such times he came early and remained late. Arrellano had found him at midnight, setting type with fresh-swollen knuckles, or mayhap it was his lip, new-split, that still bled.

II

The time of the crisis approached. Whether or not the revolution would be depended upon the Junta, and the Junta was hard-pressed. The need for money was greater than ever before, while money was harder to get. Patriots had given their last cent and now could give no more. Section-gang laborers—fugitive peons from Mexico—were contributing half their scanty wages. But more than that was needed. The heartbreaking, conspiring, undermining toil of years approached fruition. The time was ripe. The revolution hung on the balance. One shove more, one last heroic effort, and it would tremble across the scales to victory. They knew their Mexico. Once started, the revolution would take care of itself. The whole Diaz machine would go down like a house of cards. The border was ready to rise. One Yankee, with a hundred I.W.W. men, waited the word to cross over the border and begin the conquest of Lower California. But he needed guns. And clear across to the Atlantic, the Junta in touch with them all and all of them needing guns, mere adventurers, soldiers of fortune, bandits, disgruntled American union men, socialists, anarchists, roughnecks, Mexican exiles, peons escaped from bondage, whipped miners from the bullpens of Cœur d'Alene and Colorado who desired only the more vindictively to fight—all the flotsam and jetsam of wild spirits from the madly complicated modern world. And it was guns and ammunition, ammunition and guns—the unceasing and eternal cry.

Fling this heterogeneous, bankrupt, vindictive mass across the border, and the revolution was on. The customhouse, the northern ports of entry, would be captured. Diaz could not resist. He dared not throw the weight of his armies against them, for he must hold the south. And through the south the flame would spread despite. The people would rise. The defenses of city after city would crumple up. State after state would totter down. And at last, from every side, the victorious armies of the revolution would close in on the city of Mexico itself, Diaz's last stronghold.

But the money. They had the men, impatient and urgent, who would use the guns. They knew the traders who would sell and deliver the guns. But to culture the revolution thus far had exhausted the Junta. The last dollar had been spent, the last resource and the last starving patriot milked dry, and the great adventure still trembled on the scales. Guns and ammunition! The ragged battalions must be armed. But how? Ramos lamented his confiscated estates. Arrellano wailed the spend-thriftness of his youth. May Sethby wondered if it would have been different had they of the Junta been more economical in the past.

"To think that the freedom of Mexico should stand or fall on a few paltry thousands of dollars," said Paulino Vera.

Despair was in all their faces. José Amarillo, their last hope, a recent convert who had promised money, had been apprehended at his hacienda in Chihuahua and shot against his own stable wall. The news had just come through.

Rivera, on his knees, scrubbing, looked up, with suspended brush, his bare arms flecked with soapy, dirty water.

"Will five thousand do it?" he asked.

They looked their amazement. Vera nodded and swallowed. He could not speak, but he was on the instant invested with a vast faith.

"Order the guns," Rivera said, and thereupon was guilty of the longest flow of words they had ever heard him utter. "The time is short. In three weeks I shall bring you the five thousand. It is well. The weather will be warmer for those who fight. Also, it is the best I can do."

Vera fought his faith. It was incredible. Too many fond hopes had been shattered since he had begun to play the revolution game. He believed this threadbare scrubber of the revolution, and yet he dared not believe.

"You are crazy," he said.

"In three weeks," said Rivera. "Order the guns."

He got up, rolled down his sleeves, and put on his coat.

"Order the guns," he said. "I am going now."

III

After hurrying and scurrying, much telephoning and bad language, a night session was held in Kelly's office. Kelly was rushed with business; also, he was unlucky. He had brought Danny Ward out from New York, arranged the fight for him with Billy Carthey, the date was three weeks away, and for two days now, carefully concealed from the sporting writers, Carthey had been lying up, badly injured. There was no one to take his place. Kelly had been burning the wires east to every eligible lightweight, but they were tied up with dates and contracts. And now hope had revived, though faintly.

"You've got a hell of a nerve," Kelly addressed Rivera, after one look, as soon as they got together.

Hate that was malignant was in Rivera's eyes, but his face remained impassive.

"I can lick Ward," was all he said.

"How do you know? Ever see him fight?"

Rivera shook his head.

"He can beat you up with one hand and both eyes closed."

Rivera shrugged his shoulders.

"Haven't you got anything to say?" the fight promoter snarled.

"I can lick him."

"Who'd you ever fight, anyway?" Michael Kelly demanded. Michael was the promoter's brother, and ran the Yellowstone Poolrooms, where he made goodly sums on the fight game.

Rivera favored him with a bitter, unanswering stare.

The promoter's secretary, a distinctively sporty young man, sneered audibly.

"Well, you know Roberts." Kelly broke the hostile silence. "He ought to be here. I've sent for him. Sit down and wait, though from the looks of you, you haven't got a chance. I can't throw the public down with a bum fight. Ringside seats are selling at fifteen dollars, you know that."

When Roberts arrived it was patent that he was mildly drunk. He was a tall, lean, slack-jointed individual, and his walk, like his talk, was a smooth and languid drawl.

Kelly went straight to the point.

"Look here, Roberts, you've been braggin' you discovered this little Mexican. You know Carthey's broke his arm. Well, this little yellow streak has the gall to blow in today and say he'll take Carthey's place. What about it?"

"It's all right, Kelly," came the slow response. "He can put up a fight."

"I suppose you'll be sayin' next that he can lick Ward," Kelly snapped.

Roberts considered judicially.

"No, I won't say that. Ward's a topnotcher and a ring general. But he can't hash-house Rivera in short order. I know Rivera. Nobody can get his goat. He ain't got a goat that I could ever discover. And he's a two-handed fighter. He can throw in the sleep-makers from any position."

"Never mind that. What kind of a show can he put up? You've been conditioning and training fighters all your life. I take off my hat to your judgment. Can he give the public a run for its money?"

"He sure can, and he'll worry Ward a mighty heap on top of it. You don't know that boy. I do. I discovered him. He ain't got a goat. He's a devil. He's a wizzy-wooz if anybody should ask you. He'll make Ward sit up with a show of local talent that'll make the rest of you sit up. I won't say he'll lick Ward, but he'll put up such a show that you'll all know he's a comer."

"All right." Kelly turned to his secretary. "Ring up Ward. I warned him to show up if I thought it worth while. He's right across at the Yellowstone, throwin' chests and doing the popular." Kelly turned back to the conditioner. "Have a drink?"

Roberts sipped his highball and unburdened himself.

"Never told you how I discovered the little cuss. It was a couple of years ago he showed up out at the quarters. I was getting Prayne ready for his fight with Delaney. Prayne's wicked. He ain't got a tickle of mercy in his make-up. He'd chopped up his pardners something cruel, and I couldn't find a willing boy that'd work with him. I'd noticed this little starved Mexican kid hanging around, and I was desperate. So I grabbed him, slammed on the gloves, and put him in. He was tougher'n rawhide, but weak. And he didn't know the first letter in the alphabet of boxing. Prayne chopped him to ribbons. But he hung on for two sickening rounds, when he fainted. Starvation, that was all. Battered? You couldn't have recognized him. I gave him half a dollar and a square meal. You oughta seen him wolf it down. He hadn't had a bite for a couple of days. That's the end of him, thinks I. But next day he showed up, stiff an' sore, ready for another half and a square meal. And he done better as time went by. Just a born fighter, and tough beyond belief. He hasn't a heart. He's a piece of ice. And he never talked eleven words in a string since I know him. He saws wood and does his work."

"I've seen 'm," the secretary said. "He's worked a lot for you."

"All the big little fellows has tried out on him," Roberts answered. "And he's learned from 'em. I've seen some of them he could lick. But his heart wasn't in it. I reckoned he never liked the game. He seemed to act that way."

"He's been fighting some before the little clubs the last few months," Kelly said.

"Sure. But I don't know what struck 'm. All of a sudden his heart got into it. He just went out like a streak and cleaned up all the little local fellows. Seemed to want the money, and he's won a bit, though his clothes don't look it. He's peculiar. Nobody knows his business. Nobody knows how he spends his time. Even when he's on the job, he plumb up and disappears most of each day soon as his work is done. Sometimes he just blows away for weeks at a time. But he don't take advice. There's a fortune in it for the fellow that gets the job of managin' him, only he won't consider it. And you watch him hold out for the cash money when you get down to terms."

It was at this stage that Danny Ward arrived. Quite a party it was. His manager and trainer were with him, and he breezed in like a gusty draft of geniality, good nature, and all-conqueringness. Greetings flew about, a joke here, a retort there, a smile or a laugh for everybody. Yet it was his way, and only partly sincere. He was a good actor, and he had found geniality a most valuable asset in the game of getting on in the world. But down underneath he was the deliberate, cold-blooded fighter and businessman. The rest was a mask. Those who knew him or trafficked with him said that when it came to brass tacks he was Danny on the Spot. He was invariably present at all business discussions, and it was urged by some that his manager was a blind whose only function was to serve as Danny's mouthpiece.

Rivera's way was different. Indian blood, as well as Spanish, was in his veins, and he sat back in a corner, silent, immobile, only his black eyes passing from face to face and noting everything.

"So that's the guy," Danny said, running an appraising eye over his proposed antagonist. "How de do, old chap."

Rivera's eyes burned venomously, but he made no sign of acknowledgment. He disliked all gringos, but this gringo he hated with an immediacy that was unusual even in him.

"Gawd!" Danny protested facetiously to the promoter. "You ain't expectin' me to fight a deef mute." When the laughter subsided he made another hit. "Los Angeles must be on the dink when this is the best you can scare up. What kindergarten did you get 'm from?"

"He's a good little boy, Danny, take it from me," Roberts defended. "Not as easy as he looks."

"And half the house is sold already," Kelly pleaded. "You'll have to take 'm on, Danny. It's the best we can do."

Danny ran another careless and unflattering glance over Rivera and sighed.

"I gotta be easy with 'm, I guess. If only he don't blow up."

Roberts snorted.

"You gotta be careful," Danny's manager warned. "No taking chances with a dub that's likely to sneak a lucky one across."

"Oh, I'll be careful all right, all right," Danny smiled. "I'll get 'm at the start an' nurse 'm along for the dear public's sake. What d'ye say to fifteen rounds, Kelly—an' then the hay for him?"

"That'll do," was the answer. "As long as you make it realistic."

"Then let's get down to biz." Danny paused and calculated. "Of course, sixty-five per cent of gate receipts, same as with Carthey. But the split'll be different. Eighty will just about suit me." And to his manager, "That right?"

The manager nodded.

"Here, you, did you get that?" Kelly asked Rivera.

Rivera shook his head.

"Well, it's this way," Kelly exposited. "The purse'll be sixty-five per cent of the gate receipts. You're a dub, and an unknown. You and Danny split, twenty per cent goin' to you, an' eighty to Danny. That's fair, isn't it, Roberts?"

"Very fair, Rivera," Roberts agreed. "You see, you ain't got a reputation yet."

"What will sixty-five per cent of the gate receipts be?" Rivera demanded.

"Oh, maybe five thousand, maybe as high as eight thousand," Danny broke in to explain. "Something like that. Your share'll come to something like a thousand or sixteen hundred. Pretty good for takin' a licking from a guy with my reputation. What d'ye say?"

Then Rivera took their breaths away.

"Winner takes all," he said with finality.

A dead silence prevailed.

"It's like candy from a baby," Danny's manager proclaimed.

Danny shook his head.

"I've been in the game too long," he explained. "I'm not casting reflections on the referee or the present company. I'm not sayin' nothing about bookmakers an' frame-ups that sometimes happen. But what I do say is that it's poor business for a fighter like me. I play safe. There's no tellin'. Mebbe I break my arm, eh? Or some guy slips me a bunch of dope." He shook his head solemnly. "Win or lose, eighty is my split. What d'ye say, Mexican?"

Rivera shook his head.

Danny exploded. He was getting down to brass tacks now.

"Why, you dirty little greaser! I've a mind to knock your block off right now."

Roberts drawled his body to interposition between hostilities.

"Winner takes all," Rivera repeated sullenly.

"Why do you stand out that way?" Danny asked.

"I can lick you," was the straight answer.

Danny half started to take off his coat. But, as his manager knew, it was a grandstand play. The coat did not come off, and Danny allowed himself to be placated by the group. Everybody sympathized with him. Rivera stood alone.

"Look here, you little fool," Kelly took up the argument. "You're no-body. We know what you've been doing the last few months—putting away little local fighters. But Danny is class. His next fight after this will be for the championship. And you're unknown. Nobody ever heard of you out of Los Angeles."

"They will," Rivera answered with a shrug, "after this fight."

"You think for a second you can lick me?" Danny blurted in.

Rivera nodded.

"Oh, come; listen to reason," Kelly pleaded. "Think of the advertising."

"I want the money," was Rivera's answer.

"You couldn't win from me in a thousand years," Danny assured him.

"Then what are you holding out for?" Rivera countered. "If the money's that easy, why don't you go after it?"

"I will, so help me!" Danny cried with abrupt conviction. "I'll beat you to death in the ring, my boy—you monkeyin' with me this way. Make out the articles, Kelly. Winner take all. Play it up in the sportin' columns. Tell 'em it's a grudge fight. I'll show this fresh kid a few."

Kelly's secretary had begun to write, when Danny interrupted.

"Hold on!" He turned to Rivera. "Weights?"

"Ringside," came the answer.

"Not on your life, fresh kid. If winner takes all, we weigh in at 10 A.M."

"And winner takes all?" Rivera queried.

Danny nodded. That settled it. He would enter the ring in his full ripeness of strength.

"Weigh in at ten," Rivera said.

The secretary's pen went on scratching.

"It means five pounds," Roberts complained to Rivera. "You've given too much away. You've thrown the fight right there. Danny'll be as strong as a bull. You're a fool. He'll lick you sure. You ain't got the chance of a dewdrop in hell."

Rivera's answer was a calculated look of hatred. Even this gringo he despised, and him had he found the whitest gringo of them all.

IV

Barely noticed was Rivera as he entered the ring. Only a very slight and very scattering ripple of halfhearted handclapping greeted him. The house did not believe in him. He was the lamb led to slaughter at the hands of the great Danny. Besides, the house was disappointed. It had expected a rushing battle between Danny Ward and Billy Carthey, and here it must put up with this poor little tyro. Still further, it had manifested its disapproval of the change by betting two, and even three, to one on Danny. And where a betting audience's money is, there is its heart.

The Mexican boy sat down in his corner and waited. The slow minutes lagged by. Danny was making him wait. It was an old trick, but ever it worked on the young, new fighters. They grew frightened, sitting thus and facing their own apprehensions and a callous, tobacco-smoking audience. But for once the trick failed. Roberts was right. Rivera had no goat. He, who was more delicately co-ordinated, more finely nerved and strung than any of them, had no nerves of this sort. The atmosphere of foredoomed defeat in his own corner had no effect on him. His handlers were gringos and strangers. Also they were scrubs—the dirty driftage of the fight game, without honor, without efficiency. And they were chilled, as well, with certitude that theirs was the losing corner.

"Now you gotta be careful," Spider Hagerty warned him. Spider was his chief second. "Make it last as long as you can—them's my instructions from Kelly. If you don't, the papers'll call it another bum fight and give the game a bigger black eye in Los Angeles."

All of which was not encouraging. But Rivera took no notice. He despised prize fighting. It was the hated game of the hated gringo. He had taken up with it, as a chopping block for others in the training quarters, solely because he was starving. The fact that he was marvelously made for it had meant nothing. He hated it. Not until he had come in to the Junta had he fought for money, and he had found the money easy. Not first among the sons of men had he been to find himself successful at a despised vocation.

He did not analyze. He merely knew that he must win this fight. There could be no other outcome. For behind him, nerving him to this belief, were profounder forces than any the crowded house dreamed. Danny Ward fought for money and for the easy ways of life that money would bring. But the things Rivera fought for burned in his brain—blazing and terrible visions, that, with eyes wide open, sitting lonely in the corner of the ring and waiting for his tricky antagonist, he saw as clearly as he had lived them.

He saw the white-walled, water-power factories of Rio Blanco. He saw the six thousand workers, starved and wan, and the little children, seven and eight years of age, who toiled long shifts for ten cents a day. He saw the perambulating corpses, the ghastly death's heads of men who labored in the dye rooms. He remembered that he had heard his father call the dye rooms the "suicide holes," where a year was death. He saw the little patio, and his mother cooking and moiling at crude housekeeping and finding time to caress and love him. And his father he saw, large, big-mustached, and deep-chested, kindly above all men, who loved all men and whose heart was so large that there was love to overflowing still left for the mother and the little *muchacho* playing in the corner of the patio. In those days his name had not been Felipe Rivera. It had been Fernandez, his father's and mother's name. Him had they called Juan. Later he had changed it himself, for he had found the name of Fernandez hated by prefects of police, *jefes políticos,* and *rurales.*

Big, hearty Joaquin Fernandez! A large place he occupied in Rivera's visions. He had not understood at the time, but, looking back, he could understand. He could see him setting type in the little printery, or scribbling endless hasty, nervous lines on the much-cluttered desk. And he could see the strange evenings, when workmen, coming secretly in the dark like men who did ill deeds, met with his father and talked long hours where he, the muchacho, lay not always asleep in the corner.

As from a remote distance he could hear Spider Hagerty saying to him: "No layin' down at the start. Them's instructions. Take a beatin' an' earn your dough."

Ten minutes had passed, and he still sat in his corner. There were no signs of Danny, who was evidently playing the trick to the limit.

But more visions burned before the eye of Rivera's memory. The strike, or, rather, the lockout, because the workers of Rio Blanco had helped their striking brothers of Puebla. The hunger, the expeditions in the hills for berries, the roots and herbs that all ate and that twisted and pained the stomachs of all of them. And then the nightmare; the waste of ground before the company's store; the thousands of starving workers; General Rosalio Martinez and the soldiers of Porfirio Diaz; and the death-spitting rifles that seemed never to cease spitting, while the workers' wrongs were washed and washed again in their own blood. And that night! He saw the flatcars, piled high with the bodies of the slain, consigned to Vera Cruz, food for the sharks of the bay. Again he crawled over the grisly heaps, seeking and finding, stripped and mangled, his father and his mother. His mother he especially remembered—only her face projecting, her body burdened by the weight of dozens of bodies. Again the rifles of the soldiers of Porfirio Diaz cracked, and again he dropped to the ground and slunk away like some hunted coyote of the hills.

To his ears came a great roar, as of the sea, and he saw Danny Ward, leading his retinue of trainers and seconds, coming down the center aisle. The house was in wild uproar for the popular hero who was bound to win. Everybody proclaimed him. Everybody was for him. Even Rivera's own seconds warmed to something akin to cheerfulness when Danny ducked jauntily through the ropes and entered the ring. His face continually spread to an unending succession of smiles, and when Danny smiled he smiled in every feature, even to the laughter wrinkles of the corners of the eyes and into the depths of the eyes themselves. Never was there so genial a fighter. His face was a running advertisement of good feeling, of good-fellowship. He knew everybody. He joked, and laughed, and greeted his friends through the ropes. Those farther away, unable to suppress their admiration, cried loudly: "Oh, you Danny!" It was a joyous ovation of affection that lasted a full five minutes.

Rivera was disregarded. For all that the audience noticed, he did not exist. Spider Hagerty's bloated face bent down close to his.

"No gettin' scared," the Spider warned. "An' remember instructions. You gotta last. No layin' down. If you lay down, we got instructions to beat you up in the dressing rooms. Savvy? You just gotta fight."

The house began to applaud. Danny was crossing the ring to him. Danny bent over, caught Rivera's right hand in both his own and shook it with impulsive heartiness. Danny's smile-wreathed face was close to his. The audience yelled its appreciation of Danny's display of sporting spirit. He was greeting his opponent with the fondness of a brother. Danny's lips moved, and the audience, interpreting the unheard words to be those of a kindly-natured sport, yelled again. Only Rivera heard the low words.

"You little Mexican rat," hissed from between Danny's gaily smiling lips, "I'll fetch the yellow outa you."

Rivera made no move. He did not rise. He merely hated with his eyes.

"Get up, you dog!" some man yelled through the ropes from behind.

The crowd began to hiss and boo him for his unsportsmanlike conduct, but he sat unmoved. Another great outburst of applause was Danny's as he walked back across the ring.

When Danny stripped, there were ohs! and ahs! of delight. His body was perfect, alive with easy suppleness and health and strength. The skin was white as a woman's, and as smooth. All grace, and resilience, and power resided therein. He had proved it in scores of battles. His photographs were in all the physical-culture magazines.

A groan went up as Spider Hagerty peeled Rivera's sweater over his head. His body seemed leaner because of the swarthiness of the skin. He had muscles, but they made no display like his opponent's. What the audience neglected to see was the deep chest. Nor could it guess the toughness of the fiber of the flesh, the instantaneousness of the cell explosions of the muscles, the fineness of the nerves that wired every part of him into a splendid fighting mechanism. All the audience saw was a brown-skinned boy of eighteen with what seemed the body of a boy. With Danny it was different. Danny was a man of twenty-four, and his body was a man's body. The contrast was still more striking as they stood together in the center of the ring receiving the referee's last instructions.

Rivera noticed Roberts sitting directly behind the newspapermen. He was drunker than usual, and his speech was correspondingly slower.

"Take it easy, Rivera," Roberts drawled. "He can't kill you, remember that. He'll rush you at the go-off, but don't get rattled. You just cover up, and stall, and clinch. He can't hurt you much. Just make believe to yourself that he's choppin' out on you at the trainin' quarters."

Rivera made no sign that he had heard.

"Sullen little devil," Roberts muttered to the man next to him. "He always was that way."

But Rivera forgot to look his usual hatred. A vision of countless rifles blinded his eyes. Every face in the audience, far as he could see, to the high dollar seats, was transformed into a rifle. And he saw the long Mexican border arid and sun-washed and aching, and along it he saw the ragged bands that delayed only for the guns.

Back in his corner he waited, standing up. His seconds had crawled out through the ropes, taking the canvas stool with them. Diagonally across the squared ring, Danny faced him. The gong struck, and the battle was on. The audience howled its delight. Never had it seen a battle open more convincingly. The papers were right. It was a grudge fight. Three quarters of the distance Danny covered in the rush to get together, his intention to eat up the Mexican lad plainly advertised. He assailed with not one blow, nor two, nor a dozen. He was a gyroscope of blows, a whirlwind of destruction. Rivera was nowhere. He was overwhelmed, buried beneath avalanches of punches delivered from every angle and position by a past master in the art. He was overborne, swept back against the ropes, separated by the referee, and swept back against the ropes again.

It was not a fight. It was a slaughter, a massacre. Any audience, save a prize-fighting one, would have exhausted its emotions in that first minute. Danny was certainly showing what he could do—a splendid exhibition. Such was the certainty of the audience, as well as its excitement and favoritism, that it failed to take notice that the Mexican still stayed on his feet. It forgot Rivera. It rarely saw him, so closely was he enveloped in Danny's man-eating attack. A minute of this went by, and two minutes. Then, in a separation, it caught a clear glimpse of the Mexican. His lip was cut, his nose was bleeding. As he turned and staggered into a clinch the welts of oozing blood, from his contacts with the ropes, showed in red bars across his back. But what the audience did not notice was that his chest was not heaving and that his eyes were coldly burning as ever. Too many aspiring champions, in the cruel welter of the training camps, had practiced this man-eating attack on him. He had learned to live through for a compensation of from half a dollar a go up to fifteen dollars a week—a hard school, and he was schooled hard.

Then happened the amazing thing. The whirling, blurring mix-up ceased suddenly. Rivera stood alone. Danny, the redoubtable Danny, lay on his back. His body quivered as consciousness strove to return to it. He had not staggered and sunk down, nor had he gone over in a long slumping fall. The right hook of Rivera had dropped him in mid-air with the abruptness of death. The referee shoved Rivera back with one hand and stood over the fallen gladiator counting the seconds. It is the custom of prize-fighting audiences to cheer a clean knockdown blow. But this audience did not cheer. The thing had been too unexpected. It watched the toll of the seconds in tense silence, and through this silence the voice of Roberts rose exultantly:

"I told you he was a two-handed fighter!"

By the fifth second Danny was rolling over on his face, and when seven was counted he rested on one knee, ready to rise after the count of nine and before the count of ten. If his knee still touched the floor at "ten" he was considered "down" and also "out." The instant his knee left the floor he was considered "up," and in that instant it was Rivera's right to try and put him down again. Rivera took no chances. The moment that knee left the floor he would strike again. He circled around, but the referee circled in between, and Rivera knew that the seconds he counted were very slow. All gringos were against him, even the referee.

At "nine" the referee gave Rivera a sharp thrust back. It was unfair, but it enabled Danny to rise, the smile back on his lips. Doubled partly over, with arms wrapped about face and abdomen, he cleverly stumbled into a clinch. By all the rules of the game the referee should have broken it, but he did not, and Danny clung on like a surf-battered barnacle and moment by moment recuperated. The last minute of the round was going fast. If he could live to the end he would have a full minute in his corner to revive. And live to the end he did, smiling through all desperateness and extremity.

"The smile that won't come off!" somebody yelled, and the audience laughed loudly in its relief.

"The kick that greaser's got is something God-awful," Danny gasped in his corner to his adviser while his handlers worked frantically over him.

The second and third rounds were tame. Danny, a tricky and consummate ring general, stalled and blocked and held on, devoting himself to recovering from that dazing first-round blow. In the fourth round he was himself again. Jarred and shaken, nevertheless his good condition had enabled him to regain his vigor. But he tried no man-eating tactics. The Mexican had proved a tartar. Instead he brought to bear his best fighting powers. In tricks and skill and experience he was the master, and though he could land nothing vital, he proceeded scientifically to chop and wear down his opponent. He landed three blows to Rivera's one, but they were punishing blows only, and not deadly. It was the sum of many of them that constituted deadliness. He was respectful of this two-handed dub with the amazing short-arm kicks in both his fists.

In defense Rivera developed a disconcerting straight left. Again and again, attack after attack he straight-lefted away from him with accumulated damage to Danny's mouth and nose. But Danny was protean. That was why he was the coming champion. He could change from style to style of fighting at will. He now devoted himself to infighting. In this he was particularly wicked, and it enabled him to avoid the other's straight left. Here he set the house wild repeatedly, capping it with a marvelous lock-break and lift of an inside uppercut that raised the Mexican in the air and dropped him to the mat. Rivera rested on one knee, making the most of the count, and in the soul of him he knew the referee was counting short seconds on him.

Again, in the seventh, Danny achieved the diabolical inside uppercut. He succeeded only in staggering Rivera, but in the ensuing moment of defenseless helplessness he smashed him with another blow through the ropes. Rivera's body bounced on the heads of the newspapermen below, and they boosted him back to the edge of the platform outside the ropes. Here he rested on one knee, while the referee raced off the seconds. Inside the ropes, through which he must duck to enter the ring, Danny waited for him. Nor did the referee intervene or thrust Danny back.

The house was beside itself with delight.

"Kill 'm, Danny, kill 'm!" was the cry.

Scores of voices took it up until it was like a war chant of wolves.

Danny did his best, but Rivera, at the count of eight, instead of nine, came unexpectedly through the ropes and safely into a clinch. Now the referee worked, tearing him away so that he could be hit, giving Danny every advantage that an unfair referee can give.

But Rivera lived, and the daze cleared from his brain. It was all of a piece. They were the hated gringos and they were all unfair. And in the worst of it visions continued to flash and sparkle in his brain—long lines of railroad track that simmered across the desert; *rurales* and American constables; prisons and calabooses; tramps at water tanks—all the squalid and painful panorama of his odyssey after Rio Blanco and the strike. And, resplendent and glorious, he saw the great red revolution sweeping across his land. The guns were there before him. Every hated face was a gun. It was for the guns he fought. He was the guns. He was the revolution. He fought for all Mexico.

The audience began to grow incensed with Rivera. Why didn't he take the licking that was appointed him? Of course he was going to be licked, but why should he be so obstinate about it? Very few were interested in him, and they were the certain, definite percentage of a gambling crowd that plays long shots. Believing Danny to be the winner, nevertheless they had put their money on the Mexican at four to ten and one to three.

More than a trifle was up on the point of how many rounds Rivera could last. Wild money had appeared at the ringside proclaiming that he could not last seven rounds, or even six. The winners of this, now that their cash risk was happily settled, had joined in cheering on the favorite.

Rivera refused to be licked. Through the eighth round his opponent strove vainly to repeat the uppercut. In the ninth Rivera stunned the house again. In the midst of a clinch he broke the lock with a quick, lithe movement, and in the narrow space between their bodies his right lifted from the waist. Danny went to the floor and took the safety of the count. The crowd was appalled. He was being bested at his own game. His famous right uppercut had been worked back on him. Rivera made no attempt to catch him as he arose at "nine." The referee was openly blocking that play, though he stood clear when the situation was reversed and it was Rivera who required to rise.

Twice in the tenth Rivera put through the right uppercut, lifted from waist to opponent's chin. Danny grew desperate. The smile never left his face, but he went back to his man-eating rushes. Whirlwind as he would, he could not damage Rivera, while Rivera, through the blur and whirl, dropped him to the mat three times in succession. Danny did not recuperate so quickly now, and by the eleventh round he was in a serious way. But from then till the fourteenth he put up the gamest exhibition of his career. He stalled and blocked, fought parsimoniously, and strove to gather strength. Also he fought as foully as a successful fighter knows how. Every trick and device he employed, butting in the clinches with the seeming of accident, pinioning Rivera's glove between arm and body, heeling his glove on Rivera's mouth to clog his breathing. Often, in the clinches, through his cut and smiling lips he snarled insults unspeakable and vile in Rivera's ear. Everybody, from the referee to the house, was with Danny and was helping Danny. And they knew what he had in mind. Bested by this surprise box of an unknown, he was pinning all on a single punch. He offered himself for punishment, fished, and feinted, and drew, for that one opening that would enable him to whip a blow through with all his strength and turn the tide. As another and greater fighter had done before him, he might do—a right and left, to solar plexus and across the jaw. He could do it, for he was noted for the strength of punch that remained in his arms as long as he could keep his feet.

Rivera's seconds were not half caring for him in the intervals between rounds. Their towels made a showing but drove little air into his panting lungs. Spider Hagerty talked advice to him, but Rivera knew it was wrong advice. Everybody was against him. He was surrounded by treachery. In the fourteenth round he put Danny down again, and himself stood resting, hands dropped at side, while the referee counted. In the other corner Rivera had been noting suspicious whisperings. He saw Michael Kelly make his way to Roberts and bend and whisper. Rivera's ears were a cat's, desert-trained, and he caught snatches of what was said. He wanted to hear more, and when his opponent arose he maneuvered the fight into a clinch over against the ropes.

"Got to," he could hear Michael, while Roberts nodded. "Danny's got to win—I stand to lose a mint. I've got a ton of money covered—my own. If he lasts the fifteenth I'm bust. The boy'll mind you. Put something across."

And thereafter Rivera saw no more visions. They were trying to job him. Once again he dropped Danny and stood resting, his hands at his side. Roberts stood up.

"That settled him," he said. "Go to your corner."

He spoke with authority, as he had often spoken to Rivera at the training quarters. But Rivera looked hatred at him and waited for Danny to rise. Back in his corner in the minute interval, Kelly, the promoter, came and talked to Rivera.

"Throw it, damn you," he rasped in a harsh low voice. "You gotta lay down, Rivera. Stick with me and I'll make your future. I'll let you lick Danny next time. But here's where you lay down."

Rivera showed with his eyes that he heard, but he made neither sign of assent nor dissent.

"Why don't you speak?" Kelly demanded angrily.

"You lose anyway," Spider Hagerty supplemented. "The referee'll take it away from you. Listen to Kelly and lay down."

"Lay down, kid," Kelly pleaded, "and I'll help you to the championship."

Rivera did not answer.

"I will, so help me, kid."

At the strike of the gong Rivera sensed something impending. The house did not. Whatever it was, it was there inside the ring with him and very close. Danny's earlier surety seemed returned to him. The confidence of his advance frightened Rivera. Some trick was about to be worked. Danny rushed, but Rivera refused the encounter. He sidestepped away into safety. What the other wanted was a clinch. It was in some way necessary to the trick. Rivera backed and circled away, yet he knew, sooner or later, the clinch and the trick would come. Desperately he resolved to draw it. He made as if to effect the clinch with Danny's next rush. Instead, at the last instant, just as their bodies should have come together, Rivera darted nimbly back. And in the same instant Danny's corner raised a cry of foul. Rivera had fooled them. The referee paused irresolutely. The decision that trembled on his lips was never uttered, for a shrill, boy's voice from the gallery piped, "Raw work!"

Danny cursed Rivera openly, and forced him, while Rivera danced away. Also Rivera made up his mind to strike no more blows at the body. In this he threw away half his chance of winning, but he knew if he was to win at all it was with the outfighting that remained to him. Given the least opportunity, they would lie a foul on him. Danny threw all caution to the winds. For two rounds he tore after and into the boy who dared not meet him at close quarters. Rivera was struck again and again; he took blows by the dozens to avoid the perilous clinch. During this supreme final rally of Danny's the audience rose to its feet and went mad. It did not understand. All it could see was that its favorite was winning after all.

"Why don't you fight?" it demanded wrathfully of Rivera. "You're yellow! You're yellow!" "Open up, you cur! Open up!" "Kill 'm, Danny! Kill 'm!" "You sure got 'm! Kill 'm!"

In all the house, bar none, Rivera was the only cold man. By temperament and blood he was the hottest-passioned there; but he had gone through such vastly greater heats that this collective passion of ten thousand throats, rising surge on surge, was to his brain no more than the velvet cool of a summer twilight.

Into the seventeenth round Danny carried his rally. Rivera, under a heavy blow, drooped and sagged. His hands dropped helplessly as he reeled backward. Danny thought it was his chance. The boy was at his mercy. Thus Rivera, feigning, caught him off his guard, lashing out a clean drive to the mouth. Danny went down. When he arose Rivera felled him with a down-chop of the right on neck and jaw. Three times he repeated this. It was impossible for any referee to call these blows foul.

"Oh, Bill! Bill!" Kelly pleaded to the referee.

"I can't," that official lamented back. "He won't give me a chance."

Danny, battered and heroic, still kept coming up. Kelly and others near to the ring began to cry out to the police to stop it, though Danny's corner refused to throw in the towel. Rivera saw the fat police captain starting awkwardly to climb through the ropes, and was not sure what it meant. There were so many ways of cheating in this game of the gringos. Danny, on his feet, tottered groggily and helplessly before him. The referee and the captain were both reaching for Rivera when he struck the last blow. There was no need to stop the fight, for Danny did not rise.

"Count!" Rivera cried hoarsely to the referee.

And when the count was finished Danny's seconds gathered him up and carried him to his corner.

"Who wins?" Rivera demanded.

Reluctantly the referee caught his gloved hand and held it aloft.

There were no congratulations for Rivera. He walked to his corner unattended, where his seconds had not yet placed his stool. He leaned backward on the ropes and looked his hatred at them, swept it on and about him till the whole ten thousand gringos were included. His knees trembled under him, and he was sobbing from exhaustion. Before his eyes the hated faces swayed back and forth in the giddiness of nausea. Then he remembered they were the guns. The guns were his. The revolution could go on.

One of the great storytellers of all time, Damon Runyon (1884–1946) was also the most prominent reporter in the nation as a syndicated writer for the Hearst newspapers. In his fiction, which features sports such as baseball, football, and boxing, Runyon is a master of character invention, humorous dialogue, and colorful monikers. The following story is typically Runyonesque, with a race-track gambler named Hot Horse Herbie and his blonde girlfriend, Cutie Singleton, seeking in their own ways the elusive big score in life.

Damon Runyon

PICK THE WINNER (1933)

WHAT I AM DOING IN MIAMI associating with such a character as Hot Horse Herbie is really quite a long story, and it goes back to one cold night when I am sitting in Mindy's restaurant on Broadway thinking what a cruel world it is, to be sure, when in comes Hot Horse Herbie and his ever-loving fiancée, Miss Cutie Singleton.

This Hot Horse Herbie is a tall, skinny guy with a most depressing kisser, and he is called Hot Horse Herbie because he can always tell you about a horse that is so hot it is practically on fire, a hot horse being a horse that is all readied up to win a race, although sometimes Herbie's hot horses turn out to be so cold they freeze everybody within fifty miles of them.

He is following the races almost since infancy, to hear him tell it. In fact, old Captain Duhaine, who has charge of the Pinkertons around the race tracks, says he remembers Hot Horse Herbie as a little child, and that even then Herbie is a hustler, but of course Captain Duhaine does not care for Hot Horse Herbie, because he claims Herbie is nothing but a tout, and a tout is something that is most repulsive to Captain Duhaine and all other Pinkertons.

A tout is a guy who goes around a race track giving out tips on the races, if he can find anybody who will listen to his tips, especially suckers, and a tout is nearly always broke. If he is not broke, he is by no means a tout, but a handicapper, and is respected by one and all, including the Pinkertons, for knowing so much about the races.

Well, personally, I have nothing much against Hot Horse Herbie, no matter what Captain Duhaine says he is, and I certainly have nothing against Herbie's ever-loving fiancée, Miss Cutie Singleton. In fact, I am rather in favor of Miss Cutie Singleton because in all the years I know her, I wish to say I never catch Miss Cutie Singleton out of line, which is more than I can say of many other dolls I know.

She is a little, good-natured blonde doll, and by no means a crow, if you care for blondes, and some people say that Miss Cutie Singleton is pretty smart, although I never can see how this can be, as I figure a smart doll will never have any truck with a guy like Hot Horse Herbie, for Herbie is by no means a provider.

But for going on ten years Miss Cutie Singleton and Hot Horse Herbie are engaged, and it is well known to one and all that they are to be married as soon as Herbie makes a scratch.

In fact, they are almost married in New Orleans in 1928, when Hot Horse Herbie beats a good thing for eleven Cs, but the tough part of it is the good thing is in the first race, and naturally Herbie bets the eleven Cs right back on another good thing in the next race, and this good thing blows, so Herbie winds up with nothing but the morning line and is unable to marry Miss Cutie Singleton at this time.

Then again in 1929 at Churchill Downs, Hot Horse Herbie has a nice bet on Naishapur to win the Kentucky Derby, and he is so sure Naishapur cannot miss that the morning of the race he sends Miss Cutie Singleton out to pick a wedding ring. But Naishapur finishes second, so naturally Hot Horse Herbie is unable to buy the ring, and of course Miss Cutie Singleton does not wish to be married without a wedding ring.

They have another close call in 1931 at Baltimore, when Hot Horse Herbie figures Twenty Grand a standout in the Preakness, and in fact is so sure of his figures that he has Miss Cutie Singleton go down to the city hall to find out what a marriage license costs. But of course Twenty Grand does not win the Preakness, so the information Miss Cutie Singleton obtains is of no use to them, and anyway Hot Horse Herbie says he can beat the price on marriage licenses in New York.

However, there is no doubt but what Hot Horse Herbie and Miss Cutie Singleton are greatly in love, although I hear rumors that for a couple of years past Miss Cutie Singleton is getting somewhat impatient about Hot Horse Herbie not making a scratch as soon as he claims he is going to when he first meets up with her in Hot Springs in 1923.

In fact, Miss Cutie Singleton says if she knows Hot Horse Herbie is going to be so long delayed in making his scratch she will never consider becoming engaged to him, but will keep her job as a manicurist at the Arlington Hotel, where she is not doing bad, at that.

It seems that the past couple of years Miss Cutie Singleton is taking to looking longingly at the little houses in the towns they pass through going from one race track to another, and especially at little white houses with green shutters and yards and vines all around and about, and saying it must be nice to be able to live in such places instead of in a suitcase.

But of course Hot Horse Herbie does not put in with her on these ideas, because Herbie knows very well if he is placed in a little white house for more than fifteen minutes the chances are he will lose his mind, even if the house has green shutters.

Personally, I consider Miss Cutie Singleton somewhat ungrateful for thinking of such matters after all the scenery Hot Horse Herbie lets her see in the past ten years. In fact, Herbie lets her see practically all the scenery there is in this country, and some in Canada, and all she has to do in return for all this courtesy is to occasionally get out a little crystal ball and deck of cards and let on she is a fortuneteller when things are going especially tough for Herbie.

Of course, Miss Cutie cannot really tell fortunes, or she will be telling Hot Horse Herbie's fortune, and maybe her own, too, but I hear she is better than a raw hand at making people believe she is telling their fortunes, especially old maids who think they are in love, or widows who are looking to snare another husband and other such characters.

Well, anyway, when Hot Horse Herbie and his ever-loving fiancée come into Mindy's, he gives me a large hello, and so does Miss Cutie Singleton, so I hello them right back, and Hot Horse Herbie speaks to me as follows:

"Well," Herbie says, "we have some wonderful news for you. We are going to Miami," he says, "and soon we will be among the waving palms and reveling in the warm waters of the Gulf Stream."

Now of course this is a lie, because while Hot Horse Herbie is in Miami many times, he never revels in the warm waters of the Gulf Stream, because he never has time for such a thing, what with hustling around the race tracks in the daytime, and around the dog tracks and gambling joints at night, and, in fact, I will lay plenty of six to five Hot Horse Herbie cannot even point in the direction of the Gulf Stream when he is in Miami, and I will give him three points, at that.

But naturally what he says gets me to thinking how pleasant it is in Miami in the winter, especially when it is snowing up north, and a guy does not have a flogger to keep himself warm, and I am commencing to feel very envious of Hot Horse Herbie and his ever-loving fiancée when he says like this:

"But," Herbie says, "our wonderful news for you is not about us going. It is about you going," he says. "We already have our railroad tickets," he says, "as Miss Cutie Singleton, my ever-loving fiancée here, saves up three Cs for her hope chest the past summer, but when it comes to deciding between a hope chest and Miami, naturally she chooses Miami, because," Herbie says, "she claims she does not have enough hope left to fill a chest. Miss Cutie Singleton is always kidding," he says.

"Well, now," Herbie goes on, "I just run into Mr. Edward Donlin, the undertaker, and it seems that he is sending a citizen of Miami back home tomorrow night, and of course you know," he says, "that Mr. Donlin must purchase two railroad tickets for this journey, and as the citizen has no one else to accompany him, I got to thinking of you. He is a very old and respected citizen of Miami," Herbie says, "although of course he is no longer with us, except maybe in spirit."

Of course such an idea is most obnoxious to me, and I am very indignant that Hot Horse Herbie can even think I will travel in this manner, but he gets to telling me that the old and respected citizen of Miami that Mr. Donlin is sending back home is a great old guy in his day, and that for all anybody knows he will appreciate having company on the trip, and about this time Big Nig, the craps shooter, comes into Mindy's leaving the door open behind him so that a blast of cold air hits me, and makes me think more than somewhat of the waving palms and the warm waters of the Gulf Stream.

So the next thing I know, there I am in Miami with Hot Horse Herbie and it is the winter of 1931, and everybody now knows that this is the winter when the suffering among the horse players in Miami is practically horrible. In fact, it is worse than it is in the winter of 1930.

In fact, the suffering is so intense that many citizens are wondering if it will do any good to appeal to Congress for relief for the horse players, but The Dancer says he hears Congress needs a little relief itself.

Hot Horse Herbie and his ever-loving fiancée, Miss Cutie Singleton, and me have rooms in a little hotel on Flagler Street, and while it is nothing but a fleabag, and we are doing the landlord a favor by living there, it is surprising how much fuss he makes any time anybody happens to be a little short of the rent.

In fact, the landlord hollers and yells so much any time anybody is a little short of the rent that he becomes a very great nuisance to me, and I have half a notion to move, only I cannot think of any place to move to. Furthermore, the landlord will not let me move unless I pay him all I owe him, and I am not in a position to take care of this matter at the moment.

Of course I am not very dirty when I first come in as far as having any potatoes is concerned and I start off at once having a little bad luck. It goes this way a while, and then it gets worse and sometimes I wonder if I will not be better off if I buy myself a rope and end it all on a palm tree in the park on Biscayne Boulevard.

But the only trouble with the idea is I do not have the price of a rope, and anyway I hear most of the palm trees in the park are already spoken for by guys who have the same notion.

And bad off as I am, I am not half as bad off as Hot Horse Herbie, because he has his ever-loving fiancée, Miss Cutie Singleton, to think of, especially as Miss Cutie Singleton is putting up quite a beef about not having any recreation, and saying if she only has the brains God gives geese she will break off their engagement at once and find some guy who can show her a little speed, and she seems to have no sympathy whatever for Hot Horse Herbie when he tells her how many tough snoots he gets beat at the track.

But Herbie is very patient with her, and tells her it will not be long now, because the law of average is such that his luck is bound to change, and he suggests to Miss Cutie Singleton that she get the addresses of a few preachers in case they wish to locate one in a hurry.

Furthermore, Hot Horse Herbie suggests to Miss Cutie Singleton that she get out the old crystal ball and her deck of cards, and hang out her sign as a fortuneteller while they are waiting for the law of average to start working for him, although personally I doubt if she will be able to get any business telling fortunes in Miami at this time because everybody in Miami seems to know what their fortune is already.

Now I wish to say that after we arrive in Miami I have very little truck with Hot Horse Herbie because I do not approve of some of his business methods, and furthermore I do not wish Captain Duhaine and his Pinkertons at my hip all the time, as I never permit myself to get out of line in any respect, or anyway not much. But of course I see Hot Horse Herbie at the track every day, and one day I see him talking to the most innocent-looking guy I ever see in all my life.

He is a tall, spindling guy with a soft brown vandyke beard, and soft brown hair, and no hat, and is maybe forty-odd, and wears rumpled white flannel pants, and a rumpled sports coat, and big horn cheaters, and he is smoking a pipe that you can smell a block away.

He is such a guy as looks as if he does not know what time it is, and furthermore he does not look as if he has a quarter, but I can see by the way Hot Horse Herbie is warming his ear that Herbie figures him to have a few potatoes.

Furthermore, I never know Hot Horse Herbie to make many bad guesses in this respect, so I am not surprised when I see the guy pull out a long flat leather from the inside pocket of his coat and weed Herbie a banknote. Then I see Herbie start for the mutuels windows, but I am quite astonished when I see that he makes for a two-dollar window.

So I follow Hot Horse Herbie to see what this is all about, because it is certainly not like Herbie to dig up a guy with a bank roll and then only promote him for a deuce.

When I get hold of Herbie and ask him what this means, he sighs, and says to me like this:

"Well," he says, "I am just taking a chance with the guy. He may be a prospect at that," Herbie says. "You never can tell about people. This is the first bet he ever makes in his life, and furthermore," Herbie says, "he does not wish to bet. He says he knows one horse can beat another, and what of it?"

"But," Herbie says, "I give him a good story, so he finally goes for the deuce. I think he is a college professor somewhere," Herbie says, "and he is only wandering around the track out of curiosity. He does not know a soul here. Well," Herbie says, "I put him on a good hot horse, and if he wins maybe he can be developed into something. You know," Herbie says, "they can never rule you off for trying."

Well, it seems that the horse Herbie gives the guy wins all right and at a fair price, and Herbie lets it go at that for the time being, because he gets hold of a real good guy, and cannot be bothering with guys who only bet deuces. But every day the professor is at the track and I often see him wandering through the crowds, puffing at an old stinkaroo and looking somewhat bewildered.

I get somewhat interested in the guy myself, because he seems so much

out of place, but I wish to say I never think of promoting him in any respect, because this is by no means my dodge, and finally one day I get
to talking to him and he seems just as innocent as he looks.

He is a professor at Princeton, which is a college in New Jersey, and his
name is Woodhead, and he has been very sick, and is in Florida to get
well, and he thinks the track mob is the greatest show he ever sees, and
is sorry he does not study this business a little earlier in life.

Well, personally, I think he is a very nice guy, and he seems to have quite
some knowledge of this and that and one thing and another, although he
is so ignorant about racing that it is hard to believe he is a college guy.

Even if I am a hustler, I will just as soon try to hustle Santa Claus as
Professor Woodhead, but by and by Hot Horse Herbie finds things getting very desperate indeed, so he picks up the professor again and starts
working on him, and one day he gets him to go for another deuce, and
then for a fin and both times the horses Herbie gives him are winners,
which Herbie says just goes to show you the luck he is playing in, because
when he has a guy who is willing to make a bet for him, he cannot pick
one to finish fifth.

You see, the idea is when Hot Horse Herbie gives a guy a horse he ex-
pects the guy to bet for him, too, or maybe give him a piece of what he
wins, but of course Herbie does not mention this to Professor Woodhead
as yet, because the professor does not bet enough to bother with, and
anyway Herbie is building him up by degrees, although if you ask me, it
is going to be slow work, and finally Herbie himself admits as much, and
says to me like this:

"It looks as if I will have to blast," Herbie says. "The professor is a nice
guy, but," he says, "he does not loosen so easy. Furthermore," Herbie
says, "he is very dumb about horses. In fact," he says, "I never see a guy
so hard to educate, and if I do not like him personally, I will have no part
of him whatever. And besides liking him personally," Herbie says, "I get
a gander into that leather he carries the other day, and what do I see," he
says, "but some large, coarse notes in there back to back."

Well, of course, this is very interesting news, even to me, because large,
coarse notes are so scarce in Miami at this time that if a guy runs into

one he takes it to a bank to see if it is counterfeit before he changes it, and even then he will scarcely believe it.

I get to thinking that if a guy such as Professor Woodhead can be going around with large, coarse notes in his possession, I make a serious mistake in not becoming a college professor myself, and naturally after this I treat the professor with great respect.

Now what happens one evening, but Hot Horse Herbie and his ever-loving fiancée, Miss Cutie Singleton, and me are in a little grease joint on Second Street putting on the old hot tripe à la Creole, which is a very pleasant dish, and by no means expensive, when who wanders in but Professor Woodhead.

Naturally Herbie calls him over to our table and introduces Professor Woodhead to Miss Cutie Singleton and Professor Woodhead sits there with us looking at Miss Cutie Singleton with great interest, although Miss Cutie Singleton is at this time feeling somewhat peevish because it is the fourth evening running she has to eat tripe à la Creole, and Miss Cutie Singleton does not care for tripe under any circumstances.

She does not pay any attention whatever to Professor Woodhead, but finally Hot Horse Herbie happens to mention that the professor is from Princeton, and then Miss Cutie Singleton looks at the professor, and says to him like this:

"Where is this Princeton?" she says. "Is it a little town?"

"Well," Professor Woodhead says, "Princeton is in New Jersey, and it is by no means a large town, but," he says, "it is thriving."

"Are there any little white houses in this town?" Miss Cutie Singleton asks. "Are there any little white houses with green shutters and vines all around and about?"

"Why," Professor Woodhead says, looking at her with more interest than somewhat, "you are speaking of my own house," he says. "I live in a little white house with green shutters and vines all around and about, and," he says, "it is a nice place to live in, at that, although it is sometimes a little lonesome, as I live there all by myself, unless," he says, "you wish to count on old Mrs. Bixby who keeps house for me. I am a bachelor," he says.

Well, Miss Cutie Singleton does not have much to say after this, although it is only fair to Miss Cutie Singleton to state that for a doll, and especially a blonde doll, she is never so very gabby, at that, but she watches Professor Woodhead rather closely as Miss Cutie Singleton never before comes in contact with anybody who lives in a little white house with green shutters.

Finally we get through with the hot tripe à la Creole and walk around to the fleabag where Hot Horse Herbie and Miss Cutie Singleton and me are residing and the professor walks around with us.

In fact, Professor Woodhead walks with Miss Cutie Singleton, while Hot Horse Herbie walks with me, and Hot Horse Herbie is telling me that he has the very best thing of his entire life in the final race at Hialeah the next day, and he is expressing great regret that he does not have any potatoes to bet on this thing, and does not know where he can get any potatoes.

It seems that he is speaking of a horse by the name of Breezing Along, which is owned by a guy by the name of Moose Tassell, who is a citizen of Chicago, and who tells Hot Horse Herbie that the only way Breezing Along can lose the race is to have somebody shoot him at the quarter pole, and of course nobody is shooting horses at the quarter pole at Hialeah, though many citizens often feel like shooting horses at the half.

Well, by this time we get to our fleabag and we all stand there talking when Professor Woodhead speaks as follows:

"Miss Cutie Singleton informs me," he says, "that she dabbles somewhat in fortunetelling. Well," Professor Woodhead says, "this is most interesting to me, because I am by no means skeptical of fortunetelling. In fact," he says, "I make something of the study of the matter, and there is no doubt in my mind that certain human beings do have the faculty of foretelling future events with remarkable accuracy."

Now I wish to say one thing for Hot Horse Herbie, and this is that he is a quick-thinking guy when you put him up against a situation that calls for quick thinking, for right away he speaks up and says like this:

"Why, Professor," he says, "I am certainly glad to hear you make this statement, because," he says, "I am a believer in fortunetelling myself. As a matter of fact, I am just figuring on having Miss Cutie Singleton look into her crystal ball for a horse," and furthermore, it is the first time in his life that Hot Horse Herbie ever asks her to look into the crystal ball for anything whatever, except to make a few bobs for them to eat on, because Herbie by no means believes in matters of this nature.

But naturally Miss Cutie Singleton is not going to display any astonishment, and when she says she will be very glad to oblige, Professor Woodhead speaks up and says he will be glad to see this crystal gazing come off, which makes it perfect for Hot Horse Herbie.

So we all go upstairs to Miss Cutie Singleton's room, and the next thing anybody knows there she is with her crystal ball, gazing into it with both eyes.

Now Professor Woodhead is taking a deep interest in the proceedings, but, of course, Professor Woodhead does not hear what Hot Horse Herbie tells Miss Cutie Singleton in private, and as far as this is concerned neither do I, but Herbie tells me afterward that he tells her to be sure and see a breeze blowing in the crystal ball. So by and by, after gazing into the ball a long time, Miss Cutie Singleton speaks in a low voice as follows:

"I seem to see trees bending to the ground under the force of a great wind," Miss Cutie Singleton says. "I see houses blown about by the wind," she says. "Yes," Miss Cutie Singleton says, "I see pedestrians struggling along and shivering in the face of this wind, and I see waves driven high on a beach and boats tossed about like paper cups. In fact," Miss Singleton says, "I seem to see quite a blow."

Well, then it seems that Miss Cutie Singleton can see no more, but Hot Horse Herbie is greatly excited by what she sees already, and he says like this:

"It means this horse Breezing Along," he says. "There can be no doubt about it, Professor," he says, "here is the chance of your lifetime. The horse will be not less than six to one," he says. "This is the spot to bet a gob, and," he says, "the place to bet it is downtown with a bookmaker at the opening price, because there will be a ton of money for the horse in the machines. Give me five Cs," Hot Horse Herbie says, "and I will bet four for you, and one for me."

Well, Professor Woodhead seems greatly impressed by what Miss

Cutie Singleton sees in the crystal ball, but of course taking a guy from a finnif to five Cs is carrying him along too fast, especially when Herbie knows the professor does not care to bet any such money as this.

In fact, the professor does not seem anxious to bet more than a sawbuck, tops, but Herbie finally moves him up to a bet a yard, and of this yard twenty-five bobs is running for Hot Horse Herbie, as Herbie explains to the professor that a remittance he is expecting from his New York bankers fails him.

The next day Herbie takes the hundred bucks and bets it with Gloomy Gus downtown, for Herbie really has great confidence in the horse.

We are out to the track early in the afternoon and the first guy we run into is Professor Woodhead, who is very excited. We speak to him, and then we do not see him again all day.

Well, I am not going to bother telling you the details of the race, but this horse Breezing Along is nowhere. In fact he is so far back that I do not recollect seeing him finish, because by the time the third horse in the field crosses the line, Hot Horse Herbie and me are on our way back to town, as Herbie does not feel that he can face Professor Woodhead at such a time as this. In fact, Herbie does not feel that he can face anybody, so we go to a certain spot over on Miami Beach and remain there drinking beer until a late hour when Herbie happens to think of his ever-loving fiancée, Miss Cutie Singleton, and how she must be suffering from lack of food, so we return to our fleabag so Herbie can take Miss Cutie Singleton to dinner.

But he does not find Miss Cutie Singleton. All he finds from her is a note, and in this note Miss Cutie Singleton says like this: "Dear Herbie," she says, "I do not believe in long engagements any more, so Professor Woodhead and I are going to Palm Beach to be married tonight, and are leaving for Princeton, New Jersey, at once, where I am going to live in a little white house with green shutters and vines all around and about. Good-bye, Herbie," the note says. "Do not eat any bad fish. Respectfully, Mrs. Professor Woodhead."

Well, naturally this is most surprising to Hot Horse Herbie, but I never hear him mention Miss Cutie Singleton or Professor Woodhead again until a couple of weeks later when he shows me a letter from the professor.

It is quite a long letter, and it seems that Professor Woodhead wishes to apologize, and naturally Herbie has a right to think that the professor is going to apologize for marrying his ever-loving fiancée, Miss Cutie Singleton, as Herbie feels he has an apology coming on this account.

But what the professor seems to be apologizing about is not being able to find Hot Horse Herbie just before the Breezing Along race to explain a certain matter that is on his mind.

"It does not seem to me," the professor says, as near as I can remember the letter, "that the name of your selection is wholly adequate as a description of the present Mrs. Professor Woodhead's wonderful vision in the crystal ball, so," he says, "I examine the program further, and finally discover what I believe to be the name of the horse meant by the vision, and I wager two hundred dollars on this horse, which turns out to be the winner at ten to one, as you may recall. It is in my mind," the professor says, "to send you some share of the proceeds, inasmuch as we are partners in the original arrangements, but the present Mrs. Woodhead disagrees with my view, so all I can send you is an apology, and best wishes."

Well, Hot Horse Herbie cannot possibly remember the name of the winner of any race as far back as this, and neither can I, but we go over to the *Herald* office and I look at the files, and what is the name of the winner of the Breezing Along race but Mistral, and when I look in the dictionary to see what this word means, what does it mean but a violent cold and dry northerly wind.

And of course I never mention to Hot Horse Herbie or anybody else that I am betting on another horse in this race myself, and the name of the horse I am betting on is Leg Show, for how do I know for certain that Miss Cutie Singleton is not really seeing in the crystal ball just such a blow as she describes?

Originally published in Collier's, *this story features one of the great heroes of the printed word: Sherlock Holmes. With his narrator and good friend, Dr. Watson, Holmes is on the case of a star rugby player for Cambridge University who disappears on the eve of the big game with Oxford. (Rugby originated in England around 1840 and is the sport from which American football is derived. Tradition holds that rugby is a thug's game played by gentlemen, whereas soccer is a gentlemen's game played by thugs.) Sherlock Holmes appears, of course, in such other memorable stories as "A Scandal in Bohemia," "The Five Orange Pips," and "The Adventure of the Musgrave Ritual." Sir Arthur Conan Doyle (1859–1930) was a medical doctor who turned to short fiction as a hobby. As the creator of literature's most famous detective, Doyle became the toast of Victorian England, and he remains one of the world's favorite authors today.*

A. Conan Doyle
THE ADVENTURE OF THE MISSING THREE-QUARTER (1904)

WE WERE FAIRLY ACCUSTOMED TO RECEIVE WEIRD telegrams at Baker Street, but I have a particular recollection of one which reached us on a gloomy February morning some seven or eight years ago, and gave Mr. Sherlock Holmes a puzzled quarter of an hour. It was addressed to him and ran thus:

"Please await me. Terrible misfortune. Right wing. Three-quarter missing. Indispensable. Tomorrow.

"OVERTON"

"Strand post-mark and despatched 10:36," said Holmes, reading it over and over. "Mr. Overton was evidently considerably excited when he sent it, and somewhat incoherent in consequence. Well, well, he will be here, I dare say, by the time I have looked through the 'Times,' and then we shall know all about it. Even the most insignificant problem would be welcome in these stagnant days."

Things had indeed been very slow with us, and I had learned to dread such periods of inaction, for I knew by experience that my companion's brain was so abnormally active that it was dangerous to leave it without material upon which to work. For years I had gradually weaned him from that drug mania which had threatened once to check his remarkable career. Now, I knew that under ordinary conditions he no longer craved for this artificial stimulus, but I was well aware that the fiend was not dead, but sleeping; and I have known that the sleep was a light one, and the waking near, when, in periods of idleness, I have seen the drawn look upon Holmes's ascetic face and the brooding of his deep-set and inscrutable eyes. Therefore I blessed this Mr. Overton, whoever he might be, since he had come with his enigmatic message to break that dangerous calm which brought more peril to my friend than all the storms of his tempestuous life.

As we had expected, the telegram was soon followed by its sender, and the card of Mr. Cyril Overton, of Trinity College, Cambridge, announced the arrival of an enormous young man, sixteen stone of solid bone and muscle, who spanned the doorway with his broad shoulders, and looked from one of us to the other with a comely face which was haggard with anxiety:

"Mr. Sherlock Holmes?"

My companion bowed.

"I've been down to Scotland Yard, Mr. Holmes. I saw Inspector Stanley Hopkins. He advised me to come to you. He said the case, so far as he could see, was more in your line than in that of the regular police."

"Pray sit down and tell me what is the matter."

"It's awful, Mr. Holmes, simply awful! I wonder my hair isn't gray. Godfrey Staunton—you've heard of him, of course. He's simply the hinge that the whole team turns on. I'd rather spare two from the pack, and have Godfrey for my three-quarter line. Whether it's passing, or tackling, or dribbling, there's no one to touch him; and then he's got the head, and can hold us all together. What am I to do? That's what I ask you, Mr. Holmes. There's Moorhouse, first reserve, but he is trained as a half, and he always edges right in on to the scrum, instead of keeping out on the touch line. He's a fine place-kick, it's true, but then he has no judgment, and he can't sprint for nuts. Why, Morton or Johnson, the Oxford fliers, could romp round him. Stevenson is fast enough, but he couldn't drop from the twenty-five line, and a three-quarter who can't either punt or drop isn't worth a place for pace alone. No, Mr. Holmes, we are done, unless you can help me to find Godfrey Staunton."

My friend had listened with amused surprise to this long speech, which was poured forth with extraordinary vigor and earnestness, every point being driven home by the slapping of a brawny hand upon the speaker's knee. When our visitor was silent, Holmes stretched out his hand and took down letter "S" of his commonplace book. For once he dug in vain into that mine of varied information.

"There is Arthur H. Staunton, the rising young forger," said he, "and there was Henry Staunton, whom I helped to hang, but Godfrey Staunton is a new name to me."

It was our visitor's turn to look surprised.

"Why, Mr. Holmes, I thought you knew things," said he. "I suppose, then, if you have never heard of Godfrey Staunton, you don't know Cyril Overton, either?"

Holmes shook his head good-humoredly.

"Great Scott!" cried the athlete. "Why, I was first reserve for England against Wales, and I've skippered the Varsity all this year. But that's nothing! I didn't think there was a soul in England who didn't know Godfrey Staunton, the crack three-quarter, Cambridge, Blackheath, and five Internationals. Good Lord! Mr. Holmes, where *have* you lived?"

Holmes laughed at the young giant's naïve astonishment.

"You live in a different world to me, Mr. Overton, a sweeter and healthier one. My ramifications stretch out into many sections of society, but never, I am happy to say, into amateur sport, which is the best and soundest thing in England. However, your unexpected visit this morning shows me that even in that world of fresh air and fair play there may be work for me to do; so now, my good sir, I beg you to sit down and to tell me slowly and quietly, exactly what it is that has occurred, and how you desire that I should help you."

Young Overton's face assumed the bothered look of the man who is more accustomed to using his muscles than his wits, but by degrees, with many repetitions and obscurities which I may omit from his narrative, he laid his strange story before us:

"It's this way, Mr. Holmes. As I have said, I am the skipper of the Rugger team of Cambridge Varsity, and Godfrey Staunton is my best man. To-morrow we play Oxford. Yesterday we all came up, and we settled at Bentley's private hotel. At ten o'clock I went round and saw that all the fellows had gone to roost, for I believe in strict training and plenty of sleep to keep a team fit. I had a word or two with Godfrey before he turned in. He seemed to me to be pale and bothered. I asked him what was the matter. He said he was all right—just a touch of headache. I bade him good-night and left him. Half an hour later the porter tells me that a rough-looking man with a beard called with a note for Godfrey. He had not gone to bed, and the note was taken to his room. Godfrey read it and fell back in a chair as if he had been pole-axed. The porter was so scared that he was going to fetch me, but Godfrey stopped him, had a drink of water and pulled himself together. Then he went downstairs, said a few words to the man who was waiting in the hall, and the two of them went off together. The last that the porter saw of them, they were almost running down the street in the direction of the Strand. This morning, Godfrey's room was empty, his bed had never been slept in, and his things were all just as I had seen them the night before. He had gone off at a moment's notice with this stranger, and no word has come from him since. I don't believe he will ever come back. He was a sportsman, was Godfrey, down to his marrow, and he wouldn't have stopped his training and let in his skipper, if it were not for some cause that was too strong for him. No, I feel as if he were gone for good and we should never see him again."

Sherlock Holmes listened with the deepest attention to this singular narrative.

"What did you do?" he asked.

"I wired to Cambridge to learn if anything had been heard of him there. I have had an answer. No one has seen him."

"Could he have got back to Cambridge?"

"Yes, there is a late train—quarter past eleven."

"But as far as you can ascertain he did not take it?"

"No, he has not been seen."

"What did you do next?"

"I wired to Lord Mount-James."

"Why to Lord Mount-James?"

"Godfrey is an orphan, and Lord Mount-James is his nearest relative—his uncle, I believe."

"Indeed! This throws new light upon the matter. Lord Mount-James is one of the richest men in England."

"So I've heard Godfrey say."

"And your friend was closely related?"

"Yes, he was his heir, and the old boy is nearly eighty—cram full of gout, too. They say he could chalk his billiard-cue with his knuckles. He never allowed Godfrey a shilling in his life, for he is an absolute miser, but it will all come to him right enough."

"Have you heard from Lord Mount-James?"

"No."

"What motive could your friend have in going to Lord Mount-James?"

"Well, something was worrying him the night before, and if it was to do with money, it is possible that he would make for his nearest relative, who had so much of it; though, from all I have heard he would not have much chance of getting it. Godfrey was not fond of the old man. He would not go if he could help it."

"Well, we can soon determine that. If your friend was going to his relative, Lord Mount-James, you have then to explain the visit of this rough-looking fellow at so late an hour, and the agitation that was caused by his coming."

Cyril Overton pressed his hands to his head. "I can make nothing of it," said he.

"Well, well, I have a clear day, and I shall be happy to look into the matter," said Holmes. "I should strongly recommend you to make your preparations for your Match without reference to this young gentleman. It must, as you say, have been an overpowering necessity which tore him away in such a fashion, and the same necessity is likely to hold him away. Let us step round together to the hotel, and see if the porter can throw any fresh light upon the matter."

Sherlock Holmes was a past master in the art of putting a humble witness at his ease; and very soon in the privacy of Godfrey Staunton's abandoned room he had extracted all that the porter had to tell. The visitor of the night before was not a gentleman, neither was he a workingman. He was simply what the porter described as a "medium-looking chap"; a man of fifty, beard grizzled, pale face, quietly dressed. He seemed himself to be agitated. The porter had observed his hand trembling when he held out the note. Godfrey Staunton had crammed the note into his pocket. Staunton had not shaken hands with the man in the hall. They had exchanged a few sentences, of which the porter had only distinguished the one word "time." Then they had hurried off in the manner described. It was just half-past ten by the hall clock.

"Let me see!" said Holmes, seating himself on Staunton's bed. "You are the day porter, are you not?"

"Yes, sir, I go off duty at eleven."

"The night porter saw nothing, I suppose?"

"No, sir; one theatre party came in late. No one else."

"Were you on duty all day yesterday?"

"Yes, sir."

"Did you take any messages to Mr. Staunton?"

"Yes, sir, one telegram."

"Ah! that's interesting. What o'clock was this?"

"About six."

"Where was Mr. Staunton when he received it?"

"Here in his room."

"Were you present when he opened it?"

"Yes, sir; I waited to see if there was an answer."

"Well, was there?"

"Yes, sir. He wrote an answer."

"Did you take it?"

"No, he took it himself."

"But he wrote it in your presence?"

"Yes, sir. I was standing by the door, and he with his back turned at that table. When he had written it he said: 'All right, porter, I will take this myself.'"

"What did he write it with?"

"A pen, sir."

"Was the telegraphic form one of these on the table?"

"Yes, sir, it was the top one."

Holmes rose. Taking the forms, he carried them over to the window, and carefully examined that which was uppermost.

"It is a pity he did not write in pencil," said he, throwing them down again with a shrug of disappointment. "As you have no doubt frequently observed, Watson, the impression usually goes through, a fact which has dissolved many a happy marriage. However, I can find no trace here. I rejoice, however, to perceive that he wrote with a broad-pointed quill pen, and I can hardly doubt that we will find some impression upon this blotting-pad. Ah, yes, surely this is the very thing!"

He tore off a strip of the blotting-paper and turned toward us the following hieroglyphic:

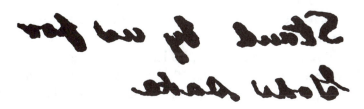

Cyril Overton was much excited. "Hold it to the glass!" he cried.

"That is unnecessary," said Holmes. "The paper is thin, and the reverse will give the message. Here it is." He turned it over and we read:

"So that is the tail-end of the telegram which Godfrey Staunton despatched within a few hours of his disappearance. There are at least six words of the message which have escaped us; but what remains, 'Stand by us, for God's sake,' proves that this young man saw a formidable danger which approached him, and from which someone else could protect him. '*Us*,' mark you! Another person was involved. Who should it be but the pale-faced, bearded man, who seemed himself in so nervous a state. What, then, is the connection between Godfrey Staunton and the bearded man? And what is the third source from which each of them sought for help against pressing danger? Our inquiry has already narrowed down to that."

"We have only to find to whom that telegram is addressed," I suggested.

"Exactly, my dear Watson. Your reflection, though profound, had already crossed my mind. But I daresay it may have come to your notice that, if you walk into a post office and demand to see the counterfoil of another man's message, there may be some disinclination on the part of the officials to oblige you. There is so much red tape in these matters! However, I have no doubt that, with a little delicacy and finesse, the end may be attained. Meanwhile, I should like, in your presence, Mr. Overton, to go through these papers which have been left upon the table."

There were a number of letters, bills, and note-books which Holmes turned over and examined with quick, nervous fingers and darting, penetrating eyes. "Nothing here," he said at last. "By the way, I suppose your friend was a healthy young fellow—nothing amiss with him?"

"Sound as a bell."

"Have you ever known him ill?"

"Not a day. He has been laid up with a hack, and once he slipped his knee-cap, but that was nothing."

"Perhaps he was not as strong as you suppose. I should think he may have had some secret trouble. With your assent, I will put one or two of these papers in my pocket, in case they should bear upon our future inquiry."

"One moment, one moment!" cried a querulous voice; and we looked up to find a queer little old man, jerking and twitching in the doorway. He was dressed in rusty black, with a very broad-brimmed top-hat and a loose white necktie—the whole effect being that of a very rustic parson or of an undertaker's mute. Yet, in spite of his shabby and even absurd appearance, his voice had a sharp crackle, and his manner a quick intensity which commanded attention.

"Who are you, sir, and by what right do you touch this gentleman's papers?" he asked.

"I am a private detective, and I am endeavoring to explain his disappearance."

"Oh, you are, are you? And who instructed you, eh?"

"This gentleman, Mr. Staunton's friend, was referred to me by Scotland Yard."

"Who are you, sir?"

"I am Cyril Overton."

"Then it is you who sent me a telegram. My name is Lord Mount-James. I came round as quickly as the Bayswater 'bus would bring me. So you have instructed a detective?"

"Yes, sir."

"And are you prepared to meet the cost?"

"I have no doubt, sir, that my friend Godfrey, when we find him, will be prepared to do that."

"But if he is never found, eh? Answer me that!"

"In that case, no doubt his family—"

"Nothing of the sort, sir!" screamed the little man. "Don't look to me for a penny—not a penny! You understand that, Mr. Detective! I am all the family that this young man has got, and I tell you that I am not responsible. If he has any expectations, it is due to the fact that I have never wasted money, and I do not propose to begin to do so now. As to those papers with which you are making so free, I may tell you that, in case there should be anything of any value among them, you will be held strictly to account for what you do with them."

"Very good, sir," said Sherlock Holmes. "May I ask, in the meanwhile, whether you have yourself any theory to account for this young man's disappearance?"

"No, sir, I have not. He is big enough and old enough to look after himself, and if he is so foolish as to lose himself, I entirely refuse to accept the responsibility of hunting for him."

"I quite understand your position," said Holmes, with a mischievous twinkle in his eyes. "Perhaps you don't quite understand mine. Godfrey Staunton appears to have been a poor man. If he has been kidnapped, it could not have been for anything which he himself possesses. The fame of your wealth has gone abroad, Lord Mount-James, and it is entirely possible that a gang of thieves have secured your nephew in order to gain from him some information as to your house, your habits, and your treasure."

The face of our unpleasant little visitor turned as white as his neckcloth.

"Good God, sir, what an idea! I never thought of such villainy! What inhuman rogues there are in the world! But Godfrey is a fine lad—a stanch lad. Nothing would induce him to give his old uncle away. I'll have the plate moved over to the Bank this evening. In the meantime, spare no pains, Mr. Detective! I beg you to leave no stone unturned to bring him safely back. As to money, well, so far as a fiver, or even a tener, goes, you can always look to me."

Even in his chastened frame of mind the noble miser could give us no information which could help us, for he knew little of the private life of his nephew. Our only clew lay in the truncated telegram; and with a copy of this in his hand, Holmes set forth to find a second link for his chain.

We had shaken off Lord Mount-James, and Overton had gone to consult with the other members of his team over the misfortune which had befallen them.

There was a telegraph office at a short distance from the hotel. We halted outside it.

"It's worth trying, Watson," said he. "Of course, with a warrant we could demand to see the counterfoils, but we have not reached that stage yet. I don't suppose they remember faces in so busy a place. Let us venture it."

"I am sorry to trouble you," said Holmes, in his blandest manner, to the young woman behind the grating, "there is some small mistake about a telegram I sent yesterday. I have had no answer, and I very much fear that I must have omitted to put my name at the end. Could you tell me if this was so?"

The young woman turned over a sheaf of counterfoils.

"What o'clock was it?" she asked.

"A little after six."

"Whom was it to?"

Holmes put his finger to his lips, and glanced at me. "The last words in it were 'for God's sake,'" he whispered confidentially; "I am very anxious at getting no answer."

The young woman separated one of the forms.

"This is it. There is no name," said she, smoothing it out upon the counter.

"Then that, of course, accounts for my getting no answer," said Holmes. "Dear me, how very stupid of me, to be sure! Good-morning, Miss, and many thanks for having relieved my mind." He chuckled and rubbed his hands when we found ourselves in the street once more.

"Well?" I asked.

"We progress, my dear Watson, we progress. I had seven different schemes for getting a glimpse of that telegram, but I could hardly hope to succeed the very first time."

"And what have you gained?"

"A starting-point for our investigation." He hailed a cab. "King's Cross Station," said he.

"We have a journey, then?"

"Yes, I think we must run down to Cambridge together. All the indications seem to me to point in that direction."

"Tell me," I asked, as we rattled up Grey's Inn Road, "have you any suspicion yet as to the cause of the disappearance? I don't think that among all our cases I have known one where the motives are more obscure. Surely you don't imagine that he may be kidnapped in order to give information against his wealthy uncle?"

"I confess, my dear Watson, that that does not appeal to me as a very probable explanation. It struck me, however, as being the one which was most likely to interest that exceedingly unpleasant old person."

"It certainly did that. But what are your alternatives?"

"I could mention several. You must admit that it is curious and suggestive that this incident should occur on the eve of this important match, and should involve the only man whose presence seems essential to the success of the side. It may, of course, be coincidence, but it is interesting. Amateur sport is free from betting, but a good deal of outside betting goes on among the public, and it is possible that it might be worth someone's while to get at a player as the ruffians of the turf get at a race-horse. There is one explanation. A second very obvious one is that this young man really is the heir of a great property, however modest his means may at present be, and it is not impossible that a plot to hold him for ransom might be concocted."

"These theories take no account of the telegram."

"Quite true, Watson. The telegram still remains the only solid thing with which we have to deal, and we must not permit our attention to wander away from it. It is to gain light upon the purpose of this telegram that we are now upon our way to Cambridge. The path of our investigation is at present obscure, but I shall be very much surprised if before evening we have not cleared it up, and made a considerable advance along it."

It was already dark when we reached the old University city. Holmes took a cab at the station, and ordered the man to drive to the house of Dr. Leslie Armstrong. A few minutes later we had stopped at a large mansion in the busiest thoroughfare. We were shown in, and after a long wait were at last admitted into the consulting-room, where we found the Doctor, seated behind his table.

It argues the degree in which I had lost touch with my profession that the name of Leslie Armstrong was unknown to me. Now, I am aware that he is not only one of the heads of the medical school of the University, but a thinker of European reputation in more than one branch of science. Yet even without knowing his brilliant record one could not fail to be impressed by a mere glance at the man, the square, massive face, the brooding eyes under the thatched brows, and the granite molding of the inflexible jaw. A man of deep character, a man with an alert mind, grim, ascetic, self-contained, formidable—so I read Dr. Leslie Armstrong. He held my friend's card in his hand, and he looked up with no very pleased expression upon his dour features.

"I have heard your name, Mr. Sherlock Holmes, and I am aware of your profession, one of which I by no means approve."

"In that, Doctor, you will find yourself in agreement with every criminal in the country," said my friend, quietly.

"So far as your efforts are directed toward the suppression of crime, sir, they must have the support of every reasonable member of the community, though I can not doubt that the official machinery is amply sufficient for the purpose. Where your calling is more open to criticism is when you pry into the secrets of private individuals, when you rake up family matters which are better hidden, and when you incidentally waste the time of men who are more busy than yourself. At the present moment, for example, I should be writing a treatise instead of conversing with you."

"No doubt, Doctor, and yet the conversation may prove more important than the treatise. Incidentally, I may tell you that we are doing the reverse of what you very justly blame, and that we are endeavoring to prevent anything like public exposure of private matters which must necessarily follow when once the case is fairly in the hands of the official police. You may look upon me simply as an irregular pioneer who goes in front of the regular forces of the country. I have come to ask you about Mr. Godfrey Staunton."

"What about him?"

"You know him, do you not?"

"He is an intimate friend of mine."

"You are aware that he has disappeared?"

"Ah, indeed!" There was no change of expression in the rugged features of the Doctor.

"He left his hotel last night. He has not been heard of."

"No doubt he will return."

"To-morrow is the Varsity football match."

"I have no sympathy with these childish games. The young man's fate interests me deeply, since I know him and like him. The football match does not come within my horizon at all."

"I claim your sympathy then in my investigation of Mr. Staunton's fate. Do you know where he is?"

"Certainly not."

"You have not seen him since yesterday?"

"No, I have not."

"Was Mr. Staunton a healthy man?"

"Absolutely."

"Did you ever know him ill?"

"Never."

Holmes popped a sheet of paper before the Doctor's eyes. "Then perhaps you will explain this receipted bill for thirteen guineas, paid by Mr. Godfrey Staunton last month to Dr. Leslie Armstrong of Cambridge. I picked it out from among the papers upon his desk."

The Doctor flushed with anger.

"I do not feel that there is any reason why I should render an explanation to you, Mr. Holmes."

Holmes replaced the bill in his note-book. "If you prefer a public explanation it must come sooner or later," said he. "I have already told you that I can hush up that which others will be bound to publish, and you would really be wiser to take me into your complete confidence."

"I know nothing about it."

"Did you hear from Mr. Staunton in London?"

"Certainly not."

"Dear me, dear me, the post-office again!" Holmes sighed wearily. "A most urgent telegram was despatched to you from London by Godfrey Staunton at six-fifteen yesterday evening—a telegram which is undoubtedly associated with his disappearance—and yet you have not had it. It is most culpable. I shall certainly go down to the office here and register a complaint."

Dr. Leslie Armstrong sprang up from behind his desk, and his dark face was crimson with fury.

"I'll trouble you to walk out of my house, sir," said he. "You can tell your employer, Lord Mount-James, that I do not wish to have anything to do either with him or with his agents. No, sir, not another word!" He rang the bell furiously. "John, show these gentlemen out!" A pompous butler ushered us severely to the door, and we found ourselves in the street. Holmes burst out laughing.

"Dr. Leslie Armstrong is certainly a man of energy and character," said he. "I have not seen a man who if he turned his talents that way, was more calculated to fill the gap left by the illustrious Moriarty. And now, my poor Watson, here we are stranded and friendless in this inhospitable town, which we can not leave without abandoning our case. This little inn just opposite Armstrong's house is singularly adapted to our needs. If you would engage a front room, and purchase the necessaries for the night, I may have time to make a few inquiries."

These few inquiries proved, however, to be a more lengthy proceeding than Holmes had imagined, for he did not return to the inn until nearly nine o'clock. He was pale and dejected, stained with dust, and exhausted with hunger and fatigue. A cold supper was ready upon the table, and when his needs were satisfied and his pipe alight he was ready to take that half-comic and wholly philosophic view which was natural to him when his affairs were going awry. The sound of carriage wheels caused him to rise and glance out of the window. A brougham and pair of grays, under the glare of a gas-lamp, stood before the Doctor's door.

"It's been out three hours," said Holmes; "started at half past six, and here it is back again. That gives a radius of ten or twelve miles, and he does it once or sometimes twice a day."

"No unusual thing for a doctor in practice."

"But Armstrong is not really a doctor in practice. He is a lecturer and a consultant, but he does not care for general practice, which distracts him from his literary work. Why, then, does he make these long journeys, which must be exceedingly irksome to him, and who is it that he visits?"

"His coachman—?"

"My dear Watson, can you doubt that it was to him that I first applied? I do not know whether it came from his own innate depravity, or from the promptings of his master, but he was rude enough to set a dog at me. Neither dog nor man liked the look of my stick, however, and the matter fell through. Relations were strained after that, and further inquiries out of the question. All that I have learned I got from a friendly native in the yard of our own inn. It was he who told me of the Doctor's habits, and of his daily journey. At that instant, to give point to his words, the carriage came round to the door."

"Could you not follow it?"

"Excellent Watson! You are scintillating this evening. The idea did cross my mind. There is, as you may have observed, a bicycle shop next to our inn. Into this I rushed, engaged a bicycle, and was able to get started before the carriage was quite out of sight. I rapidly overtook it, and then, keeping at a discreet distance of a hundred yards or so, I followed its lights, until we were clear of the town. We had got well out on the country road when a somewhat mortifying incident occurred. The carriage stopped, the Doctor alighted, walked swiftly back to where I had also halted, and told me in an excellent sardonic fashion that he feared the road was narrow, and that he hoped his carriage did not impede the passage of my bicycle. Nothing could have been more admirable than his way of putting it. I at once rode past the carriage, and, keeping to the main road, I went on for a few miles, and then halted in a convenient place to see if the carriage passed. There was no sign of it, however, and so it became evident that it had turned down one of several side roads which I had observed. I rode back, but again saw nothing of the carriage, and now, as you perceive, it has returned after me. Of course, I had at the outset no particular reason to connect these journeys with the disappearance of Godfrey Staunton, and was only inclined to investigate them on the general grounds that everything which concerns Dr. Armstrong is at present of interest to us; but, now that I find that he keeps so keen a lookout upon any one who may follow him on these excursions, the affair appears more important, and I shall not be satisfied until the matter is clear."

"We can follow him to-morrow?"

"Can we? It is not so easy as you seem to think. You are not familiar with Cambridgeshire scenery, are you? It does not lend itself to concealment. All this country that I passed over to-night is as flat and clean as the palm of your hand, and the man we are following is no fool, as he very clearly showed to-night. I have wired to Overton to let us know any fresh London developments at this address, and in the meantime we can only concentrate our attention upon Dr. Armstrong, whose name the obliging young lady at the office allowed me to read upon the counterfoil of Staunton's urgent message. He knows where the young man is—to that I'll swear—and if he knows, then it must be our own fault if we can not manage to know it also. At present it must be admitted that the odd trick is in his possession, and, as you are aware, Watson, it is not my habit to leave the game in that condition."

And yet the next day brought us no nearer to the solution of the mystery. A note was handed in after breakfast, which Holmes passed across to me with a smile.

"Sir," it ran, "I can assure you that you are wasting your time in dogging my movements. I have, as you discovered last night, a window at the back of my brougham, and if you desire a twenty-mile ride which will lead you to the spot from which you started, you have only to follow me. Meanwhile I can inform you that no spying upon me can in any way help Mr. Godfrey Staunton, and I am convinced that the best service you can do to that gentleman is to return at once to London and to report to your employer that you are unable to trace him. Your time in Cambridge will certainly be wasted.

Yours faithfully,
"LESLIE ARMSTRONG"

"An outspoken, honest antagonist is the Doctor," said Holmes. "Well, well, he excites my curiosity, and I must really know more before I leave him."

"His carriage is at his door now," said I. "There he is stepping into it. Suppose I try my luck upon the bicycle!"

"No, no, my dear Watson! With all respect for your natural acumen, I do not think that you are quite a match for the worthy doctor. I think that possibly I can attain our end by some independent explorations of my own. I am afraid that I must leave you to your own devices, as the appearance of *two* inquiring strangers upon a sleepy countryside might excite more gossip than I care for. No doubt you will find some sights to amuse you in this venerable city, and I hope to bring back a more favorable report to you before evening."

Once more, however, my friend was destined to be disappointed. He came back at night weary and unsuccessful.

"I have had a blank day, Watson. Having got the Doctor's general direction, I spent the day in visiting all the villages upon that side of Cambridge, and comparing notes with publicans and other local news agencies. I have covered some ground: Chesterton, Histon, Waterbeach, and Oakington have each been explored, and have each proved disappointing. The daily appearance of a brougham and pair could hardly have been overlooked in such sleepy hollows. The Doctor has scored once more. Is there a telegram for me?"

"Yes, I opened it. Here it is: 'Ask for Pompey from Jeremy Dixon, Trinity College.' I don't understand it."

"Oh, it is clear enough. It is from our friend Overton, and is in answer to a question from me. I'll just send round a note to Mr. Jeremy Dixon, and then I have no doubt that our luck will turn. By the way, is there any news of the match?"

"Yes, the local evening paper has an excellent account in its last edition. Oxford won by a goal and two tries. The last sentences of the description says: 'The defeat of the Light Blues may be entirely attributed to the unfortunate absence of the crack International Godfrey Staunton, whose want was felt at every instant of the game. The lack of combination in the three-quarter line and their weakness both in attack and defence more than neutralized the efforts of a heavy and hard-working pack."

"Then our friend Overton's forebodings have been justified," said Holmes. "Personally, I am in agreement with Dr. Armstrong, and football does not come within my horizon. Early to bed to-night, Watson, for I foresee that to-morrow may be an eventful day."

I was horrified by my first glimpse of my friend next morning, for he sat by the fire holding his tiny hypodermic syringe. I associated that instrument with the single weakness of his nature, and I feared the worst when I saw it glittering in his hand. He laughed at my expression of dismay, and he laid it upon the table.

"No, no, my dear fellow, there is no cause for alarm. It is not upon this occasion the instrument of evil, but it will rather prove to be the key which will unlock our mystery. On this syringe I base all my hopes. I have just returned from a small scouting expedition, and everything is favorable. Eat a good breakfast, Watson, for I propose to get upon Dr. Armstrong's trail to-day, and once on it I will not stop for rest or food until I run him to his burrow."

"In that case," said I, "we had best carry our breakfast with us, for he is making an early start. His carriage is at the door."

"Never mind. Let him go. He will be clever if he can drive where I can not follow him. When you have finished come downstairs with me, and I will introduce you to a detective who is a very eminent specialist in the work that lies before us."

When we descended I followed Holmes into the stable yard, where he opened the door of a loose box, and let out a squat, lop-eared, white-and-tan dog, something between a beagle and a foxhound.

"Let me introduce you to Pompey," said he. "Pompey is the pride of the local draghounds, no very great flier, as his build will show, but a stanch hound on a scent. Well, Pompey, you may not be fast, but I expect you will be too fast for a couple of middle-aged London gentlemen, so I will take the liberty of fastening this leather leash to your collar. Now, boy, come along and show what you can do." He led him across to the

Doctor's door. The dog sniffed round for an instant, and then with a shrill whine of excitement started off down the street, tugging at his leash in his efforts to go faster. In half an hour we were clear of the town, and hastening down a country road.

"What have you done, Holmes?" I asked.

"A threadbare and venerable device, but useful upon occasion. I walked into the Doctor's yard this morning and shot my syringe full of aniseed over the hindwheel. A draghound will follow aniseed from here to John O'Groat's, and our friend Armstrong would have to drive through the Cam before he could shake Pompey off his trail. Oh, the cunning rascal—this is how he gave me the slip the other night!"

The dog had suddenly turned out of the main road into a grass-grown lane. Half a mile further this opened into another broad road, and the trail turned hard to the right in the direction of the town, which we had just quitted. The road took a sweep to the south of the town and continued in the opposite direction to that in which we started.

"This detour has been entirely for our benefit, then," said Holmes."No wonder that my inquiries among those villages led to nothing. The Doctor has certainly played the game for all it is worth, and one would like to know the reason for such elaborate deception. This should be the village of Trumpington to the right of us. And by Jove, here is the brougham coming round the corner! Quick, Watson, quick, or we are done!"

He sprang through a gate into a field, dragging the reluctant Pompey after him. We had hardly got under the shelter of the hedge when the carriage rattled past.

"I fear there is some dark ending to our quest," said he. "It can not be long before we know it. Come, Pompey! Ah, it is the cottage in the field!"

There could be no doubt that we had reached the end of our journey. Pompey ran about and whined eagerly outside the gate where the marks of the brougham's wheels were still to be seen. A footpath led across to the lonely cottage. Holmes tied the dog to the hedge, and we hastened onward. My friend knocked at the little rustic door and knocked again without response. And yet the cottage was not deserted, for a low sound came to our ears, a kind of drone of misery and despair which was indescribably melancholy. Holmes paused irresolute, and then he glanced back at the road which we had just traversed. A brougham was coming down it, and there could be no mistaking those gray horses.

"By Jove, the Doctor is coming back!" cried Holmes. "That settles it. We shall see what it means before he comes."

He opened the door, and we stepped into the hall. The droning sound swelled louder upon our ears until it became one long deep wail of distress. It came from upstairs. Holmes darted up and I followed him. He pushed open a half-closed door and we both stood appalled at the sight before us.

A woman, young and beautiful, was lying dead upon the bed. Her calm pale face, with dim, wide-opened blue eyes, looked upward from amid a great tangle of golden hair. At the foot of the bed, half sitting, half kneeling, his face buried in the clothes, was a young man whose frame was racked by his sobs. So absorbed was he by his bitter grief that he never looked up until Holmes's hand was on his shoulder.

"Are you Mr. Godfrey Staunton?"

"Yes, yes, I am—but you are too late. She is dead."

The man was so dazed that he could not be made to understand that we were anything but doctors who had been sent to his assistance. Holmes was endeavoring to suggest a few words of consolation, and to explain the alarm which had been caused to his friends by his sudden disappearance, when there was a step upon the stairs, and there was the heavy, stern, questioning face of Dr. Armstrong at the door.

"So, gentlemen," said he, "you have attained your end, and have certainly chosen a particularly delicate moment for your intrusion. I would not brawl in the presence of death, but I can assure you that if I were a younger man your monstrous conduct would not pass with impunity."

"Excuse me, Dr. Armstrong. I think we are a little at cross purposes," said my friend, with dignity. "If you could step downstairs with us we may each be able to give some light to the other upon this miserable affair."

A minute later the grim Doctor and ourselves were in the sitting-room below.

"Well, sir?" said he.

"I wish you to understand, in the first place, that I am not employed by Lord Mount-James, and that my sympathies in this matter are entirely against that nobleman. When a man is lost it is my duty to ascertain his fate, but having done so the matter ends so far as I am concerned, and so long as there is nothing criminal I am much more anxious to hush up private scandals than to give them publicity. If, as I imagine, there is no breach of the law in this matter, you can absolutely depend upon my discretion and my co-operation in keeping the facts out of the papers."

Dr. Armstrong took a quick step forward and wrung Holmes by the hand.

"You are a good fellow," said he. "I had misjudged you. I thank Heaven that my compunction at leaving poor Staunton all alone in this plight caused me to turn my carriage back and so to make your acquaintance. Knowing as much as you do, the situation is very easily explained. A year ago Godfrey Staunton lodged in London for a time, and became passionately attached to his landlady's daughter, whom he married. She was as good as she was beautiful, and as intelligent as she was good. No man need be ashamed of such a wife. But Godfrey was the heir to this crabbed old nobleman, and it was quite certain that the news of his marriage would have been the end of his inheritance. I knew the lad well, and I loved him for his many excellent qualities. I did all I could to help him to keep things straight. We did our very best to keep the thing from everyone, for, when once such a whisper gets about it is not long before everyone has heard it. Thanks to this lonely cottage and his own discretion, Godfrey has succeeded up to now. Their secret was known to no one save to me and to one excellent servant, who has at present gone for assistance to Trumpington. But at last there came a terrible blow in the shape of dangerous illness to his wife. It was consumption of the most virulent kind. The poor boy was half-crazed with grief, and yet he had to go to London to play this match, for he could not get out of it without explanations which would expose his secret. I tried to cheer him up by wire, and he sent me one in reply imploring me to do all I could. This was the telegram which you appear in some inexplicable way to have seen. I did not tell him how urgent the danger was, for I knew that he could do no good here, but I sent the truth to the girl's father, and he very injudiciously communicated it to Godfrey. The result was that he came straight away in a state bordering on frenzy, and has remained in the same state, kneeling at the end of her bed, until this morning death put an end to her sufferings. That is all, Mr. Holmes, and I am sure that I can rely upon your discretion, and that of your friend."

Holmes grasped the Doctor's hand.

"Come, Watson," said he, and we passed from that house of grief into the pale sunlight of the winter day.

In this brief story we meet an irascible spitball pitcher intent on making it back to the major leagues. The author treats the reader to a surprise ending. The story was originally published in Esquire.

James Kieran

RETURN OF A TROUBLE MAKER (1943)

WHEN THEY BARRED THE SPITTER everybody said Phil was through, but he was a foxy devil and he worked up a new curve and a change of pace and he kept hanging on year after year.

But when we made the first western trip that year you could see he was all washed up and in Cincinnati, George O'Leary called Phil in and told him to pack his bag for Kansas City. He was a ten-year man and didn't have to go unless he wanted to, but I guess he had to have a job.

Going through the lobby he waved to Frank Johnson and me. "I'll be back," he said.

"How come?" Frank Johnson said.

"Cause I've got a wife and four kids and you can't send girls to college on no minor league salary."

"Good luck, Phil," I said.

"I don't want no good wishes from you young punks," Phil said. He glared at me. "And if you don't like it you can go to hell."

"O.K., Phil, take it easy," Frank Johnson said.

"O.K.," Phil said as he left.

That was the trouble with Phil. He could have been a coach because he knew the game inside out and he'd been in the league a long while and had every hitter pegged. But he couldn't get along with anybody. He always wanted to start a fight.

We were sorry to see him go though, and even missed the fights he used to start. We got going good that year and by the Fourth we were up there one, two, three. It was a hot summer but we played in luck and when we hit Labor Day we were still in there.

We finished up the last western trip half a game in front and on the train back that night, I saw a little dispatch in the paper from Kansas City about Phil being unconditionally released. "The action followed rumors of a recent club house row," the story read.

"The same old army game," Frank said.

All we were thinking about was that final home stand and that half game edge we had.

And then Bill Jolson slipped, trying to field a bunt when the grass was wet. Bill had won twenty-two games for us and the sports writers were saying he would pitch us right into the Series. When he slipped, he fractured his ankle and that seemed to fracture our pennant chances too.

We broke even with the Braves in a double header the next day and when we got back to the club house who was standing there but Phil. We were feeling pretty good and we all said hello but Phil just stared at us.

I was walking past George O'Leary's cubbyhole when I saw Phil saying to George that George needed a tough experienced pitcher for the home stretch, and O'Leary sighed and he said:

"I'll tell you what I'll do, Phil. You and me seem to be able to get along even if nobody else could do it with you. I'm not kidding you, my job depends on coming through this year. I'll take you on and if you can really help us come through before the end of the season, I'll have a good chance of getting you on as coach."

I heard Phil growling and I wondered why he should kick about a proposition like that. But he took it because he was in uniform the next day.

"Well, you had to call on the Old Timer," he said. "I told you I'd be back."

His voice was jeering and sharp and a few of the boys stopped dressing to look at him hard. They let it drop. We had plenty of worrying to do about hanging on ourselves and somehow we did, even with Phil complaining all the time because George didn't have to put him in, not even once. When the Cards came east for the final series it was us or the Bucs. If we won the last two games from the Cards we'd finish a couple of percentage points in front.

We pulled through in the first game two to one and Ed Corwin went all the way for us. Phil kept grousing about getting a chance.

The next afternoon, we stood to win or lose the flag. George told Phil to get out to the bull pen as usual and Phil began to grouse about what was the use of throwing them in that hot sun in the bull pen and stuff like that.

We did all right. Frank Johnson hit one into the right field boxes in the fourth and that put us three runs ahead. But the Cards picked up a couple in the sixth and in the seventh they would have gone ahead because Jack Marshbanks passed two men and it was only a running catch near the wall by Charley that kept us out of the soup.

In the eighth Marshbanks gave another pass. A single and another pass filled the bases. George waved Marshbanks out, and in from left field comes old Phil.

George O'Leary came over from the bench and said: "Well, here's what you been asking for. Now let's see it." Phil only looked at him.

We had two out, but Al Breslow, the Cards' first baseman, could powder that old apple. A hit would mean the ball game for the Cards. Phil took his time warming up. He slipped one in, lost his man and finally got it up to two and two. Breslow fouled a couple off and Phil was standing on the hill watching Breslow, when suddenly he walked back toward second base. He started over toward me.

"Why the hell don't you get in position?" he shouted.

I didn't know what he was talking about. He kept on coming toward me still shouting and waving his arms. Nick trotted across from short-stop.

"You can't do that to me!" Phil kept shouting.

It didn't make any sense. Two umpires came over and then Phil gave me a stiff push and I nearly knocked the umpires over. Nobody knew what it was all about.

The fight stopped as quick as it began and Phil went back on the mound. He wound up and sent as sharp a breaking curve as you would want to see right past Breslow and Breslow swung hard and missed. He left the bases loaded when he missed that third one.

The crowd went wild. We pushed another run over and the next inning held them tight and when the crowd poured out of the stands we were in.

Half a dozen of us made for Dinty's that night. As I was coming in I ran into Phil.

"You sure did it," I said. "But let me in on something. What were you doing when you tried to start a fight in the eighth?"

"Hell, boy," he said. "I'm supposed to be a trouble maker, ain't I? And the umpires watch pretty close, don't they?"

"Yeah," I said. "So what?"

"Well," Phil said, "the spitter's barred so I just started a row and everybody gets excited and the umpires are watching something else and I put the old spit on her and I breeze that curve past Breslow."

I guess the girls will get through college all right and I guess Phil will be a mighty valuable man to have around as coach next year because you can't beat an old trouble maker like that.

According to writer George Plimpton, the smaller the ball, the more creative writing there is on the sport. Thus we have many great stories on golf and baseball but hardly any on basketball—and none on beachball. The story here, originally published in Redbook, is a rarity, one of the few and certainly the best on the sport of basketball. Although basketball plays a key role in the story, it is more about the relationship between a father and his medical student son. Author Ethan Canin has a special talent for this kind of writing. He has a degree from Harvard Medical School and his books and stories display an extraordinary understanding of family. His first published collection of short stories, Emperor of the Air (1988), was called "the work of a phenomenally skilled writer" by the London Sunday Times. His other books include Blue River (1991), The Palace Thief (1994), and For Kings and Planets (1998). Canin is currently a professor at the University of Iowa Writers' Workshop.

Ethan Canin

THE CARNIVAL DOG, THE BUYER OF DIAMONDS (1988)

WHAT'S THE ONE THING you should never do? Quit? Depends on who you talk to. Steal? Cheat? Eat food from a dented can? Myron Lufkin's father, Abe, once told him never get your temperature taken at the hospital. Bring your own thermometer, he said; you should see how they wash theirs. He ought to have known; when he was at Yeshiva University he worked as an orderly in the hospital, slid patients around on gurneys, cleaned steelware. Myron knows all his father's hospital stories and all his rules. On the other hand, there are things you *should* do. Always eat sitting down. Wear a hat in the rain. What else? Never let the other guy start the fight. Certain inviolable commandments. In thirty-two years Myron Lufkin had never seen his father without an answer.

That is, until the day five years ago when Myron called home from Albert Einstein College of Medicine and told his father he had had enough, was quitting, leaving, *kaput,* he said. Now, Myron, living in Boston, sometime Jew, member of the public gym where he plays basketball and swims in the steamy pool after rounds, still calls home every other week. The phone calls, if he catches his father asleep, remind him of the day five years ago when he called to say that he was not, after all, going to be a doctor.

It was not the kind of thing you told Abe Lufkin. Abe Lufkin, a man who once on Election Day put three twelve-pound chains across his chest and dove into San Francisco Bay at Aquatic Park, to swim most of the mile and three-quarters across to Marin. As it turned out they had to pull him from the frothy cold water before he made the beach—but to give him credit, he was not a young man. In the *Chronicle* the next day there he was on an inside page, sputtering and shaking on the sand, steam rising off his body. Rachel, Myron's mother, is next to him in a sweater and baggy wool pants. Myron still has the newspaper clipping in one of his old butterfly display cases wrapped in tissue paper in a drawer in Boston.

On the day Myron called home from Albert Einstein to say that three years of studying and money, three years of his life, had been a waste, he could imagine the blood-rush in his father's head. But he knew what to expect. He kept firm, though he could feel the pulse in his own neck. Itzhak, his roommate at medical school, had stood behind him with his hand on Myron's shoulder, smoking a cigarette. But Abe simply did not believe it.

Myron didn't expect him to believe it: Abe, after all, didn't understand quitting. If his father had been a sea captain, Myron thought, he would have gone down with his ship—singing, boasting, denying the ocean that closed over his head—and this was not, in Myron's view, a glorious death.

It just showed stubbornness. His father was stubborn about everything. When he was young, for example, when stickball was what you did in the Bronx, Abe played basketball. Almost nobody else played. In those days, Abe told Myron, you went to the Yankee games when Detroit was in town and rooted for Hank Greenberg to hit one out, and when he did you talked about it and said how the *goyishe* umpires would have ruled it foul if they could have, if it hadn't been to center field. In Abe's day, baseball was played by men named McCarthy, Murphy, and Burdock, and basketball wasn't really played at all, except by the very very tall, awkward kids. But not Abe Lufkin. He was built like a road-show wrestler and he kept a basketball under his bed. It was his love for the game, maybe, that many years later made him decide to have a kid. When Myron was born, Abe nailed a backboard to the garage. This is my boy, he said, my *mensch*. He began playing basketball with his son when Myron was nine. But really, what they did was not playing. By the time Myron was in the fifth grade Abe had visions in his already balding pharmacist's head. He sat in the aluminum lawn furniture before dinner and counted out the one hundred layups Myron had to do from each side of the basket. One hundred from the left. One hundred from the right. No misses.

But it paid off. At Woodrow Wilson High, Myron was the star. Myron hitting a twenty-foot bank shot. Myron slipping a blind pass inside, stealing opponents' dribbles so their hands continued down, never realizing the ball was gone. Myron blocking the last-second shot. It was a show. Before the games he stood alone under the basket, holding his toes and stretching loose the muscles in his thighs. He knew Abe was sitting in the stands. His father always got there before the teams even came upstairs to the gym. He took the front-row seat at one corner and made Rachel take the one at the opposite corner. Then at halftime they switched. This way Abe could always see the basket his son was shooting at. After the games Abe waited in the car for Myron. Rachel sat in the back, and when Myron got in, Abe talked about the game until the windows steamed or Rachel finally said that it was unhealthy to sit like this in the cold. Then Abe wiped the windows and started the car, and they drove home with the heater blasting up warm air between the seats.

Abe had always believed the essence of the body was in the lungs, and sometimes, to keep Myron in shape for basketball, he challenged him to breath-holding contests. They sat facing each other across the kitchen table without breathing while an egg timer ran down between them. Myron could never beat his father, though; Abe held his breath like a blow-fish at low tide. Myron's eyes teared, his heart pounded in his head, his lungs swelled to combustion, while all the time his father just stared at him, winking. He made Myron admit defeat out loud. "Do you give?" Abe whispered when half the sand had run down through the timer. Myron swallowed, pressed his lips together, stared at the sand falling through the narrow neck. A few seconds later, Abe said it again: "Do you give?" Myron squeezed his legs together, held his hands over his mouth, stood up, sat down, and finally let his breath explode out. "I give," he said, then sat there until the egg timer ran down and Abe exhaled.

There was always this obsession in the Lufkin family, this holiness about the affairs of the body. What were wars or political speeches next to the importance of body heat, expansive lungs, or leg muscles that could take you up the stairs instead of the elevator? Abe told hospital stories because to him there was no more basic truth than keeping your bronchial tubes cleared, or drying between your toes. Any questions of the body were settled quickly and finally when Abe showed Myron the smelly fungus between his own toes, or opened the *Encyclopaedia Britannica* to pictures of stomach worms, syphilis, or skin rash.

Any religious fervor in the family went instead into this worship of the body. Rachel did not light candles on Friday nights, and Myron was never *bar-mitzvahed*. Instead there was health to be zealous about. It was Abe's way. But at times he wavered, and these were nearly the only times Myron ever saw him unsure—in the evenings when he read the newspaper and talked about the State of Israel, or on Friday nights sometimes when he stood in the living room with the lights off, staring out at the sidewalk as the congregation filtered by in wool coats and *yarmulkes*. It put Abe into a mood. The spring after Myron's fifteenth birthday he told Myron he was sending him to a Judaism camp in the mountains for the month of July. They were outside on the porch when Abe told him.

"What? A Judaism camp? I don't believe it."

"What don't you believe?"

"I'm not going to a Judaism camp."

"What's this? Yes, you're going. You've got no more religion than *goyim*. I've already sent the money."

"How much money?"

"Fifty dollars."

Then Abe went in from the porch, and that was the end of the argument. Myron knew he would have to go off in the hot, bright month of July. That was how Abe argued. He wasn't wordy. If you wanted to change his mind you didn't argue, you fought him with your fists or your knees. This was what he expected from the world, and this was what he taught his son. Once, when Myron was fourteen, Abe had taken him to a bar, and when the bouncer hadn't wanted to let him in Abe said, "This is my *mensch;* he's not going to drink," and had pushed Myron in front of him through the door. Later, when they stood in line to pee away their drinks, Abe told him you can do what you want with strangers because they don't want to fight. "Remember that," he said.

But the day after he told Myron about the Judaism camp, Abe came out on the porch and said, "Myron, you're a man now and we're going to decide about camp like men."

"What?"

"We're going to decide like men. We're going to have a race."

"We can't race."

"What do you mean, we can't race? We sure can. A footrace, from here to the end of the block. I win, you go to camp."

"I don't want to do it."

"What, do you want it longer? We can do what you want. We can make it two times to the corner."

Then Abe went into the house, and Myron sat on the porch. He didn't want to learn religion during the hottest month of the year, but also, he knew, there was something in beating his father that was like the toppling of an ancient king. What was it for him to race an old man? He walked down to the street, stretched the muscles in his legs, and sprinted up to the corner. He sprinted back down to the house, sat down on the steps, and decided it wasn't so bad to go to the mountains in July. That afternoon Abe came out of the house in long pants and black, rubber-soled shoes, and he and Myron lined up on one of the sidewalk lines and raced, and Abe won going away. The sound of Abe's fierce breathing and his hard shoes pounding the cement hid the calmness of Myron's own breath. That July Myron packed Abe's old black cloth traveling bag and got on the bus to the mountains.

But what Abe taught Myron was more than just competition; it was everything. It was the way he got to work every day for thirty-seven years without being late, the way he treated Rachel, his bride of uncountable years, who sewed, cooked, cleaned for him, in return for what? For Sunday night dinners out every single week, a ritual so ancient that Myron couldn't break it even after he moved out of the house. For Sunday dinners out, and a new diamond each year. It was a point of honor, an expectation. Obviously on a pharmacist's salary Abe couldn't afford it. He bought her rings, necklaces, bracelets, brooches, hairpins, earrings, lockets—one gift at the end of each year for, what is it, almost forty years? One year Rachel was sick with mild hepatitis and spent the holidays in the hospital. On the first evening of Chanukah Abe took Myron with him to visit her, and in the hospital room he pulled out a small bracelet strung with a diamond and gave it to her, his wife, as she lay in the bed. But what is the value of a diamond, he later asked Myron in the car, next to the health of the body?

It was two years later that Abe tried the swim across San Francisco Bay. But there were other things before that. At the age of fifty-four he fought in a bar over politics. Yes, fought. He came home with his knuckles wrapped in a handkerchief. On his cheek there was a purple bruise that even over the years never disappeared, only gradually settled down the side of his face and formed a black blotch underneath his jaw. That was when he told Myron never to let the other guy start the fight. Always get the first punch, he said. Myron was sixteen then, sitting in the kitchen watching his father rub iodine into the split skin behind his knuckles. The smell stayed in the kitchen for days, the smell of hospitals that later came to be the smell of all his father's clothes, and of his closet. Maybe Myron had just never noticed it before, but on that day his father began to smell old.

Myron was startled. Even then he had been concerned with life. He was a preserver, a collector of butterflies that he caught on the driving trips the family took in the summers. The shelves in his bedroom were lined with swallowtails and monarchs pressed against glass panes, the crystal dust still on their wings. Later, in college, he had studied biology, zoology, entomology, looking inside things, looking at life. Once, on a driving trip through Colorado when Myron was young, Abe had stopped the car near the lip of a deep gorge. Across from where they got out and stood, the cliffs extended down a quarter of a mile, colored with clinging green brush, wildflowers, shafts of red clay, and, at the bottom, a turquoise river. But there were no animals on the sheer faces, no movement anywhere in the gorge. Abe said that life could survive anywhere, even on cliffs like these, and that this was a miracle. But Myron said nothing. To him, anything that couldn't move, that couldn't fly or swim or run, was not really alive. Real life interested him. His father interested him, with his smells and exertions, with the shifting bruise on his jaw.

Years later, on his first day at Albert Einstein medical school, the thing Myron noticed was the smell, the pungency of the antiseptics, like the iodine Abe had once rubbed into his knuckles. On that first day when a whole class of new medical students listened to an address by the dean of the medical college, the only thing Myron noticed was that the room smelled like his father.

Medical school was a mountain of facts, a giant granite peak full of outcroppings and hidden crevices. Physiology. Anatomy. Histology. More facts than he could ever hope to remember. To know the twenty-eight bones of the hand seemed to Myron a rare and privileged knowledge, but then there were the arms and shoulders with their bones and tendons and opposing muscles, then the whole intricate, extravagant cavity of the chest, and then the head and the abdomen and the legs. Myron never really tried to learn it all. It wasn't the volume of knowledge so much as it was the place where he had to be in order to learn it. The anatomy labs reeked of formaldehyde, the hospitals of a mixture of cleanliness and death. All of it reminded Myron of men getting old, and that is why in three years of medical school he made the minuscule but conscious effort not to study enough. He let the knowledge collect around him, in notebooks, binders, pads, on napkins and checks, everywhere except in his brain. His room was strewn with notes he never studied. Once in a letter home he said learning medicine was like trying to drink water from a fire hose.

But that was something Abe would want to hear. Once on a driving trip through the Florida deltas, Abe came upon three men trying to lift an abandoned car from a sludge pit with a rope they had looped around it. Only the roof and the tops of the windows were showing above the mud, but Abe got out anyway and helped the men pull. His face turned red and the muscles in his belly shook so much Myron could see them through his shirt. Myron didn't understand the futility of his father's effort, or even know why he helped save a useless car for men he didn't know, until years later. Abe did things like that; he loved doing things like that.

Myron, on the other hand, just didn't want to study. His weren't the usual reasons for quitting medical school. It wasn't the hours, and really, it wasn't the studying and the studying. It was something smaller, harder, that in a vague way he knew had to do with Abe. Perhaps he saw his own father in the coughing middle-aged men whose hearts he watched flutter across oscilloscope screens. But it was not Abe's death that he feared. Heart stoppage or brain tumors or sudden clots of blood were reactions of the body, and thus, he had always believed, they were good. Death, when it was a fast action, didn't bother him. The fatty cadavers in anatomy labs were no more than objects to Myron, and it meant nothing to him that they were dead. The only time in his life that he had had to really think about death was in his childhood, when the phone rang in the middle of the night to tell Abe about his aunt in Miami Beach. The next morning Myron had found his father downstairs drinking coffee. "Life is for the living," Abe had said, and even then Myron could weigh the seriousness in his voice. It was plain that death meant only a little if you still had the good muscles in your own heart, and that people's bodies, once under ground, were not to be mourned. And besides, there really was no blood in the medical school anatomy classes. The cadavers were gray, no different when you cut them than the cooked leg of a turkey. They had none of the pliable fleshiness, none of the pink, none of the smells and secretions that told you of life.

No, it wasn't death that bothered Myron; it was the downhill plunge of the living body—the muscles that stretched off the bones into folds, the powdery flesh odors of middle-aged men. He longed for some octogenarian to stand up suddenly from a wheelchair and run the length of a corridor. Once, a drugged coronary patient, a sixty-year-old man, had unhooked an IV cart and caromed on it through the corridor until Myron cornered him. When Myron looked at the blood spots that were in the old man's eyes, he wanted to take him in his own arms then and there, in his triumph. That was why Myron wanted to quit medical school. He hated the demise of the spirit.

So he let the work pile up around him. In this third year he felt the walls of the lecture halls and the sponged hospital floors to be somehow holding him against his will. Fifty-year-old men who could no longer walk, or whose intestines bled and collapsed, Myron felt, were betrayers of the human race. He was convinced of the mind's control over the flesh.

In the winter of his third year he started jogging. First two, three miles a day, then, later, long six-mile runs into the hills and neighborhoods around the medical school. He left in the early mornings and ran in the frozen air so that he could feel the chill in his lungs. He ran every morning through November and December, and then January after the holidays, until one morning in February, when the grass was still breaking like needles underneath his feet, he realized he could run forever. That morning he just kept running. He imagined Itzhak sitting with two cups of coffee at the table, but he ran to the top of a hill and watched the streets below him fill with morning traffic. Then onward he went, amidst the distant bleating of car horns and the whistling wind. He thought of the hospital, of the arriving interns, sleepless, pale, and of the third-year students following doctors from room to room. He ran on the balls of his feet and never got tired.

When he returned to the apartment Itzhak was at the table eating lunch. Myron took a carton of milk from the refrigerator and drank standing up, without a glass.

"You ever think about passing infection that way?"

Myron put down the carton and looked at the muscles twitching in his thighs. Itzhak lit a cigarette.

"You're a real one," Itzhak said. "Where the hell were you?"

"Hypoxia. No oxygen to the brain. You know how easy it is to forget what time it is."

"Watch it," Itzhak said. "You'll get into trouble."

The next day Myron went to classes and to rounds, but that night he ran again, stumbling in the unlit paths, and after that, over the next weeks of frozen, windless days, he ran through his morning assignments and spent the afternoons in a park near his apartment. There was a basketball hoop there, a metal backboard with a chain net, and sometimes he shot with a group of kids or joined their half-court games. Afterward, he always ran again. He loved to sweat when the air was cold enough to turn the grass brittle, when a breath of air felt like a gulp of cold water. After a while, Itzhak began to ignore his disappearances. One day when Myron returned from running, Itzhak took his pulse. "Damn, Myron," he said, "you *are* running." His professors tried to take him aside, and Myron could see them looking into his pupils when they spoke. But he ignored them. One night he returned late from running, still dripping sweat, picked up the telephone and dialed, and heard his father's sleepy voice on the other end of the line. "Pa," he said, "it's *kaput* here."

So why the quitting now? Why the phone call at ten-thirty on a Thursday night when Abe and Rachel were just going into their dream sleep? Myron could hear the surprise, the speechlessness. He heard Rachel over the line telling Abe to calm himself, to give her the phone. He imagined the blood rushing to Abe's face, the breathing starting again the way he breathed the morning they pulled him from the frothy water in San Francisco Bay. Rachel took the phone and spoke, and Myron, because he had lived with his father for most of his life, knew Abe was taking black socks from the drawer and stretching them over his feet.

The next morning at seven Myron opened the apartment door and Abe was sitting there in a chair with the black cloth traveling bag on his lap. He was wide awake, blocking the passage out of the apartment.

"For crying out loud!"

"Who else did you expect? Am I supposed to let you throw away everything?"

"Pa, I didn't expect *anybody*."

"Well, I came, and I'm here, and I spent like a madman to get a flight. You think I don't have the lungs to argue with my son?"

"I was about to go running."

"I'll come along. We're going to settle this thing."

"Okay," Myron said, "come," and in his sweatsuit, hooded and wrapped against the cold, he led Abe down through the corridors of the building and out into the street. The ground outside was frozen from the night, the morning icy cold and without wind. Abe held the black traveling bag at his side as they stood under the entrance awning.

"I was planning to run."

"It won't hurt you to walk a few blocks."

It was cold, so they walked quickly. Abe was wearing what he always wore in the winter, a black hat, gloves, galoshes, an overcoat that smelled of rain. Myron watched him out of the side of his vision. He tried to look at his father without turning around—at the face, at the black bruise under the jaw, at the shoulders. He tried to see the body beneath the clothing. Abe's arm swung with the weight of the traveling bag, and for the first time, as he watched through the corner of his eye, Myron noticed the faint spherical outline inside the cloth.

They walked wordlessly, Myron watching Abe's breath come out in clouds. By now the streets had begun to move with traffic, and the ice patches, black and treacherous, crackled underneath their feet. The streetlamps had gone off and in the distance dogs barked. They came to the park where Myron played basketball in the afternoons.

"So you brought the ball," Myron said.

"Maybe you want some shooting to calm you."

"You're not thinking of any games, are you?"

"I just brought it in case you wanted to shoot."

Abe unzipped the bag and pulled out the basketball. They went into the court. He bounced the ball on the icy pavement, then handed it to Myron. Myron spun it on his finger, dribbled it off the ice. He was watching Abe. He couldn't see beneath the overcoat, but Abe's face seemed drawn down, the cheeks puffier, the dark bruise lax on his jaw.

"Pa, why don't you shoot some? It would make you warm."

"You think you have to keep me warm? Look at this." He took off the overcoat. "Give me the ball."

Myron threw it to him, and Abe dribbled it in his gloved hands. Abe was standing near the free-throw line, and he turned then, brought the ball to his hip, and shot it, and as his back was turned to watch the shot, Myron did an incredible thing—he crouched, took three lunging steps, and dove into the back of his father's thin, tendoned knees. Abe tumbled backward over him. What could have possessed Myron to do such a thing? A medical student, almost a doctor—what the hell was he doing? But Myron knew his father. Abe was a prizefighter, a carnival dog. Myron knew he would protect the exposed part of his skull, that he would roll and take the weight on his shoulders, that he would be up instantly, crouched and ready to go at it. But Myron had slid on the ice after the impact, and when he scrambled back up and turned around, his father was on his back on the icy pavement. He was flat out.

"Pa!"

Abe was as stiff and extended as Myron had ever seen a human being. He was like a man who had laid out his own body.

"What kind of crazy man are you?" Abe said hoarsely. "I think it's broken."

"What? What's broken?"

"My back. You broke your old man's back."

"Oh no, Pa, I couldn't have! Can you move your toes?"

But the old man couldn't. He lay on the ground staring up at Myron like a beached sea animal. Oh, Pa. Myron could see the unnatural stiffness in his body, in the squat legs and the hard, protruding belly.

"Look," Myron said, "don't move." Then he turned and started back to get his father's coat, and he had taken one step when Abe—Abe the carnival dog, the buyer of diamonds and the man of endurance—hooked his hand around Myron's ankles and sent him tumbling onto the ice. Bastard! Pretender! He scrambled up and pinned Myron's shoulders against the pavement. "Faker!" Myron cried. He grappled with the old man, butted him with his head and tried to topple his balance, but Abe clung viciously and set the weight of his chest against Myron's shoulders. "Fraud!" shouted Myron. "Cheat!" He shifted his weight and tried to roll Abe over, but his father's legs were spread wide and he had pinned Myron's hands. "Coward," Myron said. Abe's wrists pressed into Myron's arms. His knees dug into Myron's thighs. "Thief," Myron whispered. "Scoundrel." Cold water was spreading upward through Myron's clothes and Abe was panting hoarse clouds of steam into his face when Myron realized his father was leaning down and speaking into his ear.

"Do you give?"

"What?"

"Do you give?"

"You mean, will I go back to school?"

"That's what I mean."

"Look," Myron said, "you're crazy."

"Give me your answer."

Myron thought about this. While his father leaned down over him, pressed into him with his knees and elbows, breathed steam into his face, he thought about it. As he lay there he thought about other things too: This is my father, he thought. Then: This is my life. For a while, as the cold water spread through his clothes, he lay there and remembered things—the thousands and thousands of layups, the smell of a cadaver, the footrace on a bright afternoon in April. Then he thought: What can you do? These are clouds above us, and below us there is ice and the earth. He said, "I give."

Mark Twain (Samuel Langhorne Clemens), 1835–1910, was once described as "representing the single most important contribution of the frontier to American literature." Born in Missouri, he grew up in the Mississippi River town of Hannibal and became a pilot on the famous waterway. Twain's adventures in the mining camps and cities of the far West are recounted in Roughing It *(1871). His most famous novels are* The Adventures of Tom Sawyer *(1876),* The Adventures of Huckleberry Finn *(1884), and* A Connecticut Yankee in King Arthur's Court *(1889). The frog-jumping episode found here is a masterpiece of humorous storytelling. It originally came out in the New York* Saturday Press *and was Twain's first published story. For many years the yarn has been celebrated by a real frog-jumping contest in Angel's Camp, California, which is located in Calaveras County.*

Mark Twain

THE CELEBRATED JUMPING FROG OF CALAVERAS COUNTY (1865)

IN COMPLIANCE WITH THE REQUEST OF A FRIEND of mine, who wrote me from the East, I called on good-natured, garrulous old Simon Wheeler, and inquired after my friend's friend, Leonidas W. Smiley, as requested to do, and I hereunto append the result. I have a lurking suspicion that *Leonidas W.* Smiley is a myth; and that my friend never knew such a personage; and that he only conjectured that if I asked old Wheeler about him, it would remind him of his infamous *Jim* Smiley, and he would go to work and bore me to death with some exasperating reminiscence of him as long and as tedious as it should be useless to me. If that was the design, it succeeded.

I found Simon Wheeler dozing comfortably by the bar-room stove of the dilapidated tavern in the decayed mining camp of Angel's, and I noticed that he was fat and bald-headed, and had an expression of winning gentleness and simplicity upon his tranquil countenance. He roused up, and gave me good-day. I told him a friend had commissioned me to make some inquiries about a cherished companion of his boyhood named *Leonidas W.* Smiley—*Rev. Leonidas W.* Smiley, a young minister of the Gospel, who he had heard was at one time a resident of Angel's Camp. I added that if Mr. Wheeler could tell me anything about this Rev. Leonidas W. Smiley, I would feel under many obligations to him.

Simon Wheeler backed me into a corner and blockaded me there with his chair, and then sat down and reeled off the monotonous narrative which follows this paragraph. He never smiled, he never frowned, he never changed his voice from the gentle-flowing key to which he tuned his initial sentence, he never betrayed the slightest suspicion of enthusiasm; but all through the interminable narrative there ran a vein of impressive earnestness and sincerity, which showed me plainly that, so far from his imagining that there was anything ridiculous or funny about his story, he regarded it as a really important matter, and admired its two heroes as men of transcendent genius in *finesse*. I let him go on in his own way, and never interrupted him once:

Rev. Leonidas W. H'm, Reverend Le—well, there was a feller here once by the name of Jim Smiley, in the winter of '49—or maybe it was the spring of '50—I don't recollect exactly, somehow, though what makes me think it was one or the other is because I remember the big flume warn't finished when he first came to the camp; but any way, he was the curiousest man about always betting on anything that turned up you ever see, if he could get anybody to bet on the other side; and if he couldn't he'd change sides. Any way that suited the other man would suit *him*—any way just so's he got a bet, *he* was satisfied. But still he was lucky, uncommon lucky; he most always come out winner. He was always ready and laying for a chance; there couldn't be no solit'ry thing mentioned but that feller'd offer to bet on it, and take any side you please, as I was just telling you. If there was a horserace, you'd find him flush or you'd find him busted at the end of it; if there was a dog-fight, he'd bet on it; if there was a cat-fight, he'd bet on it; if there was a chicken-fight, he'd bet on it; why, if there was two birds setting on a fence, he would bet you which one would fly first; or if there was a camp-meeting, he would be there reg'lar to bet on Parson Walker, which he judged to be the best exhorter about here, and he was, too, and a good man. If he even see a straddle-bug start to go anywheres, he would bet you how long it would take him to get to—to wherever he was going to, and if you took him up, he would foller that straddle-bug to Mexico but what he would find out where he was bound for and how long he was on the road. Lots of the boys here has seen that Smiley and can tell you about him. Why, it never made no difference to *him*—he'd bet on *any* thing—the dangest feller. Parson Walker's wife laid very sick once, for a good while, and it seemed as if they warn't going to save her; but one morning he come in, and Smiley up and asked him how she was, and he said she was considerable better—thank the Lord for his inf'nit' mercy—and coming on so smart that with the blessing of Prov'dence she'd get well yet; and Smiley, before he thought, says, "Well, I'll risk two-and-a-half she don't anyway."

Thish-yer Smiley had a mare—the boys called her the fifteen-minute nag, but that was only in fun, you know, because, of course, she was faster than that—and he used to win money on that horse, for all she was so slow and always had the asthma, or the distemper, or the consumption, or something of that kind. They used to give her two or three hundred yards start, and then pass her under way; but always at the fag-end of the race she'd get excited and desperate-like, and come cavorting and straddling up, and scattering her legs around limber, sometimes in the air, and sometimes out to one side amongst the fences, and kicking up m-o-r-e dust and raising m-o-r-e racket with her coughing and sneezing and blowing her nose—and *always* fetch up at the stand just about a neck ahead, as near as you could cipher it down.

And he had a little small bull-pup, that to look at him you'd think he warn't worth a cent but to set around and look ornery and lay for a chance to steal something. But as soon as money was upon him he was a different dog; his under-jaw'd begin to stick out like the fo'-castle of a steamboat, and his teeth would uncover and shine like the furnaces. And a dog might tackle him and bully-rag him, and bite him, and throw him over his shoulder two or three times, and Andrew Jackson—which was the name of the pup—Andrew Jackson would never let on but what he was satisfied, and hadn't expected nothing else—and the bets being doubled and doubled on the other side all the time, till the money was all up; and then all of a sudden he would grab that other dog jest by the j'int of his hind leg and freeze to it—not chaw, you understand, but only just grip and hang on till they throwed up the sponge, if it was a year. Smiley always come out winner on that pup, till he harnessed a dog once that didn't have no hind legs, because they'd been sawed off in a circular saw, and when the thing had gone along far enough, and the money was all up, and he come to make a snatch for his pet holt, he see in a minute how he'd been imposed on, and how the other dog had him in the door, so to speak, and he 'peared surprised, and then he looked sorter discouraged-like, and didn't try no more to win the fight and so he got shucked out bad. He gave Smiley a look, as much as to say his heart was broke, and it was *his* fault, for putting up a dog that hadn't no hind legs for him to take holt of, which was his main dependence in a fight, and then he limped off a piece and laid down and died. It was a good pup, was that Andrew Jackson, and would have made a name for hisself if he'd lived, for the stuff was in him and he had genius—I know it, because he hadn't no opportunities to speak of, and it don't stand to reason that a dog could make such a fight as he could under them circumstances if he hadn't no talent. It always makes me feel sorry when I think of that last fight of his'n, and the way it turned out.

Well, thish-yer Smiley had rat-tarriers, and chicken cocks, and tomcats and all of them kind of things, till you couldn't rest, and you couldn't fetch nothing for him to bet on but he'd match you. He ketched a frog one day, and took him home, and said he cal'lated to educate him; and so he never done nothing for three months but set in his back yard and learn that frog to jump. And you bet you he *did* learn him, too. He'd give him a little punch behind, and the next minute you'd see that frog whirling in the air like a doughnut—see him turn one summerset, or maybe a couple, if he got a good start, and come down flat-footed and all right, like a cat. He got him up so in the matter of ketching flies, and kep' him in practice so constant, that he'd nail a fly every time as fur as he could see him. Smiley said all a frog wanted was education, and he could do 'most anything—and I believe him. Why, I've seen him set Dan'l Webster down here on this floor—Dan'l Webster was the name of the frog—and sing out, "Flies, Dan'l, flies!" and quicker'n you could wink he'd spring straight up and snake a fly off'n the counter there, an' flop down on the floor ag'in as solid as a gob of mud, and fall to scratching the side of his head with his hind foot as indifferent as if he hadn't no idea he'd been doin' any more'n any frog might do. You never see a frog so modest and straightfor'ard as he was, for all he was so gifted. And when it come to fair and square jumping on a dead level, he could get over more ground at one straddle than any animal of his breed you ever see. Jumping on a dead level was his strong suit, you understand; and when it come to that, Smiley would ante up money on him as long as he had a red. Smiley was monstrous proud of his frog, and well he might be, for fellers that had travelled and been everywheres, all said he laid over any frog that ever *they* see.

Well, Smiley kep' the beast in a little lattice box, and he used to fetch him downtown sometimes and lay for a bet. One day a feller—a stranger in the camp, he was—come acrost him with his box, and says:

"What might be that you've got in the box?"

And Smiley says, sorter indifferent-like, "It might be a parrot, or it might be a canary, maybe, but it ain't—it's only just a frog."

And the feller took it, and looked at it careful, and turned it round this way and that, and says, "H'm—so 'tis. Well, what's *he* good for?"

"Well," Smiley says, easy and careless, "he's good enough for *one* thing, I should judge—he can outjump any frog in Calaveras County."

The feller took the box again, and took another long, particular look, and give it back to Smiley, and says, very deliberate, "Well," he says, "I don't see no p'ints about that frog that's any better'n any other frog."

"Maybe you don't," Smiley says. "Maybe you understand frogs and maybe you don't understand 'em; maybe you've had experience, and maybe you ain't only a amature, as it were. Anyways, I've got *my* opinion and I'll risk forty dollars that he can outjump any frog in Calaveras County."

And the feller studied a minute, and then says, kinder sad like, "Well, I'm only a stranger here, and I ain't got no frog; but if I had a frog, I'd bet you."

And then Smiley says, "That's all right—that's all right—if you'll hold my box a minute, I'll go and get you a frog." And so the feller took the box, and put up his forty dollars along with Smiley's and set down to wait.

So he set there a good while thinking and thinking to hisself, and then he got the frog out and prized his mouth open and took a teaspoon and filled him full of quail shot—filled him pretty near up to his chin—and set him on the floor. Smiley he went to the swamp and slopped around in the mud for a long time, and finally he ketched a frog, and fetched him in, and give him to this feller, and says:

"Now, if you're ready, set him alongside of Dan'l, with his forepaws just even with Dan'l's, and I'll give the word." Then he says, "One—two—three—*git!*" and him and the feller touched up the frogs from behind, and the new frog hopped off lively, but Dan'l give a heave, and hysted up his shoulders—so—like a Frenchman, but it warn't no use—he couldn't budge; he was planted as solid as a church, and he couldn't no more stir than if he was anchored out. Smiley was a good deal surprised, and he was disgusted too, but he didn't have no idea what the matter was, of course.

The feller took the money and started away; and when he was going out at the door, he sorter jerked his thumb over his shoulder—so—at Dan'l, and says again, very deliberate, "Well," he says, "*I* don't see no p'ints about that frog that's any better'n any other frog."

Smiley he stood scratching his head and looking down at Dan'l a long time, and at last says, "I do wonder what in the nation that frog throwed off for—I wonder if there ain't something the matter with 'im—he 'pears to look mighty baggy, somehow." And he ketched Dan'l up by the nap of the neck, and hefted him, and says, "Why blame my cats if he don't weigh five pounds!" and turned him upside down and he belched out a double handful of shot. And then he see how it was, and he was the maddest man—he set the frog down and took out after that feller, but he never ketched him. And—

(Here Simon Wheeler heard his name called from the front yard, and got up to see what was wanted.) And turning to me as he moved away, he said: "Jest set where you are, stranger, and rest easy—I ain't going to be gone a second."

But, by your leave, I did not think that a continuation of the history of the enterprising vagabond *Jim* Smiley would be likely to afford me much information concerning the Rev. *Leonidas W.* Smiley, and so I started away.

At the door I met the sociable Wheeler returning, and he buttonholed me and recommenced:

"Well, thish-yer Smiley had a yaller, one-eyed cow that didn't have no tail, only jest a short stump like a bannanner, and—"

However, lacking both time and inclination, I did not wait to hear about the afflicted cow, but took my leave.

While sports are supposed to mold character, they can also reveal it. This lovely tennis story is a good example, where playing mixed doubles reveals a flawed character and a strained marital relationship. The story was originally published in The New Yorker. *Author Irwin Shaw (1913–1984) was one of the greatest writers of his generation. He played football at Brooklyn College and served in World War II. Shaw's* Selected Short Stories *were published in 1961 by the prestigious Modern Library. Many of Shaw's works have been made into movies and television miniseries. His best-known novel,* The Young Lions *(1948), became an excellent war movie with Marlon Brando, Montgomery Clift, and Dean Martin.*

Irwin Shaw

MIXED DOUBLES
(1947)

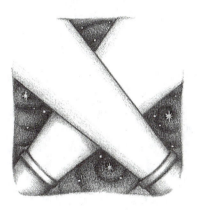

AS JANE COLLINS WALKED OUT onto the court behind her husband, she felt once more the private, strong thrill of pride that had moved her again and again in the time she had known him. Jane and Stewart had been married six years, but even so, as she watched him stride before her in that curious upright, individual, half-proud, half-comic walk, like a Prussian drill sergeant on his Sunday off, Jane felt the same mixture of amusement and delight in him that had touched her so strongly when they first met. Stewart was tall and broad and his face was moody and good-humored and original, and Jane felt that even at a distance of five hundred yards and surrounded by a crowd of people, she could pick him out unerringly. Now, in well-cut white trousers and a long-sleeved Oxford shirt, he seemed elegant and a little old-fashioned among the other players, and he looked graceful and debonair as he hit the first few shots in the preliminary rallying.

Jane was sensibly dressed, in shorts and tennis shirt, and her hair was imprisoned in a bandanna, so that it wouldn't get into her eyes. She knew that the shorts made her look a little dumpy and that the handkerchief around her head gave her a rather skinned and severe appearance, and she had a slight twinge of female regret when she looked across the net and saw Eleanor Burns soft and attractive in a prettily cut tennis dress and with a red ribbon in her hair, but she fought it down and concentrated on keeping her eye on the ball as Mr. Croker, Eleanor's partner, sliced it back methodically at her.

Mr. Croker, a vague, round, serious little man, was a neighbor of the Collinses' hosts. His shorts were too tight for him, and Jane knew, from having watched him on previous occasions, that his face would get more serious and more purple as the afternoon wore on, but he played a steady, dependable game and he was useful when other guests were too lazy or had drunk too much at lunch to play in the afternoon.

Two large oak trees shaded part of the court, and the balls flashed back and forth, in light and shadow, making guitarlike chords as they hit the rackets, and on the small terrace above the court, where the other guests were lounging, there was the watery music of ice in glasses and the bright flash of summer colors as people moved about.

How pleasant this was, Jane thought—to get away from the city on a week end, to this cool, tree-shaded spot, to slip all the stiff bonds of business and city living and run swiftly on the springy surface of the court, feeling the country wind against her bare skin, feeling youth in her legs, feeling, for this short Sunday hour at least, free of desks and doors and weekday concrete.

Stewart hit a tremendous overhead smash, whipping all the strength of his long body into it, and the ball struck the ground at Eleanor's feet and slammed high in the air. He grinned. "I'm ready," he said.

"You're not going to do that to me in the game, are you?" Eleanor asked.

"I certainly am," Stewart said. "No mercy for women. The ancient motto of the Collins family."

They tossed for service, and Stewart won. He served and aced Eleanor with a twisting, ferocious shot that spun off at a sharp angle.

"Jane, darling," he said, grinning, as he walked to the other side, "we're going to be sensational today."

They won the first set with no trouble. Stewart played very well. He moved around the court swiftly and easily, hitting the ball hard in loose, well-coached strokes, with an almost exaggerated grace. Again and again, the people watching applauded or called out after one of his shots, and he waved his racket, smiling at them, and said, "Oh, we're murderous today." He kept humming between shots—a tuneless, happy composition of his own—like a little boy who is completely satisfied with himself, and Jane couldn't help smiling and adoring him as he lightheartedly dominated the game and the spectators and the afternoon, brown and dashing and handsome in his white clothes, with the sun flooding around him like a spotlight on an actor in the middle of the stage.

Occasionally, when Stewart missed a shot, he would stand, betrayed and tragic, and stare up at the sky and ask with mock despair, "Collins, why don't you just go home?" And then he would turn to Jane and say, "Janie, darling, forgive me. Your husband's just no good."

And even as she smiled at him and said, "You're so right," she could sense the other women, up on the terrace, looking down at him, their eyes speculative and veiled and lit with invitation as they watched.

Jane played her usual game, steady, unheroic, getting almost everything back quite sharply, keeping the ball in play until Stewart could get his racket on it and kill it. They were a good team. Jane let Stewart poach on her territory for spectacular kills, and twice Stewart patted her approvingly on the behind after she had made difficult saves, and there were appreciative chuckles from the spectators at the small domestic vulgarity.

Stewart made the last point of the set on a slamming deep backhand that passed Eleanor at the net. Eleanor shook her head and said, "Collins, you're an impossible man," and Croker said stolidly, "Splendid. Splendid," and Stewart said, grinning, "Something I've been saving for this point, old man."

They walked off and sat down on a bench in the shade between sets, and Croker and Jane had to wipe their faces with towels and Croker's alarming purple died a little from his cheeks.

"That overhead!" Eleanor said to Stewart. "It's absolutely frightening. When I see you winding up, I'm just tempted to throw away my poor little racket and run for my life."

Jane lifted her head and glanced swiftly at Stewart to see how he was taking it. He was taking it badly, smiling a little too widely at Eleanor, being boyish and charming. "It's nothing," he said. "Something I picked up on Omaha Beach."

That, too, Jane thought bitterly. Foxhole time, too. She ducked her head into her towel to keep from saying something wifely. This is the last time, she thought, feeling the towel sticky against her sweaty forehead, the last time I am coming to any of these week-end things, always loaded with unattached or semi-attached, man-hungry, half-naked, honey-mouthed girls. She composed her face, so that when she looked up from the towel she would look like a nice, serene woman who merely was interested in the next set of tennis.

Eleanor, who had wide green eyes, was staring soberly and unambiguously over the head of her racket at Stewart, and Stewart, fascinated, as always, and a little embarrassed, was staring back. Oh, God, Jane thought, the long stare, too.

"Well," she said briskly, "I'm ready for one more set."

"What do you say," Stewart asked, "we divide up differently this time? Might make it more even. Croker and you, Jane, and the young lady and me."

"Oh," said Eleanor, "I'd be a terrible drag to you, Stewart. And besides, I'm sure your wife loves playing on your side."

"Not at all," Jane said stiffly. The young lady! How obvious could a man be?

"No," said Croker surprisingly. "Let's stay the way we are." Jane wanted to kiss the round purple face, a bleak, thankful kiss. "I think we'll do better this time. I've been sort of figuring out what to do with you, Collins."

Stewart looked at him briefly and unpleasantly, then smiled charmingly. "Anything you say, old man. I just thought . . ."

"I'm sure we'll do better," Croker said firmly. He stood up. "Come on, Eleanor."

Eleanor stood up, lithe and graceful in her short dress, which whipped around her brown legs in the summer wind. Never again, Jane thought, will I wear shorts. Dresses like that, even if they cost fifty dollars apiece, and soft false bosoms to put in them, too, and no bandanna, even if I'm blinded on each shot.

Stewart watched Eleanor follow Croker onto the court, and Jane could have brained him for the buried, measuring glint in his eye.

"Let's go," Stewart said, and under his breath, as they walked to their positions on the base line. He added, "Let's really show the old idiot this time, Jane."

"Yes, dear," Jane said, and pulled her bandanna straight and tight around her hair.

The first three games were ludicrously one-sided. Stewart stormed the net, made sizzling, malicious shots to Croker's feet, and purposely made him run, so that he panted pitifully and grew more purple than ever, and from time to time muttered to Jane, "Ridiculous old windbag," and "I thought he had me figured out," and "Don't let up, Janie, don't let up."

Jane played as usual, steady, undeviating, as predictably and sensibly as she always played. She was serving in the fourth game and was at 40–15 when Stewart dropped a shot just over the net, grinning as Croker galloped heavily in and barely got his racket on it. Croker's return wobbled over Stewart's head and landed three inches beyond the base line.

"Nice shot," she heard Stewart say. "Just in."

She looked at him in surprise. He was nodding his head emphatically at Croker.

Eleanor was at the net on the other side, looking at Stewart. "It looked out to me," she said.

"Not at all," Stewart said. "Beautiful shot. Serve them up, Janie."

Oh, Lord, Jane thought, now he's being sporting.

Jane made an error on the next point and Croker made a placement for advantage and Stewart hit into the net for the last point, and it was Croker's and Eleanor's game. Stewart came back to receive the service, not humming any more, his face irritable and dark.

Croker suddenly began to play very well, making sharp, sliding, slicing shots that again and again forced Stewart and Jane into errors. As they played, even as she swung at the ball, Jane kept remembering the shot that Stewart had called in, that had become the turning point of the set. He had not been able to resist the gallant gesture, especially when Eleanor had been standing so close, watching it all. It was just like Stewart. Jane shook her head determinedly, trying to concentrate on the game. This was no time to start dissecting her husband. They had had a lovely week end till now and Stewart had been wonderful, gay and funny and loving, and criticism could at least be reserved for weekdays, when everything else was dreary, too. But it *was* just like Stewart. It was awful how everything he did was all of a piece. His whole life was crowded with gestures. Hitting his boss that time in the boss's own office with three secretaries watching, because the boss had bawled him out. Giving up his R.O.T.C. commission and going into the Army as a private, in 1942. Giving five thousand dollars, just about the last of their savings, to Harry Mather, for Mather's business, just because they had gone to school together, when everyone knew Mather had become a hopeless drunk and none of his other friends would chip in. To an outsider, all these might seem the acts of a generous and rather noble character, but to a wife, caught in the consequences . . .

"Damn these pants," Stewart was muttering after hitting a ball into the net. "I keep tripping over them all the time."

"You ought to wear shorts, like everyone else," Jane said.

"I will. Buy me some this week," Stewart said, taking time out and rolling his cuffs up slowly and obviously. Jane had bought him three pairs of shorts a month before, but he always pretended he couldn't find them, and wore the long trousers. His legs are surprisingly skinny, Jane thought, hating herself for thinking it, and they're hairy, and his vanity won't let him. . . . She started to go for a ball, then stopped when she saw Stewart going for it.

He hit it out to the backstop. "Janie, darling," he said, "at least stay out of my way."

"Sorry," she said. Stewie, darling, she thought, Stewie, be careful. Don't lay it on. You're not really like this. I know you're not. Even for a moment, don't make it look as though you are.

Stewart ended the next rally by hitting the ball into the net. He stared unhappily at the ground. "The least they might do," he said in a low voice to Jane, "is roll the court if they invite people to play on it."

Please, Stewie, Jane begged within herself, don't do it. The alibis. The time he forgot to sign the lease for the apartment and they were put out and he blamed it on the lawyer, and the time he lost the job in Chicago and it was because he had gone to the wrong college, and the time . . . By a rigorous act of will, Jane froze her eyes on the ball, kept her mind blank as she hit it back methodically again and again.

Eleanor and Croker kept winning points. Croker had begun to chop every ball, spinning soft, deceptive shots that landed in midcourt and hardly bounced before they fell a second time. The only way that Jane could return them was to hit them carefully, softly, just getting them back. But Stewart kept going in on them furiously, taking his full, beautiful swing, sending the ball whistling into the net or over the court into the backstop. He looked as pretty and expert as ever as he played, but he lost point after point.

"What a way to play tennis," he grumbled, with his back to his opponents. "Why doesn't he play ping-pong or jacks?"

"You can't slam those dinky little shots like that," Janie said. "You have to get them back soft."

"You play your game," Stewart said, "and I'll play mine."

"Sorry," Jane said. Oh, Stewart, she mourned within her.

Stewart went after two more of Croker's soft chops, each time whipping his backhand around in his usual, slightly exaggerated, beautiful stroke, and each time knocking the ball into the net.

I can't help it, Jane thought. That *is* the way he is. Form above everything. If he were hanging over a cliff, he'd let himself fall to the rocks below rather than risk being ungraceful climbing to safety to save his life. He always has to pick up the check in bars and restaurants, no matter whom he is with or how many guests there are at the table, always with the same lordly, laughing, slightly derisive manner, even if we are down to our last fifty dollars. And when they had people in to dinner, there had to be two maids to wait on table, and French wines, and there always had to be those special bottles of brandy that cost as much as a vacation in the country. And he became so cold and remote when Jane argued with him about it, reminding him they were not rich and there was no sense in pretending they were. And his shoes. She blinked her eyes painfully, getting a sudden vision, there in the sun and shadow, of the long row of exquisite shoes, at seventy dollars a pair, that he insisted upon having made to his order. How ridiculous, she thought, to allow yourself to be unnerved at your husband's taste in shoes, and she loyally reminded herself how much a part of his attraction it had been in the beginning that he was always so beautifully dressed and so easy and graceful and careless of money.

The score was 4–3 in favor of Eleanor and Croker. Stewart's shots suddenly began to work again, and he and Jane took the next game with ease. Stewart's grin came back then, and he cheerfully reassured Jane, "Now we're going to take them." But after winning the first two points of the next game he had a wild streak and missed the base line by a few inches three times in a row, and they eventually lost the game.

I will make no deductions from this, Jane told herself stonily as she went up to the net for Stewart's serve. Anybody is liable to miss a few shots like that—anybody. And yet, how like Stewart! Just when it was most important to be steady and dependable. . . . The time she'd been so sick and the maid had quit, and Jane lay, broken and miserable, in bed for three weeks, with no one to take care of her except Stewart . . . He had been charming and thoughtful for the first week, fixing her meals, reading to her, sitting at her side for hours on end, cheerful and obliging, making her illness gently tolerable. And then he had suddenly grown nervous and abrupt, made vague excuses to leave her alone, and vanished for hours at a time, only to come back and hastily attend her for a few moments and vanish again, leaving her there in the rumpled bed, staring, lonely and shaken, at the ceiling as dusk faded into night and night into morning. She had been sure there was another girl then and she had resolved that when she was well and able to move around again, she would come to some decision with him, but as unpredictably as his absences had begun, they stopped. Once more he was tender and helpful, once more he sat at her side and nursed her and cheered her, and out of gratitude and love she had remained quiet and pushed her doubts deep to the back of her mind. And here they were again, in the middle of a holiday afternoon, foolishly, in this most unlikely place, during this mild, pointless game, with half a dozen people lazily watching, laughing and friendly, over their drinks.

She looked at him a few moments later, handsome and dear and familiar at her side, and he grinned back at her, and she was ashamed of herself for the thoughts that had been flooding through her brain. It was that silly girl on the other side of the net who had started it all, she thought. That practiced, obvious, almost automatic technique of flattering the male sex. That meaningless, rather pitiful flirtatiousness. It was foolish to allow it to throw her into the bitter waters of reflection. Marriage, after all, was an up-and-down affair and in many ways a fragile and devious thing, and was not to be examined too closely. Marriage was not a bank statement or a foreign policy or an X-ray photograph in a doctor's hand. You took it and lived through it, and maybe, a long time later—perhaps the day before you died—you totalled up the accounts, if you were of that turn of mind, but not before. And if you were a reasonable, sensible, mature woman, you certainly didn't do your additions and subtractions on a tennis court every time your husband hit a ball into the net. Jane smiled at herself and shook her head.

"Nice shot," she said warmly to Stewart as he swept a forehand across court, past Croker, for a point.

But it was still set point. Croker placed himself to receive Stewart's service, tense and determined and a little funny-looking, with his purple face and his serious round body a little too tight under his clothes. The spectators had fallen silent, and the wind had died, and there was a sense of stillness and expectancy as Stewart reared up and served.

Jane was at the net and she heard the sharp twang of Stewart's racket hitting the ball behind her and the riflelike report as it hit the tape and fell away. He had just missed his first service.

Jane didn't dare look around. She could feel Stewart walking into place, in that stiff-backed, pleasant way of his, and feel him shuffling around nervously, and she couldn't look back. Please, she thought, please get this one in. Helplessly, she thought of all the times when, just at the crucial moment, he had failed. Oh, God, this is silly, she thought. I mustn't do this. The time he had old man Sawyer's account practically in his hands and he got drunk. On the sporting pages, they called it coming through in the clutch. There were some players who did and some players who didn't, and after a while you got to know which was which. If you looked at it coldly, you had to admit that until now Stewart had been one of those who didn't. The time her father died, just after her sister had run off with the vocalist in that band, and if there had been a man around, taking hold of things, her father's partner wouldn't't've been able to get away with most of the estate the way he did, and the vocalist could have been frightened off. One day's strength and determination, one day of making the right move at the right time . . . But after the funeral, Stewart had pulled out and gone to Seattle on what he had said was absolutely imperative business, but that had never amounted to anything anyway, and Jane's mother and sister, and Jane, too, were still paying for that day of failure.

She could sense Stewart winding up for his service behind her back. Somewhere in her spine she felt a sense of disaster. It was going to be a double fault. She knew it. No, she thought, I mustn't. He isn't really like that. He's so intelligent and talented and good, he can go so far. She must not make this terrible judgment on her husband just because of the way he played tennis. And yet, his tennis was so much like his life. Gifted, graceful, powerful, showy, flawed, erratic . . .

Please, she thought, make this one good. Childishly, she felt, If this one is good it will be a turning point, a symbol, his whole life will be different. She hated herself for her thoughts and stared blankly at Eleanor, self-consciously alert and desirable in her pretty dress.

Why the hell did she have to come here this Sunday? Jane thought despairingly.

She heard the crack of the racket behind her. The ball whistled past her, hit the tape, rolled undecidedly on top of the net for a moment, then fell back at her feet for a double fault and the set.

"Too bad." She turned and smiled at Stewart, helplessly feeling herself beginning to wonder how she would manage to find the six weeks it would take in Reno. She shook her head, knowing that she wasn't going to Reno, but knowing, too, that the word would pass through her thoughts again and again, more and more frequently, with growing insistence, as the days went by.

She walked off the court with Stewart, holding his hand.

"The shadows," Stewart was saying. "Late in the afternoon, like this. It's impossible to see the service line."

"Yes, dear," Jane said.

Rudyard Kipling (1865–1936), while barely in his forties, became the first English writer to win the Nobel Prize for literature in 1907. Kipling's name was synonymous with British imperialism. His literary reputation rose with the prominence of the British Empire, and later fell as colonialism receded. Nonetheless, Kipling's best known books are today considered literary classics: Soldiers Three *(1888),* The Jungle Books *(1894–1895),* Captains Courageous *(1897), and* Kim *(1901). A recent biography is* Rudyard Kipling: A Life *(2000), by Harry Ricketts. The protagonist of the following story, set in old colonial India, is a polo pony. That horses can talk and express human emotions is a novelty that Kipling carries off surprisingly well. The reader learns about the game of polo while enjoying a rousing tale of courage and competition.*

Rudyard Kipling

THE MALTESE CAT (1895)

THEY HAD GOOD REASON TO BE PROUD, and better reason to be afraid, all twelve of them; for though they had fought their way, game by game, up the teams entered for the polo tournament, they were meeting the Archangels that afternoon in the final match; and the Archangels men were playing with half a dozen ponies apiece. As the game was divided into six quarters of eight minutes each, that meant a fresh pony after every halt. The Skidars' team, even supposing there were no accidents, could only supply one pony for every other change; and two to one is heavy odds. Again as Shiraz, the grey Syrian, pointed out, they were meeting the pink and pick of the polo-ponies of Upper India, ponies that had cost from a thousand rupees each, while they themselves were a cheap lot gathered often from country-carts, by their masters, who belonged to a poor but honest native infantry regiment.

"Money means pace and weight," said Shiraz, rubbing his black-silk nose dolefully along his neat-fitting boot, "and by the maxims of the game as I know it—"

"Ah, but we aren't playing the maxims," said The Maltese Cat. "We're playing the game; and we've the great advantage of knowing the game. Just think a stride, Shiraz! We've pulled up from bottom to second place in two weeks against all those fellows on the ground here. That's because we play with our heads as well as our feet."

"It makes me feel undersized and unhappy all the same," said Kittiwynk, a mouse-colored mare with a red brow-band and the cleanest pair of legs that ever an aged pony owned. "They've twice our style, these others."

Kittiwynk looked at the gathering and sighed. The hard, dusty polo-ground was lined with thousands of soldiers, black and white, not counting hundreds and hundreds of carriages and drags and dog-carts, and ladies with brilliant-colored parasols, and officers in uniform and out of it and crowds of natives behind them; and orderlies on camels, who had halted to watch the game, instead of carrying letters up and down the station; and native horse-dealers running about on thineared Biluchi mares, looking for a chance to sell a few first-class polo-ponies. Then there were the ponies of thirty teams that had entered for the Upper India Free-for-All Cup—nearly every pony of worth and dignity, from Mhow to Peshawar, from Allahabad to Multan; prize ponies, Arabs, Syrian, Barb, Country-bred, Deccanee, Waziri, and Kabul ponies of every color and shape and temper that you could imagine. Some of them were in mat-roofed stables, close to the polo-ground, but most were under saddle, while their masters, who had been defeated in the earlier games, trotted in and out and told the world exactly how the game should be played.

It was a glorious sight, and the come and go of the little, quick hooves, and the incessant salutations of ponies that had met before on other polo-grounds or racecourses were enough to drive a four-footed thing wild.

But the Skidars' team were careful not to know their neighbors, though half the ponies on the ground were anxious to scrape acquaintance with the little fellows that had come from the North, and, so far, had swept the board.

"Let's see," said a soft gold-colored Arab, who had been playing very badly the day before, to The Maltese Cat; "didn't we meet in Abdul Rahman's stable in Bombay, four seasons ago? I won the Paikpattan Cup next season, you may remember?"

"Not me," said The Maltese Cat, politely. "I was at Malta then, pulling a vegetable-cart. I don't race. I play the game."

"Oh!" said the Arab, cocking his tail and swaggering off.

"Keep yourselves to yourselves," said The Maltese Cat to his companions. "We don't want to rub noses with all those goose-rumped half-breeds of Upper India. When we've won this Cup they'll give their shoes to know *us*."

"We sha'n't win the Cup," said Shiraz. "How do you feel?"

"Stale as last night's feed when a muskrat has run over it," said Polaris, a rather heavy-shouldered grey; and the rest of the team agreed with him.

"The sooner you forget that the better," said The Maltese Cat, cheerfully. "They've finished tiffin in the big tent. We shall be wanted now. If your saddles are not comfy, kick. If your bits aren't easy, rear, and let the *saises* know whether your boots are tight."

Each pony had his *sais,* his groom, who lived and ate and slept with the animal, and had betted a good deal more than he could afford on the result of the game. There was no chance of anything going wrong, but to make sure, each *sais* was shampooing the legs of his pony to the last minute. Behind the *saises* sat as many of the Skidars' regiment as had leave to attend the match—about half the native officers, and a hundred or two dark, black-bearded men with the regimental pipers nervously fingering the big, beribboned bagpipes. The Skidars were what they call a Pioneer regiment, and the bagpipes made the national music of half their men. The native officers held bundles of polo-sticks, long cane-handled mallets, and as the grandstand filled after lunch they arranged themselves by ones and twos at different points round the ground, so that if a stick were broken the player would not have far to ride for a new one. An impatient British Cavalry Band struck up "If you want to know the time, ask a p'leeceman!" and the two umpires in light dust-coats danced out on two little excited ponies. The four players of the Archangels' team followed, and the sight of their beautiful mounts made Shiraz groan again.

"Wait till we know," said The Maltese Cat. "Two of 'em are playing in blinkers, and that means they can't see to get out of the way of their own side, or they *may* shy at the umpires' ponies. They've *all* got white web-reins that are sure to stretch or slip!"

"And," said Kittiwynk, dancing to take the stiffness out of her, "they carry their whips in their hands instead of on their wrists. Hah!"

"True enough. No man can manage his stick and his reins and his whip that way," said The Maltese Cat. "I've fallen over every square yard of the Malta ground, and I ought to know."

He quivered his little, flea-bitten withers just to show how satisfied he felt; but his heart was not so light. Ever since he had drifted into India on a troop-ship, taken, with an old rifle, as part payment for a racing debt, The Maltese Cat had played and preached polo to the Skidars' team on the Skidars' stony polo-ground. Now a polo-pony is like a poet. If he is born with a love for the game, he can be made. The Maltese Cat knew that bamboos grew solely in order that polo-balls might be turned from their roots, that grain was given to ponies to keep them in hard condition, and that ponies were shod to prevent them slipping on a turn. But, besides all these things, he knew every trick and device of the finest game in the world, and for two seasons had been teaching the others all he knew or guessed.

"Remember," he said for the hundredth time, as the riders came up, "you *must* play together, and you *must* play with your heads. Whatever happens, follow the ball. Who goes out first?"

Kittiwynk, Shiraz, Polaris, and a short high little bay fellow with tremendous hocks and no withers worth speaking of (he was called Corks) were being girthed up, and the soldiers in the background stared with all their eyes.

"I want you men to keep quiet," said Lutyens, the captain of the team, "and especially not to blow your pipes."

"Not if we win, Captain Sahib?" asked the piper.

"If we win you can do what you please," said Lutyens, with a smile, as he slipped the loop of his stick over his wrist, and wheeled to canter to his place. The Archangels' ponies were a little bit above themselves on account of the many-colored crowds so close to the ground. Their riders were excellent players, but they were a team of crack players instead of a crack team; and that made all the difference in the world. They honestly meant to play together, but it is very hard for four men, each the best of the team he is picked from, to remember that in polo no brilliancy in hitting or riding makes up for playing alone. Their captain shouted his orders to them by name, and it is a curious thing that if you call his name aloud in public after an Englishman you make him hot and fretty. Lutyens said nothing to his men because it had all been said before. He pulled up Shiraz, for he was playing "back," to guard the goal. Powell on Polaris was half-back, and Macnamara and Hughes on Corks and Kittiwynk were forwards. The tough, bamboo ball was set in the middle of the ground, one hundred and fifty yards from the ends, and Hughes crossed sticks, heads up, with the Captain of the Archangels, who saw fit to play forward; that is a place from which you cannot easily control your team. The little click as the cane-shafts met was heard all over the ground, and then Hughes made some sort of quick wrist-stroke that just dribbled the ball a few yards. Kittiwynk knew that stroke of old, and followed as a cat follows a mouse. While the Captain of the Archangels was wrenching his pony round, Hughes struck with all his strength, and next instant Kittiwynk was away, Corks following close behind her, their little feet pattering like raindrops on glass.

"Pull out to the left," said Kittiwynk between her teeth; "it's coming your way, Corks!"

The back and half-back of the Archangels were tearing down on her just as she was within reach of the ball. Hughes leaned forward with a loose rein, and cut it away to the left almost under Kittiwynk's foot, and it hopped and skipped off to Corks, who saw that, if he was not quick it would run beyond the boundaries. That long bouncing drive gave the Archangels time to wheel and send three men across the ground to head off Corks. Kittiwynk stayed where she was; for she knew the game. Corks was on the ball half a fraction of a second before the others came up, and Macnamara, with a backhanded stroke, sent it back across the ground to Hughes, who saw the way clear to the Archangels' goal, and smacked the ball in before any one quite knew what had happened.

"That's luck," said Corks, as they changed ends. "A goal in three minutes for three hits, and no riding to speak of."

"Don't know," said Polaris. "We've made them angry too soon. Shouldn't wonder if they tried to rush us off our feet next time."

"Keep the ball hanging, then," said Shiraz. "That wears out every pony that is not used to it."

Next time there was no easy galloping across the ground. All the Archangels closed up as one man, but there they stayed, for Corks, Kittiwynk, and Polaris were somewhere on the top of the ball marking time among the rattling sticks, while Shiraz circled about outside, waiting for a chance.

"We can do this all day," said Polaris, ramming his quarters into the side of another pony. "Where do you think you're shoving to?"

"I'll–I'll be driven in an *ekka* if I know," was the gasping reply, "and I'd give a week's feed to get my blinkers off. I can't see anything."

"The dust is rather bad. Whew! That was one for my off-hock. Where's the ball, Corks?"

"Under my tail. At least the man's looking for it there! This is beautiful. They can't use their sticks, and it's driving 'em wild. Give old Blinkers a push and then he'll go over."

"Here, don't touch me! I can't see. I'll–I'll back out, I think," said the pony in blinkers, who knew that if you can't see all round your head, you cannot prop yourself against the shock.

Corks was watching the ball where it lay in the dust, close to his near fore-leg, with Macnamara's shortened stick tap-tapping it from time to time. Kittiwynk was edging her way out of the scrimmage, whisking her stump of a tail with nervous excitement.

"Ho! They've got it," she snorted. "Let me out!" and she galloped like a rifle-bullet just behind a tall lanky pony of the Archangels, whose rider was swinging up his stick for a stroke.

"Not today, thank you," said Hughes, as the blow slid off his raised stick, and Kittiwynk laid her shoulder to the tall pony's quarters, and shoved him aside just as Lutyens on Shiraz sent the ball where it had come from, and the tall pony went skating and slipping away to the left. Kittiwynk, seeing that Polaris had joined Corks in the chase for the ball up the ground, dropped into Polaris' place, and then "time" was called.

The Skidars' ponies wasted no time in kicking or fuming. They knew that each minute's rest meant so much gain, and trotted off to the rails, and their *saises* began to scrape and blanket and rub them at once.

"Whew!" said Corks, stiffening up to get all the tickle of the big vulcanite scraper. "If we were playing pony for pony, we would bend those Archangels double in half an hour. But they'll bring up fresh ones and fresh ones and fresh ones after that—you see."

"Who cares?" said Polaris. "We've drawn first blood. Is my hock swelling?"

"Looks puffy," said Corks. "You must have had rather a wipe. Don't let it stiffen. You'll be wanted again in half an hour."

"What's the game like?" said The Maltese Cat.

"Ground's like your shoe, except where they put too much water on it, said Kittiwynk. "Then it's slippery. Don't play in the centre. There's a bog there. I don't know how their next four are going to behave, but we kept the ball hanging, and made 'em lather for nothing. Who goes out? Two Arabs and a couple of country-breds! That's bad. What a comfort it is to wash your mouth out!"

Kitty was talking with a neck of a lather-covered soda-water bottle between her teeth, and trying to look over withers at the same time. This gave her a very coquettish air.

"What's bad?" said Grey Dawn, giving to the girth and admiring his well-set shoulders.

"You Arabs can't gallop fast enough to keep yourselves warm—that's what Kitty means," said Polaris, limping to show that his hock needed attention. "Are you playing back, Grey Dawn?"

"Looks like it," said Grey Dawn, as Lutyens swung himself up. Powell mounted The Rabbit, a plain bay country-bred much like Corks, but with mulish ears. Macnamara took Faiz-Ullah, a handy, short-backed little red Arab with a long tail, and Hughes mounted Benami, an old and sullen brown beast, who stood over in front more than a polo-pony should.

"Benami looks like business," said Shiraz. "How's your temper, Ben?" The old campaigner hobbled off without answering, and The Maltese Cat looked at the new Archangel ponies prancing about on the ground. They were four beautiful blacks, and they saddled big enough and strong enough to the Skidar's team and gallop away with the meal inside them.

"Blinkers again," said The Maltese Cat. "Good enough!"

"They're chargers—cavalry chargers!" said Kittiwynk, indignantly. "*They'll* never see thirteen-three again."

"They've all been fairly measured, and they've all got their certificates," said The Maltese Cat, "or they wouldn't be here. We must take things as they come along, and keep your eyes on the ball."

The game began, but this time the Skidars were penned to their own end of the ground, and the watching ponies did not approve of that.

"Faiz-Ullah is shirking—as usual," said Polaris, with a scornful grunt.

"Faiz-Ullah is eating whip," said Corks. They could hear the leather-thonged polo-quirt lacing the little fellow's well-rounded barrel. Then The Rabbit's shrill neigh came across the ground.

"I can't do all the work," he cried, desperately.

"Play the game—don't talk." The Maltese Cat whickered; and all the ponies wriggled with excitement, and the soldiers and the grooms gripped the railings and shouted. A black pony with blinkers had singled out old Benami, and was interfering with him in every possible way. They could see Benami shaking his head up and down and flapping his under lip.

"There'll be a fall in a minute," said Polaris. "Benami is getting stuffy."

The game flickered up and down between goal-post and goal-post, and the black ponies were getting more confident as they felt they had the legs of the others. The ball was hit out of a little scrimmage, and Benami and The Rabbit followed it, Faiz-Ullah only too glad to be quiet for an instant.

The blinkered black pony came up like a hawk, with two of his own side behind him, and Benami's eye glittered as he raced. The question was which pony should make way for the other, for each rider was perfectly willing to risk a fall in a good cause. The black, who had been driven nearly crazy by his blinkers, trusted to his weight and his temper; but Benami knew how to apply his weight and how to keep his temper. They met, and there was a cloud of dust. The black was lying on his side, all the breath knocked out of his body. The Rabbit was a hundred yards up the ground with the ball, and Benami was sitting down. He had slid nearly ten yards on his tail, but he had had his revenge and sat cracking his nostrils till the black pony rose.

"That's what you get for interfering. Do you want any more?" said Benami, and he plunged into the game. Nothing was done that quarter, because Faiz-Ullah would not gallop, though Macnamara beat him whenever he could spare a second. The fall of the black pony had impressed his companions tremendously, and so the Archangels could not profit by Faiz-Ullah's bad behaviour.

But as The Maltese Cat said when "time" was called, and the four came back blowing and dripping, Faiz-Ullah ought to have been kicked all round Umballa. If he did not behave better next time The Maltese Cat promised to pull out his Arab tail by the roots and—eat it.

There was no time to talk, for the third four were ordered out.

The third quarter of a game is generally the hottest, for each side thinks that the others must be pumped; and most of the winning play in a game is made about that time.

Lutyens took over The Maltese Cat with a pat and a hug, for Lutyens valued him more than anything else in the world; Powell had Shikast, a little grey rat with no pedigree and no manners outside polo; Macnamara mounted Bamboo, the largest of the team; and Hughes Who's Who, alias The Animal. He was supposed to have Australian blood in his veins, but he looked like a clothes-horse and you could whack his legs with an iron crow-bar without hurting him.

They went out to meet the very flower of the Archangels' team; and when Who's Who saw their elegantly booted legs and their beautiful satin skins, he grinned a grin through his light, well-worn bridle.

"My word!" said Who's Who. "We must give 'em a little football. These gentlemen need a rubbing down."

"No biting," said The Maltese Cat, warningly; for once or twice in his career Who's Who had been known to forget himself in that way.

"Who said anything about biting? I'm not playing tiddly-winks. I'm playing the game."

The Archangels came down like a wolf on the fold, for they were tired of football, and they wanted polo. They got it more and more. Just after the game began, Lutyens hit a ball that was coming towards him rapidly, and it rolled in the air, as a ball sometimes will, with the whirl of a frightened partridge. Shikast heard but could not see it for the minute though he looked everywhere and up into the air as The Maltese Cat had taught him. When he saw it ahead and overhead he went forward with Powell, as fast as he could put foot to ground. It was then that Powell, a quiet and level-headed man as a rule, became inspired, and played a stroke that sometimes comes off successfully after long practice. He took his stick in both hands, and, standing up in his stirrups, swiped at the ball in the air, Munipore fashion. There was one second of paralyzed astonishment, and then all four sides of the ground went up in a yell of applause and delight as the ball flew true (you could see the amazed Archangels ducking in their saddles to dodge the line of flight, and looking at it with open mouths), and the regimental pipes of the Skidars squealed from the railings as long as the pipers had breath.

Shikast heard the stroke; but he heard the head of the stick fly off at the same time. Nine hundred and ninety-nine ponies out of a thousand would have gone tearing on after the ball with a useless player pulling at their heads; but Powell knew him, and he knew Powell; and the instant he felt Powell's right leg shift a trifle on the saddle-flap, he headed to the boundary, where a native officer was frantically waving a new stick. Before the shouts had ended, Powell was armed again.

Once before in his life The Maltese Cat had heard that very same stroke played off his own back, and had profited by the confusion it wrought. This time he acted on experience, and leaving Bamboo to guard the goal in case of accidents, came through the others like a flash, head and tail low—Lutyens standing up to ease him—swept on and on before the other side knew what was the matter, and nearly pitched on his head between the Archangels's goal-post as Lutyens kicked the ball in after a straight scurry of a hundred and fifty yards. If there was one thing more than another upon which The Maltese Cat prided himself, it was on this quick, streaking kind of run half across the ground. He did not believe in taking balls round the field unless you were clearly overmatched. After this they gave the Archangels five-minutes of football; and an expensive fast pony hates football because it rumples his temper.

Who's Who showed himself even better than Polaris in this game. He did not permit any wriggling away, but bored joyfully into the scrimmage as if he had his nose in a feed-box and was looking for something nice. Little Shikast jumped on the ball the minute it got clear, and every time an Archangel pony followed it, he found Shikast standing over it, asking what was the matter.

"If we can live through this quarter," said The Maltese Cat, "I sha'n't care. Don't take it out of yourselves. Let them do the lathering."

So the ponies, as their riders explained afterwards, "shut-up." The Archangels kept them tied fast in front of their goal, but it cost the Archangels' ponies all that was left of their tempers; and ponies began to kick, and men began to repeat compliments, and they chopped at the legs of Who's Who, and he set his teeth and stayed where he was, and the dust stood up like a tree over the scrimmage until that hot quarter ended.

They found the ponies very excited and confident when they went to their *saises*; and The Maltese Cat had to warn them that the worst of the game was coming.

"Now *we* are all going in for the second time," said he, "and *they* are trotting out fresh ponies. You think you can gallop, but you'll find you can't; and then you'll be sorry."

"But two goals to nothing is a halter-long lead," said Kittiwynk, prancing.

"How long does it take to get a goal?" The Maltese Cat answered. "For pity's sake, don't run away with a notion that the game is half-won just because we happen to be in luck *now!* They'll ride you into the grandstand, if they can; you must not give 'em a chance. Follow the ball."

"Football, as usual?" said Polaris. "My hock's half as big as a nose-bag."

"Don't let them have a look at the ball, if you can help it. Now leave me alone. I must get all the rest I can before the last quarter."

He hung down his head and let all his muscles go slack, Shikast, Bamboo, and Who's Who copying his example.

"Better not watch the game," he said. "We aren't playing, and we shall only take it out of ourselves if we grow anxious. Look at the ground and pretend it's fly-time."

They did their best, but it was hard advice to follow. The hooves were drumming and the sticks were rattling all up and down the ground, and yells of applause from the English troops told that the Archangels were pressing the Skidars hard. The native soldiers behind the ponies groaned and grunted, and said things in undertones, and presently they heard a long-drawn shout and a clatter of hurrahs.

"One to the Archangels," said Shikast, without raising his head. "Time's nearly up. Oh, my sire—and dam!"

"Faiz-Ullah," said The Maltese Cat, "if you don't play to the last nail in your shoes this time, I'll kick you on the ground before all the other ponies."

"I'll do my best when the time comes," said the little Arab sturdily.

The *saises* looked at each other gravely as they rubbed their ponies' legs. This was the time when long purses began to tell, and everybody knew it. Kittiwynk and the others came back, the sweat dripping over their hooves and their tails telling sad stories.

"They're better than we are," said Shiraz. "I knew how it would be."

"Shut your big head," said The Maltese Cat; "we've one goal to the good yet."

"Yes; but it's two Arabs and two country-breds to play now," said Corks. "Faiz-Ullah, remember!" He spoke in a biting voice.

As Lutyens mounted Grey Dawn he looked at his men, and they did not look pretty. They were covered with dust and sweat in streaks. Their yellow boots were almost black, their wrists were red and lumpy, and their eyes seemed two inches deep in their heads; but the expression in the eyes was satisfactory.

"Did you take anything at tiffin?" said Lutyens; and the team shook their heads. They were too dry to talk.

"All right. The Archangels did. They are worse pumped than we are."

"They've got the better ponies," said Powell. "I sha'n't be sorry when this business is over."

That fifth quarter was a painful one in every way. Faiz-Ullah played like a little red demon, and The Rabbit seemed to be everywhere at once, and Benami rode straight at anything and everything that came in his way; while the umpires on their ponies wheeled like gulls outside the shifting game. But the Archangels had the better mounts—they had kept their racers till late in the game—and never allowed the Skidars to play football. They hit the ball up and down the width of the ground till Benami and the rest were outpaced. Then they went forward, and time and again Lutyens and Grey Dawn were just, and only just, able to send the ball away with a long, spitting backhander. Grey Dawn forgot that he was an Arab, and turned from grey to blue as he galloped. Indeed, he forgot too well, for he did not keep his eyes on the ground as an Arab should, but stuck out his nose and scuttled for the dear honor of the game. They had watered the ground once or twice between the quarters, and a careless waterman had emptied the last of his skinful all in one place near the Skidars' goal. It was close to the end of the play, and for the tenth time Grey Dawn was bolting after the ball, when his near hind-foot slipped on the greasy mud, and he rolled over and over, pitching Lutyens just clear of the goal-post; and the triumphant Archangels made their goal. Then "time" was called—two goals all; but Lutyens had to be helped up, and Grey Dawn rose with his near hindleg strained somewhere.

"What's the damage?" said Powell, his arm around Lutyens.

"Collar-bone, *of course*," said Lutyens, between his teeth. It was the third time he had broken it in two years, and it hurt him.

Powell and the others whistled.

"Game's up," said Hughes.

"Hold on. We've five good minutes yet, and it isn't my right hand. We'll stick it out."

"I say," said the Captain of the Archangels, trotting up, "are you hurt, Lutyens? We'll wait if you care to put in a substitute. I wish—I mean—the fact is, you fellows deserve this game if any team does. Wish we could give you a man, or some of our ponies—or something."

"You're awfully good, but we'll play it to a finish, I think."

The captain of the Archangels stared for a little. "That's not half bad," he said, and went back to his own side, while Lutyens borrowed a scarf from one of his native officers and made a sling of it. Then an Archangel galloped up with a big bath-sponge, and advised Lutyens to put it under his armpit to ease his shoulder and between them they tied up his left arm scientifically; and one of the native officers leaped forward with four long glasses that fizzed and bubbled.

The team looked at Lutyens piteously, and he nodded. It was the last quarter, and nothing would matter after that. They drank out the dark golden drink, and wiped their moustaches, and things looked more hopeful.

The Maltese Cat had put his nose into the front of Lutyens' shirt and was trying to say how sorry he was.

"He knows," said Lutyens, proudly. "The beggar knows. I've played him without a bridle before now—for fun."

"It's no fun now," said Powell. "But we haven't a decent substitute."

"No," said Lutyens. "It's the last quarter, and we've got to make our goal and win. I'll trust The Cat."

"If you fall this time, you'll suffer a little," said Macnamara.

"I'll trust The Cat," said Lutyens.

"You hear that?" said The Maltese Cat, proudly, to the others. "It's worth while playing polo for ten years to have that said of you. Now then, my sons, come along. We'll kick up a little bit, just to show the Archangels this team haven't suffered."

And, sure enough, as they went on to the ground, The Maltese Cat, after satisfying himself that Lutyens was home in the saddle, kicked out three or four times, and Lutyens laughed. The reins were caught up anyhow in the tips of his strapped left hand, and he never pretended to rely on them. He knew The Cat would answer to the least pressure of the leg, and by way of showing off—for his shoulder hurt him very much—he bent the little fellow in a close figure-of-eight in and out between the goal-posts. There was a roar from the native officers and men, who dearly loved a piece of *dagabashi* (horse-trick work), as they called it, and the pipes very quietly and scornfully droned out the first bars of a common bazaar tune called "Freshly Fresh and Newly New," just as a warning to the other regiments that the Skidars were fit. All the natives laughed.

"And now," said The Maltese Cat, as they took their place, "remember that this is the last quarter, and follow the ball!"

"Don't need to be told," said Who's Who.

"Let me go on. All those people on all four sides will begin to crowd in—just as they did at Malta. You'll hear people calling out, and moving forward and being pushed back; and that is going to make the Archangel ponies very unhappy. But if a ball is struck to the boundary, you go after it, and let the people get out of your way. I went over the pole of a four-in-hand once, and picked a game out of the dust by it. Back me up when I run, and follow the ball."

There was a sort of an all-round sound of sympathy and wonder as the last quarter opened, and then there began exactly what The Maltese Cat had foreseen. People crowded in close to the boundaries, and the Archangels' ponies kept looking sideways at the narrowing space. If you know how a man feels to be cramped at tennis—not because he wants to run out of the court, but because he likes to know that he can at a pinch—

you will guess how ponies must feel when they are playing in a box of human beings.

"I'll bend some of those men if I can get away," said Who's Who, as he rocketed behind the ball; and Bamboo nodded without speaking. They were playing the last ounce in them, and The Maltese Cat had left the goal undefended to join them. Lutyens gave him every order that he could to bring him back, but his was the first time in his career that the little wise grey had ever played polo on his own responsibility, and he was going to make the most of it.

"What are you doing here?" said Hughes, as The Cat crossed in front of him and rode off an Archangel.

"The Cat's in charge—mind the goal!" shouted Lutyens, and bowing forward hit the ball full, and followed on, forcing the Archangels towards their own goal.

"No football," said The Maltese Cat. "Keep the ball by the boundaries and cramp 'em. Play open order, and drive 'em to the boundaries."

Across and across the ground in big diagonals flew the ball, and whenever it came to a flying rush and a stroke close to the boundaries the Archangel ponies moved stiffly. They did not care to go headlong at a wall of men and carriages, though if the ground had been open they could have turned on a sixpence.

"Wriggle her up the sides," said The Cat. "Keep her close to the crowd. They hate the carriages. Shikast, keep her up this side."

Shikast and Powell lay left and right behind the uneasy scuffle of an open scrimmage, and every time the ball was hit away Shikast galloped on it at such an angle that Powell was forced to hit it towards the boundary; and when the crowd had been driven away from that side, Lutyens would send the ball over to the other, and Shikast would slide desperately after it till his friends came down to help. It was billiards, and no football, this time—billiards in a corner pocket; and the cues were not well chalked.

"If they get us out in the middle of the ground they'll walk away from us. Dribble her along the sides," cried The Maltese Cat.

So they dribbled all along the boundary, where a pony could not come on their right-hand side; and the Archangels were furious and the umpires had to neglect the game to shout at the people to get back, and several blundering mounted policemen tried to restore order, all close to the scrimmage, and the nerves of the Archangels' ponies stretched and broke like cobwebs.

Five or six times an Archangel hit the ball up into the middle of the ground, and each time the watchful Shikast gave Powell his chance to send it back, and after each return, when the dust had settled, men could see that the Skidars had gained a few yards.

Every now and again there were shouts of "Side! Off side!" from the spectators; but the teams were too busy to care, and the umpires had all they could do to keep their maddened ponies clear of the scuffle.

At last Lutyens missed a short easy stroke, and the Skidars had to fly back helter-skelter to protect their own goal, Shikast leading. Powell stopped the ball with a backhander when it was not fifty yards from the goal-posts, and Shikast spun round with a wrench that nearly hoisted Powell out of his saddle.

"Now's our last chance," said The Cat, wheeling like a cockchafer on a pin. "We've got to ride it out. Come along."

Lutyens felt the little chap take a deep breath, and, as it were, crouch under his rider. The ball was hopping towards the right-hand boundary, an Archangel riding for it with both spurs and a whip; but neither spur nor whip would make his pony stretch himself as he neared the crowd. The Maltese Cat glided under his very nose, picking up his hind legs sharp, for there was not a foot to spare between his quarters and the other pony's bit. It was as neat an exhibition as fancy figure-skating. Lutyens hit with all the strength he had left, but the stick slipped a little in his hand, and the fall flew off to the left instead of keeping close to the boundary. Who's Who was far across the ground, thinking hard as he galloped. He repeated stride for stride The Cat's maneuvres with another Archangel pony, nipping the ball away from under his bridle, and clearing his opponent by half a fraction of an inch, for Who's Who was clumsy behind. Then he drove away towards the right as The Maltese Cat came up from the left; and Bamboo held a middle course exactly between them. The three were making a sort of Government-broad-arrow-shaped attack; and there was only the Archangels' back to guard the goal; but immediately behind them were three Archangels racing all they knew, and mixed up with them was Powell sending Shikast along on what he felt was their last hope. It takes a very good man to stand up to the rush of seven crazy ponies in the last quarters of a Cup game, when men are riding with their necks for sale, and the ponies are delirious. The Archangels' back missed his stroke and pulled aside just in time to let the rush go by. Bamboo and Who's Who shortened stride to give The Cat room, and Lutyens got the goal with a clean, smooth, smacking stroke that was heard all over the field. But there was no stopping the ponies. They poured through the goal-posts in one mixed mob, winners and losers together, for the pace had been terrific. The Maltese Cat knew by experience what would happen, and, to save Lutyens, turned to the right with one last effort, that strained a back-sinew beyond hope of repair. As he did so he heard the right-hand goal-post crack as a pony cannoned into it—crack, splinter and fall like a mast. It had been sawed three parts through in cases of accidents, but it upset the pony nevertheless, and he blundered into another, who blundered into the left-hand post, and then there was confusion and dust and wood. Bamboo was lying on the ground seeing stars; an Archangel pony rolled beside him, breathless and angry; Shikast had sat down dog-fashion to avoid falling over the others, and was sliding along on his little bobtail in a cloud of dust; and Powell was sitting on the ground hammering with his stick and trying to cheer. All the others were shouting at the top of what was left of their voices, and the men who had been split were shouting too. As soon as the people saw no one was hurt, ten thousand natives and English shouted and clapped and yelled, and before any one could stop them the pipers of the Skidars broke on to the ground, with all the native officers and men behind them, and marched up and down, playing a wild Northern tune called "Zakhme Bagán," and through the insolent blaring of the pipes and the high-pitched native yells you could hear the Archangels' band hammering, "For they are all jolly good fellows," and then reproachfully to the losing team, "Ooh, Kafoozalum! Kafoozalum! Kafoozalum!"

Besides all these things and many more, there was a Commander-in-chief, and an Inspector-General of Cavalry, and the principal veterinary officer of all India standing on the top of a regimental coach, yelling like school-boys; and brigadiers and colonels and commissioners, and hundreds of pretty ladies joined the chorus. But The Maltese Cat stood with his head down, wondering how many legs were left to him; and Lutyens watched the men and ponies pick themselves out of the wreck of the two goal-posts, and he patted The Maltese Cat very tenderly.

"I say," said the Captain of the Archangels, spitting a pebble out of his mouth, "will you take three thousand for that pony—as he stands?"

"No thank you. I've an idea he's saved my life," said Lutyens, getting off and lying down at full length. Both teams were on the ground too, waving their boots in the air, and coughing and drawing deep breaths, as the *saises* ran up to take away the ponies, and an officious water-carrier sprinkled the players with dirty water till they sat up.

"My aunt!" said Powell, rubbing his back, and looking at the stumps of the goal-posts. "That was a game!"

They played it over again, every stroke of it, that night at the big dinner, when the Free-for-All Cup was filled and passed down the table, and emptied and filled again, and everybody made most eloquent speeches. About two in the morning, when there might have been some singing, a wise little, plain little, grey little head looked in through the open door.

"Hurrah! Bring him in," said the Archangels; and his *sais*, who was very happy indeed, patted The Maltese Cat on the flank, and he limped in to the blaze of light and the glittering uniforms looking for Lutyens. He was used to messes, and men's bedrooms, and places where ponies are not usually encouraged, and in his youth had jumped on and off a mess-table for a bet. So he behaved himself very politely, and ate bread dipped in salt, and was petted all round the table, moving gingerly; and they drank his health, because he had done more to win the Cup than any man or horse on the ground.

That was glory and honor enough for the rest of his days, and The Maltese Cat did not complain much when the veterinary surgeon said that he would be no good for polo any more. When Lutyens married, his wife did not allow him to play, so he was forced to be an umpire; and his pony on these occasions was flea-bitten grey with a neat polo-tail, lame all round, but desperately quick on his feet, and, as everybody knew, Past Pluperfect Prestissimo Player of the Game.

It takes a little while for the sports aspect of this story—some trout fishing—to develop. Set in small-town Montana during hard times, it is about ordinary people doing nothing special. Yet its compelling dialogue is a literary treat from one of America's most accomplished writers. Richard Ford's stories have appeared in Esquire *(where this story came from),* The New Yorker, *and* Tri-Quarterly. *Among his books are* The Sportswriter *(1986),* Rock Springs: Stories *(1987), and* Independence Day, *which won a Pulitzer Prize in 1996. Ford's most recent collection is* Women with Men *(1997).*

Richard Ford

WINTERKILL
(1983)

I HAD NOT BEEN BACK IN TOWN LONG. Maybe a month was all. The work had finally given out for me down at Silver Bow, and I had quit staying down there when the weather turned cold, and come back to my mother's, on the Bitterroot, to lay up and set my benefits aside for when things got worse.

My mother had her boyfriend then, an old wildcatter named Harley Reeves. And Harley and I did not get along, though I don't blame him for that. He had been laid off himself down near Gillette, Wyoming, where the boom was finished. And he was just doing what I was doing and had arrived there first. Everyone was laid off then. It was not a good time in that part of Montana, nor was it going to be. The two of them were just giving it a final try, both of them in their sixties, strangers together in the little house my father had left her.

So in a week I moved up to town, into a little misery flat across from the Burlington Northern yards, and began to wait. There was nothing to do. Watch TV. Stop in a bar. Walk down to the Clark Fork and fish where they had built a little park. Just find a way to spend the time. You think you'd like to have all the time be your own, but that is a fantasy. I was feeling my back to the wall then, and didn't know what would happen to me in a week's time, which is a feeling to stay with you and make being cheerful hard. And no one can like that.

I was at the Top Hat having a drink with Little Troy Burnham, talking about the deer season, when a woman who had been sitting at the front of the bar got up and came over to us. I had seen this woman other times in other bars in town. She would be there in the afternoons around three, and then sometimes late at night when I would be cruising back. She danced with some men from the air base, then sat drinking and talking late. I suppose she left with someone finally. She wasn't a bad-looking woman at all–blond, with wide, dark eyes set out, wide hips and dark eyebrows. She could've been thirty-four years old, although she could've been forty-four or twenty-four, because she was drinking steady, and steady drink can do both to you, especially to women. But I had thought the first time I saw her: Here's one on the way down. A miner's wife drifted up from Butte, or a rancher's daughter just suddenly run off, which can happen. Or worse. And I hadn't been tempted. Trouble comes cheap and leaves expensive, is a way of thinking about that.

"Do you suppose you could give me a light?" the woman said to us. She was standing at our table. Nola was her name. Nola Foster. I'd heard that around. She wasn't drunk. It was four o'clock in the afternoon, and no one was there but Troy Burnham and me.

"If you'll tell me a love story, I'd do anything in the world for you," Troy said. It was what he always said to women. He'd do anything in the world for something. Troy sits in a wheelchair due to a smoke jumper's injury, and can't do very much. We had been friends since high school and before. He was always short, and I was tall. But Troy had been an excellent wrestler and won awards in Montana, and I had done little of that—some boxing once was all. We had been living, recently, in the same apartments on Ryman Street, though Troy lived there permanently and drove a Checker cab to earn a living, and I was hoping to pass on to something better. "I *would* like a little love story," Troy said, and called out for whatever Nola Foster was drinking.

"Nola, Troy. Troy, Nola," I said and lit her cigarette.

"Have we met?" Nola said, taking a seat and glancing at me.

"At the East Gate. Some time ago," I said.

"That's a very nice bar," she said in a cool way. "But I hear it's changed hands."

"I'm glad to make an acquaintance," Troy said, grinning and adjusting his glasses. "Now let's hear that love story." He pulled up close to the table so that his head and his big shoulders were above the tabletop. Troy's injury had caused him not to have any hips left. There is some- thing there, but not hips. He needs bars and a special seat in his cab. He is both frail and strong at once, though in most ways he gets on like everybody else.

"I *was* in love," Nola said quietly as the bartender set her drink down and she took a sip. "And now I'm not."

"That's a short love story," I said.

"There's more to it," Troy said, grinning. "Am I right about that? Here's cheers to you," he said, and raised his glass.

Nola glanced at me again. "All right. Cheers," she said and took an- other drink.

Two men had started playing a pool game at the far end of the room. They had turned on the table light, and I could hear the balls click and someone say, "Bust 'em up, Craft." And then the smack.

"You don't want to hear about that," Nola said. "You're drunk men, that's all."

"We do too," Troy said. Troy always has enthusiasm. He could very easily complain, but I have never heard it come up. And I believe he has a good heart.

"What about you? What's your name?" Nola said to me.

"Les," I said.

"Les, then," she said. "You don't want to hear this, Les."

"Yes he does," Troy said, putting his elbows on the table and raising himself. Troy was a little drunk. Maybe we all were a little.

"Why not?" I said.

"See? Sure. Les wants more. He's like me."

Nola was actually a pretty woman, with a kind of dignity to her that wasn't at once so noticeable, and Troy was thrilled by her.

"All right," Nola said, taking another sip.

"What'd I tell you?" Troy said.

"I had really thought he was dying," Nola said.

"Who?" I said.

"My husband. Harry Lyons. I don't use that name now. Someone's told you this story before, haven't they?"

"Not me. Goddamn!" Troy said. "I *want* to hear this story."

I said I hadn't heard it either, though I had heard there was a story.

She had a puff on her cigarette and gave us both a look that said she didn't believe us. But she went on. Maybe she'd thought about another drink by then.

"He had this death look. Ca-shit-ic, they call it. He was pale, and his mouth turned down like he could see death. His heart had already gone out once in June, and I had the feeling I'd come in the kitchen some morning and he'd be slumped on his toast."

"How old was this Harry?" Troy said.

"Fifty-three years old. Older than me by a lot."

"That's cardiac alley there," Troy said and nodded at me. Troy has trouble with his own organs now and then. I think they all moved lower when he hit the ground.

"A man gets strange when he's going to die," Nola said in a quiet voice. "Like he's watching it come. Though Harry was still going to work out at Champion's every day. He was an estimator. Plus he watched *me* all the time. Watched to see if I was getting ready, I guess. Checking the insurance, balancing the checkbook, locating the safe-deposit key. All that. Though I would, too. Who wouldn't?"

"Bet your ass," Troy said and nodded again. Troy was taking this all in, I could see that.

"And I admit it, I *was*," Nola said. "I loved Harry. But if he died, where was I going? Was I supposed to die, too? I had to make some plans for myself. I had to think Harry was expendable at some point. To *my* life, anyway."

"Probably that's why he was watching you," I said. "He might not have felt expendable in *his* life."

"I know." Nola looked at me seriously and smoked her cigarette. "But I had a friend whose husband killed himself. Went into the garage and left the motor running. And his wife was *not* ready. Not in her mind. She thought he was out putting on brakeshoes. And there he was dead when she went out there. She ended up having to move to Washington, D.C. Lost her balance completely over it. Lost her house, too."

"All bad things," Troy agreed.

"And that just wasn't going to be me, I thought. And if Harry had to get wind of it, well, so be it. Some days I'd wake up and look at him in bed and I'd think, Die, Harry, quit worrying about it."

"I thought this was a love story," I said. I looked down at where the two men were playing an eight-ball rack. One man was chalking a cue while the other man was leaning over to shoot.

"It's coming," Troy said. "Just be patient, Les."

Nola drained her drink. "I'll guarantee it is."

"Then let's hear it," I said. "Get on to the love part."

Nola looked at me strangely then, as if I really did know what she was going to tell, and thought maybe I might tell it first myself. She raised her chin at me. "Harry came home one evening from work, right?" she said. "Just death as usual. Only he said to me, 'Nola, I've invited some friends over, sweetheart. Why don't you go out and get a flank steak at Albertson's.' I asked when were they coming? He said, in an hour. And I thought, An hour! Because he never brought people home. We went to bars, you know. We didn't entertain. But I said, 'All right. I'll go get a flank steak.' And I got in the car and went out and bought a flank steak. I thought Harry ought to have what he wants. If he wants to have friends and steak he ought to be able to. Men, before they die, will want strange things."

"That's a fact, too," Troy said seriously. "I was full dead all of four minutes when I hit. And I dreamed about nothing but lobster the whole time. And I'd never even seen a lobster, though I have now. Maybe that's what they serve in heaven." Troy grinned at both of us.

"Well, this wasn't heaven," Nola said and signaled for another drink. "So when I got back, there was Harry with three Crow Indians, in my house, sitting in the living room drinking mai tais. A man and two women. His *friends*, he said. From the mill. He wanted to have his friends over, he said. And Harry was raised a strict Mormon. Not that it matters."

"I guess he had a change of heart," I said.

"That'll happen, too," Troy said gravely. "LDS's aren't like they used to be. They used to be bad, but that's all changed. Though I guess coloreds still can't get inside the temple all the way."

"These three were inside my house, though. I'll just say that. And I'm not prejudiced about it. Leopards with spots, leopards without. All the same to me. But I was nice. I went right in the kitchen and put the flank steak in the oven, put some potatoes in water, got out some frozen peas. And went back in to have a drink. And we sat around and talked for half an hour. Talked about the mill. Talked about Marlon Brando. The man and one of the women were married. He worked with Harry. And the other woman was her sister, Winona. There's a town in Mississippi with the same name. I looked it up. So after a while—all nice and friends—I went in to peel my potatoes. And this other woman, Bernie, came in with me to help, I guess. And I was standing there cooking over a little range, and this Bernie said to me, 'I don't know how you do it, Nola.' 'Do what, Bernie?' I said. 'Let Harry go with my sister like he does and you stay so happy about it. I couldn't ever stand that with Claude.' And I just turned around and looked at her. *Winona is what?* I thought. That name seemed so unusual for an Indian. And I just started yelling it. 'Winona, Winona,' at the top of my lungs right at the stove. I just went crazy a minute, I guess. Screaming, holding a potato in my hand, hot. The man came running into the kitchen. Claude Smart Enemy. Claude was awfully nice. He kept me from harming myself. But when I started yelling, Harry, I guess, figured everything was all up. And he and his Winona woman went right out the door. And he didn't get even to the car when his heart went. He had a myocardial infarction right out on the sidewalk at this Winona's feet. I guess he thought everything was going to be just great. We'd all have dinner together. And I'd never know what was what. Except he didn't count on Bernie saying something."

"Maybe he was trying to make you appreciate him more," I said. "Maybe he didn't like being expendable and was sending you a message."

Nola looked at me seriously again. "I thought of that," she said. "I thought about that more than once. But that would've been hurtful. And Harry Lyons wasn't a man to hurt you. He was more of a sneak. I just think he wanted us all to be friends."

"That makes sense." Troy nodded and looked at me.

"What happened to Winona," I asked.

"What happened to Winona?" Nola took a drink and gave me a hard look. "Winona moved herself to Spokane. What happened to me is a better question."

"Why? You're here with us," Troy said enthusiastically. "You're doing great. Les and me ought to do as well as you're doing. Les is out of work. And I'm out of luck. You're doing the best of the three of us, I'd say."

"I wouldn't," Nola said frankly, then turned and stared down at the men playing pool.

"What'd he leave you?" I said. "Harry."

"Two thousand," Nola said coldly.

"That's a small amount," I said.

"And it's a sad love story, too," Troy said, shaking his head. "You loved him and it ended rotten. That's like Shakespeare."

"I loved him enough," Nola said.

"How about sports. Do you like sports?" Troy said.

Nola looked at Troy oddly then. In his chair Troy doesn't look exactly like a whole man, and sometimes simple things he'll say will seem surprising. And what he'd said then surprised Nola. I've gotten used to it, myself, after all these years.

"Did you want to try skiing?" Nola said and glanced at me.

"Fishing," Troy said, up on his elbows again. "Let's all of us go fishing. Put an end to old gloomy." Troy seemed like he wanted to pound the table. And I wondered when was the last time he had slept with a woman. Fifteen years ago, maybe. And now that was all over for him. But he was excited just to be here and get to talk to Nola Foster, and I wasn't going to be in his way. "No one'll be there now," he said. "We'll catch a fish and cheer ourselves up. Ask Les. He caught a fish."

I had been going mornings in those days, when the *Today* show got over. Just to kill an hour. The river runs through the middle of town, and I could walk over in five minutes and fish downstream below the motels that are there, and could look up at the blue and white mountains up the Bitterroot, toward my mother's house, and sometimes see the geese coming back up their flyway. It was a strange winter. January was like a spring day, and the Chinook blew down over us a warm wind from the eastern slopes. Some days were cool or cold, but many days were warm, and the only ice you'd see was in the lows where the sun didn't reach. You could walk right out to the river and make a long cast to where the fish were deep down in the cold pools. And you could even think things might turn out better.

Nola turned and looked at me. The thought of fishing was seeming like a joke to her, I know. Though maybe she didn't have money for a meal and thought we might buy her one. Or maybe she'd never even been fishing. Or maybe she knew that she was on her way to the bottom, where everything is the same, and here was this something different being offered, and it was worth a try.

"Did you catch a big fish, Les," she asked.

"Yes," I said.

"See?" Troy said. "Am I a liar? Or am I not?"

"You might be." Nola looked at me oddly then, but I thought sweetly, too. "What kind of fish was it?"

"A brown trout. Caught deep, on a hare's ear," I said.

"I don't know what that is," Nola said and smiled. I could see that she wasn't minding any of this because her face was flushed, and she looked pretty.

"Which," I asked. "A brown trout? Or a hare's ear?"

"That's it," she said.

"A hare's ear is a kind of fly," I said.

"I see," Nola said.

"Let's get out of the bar for once," Troy said loudly, running his chair backwards and forwards. "We'll go fish, then we'll have chicken-in-the-ruff. Troy's paying."

"What'll I lose?" Nola said and shook her head. She looked at both of us, smiling as though she could think of something that might be lost.

"You got it all to win," Troy said. "Let's go."

"Whatever," Nola said. "Sure."

And we went out of the Top Hat, with Nola pushing Troy in his chair and me coming on behind.

On Front Street the evening was as warm as May, though the sun had gone behind the peaks already, and it was nearly dark. The sky was deep blue in the east behind the Sapphires, where the darkness was, but salmon pink above the sun. And we were in the middle of it. Half-drunk, trying to be imaginative in how we killed our time.

Troy's Checker was parked in front, and Troy rolled over to it and spun around.

"Let me show you this great trick," he said and grinned. "Get in and drive, Les. Stay there, sweetheart, and watch me."

Nola had kept her drink in her hand, and she stood by the door of the Top Hat. Troy lifted himself off his chair onto the concrete. I got in beside Troy's bars and his raised seat, and started the cab with my left hand.

"Ready," Troy shouted. "Ease forward. Ease up."

And I eased the car up.

"Oh my God," I heard Nola say and saw her put her palm to her forehead and look away.

"*Yaah. Ya-hah*," Troy yelled.

"Your poor foot," Nola said.

"It doesn't hurt me," Troy yelled. "It's just like a pressure." I couldn't see him from where I was.

"Now I know I've seen it all," Nola said. She was smiling.

"Back up, Les. Just ease it back again," Troy called out.

"Don't do it again," Nola said.

"One time's enough, Troy," I said. No one else was in the street. I thought how odd it would be for anyone to see that, without knowing something in advance. A man running over another man's foot for fun. Just drunks, you'd think, and be right.

"Sure. Okay," Troy said. I still couldn't see him. But I put the cab back in park and waited. "Help me, sweetheart, now," I heard Troy say to Nola. "It's easy getting down, but old Troy can't get up again by himself. You have to help him."

And Nola looked at me in the cab, the glass still in her hand. It was a peculiar look she gave me, a look that seemed to ask something of me, but I did not know what it was and couldn't answer. And then she put her glass on the pavement and went to put Troy back in his chair.

When we got to the river it was as good as dark, and the river was only a big space you could hear, with the south-of-town lights up behind it and the three bridges and Champion's Paper downstream a mile. And it was cold with the sun gone, and I thought there would be fog in before morning.

Troy had insisted on driving with us in the back, as if we'd hired a cab to take us fishing. On the way down he sang a smoke jumper's song, and Nola sat close to me and let her leg be beside mine. And by the time we stopped by the river, below the Lion's Head motel, I had kissed her twice, and knew all that I could do.

"I think I'll go fishing," Troy said from his little raised-up seat in front. "I'm going night fishing. And I'm going to get my own chair out and my rod and all I need. I'll have a time."

"How do you ever change a tire?" Nola said. She was not moving. It was just a question she had. People say all kinds of things to cripples.

Troy whipped around suddenly, though, and looked back at us where we sat on the cab seat. I had put my arm around Nola, and we sat there looking at his big head and big shoulders, below which there was only half a body any good to anyone. "Trust Mr. Wheels," Troy said. "Mr. Wheels can do anything a whole man can." And he smiled at us a crazy man's smile.

"I think I'll just stay in the car," Nola said. "I'll wait for chicken-in-the-ruff. That'll be my fishing."

"It's too cold for ladies now anyway," Troy said gruffly. "Only men. Only men in wheelchairs is the new rule."

I got out of the cab with Troy then and set up his chair and put him in it. I got his fishing gear out of the trunk and strung it up. Troy was not a man to fish flies, and I put a silver dace on his spin line and told him to hurl it far out and let it flow for a time into the deep current and then to work it, and work it all the way in. I said he would catch a fish with that strategy in five minutes, or ten.

"Les," Troy said to me in the cold dark behind the cab.

"What?" I said.

"Do you ever just think of just doing a criminal thing sometime? Just do something terrible. Change everything."

"Yes," I said. "I think about that."

Troy had his fishing rod across his chair now, and he was gripping it and looking down the sandy bank toward the dark and sparkling water.

"Why don't you do it?" he said.

"I don't know what I'd choose to do," I said.

"Mayhem," Troy said. "Commit mayhem."

"And go to Deer Lodge forever," I said. "Or maybe they'd hang me and let me dangle. That would be worse than this."

"Okay, that's right," Troy said, still staring. "But *I* should do it, shouldn't I? I should do the worst thing there is."

"No, you shouldn't," I said.

And then he laughed. "Hah. Right. Never do that," he said. And he wheeled himself down toward the river into the darkness, laughing all the way.

In the cold cab, after that, I held Nola Foster for a long time. Just held her with my arms around her, breathing and waiting. From the back window I could see the Lion's Head motel, see the restaurant there that faces the river and that is lighted with candles, and where people were eating. I could see the WELCOME out front, though not who was welcomed. I could see cars on the bridge going home for the night. And it made me think of Harley Reeves in my father's little house on the Bitterroot. I thought about him in bed with my mother. Warm. I thought about the faded old tattoo on Harley's shoulder. VICTORY, that said. And I could not connect it easily with what I knew about Harley Reeves, though I thought possibly that he had won a victory of kinds over me just by being where he was.

"A man who isn't trusted is the worst thing," Nola Foster said. "You know that, don't you?" I suppose her mind was wandering. She was cold, I could tell by the way she held me. Troy was gone out in the dark now. We were alone, and her skirt had come up a good ways.

"Yes, that's bad," I said, though I couldn't think at that moment of what trust could mean to me. It was not an issue in my life, and I hoped it never would be. "You're right," I said to make her happy.

"What was your name again?"

"Les," I said. "Lester Snow. Call me Les."

"Les Snow," Nola said. "Do you like less snow?"

"Usually I do." And I put my hand then where I wanted it most.

"How old are you, Les?" she said.

"Thirty-seven."

"You're an old man."

"How old are you?" I said.

"It's my business, isn't it?"

"I guess it is," I said.

"I'll do this, you know," Nola said, "and not even care about it. Just do a thing. It means nothing more than how I feel at this time. You know? Do you know what I mean, Les?"

"I know it," I said.

"But *you* need to be trusted. Or you aren't anything. Do you know that too?"

We were close to each other. I couldn't see the lights of town or the motel or anything more. Nothing moved.

"I know that, I guess," I said. It was whiskey talking.

"Warm me up then, Les," Nola said. "Warm. Warm."

"You'll get warm," I said.

"I'll think about Florida."

"I'll make you warm," I said.

What I thought I heard at first was a train. So many things can sound like a train when you live near trains. This was a *woo* sound, you would say. Like a train. And I lay and listened for a long time, thinking about a train and its light shining through the darkness along the side of some mountain pass north of there and about something else I don't even remember now. And then Troy came around to my thinking, and I knew then that the *woo* sound had been him.

Nola Foster said, "It's Mr. Wheels. He's caught a fish, maybe. Or else drowned."

"Yes," I said. I sat up and looked out the window but could see nothing. It had become foggy in just that little time, and tomorrow, I thought, would be warm again, though it was cold now. Nola and I had not even taken off our clothes to do what we'd done.

"Let me see," I said.

I got out and walked into the fog to where I could only see fog and hear the river running. Troy had not made a *woo*-ing sound again, and I thought to myself, There is no trouble here. Nothing's wrong.

Though when I walked a ways up the sandy bank, I saw Troy's chair come visible in the fog. And he was not in it, and I couldn't see him. And my heart went then. I heard it go click in my chest. And I thought: This is the worst. What's happened here will be the worst. And I called out, "Troy. Where are you? Call out now."

And Troy called out, "Here I am, here."

I went for the sound, ahead of me, which was not out in the river but on the bank. And when I had gone farther, I saw him, out of his chair, of course, on his belly, holding on to his fishing rod with both hands, the line out into the river as though it meant to drag him to the water.

"Help me!" he yelled. "I've got a huge fish. Do something to help me."

"I will," I said. Though I didn't see what I could do. I would not dare to take the rod, and it would only have been a mistake to take the line. Never give a straight pull to the fish, is an old rule. So that my only choice was to grab Troy and hold him until the fish was either in or lost, just as if Troy was a part of a rod *I* was fishing with.

I squatted in the cold sand behind him, put my heels down and took up his legs, which felt like matchsticks, and began to hold him there away from the water.

But Troy suddenly twisted toward me. "Turn me loose, Les. Don't be here. Go out. It's snagged. You've got to go out."

"That's crazy," I said. "It's too deep there."

"It's not deep," Troy yelled. "I've got it in close now."

"You're crazy," I said.

"Oh, Christ, Les, go get it. I don't want to lose it."

I looked a moment at Troy's face then, in the dark. His glasses were gone off of him. His face was wet. And he had the look of a desperate man, a man who has nothing to hope for but, in some strange way, everything in the world to lose.

"Stupid. This is stupid," I said, because it seemed to me to be. But I got up, walked to the edge and stepped out into the cold water.

Then, it was at least a month before the runoff would begin in the mountains, and the water I stepped in was cold and painful as broken glass, though the wet parts of me numbed at once, and my feet felt like bricks bumping the bottom.

Troy had been wrong all the way about the depth. Because when I stepped out ten yards, keeping touch of his line with the back of my hand,

I had already gone above my knees, and on the bottom I felt large rocks, and there was a loud rushing around me that suddenly made me afraid.

But when I had gone five more yards, and the water was on my thighs and hurting, I hit the snag Troy's fish was hooked to, and I realized then I had no way at all to hold a fish or catch it with my numbed hands. And that all I could really hope for was to break the snag and let the fish slip down into the current and hope Troy could bring it in, or that I could go back and beach it.

"Can you see it, Les?" Troy yelled out of the dark. "Goddamn it."

"It isn't easy," I said, and I had to hold the snag then to keep my balance. My legs were numb. And I thought: this might be the time and the place I die. What an odd place it is. And what an odd reason for it to happen.

"Hurry up," Troy yelled.

And I wanted to hurry. Except when I ran the line as far as where the snag was, I felt something there that was not a fish and not the snag but something else entirely, some thing I thought I recognized, though I am not sure why. A man, I thought. This is a man.

Though when I reached farther into the snag branches and woods scruff, deeper into the water, what I felt was an animal. With my fingers I touched its hard rib-side, its legs, its short slick coat. I felt to its neck and head and touched its nose and teeth, and it was a deer, though not a big deer, not even a yearling. And I knew when I found where Troy's dace had gone up in the neck flesh, that he had hooked a deer already snagged here, and that he had pulled himself out of his chair trying to work it free.

"What is it? I know it's a big *Brown*. Don't tell me, Les, don't even tell me."

"I've got it," I said. "I'll bring it in."

"Sure, hell yes," Troy said out of the fog.

It was not so hard to work the deer off the snag brush and float it up free. Though once I did, it was dangerous to get turned in the current on numb legs, and hard to keep from going down, and I had to hold on to the deer to keep balance enough to heave myself into the slower water.

And as I did that, I thought: In the Clark Fork many people drown doing less dangerous things than I am doing.

"Throw it way far up," Troy shouted when he could see me. He had righted himself on the sand and was sitting up like a little doll. "Get it way up safe."

"It's safe," I said. I had the deer beside me, floating, but I knew Troy couldn't see it.

"What did I catch?" Troy yelled.

"Something unusual," I said, and with effort I hauled the little deer a foot up onto the sand, dropped it, and put my cold hands under my arms. I heard a car door close back where I had come from, up the riverbank.

"What *is* that?" Troy said and put his hand out to touch the deer's side. He looked up at me. "I can't see without my glasses."

"It's a deer," I said.

Troy moved his hand around on the deer, then looked at me again in a painful way.

"What is it?" he said.

"A deer," I said. "You caught a dead deer."

Troy looked back at the little deer for a moment, and stared as if he did not know what to say about it. And sitting on the wet sand, in the foggy night, he all at once looked scary to me, as though it was him who had washed up there and was finished. "I don't see it," he said and sat there.

"It's what you caught," I said. "I thought you'd want to see it."

"It's crazy, Les," he said. "Isn't it?" And he smiled at me in a wild, blind-eyed way.

"It's unusual," I said.

"I never shot a deer before."

"I don't believe you shot this one," I said.

He smiled at me again, but then suddenly he gasped back a sob, something I had never seen before. "Goddamn it," he said. "Just goddamn it."

"It's an odd thing to catch," I said, standing above him in the grimy fog.

"I can't change a fucking tire," he said and sobbed. "But I'll catch a fucking deer with my fucking fishing rod."

"Not everyone can say that," I said.

"Why would they want to?" He looked up at me crazy again, and broke his spinning rod into two pieces with only his hands. And I knew he must've been drunk still, because I was still drunk a little, and that by itself made me want to cry. And we were there for a time just silent.

"Who killed a deer?" Nola said. She had come behind me in the cold and was looking. I had not known, when I heard the car door, if she wasn't starting back up to town. But it was too cold for that, and I put my arm around her because she was shivering. "Did Mr. Wheels kill it?"

"It drowned," Troy said.

"And why is that?" Nola said and pushed closer to me to be warm, though that was all.

"They get weak and they fall over," I said. "It happens in the mountains. This one fell in the water and couldn't get up."

"So a gimp man can catch it on a fishing rod in a shitty town," Troy said and gasped with bitterness. Real bitterness. The worst I have ever heard from any man, and I have heard bitterness voiced, though it was a union matter then.

"Maybe it isn't so bad," Nola said.

"Hah!" Troy said from the wet ground. "Hah, hah, hah." And I wished that I had never shown him the deer, wished I had spared him that, though the river's rushing came up then and snuffed his sound right out of hearing, and drew it away from us into the foggy night beyond all accounting.

Nola and I pushed the deer back into the river while Troy watched, and then we all three drove up into town and ate chicken-in-the-ruff at the Two Fronts, where the lights were bright and they cooked the chicken fresh for you. I bought a jug of wine and we drank that while we ate, though no one talked. Each of us had done something that night. Something different. That was plain enough. And there was nothing more to talk about.

When we were finished we walked outside, and I asked Nola where she'd like to go. It was only eight o'clock, and there was no place to go but to my little room. She said she wanted to go back to the Top Hat, that she had someone to meet there later, and there was something about the band that night that she liked. She said she wanted to dance.

I told her I was not much for dancing, and she said fine. And when Troy came out from paying, we said good-bye, and she shook my hand and said that she would see me again. Then she and Troy got in the Checker and drove away together down the foggy street, leaving me alone, where I didn't mind being at all.

For a long time I just walked then. My clothes were wet, but it wasn't so cold if you kept moving, though it stayed foggy. I walked to the river again and across on the bridge and a long way down into the south part of town on a wide avenue where there were houses with little porches and little yards, all the way, until it became commercial, and bright lights lit the drive-ins and car lots. I could've walked then, I thought, clear to my mother's house twenty miles away. But I turned back, and walked the same way, only on the other side of the street. Though when I got near the bridge, I came past the Senior Citizen Recreation, where there were soft lights on inside a big room, and I could see through a window in the pinkish glow, old people dancing across the floor to a record player that played in the corner. It was a rumba or something like a rumba that was being played, and the old people were dancing the box step, smooth and graceful and courteous, moving across the linoleum like real dancers, their arms on each other's shoulders like husbands and wives. And it pleased me to see that. And I thought that it was too bad my mother and father could not be here now, too bad they couldn't come up and dance and go home happy, and have me to watch them. Or even for my mother and Harley Reeves to do that. It didn't seem like too much to wish for. Just a normal life other people had.

I stood and watched them a while, then I walked back home across the river. Though for some reason I could not sleep that night, and simply lay in bed with the radio turned on to Denver, and smoked cigarettes until it was light. Of course I thought about Nola Foster, that I didn't know where she lived, though for some reason I thought she might live in Frenchtown, near the pulp plant. Not far. Never-never land, they called that. And I thought about my father, who had once gone to Deer Lodge prison for stealing hay from a friend, and had never recovered from it, though that meant little to me now.

And I thought about the matter of trust. That I would always lie if it would save someone an unhappiness. That was easy. And that I would rather a person mistrust me than dislike me. Though I thought you could always trust me to act a certain way, to be a place, or to say a thing if it ever were to matter. You could predict within human reason what I'd do—that I would not, for example, commit a vicious crime—trust that I would risk my own life for you if I knew it meant enough. And as I lay in the gray light, smoking, while the refrigerator clicked and the switcher in the Burlington Northern yard shunted cars and made their couplings, I thought that though my life at that moment seemed to have taken a bad turn and paused, it still meant something to me as a life, and that before long it would start again in some promising way.

I know I must've dozed a little, because I woke suddenly and there was the light. Earl Nightingale was on the radio, and I heard a door close. It was that that woke me.

I knew it would be Troy, and I thought I would step out and meet him, fix coffee for us before he went to bed and slept all day, the way he always did. But when I stood up I heard Nola Foster's voice. I could not mistake that. She was drunk, and laughing about something. "Mr. Wheels," she said. Mr. Wheels this, Mr. Wheels that. Troy was laughing. And I heard them come in the little entry, heard Troy's chair bump the sill. And I waited to see if they would knock on my door. And when they didn't, and I heard Troy's door shut and the chain go up, I thought that we had all had a good night finally. Nothing had happened that hadn't turned out all right. None of us had been harmed. And I put on my pants, then my shirt and shoes, turned off my radio, went into the kitchen where I kept my fishing rod, and with it went out into the warm, foggy morning, using just this once the back door, the quiet way, so as not to see or be seen by anyone.

Stories about cross-country running are rare as hens' teeth, but this one is a dandy. A runty high schooler struggling to make the team experiences frustration and pain but is determined to somehow sip from glory's cup. This exemplifies the purity of sport and seeking to overcome life's obstacles. The story appeared initially in the Saturday Evening Post. *Author James Buechler won the O. Henry Memorial Prize Award in 1956.*

James Buechler

JOHN SOBIESKI
RUNS (1964)

ONE SEPTEMBER AFTERNOON THE DOOR of the cross-country team room at an upstate New York high school opened a little way and then closed again, admitting in that instant a very short boy who looked a little underfed even for his size. Nobody paid him the least attention. In the first place, there were only three people in the locker room. One was a member of the varsity, a dark, Italian-looking boy dressed ready to go out in sweat pants and a sweat shirt with a picture of a winged spiked shoe printed in red on its breast. He sat tying on his lightweight cross-country shoes in front of a star-spangled locker, sky-blue in color and covered with white stars, with a red-and-white stripe running around the edges of its door. Most of the lockers were dark green, but there were a half dozen or so such splashy ones. The dark boy sat on one of two wooden benches running the length of the room, about two feet out from the lockers. On the opposite bench a boy in track shorts lay stomach down, his head to one side, his arms hanging, while a serious-faced man, an assistant coach, picked with his fingers very fast at the backs of the other's legs, snick-snick-snick-snick-snick. The liniment he was using smelled sharply above the prevailing, long-accumulated odor of sweat.

Turning from the door, the short boy stepped over one of the benches in a motion remarkably easy, considering his size. With his face in the corner made by the last locker and the wall, he began to undress. He had a blue looseleaf notebook with the name of the school on it, and he laid it on the bench. Then he took off a brown knit sweater, which he folded up on top of the notebook. Under that he wore a white shirt starched so stiffly that when he took it off it held the creases of his wearing and would only fold brokenly in a high springy pile. Now he simply stood for a moment in his undershirt, with slender shoulders and brown hair about the color of his sweater, wearing a pair of darker brown pants. He looked like a boy who had been sent to the corner for something he ought to be ashamed of. He had been trying to get something out of his pocket that didn't want to come, but all at once, as he stood tugging, the thing gave, flew out—an ordinary piece of blue cloth—with a sweep and flourish that seemed to disconcert him. Immediately he loosened his belt and let his trousers fall to his ankles. He stepped out of them and into the blue cloth thing, a cheap pair of gym shorts with a string pull at the waist. These on, he was uniformed. The brown pants he rolled up with his little pile, bent and tightened the strings of his shoes, and, fixing his eyes on the door at the far end of the room, walked toward it between the lockers, a very thin boy who might have been called lanky if he had been a foot taller. He opened the door, looked out, and finding that it led to the playing field, disappeared through it, running.

In the locker room the varsity member, his dark hair hanging over his face in long Vaselined strands, had finished with his running shoes. With a shake he laid his hair back on his head in orderly lines and, at the same time, gave one single, sophisticated glance across at the coach.

Still picking away, the man said, "He could grow."

John Sobieski—this was the short boy's name—found himself running out of the school building's shadow into the warm sunlight, over hard even ground covered with short grass which stretched away, from beneath his own thin legs, into the biggest flat field he had ever seen. Moving across it, he passed over gleaming lines of white lime powder and, except for them, did not feel he was moving at all, running though he was across the big green field in the sun. He saw, far away on his left, the football players, tiny, bright-colored people, hunching and waiting, rising and moving and entangling all together in waves, heard whistles, and saw before him, past many lines and various goalposts, more boys—the running team. Many were lying all about on the ground, but many were standing up too, all upright together in a tight kind of pack that vibrated and moved around like a thing in itself, something very bright, red and white, spinning there in the sunshine on top of uncountable bare legs. As he came nearer he saw that the people on the ground were only discarded sweat suits with nobody in them; the runners were all up and gathered around a very tall man who was waving a clipboard of papers in the air above his head as he spoke. The runners had on bright red shirts with lettering across the chest and white shorts edged in red, and they shifted and pranced on their slight little running shoes as on hooves, their bright uniforms blended and mingled to make up that whirling bright-colored thing which, idling nervous and impatient in place up to now, suddenly lurched and flexed and strained within, before extending itself loosely and easily away as, on its many legs, it began trotting off over the field. John Sobieski ran as hard as he knew how; as he pounded up, the big man flagged him on with the paper-fluttering clipboard, boomed, "Right there . . . after those men!" and John Sobieski was past and pounding after the pack of runners that stretched away loose and red and white in the sunlight toward a far fence bordering the field.

So they were running, and John Sobieski was with them. But already his legs felt heavy, and he was breathing faster than he had ever breathed in his life. He had come running all the way across the big green field, only to find that they had started already. The unfairness of it made him hot and sick. He had come out for cross-country knowing he would have to run miles, but they had started before he was ready. His throat ached; his feet he raised up and clapped down like flatirons. As he ran he thought to himself, "It's not my fault, they started before I was ready. . . . I'll stop right here, somewhere."

They had come to the end of the field and passed through a gate; they were running on a sidewalk past houses. A boy in a red shirt was running not far in front of him. John Sobieski could see his own shoes hitting the sidewalk one after the other, while he himself seemed to ride above somewhere as on some funny kind of running machine. Bumping along in this way he was interested to find, after a while, that his machine seemed to be moving a little faster than the other boy's machine. Fascinated, with curiosity and detachment mixed, he watched the increasing nearness of the other boy's white pants—for some reason that was all he could see—until gradually he came alongside the other. Both of them were bouncing up and down furiously, but the other boy seemed to bounce up and down in the same spot, while John Sobieski was very slowly moving, until, gradually again, he couldn't see the other boy anymore. But it didn't make any difference; there was another boy in front of him.

And this one approached and went by, and another one sprang up. Regular as telephone poles they went slowly by him until there had been six. He counted them because he didn't have anything else to do. Then everything grew dark, and though it was only because they had entered a park and were running on a path through woods, John Sobieski didn't know it. All he knew was that he was running after a strange white flag that moved before him in the dim. Fluttering and twinkling, always ahead, it dipped and wound with the path, and John Sobieski behind. At last, after a long time, they broke out into the light. There was the fence around the shadowed green playing field and, inside it, the football players, looking weary in their dirtied uniforms, and beyond them, far across the field, the high-school building. John Sobieski's heart lifted. He saw that the white flag was nothing but another pair of the white shorts edged with red. The boy running in them was only strides in front, and, though he was tired, he set himself to beat this one boy at least. As he sprinted around the fence toward the school—which burned at its edges like a coal, blocking off the sun—it seemed to him he had just started, he was virtually flying, he would pass them all. And he did overtake the boy in the twinkling white pants, and another.

Standing up against the bricks of the school building, the assistant coach, who had just finished a rubdown in the locker room, watched the line of long-distance runners coming around the fence. They toiled with incredible slowness and suffering, each one preserving only the formal attitude of running. Long ago they had lost the speed the attitude is supposed to produce. He watched them toiling, one by one, and as he watched, one moving slightly faster than the rest strained painfully closer to the next man, painfully abreast, and in time came up behind the next runner, whom he would probably pass before reaching the school. The coach turned and walked swiftly toward a corner of the building.

Now the leaders had reached a gate by the school. There something halted them, making them run into one another in their weariness. As John Sobieski came up he stumbled and fell against the slippery neck of the boy in front of him. The boy's sweat came away on his lips, and as they passed through the gate a man shouted something at each one. John Sobieski felt his shoulder grabbed and squeezed.

"Thirteen!" the man said to him. It was the assistant coach.

Nobody was running anymore. They all walked around in circles. So did John Sobieski. He felt sick again. His chest and throat exploded every time he tried to breathe, and he was terribly hot. What he wanted most was just to be unconscious, but he couldn't bear to sit or lie down. He saw a boy crouching on the ground, retching onto the grass between his hands. Somebody had brought in the sweat clothes off the playing field, and boys were picking their own out of a pile. They hung their sweat shirts over their shoulders like capes and tied the arms in front. After a while John Sobieski began to feel better. He walked toward the locker room, more or less with five other runners. Just in front walked the boy who had vomited, with a friend supporting him on either side. A sweat shirt was thrown on John Sobieski's back; the arms came dangling down in front of him. He never saw who did it, because nobody seemed to look at him or pay much attention to him.

Back in the locker room it was strangely quiet, considering the place was filling with runners, who sat down on the benches or tinkered quietly at their locker doors. John Sobieski went to his own pile of things, turned his back, and let his blue shorts slide down to his shoes. Then, holding his brown pants open, he stepped into them, stuffed the shorts into his pocket, pulled the crackling white shirt over his undershirt and the sweater over that; and leaving the sweat shirt neatly folded on the bench, he turned around and stood, his back to the entrance door, surveying the room. It was as if he had only just come in and was looking for something. Now he smelled the perspiration smell fresh and strong and moist, mingling with the steam that clouded out from the top of the shower-room door, and mingling, too, with all the hubbub that had come up in the short time he was changing. Everybody in the steamy room seemed naked, and they all seemed unnaturally up above him, but that was only because nearly all the runners by now were standing on the two benches, which were two parallel pedestals for their sweating, moving nude bodies. John Sobieski moved between them in his brown sweater, looking very intently for something, and having no attention paid him. He even walked a little way into the shower room, clothes and shoes on and all, and peered through the steam at the runners there. But nobody seemed to notice this either.

Finally he went out by the same door he had first come in, passed through a few halls, and left the building.

"Thirty-four," he thought to himself as he stepped outside into the cold afternoon air. "I beat twenty-one at least."

He walked home. The night passed, and then the next day–but John Sobieski couldn't have said how. He was a small, thin boy sitting at back desks in various classrooms with a blue notebook open in front of him, but what he was seeing was not a teacher or a blackboard, but four or five boys in twinkling white pants running before him, and he himself coming up behind, planning how he was going to take them.

By four in the afternoon he was on the field again. The runners were warming up. Some were doing push-ups; some were lying on their backs on the damp ground and springing up in quick little sitting motions; some just stood around with serious faces, paying no attention to others; some were rotating their torsos, with hands on hips. John Sobieski looked around carefully and did some of the same things. The tall man of the day before was nowhere to be seen, but after a few minutes the assistant coach came walking out toward them with a boy on either side. His face was hard and dark, but his eyes were large and white and serious, and appeared to be considering other things even as he said something brief and imperative to the boy next to him. This boy gave one single vigorous nod and without warning whirled, and was away. Instantly the others took after him and John Sobieski, who hadn't been ready for it to happen so fast, was left doing push-ups on the ground.

He jumped up and ran after them, though he knew it was hopeless; he was already fifty yards behind the pack and at least a hundred behind the leaders. For the second time, they had started before he was ready. Before they had even left the playing field, he felt sicker than he had at any time the previous day. His body was a misery to him. He ran along beside the endless steel wire fence crying to himself, "Why did I think I could run! I can't! I'm not any good!" He ran another hundred yards and he prayed, "Please let me just finish. I don't want to beat anybody. All I want to do is just finish!" Because somewhere inside him was the idea that if he could endure it just this one time, then maybe he would get his fair chance, when he could really do something, tomorrow.

His father had warned him. At the end of summer, when John Sobieski came home one night and told his mother and father he wasn't going back to St. Stephen's anymore but was going up to the big city high school, his father had asked him: "What do you think you're going to get by going up there?"

"Everything," said the boy. "They got everything up there, so you can do what you want, when you get out. You can be whatever you want."

His father was smoking. At first he said something, muttering only to himself, while he shook out a long wooden match. "Nah—you can't do what you want, John Sobieski," he said then, and blew out smoke. "You just try it and you'll find out. You better stay around here. We'll teach you everything you need to know."

"No, I'm going up there."

His father looked straight at him over the table, with something ugly in his look. "Do you know who you are? D'you even know your own name?"

"Sure. Everybody knows who they are."

"No they don't. But you, you're John Sobieski. That was my father's name too. He came over here when he wasn't any bigger than you are. He was one of the ones that helped put up St. Stephen's in the first place. I went there myself and so did my brothers. That's where we belong—and you're just the same as we are. No use trying to be any different, because you belong around here. You ain't ever going to be any different from that."

"Yes I am," said John Sobieski. "Oh, yes I am."

And they looked at each other, the two of them almost exactly the same size except that the father was older, and so everything about him was somehow thicker, and more unwieldly. John Sobieski's mother kept out of it, away at the stove. The two looked at each other from opposing chairs until the father's expression broke, and he turned away.

"You think you can do what you want," he said, quite differently. "You start out all right with it too. You leave the house every morning and you only come back at night. You get pretty far away. After a while you think you don't have to come back at all. Then one day you get caught out there all by yourself—and you get licked, good."

"No," said John Sobieski.

"Stay where you are," his father pleaded. "It ain't so bad down around here."

"No, you talk like that because you're old. Well, I'm not old. I'm not going to listen to it!" He got up and went into his bedroom, where he could be by himself.

Struggling, spreading out, the runners pounded along upon a hard city sidewalk. They strained and reached, with knees and toes and shoulders; each step had only one job—to slide over as much ground as possible. Most of them could not see, and none paid any attention to the big car that followed along in the street keeping pace, but inside it the head coach, the tall man who usually carried the clipboard thick with papers, hovered just beyond the toil of the runners. Ahead of him, in the next block, he watched an indistinct cluster of legs and a flash of color separate themselves, as he came closer, into a runner in blue shorts and white top trailing a line of three abreast in the red-and-white uniforms. As blue-and-white closed with the red, the legs became entangled and inextricable again, until suddenly somebody got stepped on. A boy in red shirt and white pants reeled to the side, off the curb and into the road, where he fought to recover himself, climbing back to the sidewalk only to drop rapidly to the rear, his pace broken. Meantime blue-and-white had moved up between the other two, so that the three of them, bouncing up and down, remained for a long moment like a slot machine come to rest after changing, red-blue-red, until gradually blue-and-white disengaged himself again and moved out in front.

The coach accelerated and passed on, but John Sobieski didn't notice him. He had hardly even seen the three runners. His eyes were wet and partly closed as he ran, and all at once he knew that something was in front of him, preventing him. More or less, he saw them. But there wasn't anything he could do except keep running, because he knew if he were checked at all he would have to stop altogether. Then after a moment he was clear and by himself again. He ran on. No vision of the school building raised him. It was a gray, damp day. He didn't know how far they still had to go. He passed more runners, singles or straggling twos, without any struggle. He couldn't think about taking them, or of anything; they were just going slower than he was, and he moved by.

It was over abruptly. They passed through the same gate as yesterday, freely, without being stopped, the runners all streaming in and dispersing, and as soon as John Sobieski realized where they were and stopped trying to run he collapsed.

"Walk him around!" somebody shouted. It was the tall head coach. He had parked his car and now stood just inside the gate, wearing a long raincoat. "What's the trouble?"

Two runners had already lifted John Sobieski to his feet, but he was fighting them off, and they couldn't hold him; they were tired themselves.

"I don't know . . . he's talking to himself," one answered between breaths. "He's trying to say numbers."

"Walk him around," the tall man repeated. "That's the way to finish a run. There isn't a one of you should have anything left at all!"

The two of them took John Sobieski's arms across their shoulders and together they walked him around on the grass. After a while they had their own wind back, but as soon as John Sobieski got breath enough, he began to cough. The afternoon was chilly and damp. He took several wheezing breaths and then coughed again, badly. By the time the others had walked off the effects of their run, he was coughing steadily for long stretches.

The two boys took him into the locker room. They sat him on a bench in front of their own lockers and got his clothes off, while he continued coughing. They walked him with care through the jostling, sweating, strong-smelling runners into the steamy shower room, and one readied a shower while the other held John Sobieski. Then they put him under it and left him.

Later, when the two runners were dressed and ready to leave, they turned to find the small thin boy standing naked across the bench from them, dripping onto the floor.

"Feel better now?" the bigger one asked. "What's the matter, forget your towel?" He drew his own heavy damp one from his gym bag and took the one that his friend was carrying rolled up under one arm and hung them both over John Sobieski's shoulder. The small boy opened his mouth as if to say something, but instead he was overcome by a fit of coughing.

The two had to go. "Give them to us tomorrow," said the one, pausing in the locker-room door. He was a big, strong-looking boy with a very large head. "Ernest Borkmann and Joe Felice." Still John Sobieski stood, just looking at the two boys; he was fighting a rising cough, and the door had already closed before he called after them:

"John Sobieski!"

He went back to the bench with his towels. All the runners had left. He wiped himself, put on his clothes, and put his running shorts in his pocket. But he didn't leave the two towels behind; he took them along home with him. His second day's running was over.

When he reached his own street it was dark, and a cold, foggy rain was drifting down. By the light of street lights the wooden two-family houses rose high all around him, their thrusting, peaked roofs shoulder to shoulder, the mist falling from the darkness above upon their wet slate backs. Inside they were warmly lighted behind curtains.

John Sobieski went straight to his own bedroom. His mother and father, eating already, could hear him coughing behind the door. Finally he came out and sat down. A fire was going in the kitchen stove, since it was still too early in the year to light the furnace, and in the sudden, close warmth John Sobieski began to perspire and then to cough and cough. His eyes would become fixed, his face red and then contorted as he tried to stop himself, at least long enough to eat; but the thing would burst out at last and leave him shaking, his eyes watering. He drank cups and cups of coffee, which his mother poured out for him. His father read a newspaper on the other side of the table and glanced at John Sobieski when he coughed, but said nothing.

Later, as he sat on the sofa in the living room, wearing his heavy sweater, the cough subsided. His mother and father sat across from him on either side in upholstered chairs; his mother's fingers were crocheting something nimbly, and his father still had his paper. John Sobieski sat by himself on the sofa doing nothing, thinking about nothing, just sitting still under a lamp and gazing blankly at his parents. At one point, as his father folded over his paper to study the lower corner, he caught his son gazing at him.

"What now?" he demanded.

"Nothing. Can't I look?" said John Sobieski.

His mother, too, raised her head, worried-looking and sorrowful. She reminded John Sobieski of those old women with kerchiefs around their heads whom he used to see when he had been an altar boy serving early mass. They knelt and prayed, holding their beads, with a look upon their faces and in their eyes as though the whole world were filled with sorrow; and John Sobieski hated sorrow; he couldn't stand it.

"Oh, I don't like that coughing," said his mother, shaking her head.

But John Sobieski didn't mind even sorrow, now. All he wanted was to sit, just as he was, in his own house, doing nothing, thinking about nothing at all.

Then morning came again, and John Sobieski must go up to the high school. He took the two towels plus a third one for himself that he got from his mother, his running shorts, his notebook, his lunch bag, and a black umbrella of his father's, because the morning was dark and threatening rain again. By the time he reached the school his arms ached from carrying so many things, and when he thought of the running he would have to do that day he felt sorry for himself and thought, "No wonder I can't run. Nobody else has to wear themselves out just getting here!"

The rain in clinging drops or running down the panes of the windows, the shifting light and dark places in the sky—all were watched apprehensively by John Sobieski as he sat in the classrooms' dim electric light that could barely establish itself all day against the bleak light from outside. After his last class, as he walked among crowds of others through the dim and noisy corridors, Ernest Borkmann found him.

The big boy took him down to the wing of the school where the lockers were, past the door of the cross-country room and on to a further door where he left him. For one moment John Sobieski hesitated, but then he let himself inside quickly and faced the room.

In front of him, behind a desk, sat the tall man of the clipboard—a large and handsome-appearing man with long white hair combed back, seen now for the first time indoors, without his coat and hat. Leaning back with folded hands, he was talking to the smaller, darker, bony-looking young man who sat on the windowsill with his back to the rain, his knees drawn up high and his feet on the radiator.

"Is that him?" the tall man asked. "The one that runs in the blue pants?"

The other coach only nodded gloomily, watching John Sobieski, the whites of his eyes showing in his dark face.

"What do they call him, anyway?"

A little smile seemed always to be hanging at the corners of the white-haired man's eyes and lips, as though to him things were always cheerful and a bit funny somehow.

"John Sobieski," responded the boy himself.

"John Sobieski . . . I hear that John Sobieski's a pretty good runner, Stan."

"He does the best he can."

"No, sir," said the white-haired man, "he's good, because he likes to run. He likes to go out there and beat those other boys. He likes to take 'em. Now, how's he going to do it the way he's been, Stanley? That isn't right. We have to give John Sobieski a chance, the same as everybody else. You come here, John Sobieski!"

The tall man reached forward and pointed to a box at the front of his desk. Of course it had been there all along, but for John Sobieski it only came into being at that moment. The boy opened it. Inside, under tissue paper, his hands grasped a pair of the spikeless cross-country shoes.

He lifted them out. They were small in size, for his own little feet, narrow and light and pointed, with hard and sharp rubber bottoms for digging in and starting; and he could see himself already, as from some distance away, the black shoes slashing like hoofs, slashing and slashing in arcs, the shoes of John Sobieski!

"John Sobieski's going to Utica with us," said the head coach, grinning. "John Sobieski's going to run at Syracuse—John Sobieski's going to New York City!"

"Well, you get a uniform and sweat suit from the manager, John Sobieski," the younger man told him more soberly. "Put a towel around your neck when you go outside and don't try to run very hard today. It's too cold for it."

The runners jogged across the field and gathered together under the drizzling clouds. Neither coach was anywhere around. John Sobieski had been one of the first ones out, and for once, at least, he was ready. Imperceptibly this time, without a signal of any kind, the runners began their run. They went off slowly without making any sound, all the move and flash of their bright uniforms muffled within the heavy gray sweat suits. They moved at a shuffle just over a walk, then at a trot, and then a little better. In the beginning they ran very close to one another in a tight pack, and yet in rigid silence, as though pushing together against some enormous burden, one so heavy that it might never be moved at all without an effort from each so intense as to isolate him from all the others.

Once outside the fence, John Sobieski found the pack lengthening. As it stretched out gradually, it seemed to snap in two. He was the last of the line that was moving ahead, and there were nine runners in front of him. He stayed where he was without working very hard. Then all at once, when he was scarcely tired, he spied the school building ahead of him, and he pulled out and ran as fast as he could. He passed the others easily, every one—not so fast as if they were standing still, but as if he were moving about twice as fast—and entered the gate first by a long interval.

Instead of stopping, he kept running straight on into the locker room. There he took a hurried shower and had already dried himself by the time the others began to come in, talking quietly, in twos and threes. John Sobieski dressed as fast as he could, his face buried in the new locker that had been assigned to him. He was afraid to turn around because they might all be looking at him, because he had come in first. He felt as though he were charged with electricity, and the figure "1" were shining out upon his back.

He was sweating again by the time he reached home. His coughing was so continuous that he knew he would not be able to stop it, or even halt it for a few minutes, until he had something to drink. But even so he went directly to his bedroom and carefully spread out on the bed his new running things, which were now all wrinkled and damp. The unfamiliar bright-colored things attracted his mother and father, and they came in to look.

"Where can I put these to dry . . ." John Sobieski demanded. But then he closed his eyes, grasping the long bar at the foot of his bed; his upper body leaned forward, the tears pressed at his shut eyes, and the cough came rolling out of him. ". . . where nobody will touch them?"

"Touch them," said his father angrily. "What are we going to touch them for?" And he left the room.

"We can hang them up over the stove," his mother assured him with bright, grieving eyes that only made the boy furious. "Come and eat with us."

"I'll be there!" he told her. "I have to see about this stuff first."

It was a Friday night. John Sobieski had the whole weekend to dry his running things, and on Monday he went to the school equipped just like all the rest—except that he had come in first the last time they had run. But that same day the figure "1," which he could almost feel burning upon his back once he was among the runners again, faded out. Nobody paid any attention to it.

Now every day was bright and blue. The cold air burned like alcohol on the skin of his arms and legs when he took off his sweat clothes and began to run in the afternoons. He was happy just to run with the others, keeping up with them along different streets of the city that he had not known anything about before. In the first time trials he finished twelfth.

The coaches took fifteen boys to run at Utica the following Saturday. They drove a few hours in cars, got out to warm up behind a strange and brand-new high school, gathered on a line in a bunch—one of a dozen such, each in its own bright colors—and then a gun was fired, a cloud of white smoke rose above the man who had fired it, and the bunches all sprang into a forward wave to cross the field together. John Sobieski was left behind, exhausted, right at the start. He decided he would just finish the race, this one last time, and then he would never run again. He felt that way all through the unfamiliar woods and as he came down out of them onto the field again, into the mouth of the bullpen between funneling ropes that crowded him against boys in front and on both sides until he stood still with one of the coarse-fibered ropes in either hand. Somebody wrote something on his back—a piece of paper with a number on it had been pinned to his red shirt—and then he staggered away, to walk around and begin coughing.

Riding home in the head coach's car, he learned their team had won the meet. Their first five men had come in 2nd, 4th, 5th, 7th and 8th for a score of 26. John Sobieski found the number 24 written in pencil underneath the big printed number on the paper he had torn from his back. Besides that, he had a blue satin ribbon. Two hundred boys had run, but only the first twenty-five received ribbons.

Monday his name appeared in the city newspaper. "A freshman, John Sobieski, was the Red and White's tenth finisher." Ernest Borkmann had cut the story out of the paper and showed it to him in the locker room before practice.

"Where did you come in?" John Sobieski asked him.

The big boy folded the clipping carefully with large strong fingers and put it away in his wallet. "I got sick," he answered, frowning. "I didn't finish."

Saturday they ran at Syracuse, and there were twice as many runners. The high school placed second. John Sobieski, their seventh man in, finished 39th. It meant he had improved about nine places. And he beat three of their own runners who had finished ahead of him the week before.

This time he rode home with the younger coach. The other runners were subdued; John Sobieski's continual coughing was louder than all their quiet talk. It filled the car, though he strained to suppress it by sitting motionless with all the air breathed out of him, so that he would have nothing to cough with. But he had to breathe again sometime, and then the air would rush into his lungs, explode, and be thrown out once more. "Roll up your windows," the coach told the runners. Twice they stopped at gas stations to let him drink water, but even so he would only start coughing again in a few minutes.

Now John Sobieski began to notice that boys on the running team nodded or spoke to him when he saw them in the school's halls, and even a few others seemed to know who he was. He lived only for running. He got up in the morning and walked to the school for it, waiting all day for that living half hour when he emerged on the playing field and ran, suffering, until he swore he would never do it again, and at last finished somehow and returned to the locker room. His life was running. It was different now than ever before. "I only eat and sleep at home," he thought to himself as he sat and watched his father and mother in the evening. "They see me go away, and they see me come back—but they don't know what I do!"

It was five o'clock in the morning. New York City, the biggest city in America, lay more than a hundred and fifty miles away to the east and south. The head coach had already driven off with five boys, and now the other coach and two remaining runners and a manager all got into a little car that stood by itself at the curb in front of the school. John Sobieski had the front seat. He hunched down inert and from there watched the dark houses, the peaking rooftops, roll by. Nobody said anything. The manager and the runner in the back seat were both trying to sleep. Once they were well into the country, John Sobieski sat up and looked out. It was just getting light. The sky was gray, as though cloudy. In the open fields there was light, but everything else remained shadowy. Buildings that they passed stood gray and chill-appearing, except for yellow windows distinct and square in a few isolated houses. The boy was glad to see them. It struck him as cheerful somehow, for it meant that people were awake within and beginning their work for the day. Something in him yearned toward them, but he was going to New York City; and he was glad to be going to New York, but he didn't want to run there.

The next time he looked out it was fully light; the day would clear. They were driving on a parkway now, twin concrete highways that seemed to descend endlessly taking huge dips and turns. As the little car rose up with engine roaring to meet each new crest, John Sobieski waited to see if the city were ahead, but the road on the other side only plunged them downhill again, twisting out of sight among hills and woods.

He couldn't sleep, but he closed his eyes for a long, long time, hoping that when he opened them again they would be there, and he would at least have rested a little.

What made him sit up again finally was a loud whining of tires. Then outside, all around, he saw more cars, a great many of them and all going to the same place. The young coach, sitting next to him, was very busy driving. John Sobieski saw that the man's face was now intent, his eyes fiercely concentrated ahead. He was passing the other cars as though they were runners. They went between some fairly high buildings and then ran downhill across a bridge; the coach paid money out his window, they went on down the ramp, blue water came around on the right, and immediately up in front of them, very high, a suspension bridge swung across to the other side. They drove underneath it, and there were the tall buildings of New York standing out ahead as he had thought they would be—except that they weren't down close to the water, but were built on top of a steep hill rising on the left.

Just then the runner in the back seat—it was the same dark-haired boy who had been sitting on the bench when John Sobieski first entered the locker room—called out, "Hey, we're on the island!"

The older runner knew they should be running at a park somewhere back in the Bronx. The coach knew it too—he had run there himself when he had been a cross-country runner—but coming into the city he had missed his turn and was still looking for it when he had been caught among the cars rushing into Manhattan. He got off the parkway now and they ran steeply uphill between buildings, all of them bigger than John Sobieski had ever seen, but not what he had expected of New York either. They were big dirty boxes with innumerable windows in which, it looked like, people lived. It gave him a pang to think that.

They kept turning into different streets, driving fast, and then they were out of Manhattan again. All at once the coach turned off the highway and drove straight across a flat athletic field. Right where he stopped the car the runners were massed—bright-colored, moving and shifting by the hundreds, tightening up—and just as they went to get out, a shot was fired. The pack jolted, loosened, and stretched away like an expanding accordion, the farther edge moving rapidly over the field, while the near edge remained on the starting line playing out runners in waves. The coach swore aloud as he helped rip jackets and sweat clothes from John

Sobieski and the other runner. Then the two of them were on the field running, before some had even left the starting line.

And if ever they had started before John Sobieski was ready, it was this time. Next to him, in front of him, behind him, shoving him, were runners; and he himself, short and thin, unable even to see above them. He felt as though he were dying, and as a drowning person sees his whole life, he saw his running. Then he knew he couldn't run at all; he was always sick, he only beat others by tormenting himself. And he hated it, because he cared only about beating the others and not all of them either, but just those on his own team, for of the rest there were so many as to make his own struggles seem feeble, indistinguishable.

Yet even now, as though it were a thing quite separate from himself, his small body was pressing forward through the thick of the runners. His eye was caught by the flash of a red shirt that he knew must be from his own school. Slowly, he was coming up to it. He made his way sideways between two larger boys, and when another boy just ahead stumbled, sighing, and gave up, John Sobieski dodged around him and into the free pocket, darting forward unhindered until he was running behind the familiar red shirt. When it found openings, he followed after. When it forced a way, shoving runners aside, he went through as though he had done it for himself.

They had passed over the parkway on a bridge of stone arches and now they were running on a bridle path that turned and climbed upward under trees, around the bulk of a great hill on the other side. The stream of the pack had narrowed until it was only four to five runners wide, and at one edge of the hillside fell away steeply—down to John Sobieski couldn't see what, though he was running on that side himself, just within the pack.

Twisting slowly uphill, flashing gay-colored, the pack surged over the crest of the hill and slid downward again, winding around, faster and faster. Somewhere John Sobieski had left the red shirt behind and now that the race was downhill, he tried to break out and pass runners, but he couldn't. It was impossible, with the runners pounding on all sides of him; he couldn't move from his place. He stood it until he couldn't any longer; then he pulled abreast of the boy immediately in front of him and went through diagonally to the right. He saw he was free. He let himself out, his feet smashing into the ground in long downhill strides. But while he was passing, exposed out there, an impulse that originated in an obscure movement somewhere deep inside the pack suddenly reached him and struck him through the elbow of the boy beside him. For an instant he continued to run wildly along the edge of the hill, with his arms waving and snatching for balance, but he was being toppled inexorably, and he was over.

John Sobieski went down running, but he couldn't keep on his feet. A young tree caught him by the arm, spun him around and threw him, rolling, down the slope. He hit things; but the pain wasn't so great as the exhaustion and sickness that came on immediately as he ceased running. He lay on his side on dry leaves at the bottom, his body jackknifed and heaving. Overhead was the thunder of the passing pack, the rustle of their feet among fallen leaves, the muffled reverberations of the shocks of a thousand galloping legs all shod in the sharp-pointed running shoes like hoofs—passing by, pounding, and gone; a pause—a scattered hurry of stragglers—now one, now several; their breathing like the furious labor of bicycle pumps, their feet clumping—dying away; now all gone altogether—passed on.

He was left alone. Everything was quiet. A hot sickness, separate from the ache of lungs and throat, went back and forth over him, for the first time unmixed with the bustle of others walking around feeling the same way. He hated himself, he hated his body that gasped and gasped for breath among the crisp leaves. He could not bear to think that even though he had lost, he must still suffer for trying. For a while he did nothing; he didn't even try to get up, because there wasn't any use in it. But he started to feel the cold on his arms and legs and through his thin uniform. When he finally got to his feet he was so weak and listless he could hardly climb the steep bank. He pulled himself up from one young tree to another, and then clung to them on the uphill side, resting.

Up on the bridle path again, his coughing came over him. It began loud and wet, and would get worse, he knew, harsher and drier, as his running sickness improved, but now it was all the same to him. He walked downhill weakly, without purpose, staggering and coughing. As he came out of the woods, the dark-haired runner, recovered from his run, his sweat suit on, met him in the middle of the stone bridge over the parkway. Beneath them, the bright automobiles whined in both directions. John Sobieski leaned on the boy, and together they went down to the field, an enormous one big enough for twenty football games. On the far side of it the young coach's tiny car stood by itself, and, as they were crossing, the man got out and came toward them.

"Somebody pushed me . . . I fell over," John Sobieski tried to explain, between fits of coughing, but the man only scowled, glanced briefly into the face of the other runner, and didn't answer.

They got him into his sweat clothes and inside the car. They rolled up the windows and laid him by himself on the backseat, with the coats of all three boys thrown over him. The coach and the other two rode up front, mostly in silence, while John Sobieski coughed with a horrible crouping dry sound all the way back to their own city.

From where he lay he could see it growing dark outside. The shapes of roofs were sharp in the cold sky. He was aware of the fits and starts of the automobile and the traffic sounds of the city outside; of the rush of cold air entering and the voices of the two boys briefly saying good-bye; finally of the emptiness of the car with only himself and the coach remaining—when at last the car stopped for good.

"Is this where you live, John Sobieski?" the man asked from out on the sidewalk. He looked up at the gray two-family house, while the boy was climbing out over the front seat.

"You listen to me now. I want you to get into that house and not come out of it for a month. You're sick. You belong in bed, for God's sake, and not out killing yourself running. It isn't running anymore, when you have to trade on your health just to get a place. That doesn't do us any good—it isn't reliable. You go in there and get better. Forget all about running, for a while."

The man spoke angrily. He held the car door open against the wind with his back and watched John Sobieski, but the boy just stood before him saying nothing. He got back into his car and drove away.

John Sobieski made his way upstairs. He went right to his room and to bed. His mother saw at once that he was sick and looked after him.

He stayed in bed three weeks. Most of the time he slept. There was nothing he wanted to get up for. After the first week he didn't cough anymore; as long as he didn't run it would be all right. His father came in to see him after supper. The older man seemed a little embarrassed. He would bring a kitchen chair and set it just inside the bedroom door, and talk across the space at his son, who would be watching him, lying deep in his bed, his brown head on a big pillow.

"How do you feel tonight?"

"All right."

The father nodded. He wouldn't smoke in the bedroom. He sat for a while. "The one time I was in New York," he said, "I went on the train with my father. When we got there we just stood up in some place and ate sauerkraut and frankfurts. That's all I remember about it."

John Sobieski listened, but didn't say anything. After a bit his father got up to go out. "Well, stay where you are now. Rest up a while. That's the only thing."

"Listen," John Sobieski called after him, "I'm still going back there, after I get better."

His father looked down at the linoleum. "They still want you, after you got licked like that?"

"I don't know. It doesn't matter if they want me, though—I'm going to go."

His father went away.

In the dark bedroom, John Sobieski closed his eyes. He could hear the wind blowing outside between his house and the house next door. A boy moved before him in the dark; John Sobieski was coming up closer, from behind. . . . He caught himself and swore, and thrashed in the bed with regret. He couldn't remember running without remembering his failure. Yet in twenty minutes more, going off to sleep, he would see before him a boy dressed in white shorts and red shirt, and he himself, coming up behind, planning how he was going to take him.

Born in Galway, Ireland, Frank Harris (1856–1931) ran off to America as a youngster and became one of its greatest writers. He returned to Europe to become the editor of the prestigious Fortnightly Review in London. Harris later took control of the Saturday Review and made it into a legendary literary journal. His most famous work is the story here, which George Meredith, a giant of English literature in the nineteeth century, called "one of the supreme tales of our language." Probably no story on bullfighting, not even Ernest Hemingway's "The Undefeated," captures the drama of the corrida—the people, the bulls, the spirit—as well as this one.

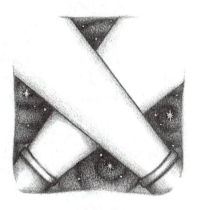

Frank Harris

MONTES: THE MATADOR (1891)

"YES! I'M BETTER, AND THE doctor tells me I've escaped once more—as if I cared! . . . And all through the fever you came every day to see me, so my niece says, and brought me the cool drink that drove the heat away and gave me sleep. You thought, I suppose, like the doctor, that I'd escape you, too. Ha! ha! And that you'd never hear old Montes tell what he knows of bullfighting and you don't. . . . Or perhaps it was kindness; though, why you, a foreigner and a heretic, should be kind to me, God knows. . . . The doctor says I've not got much more life in me, and you're going to leave Spain within the week—within the week, you said didn't you? . . . Well, then, I don't mind telling you the story.

"Thirty years ago I wanted to tell it often enough, but I knew no one I could trust. After that fit passed, I said to myself I'd never tell it; but as you're going away, I'll tell it to you, if you swear by the Virgin you'll never tell it to anyone, at least until I'm dead. You'll swear, will you? Easily enough! they all will; but as you're going away, it's much the same. Besides, you can do nothing now; no one can do anything now; no one can do anything; they never could have done anything. Why, they wouldn't believe you if you told it to them, the fools! . . . My story will teach you more about bullfighting than Frascuelo or Mazzantini, or—yes, Lagartijo knows. Weren't there Frascuelos and Mazzantinis in my day? Dozens of them. You could pick one Frascuelo out of every thousand laborers if you gave him the training and the practice, and could keep him away from wine and women. But a Montes is not to be found every day, if you searched all Spain for one. . . . What's the good of bragging? I never bragged when I was at work; the deed talks—louder than any words. Yet I think, no one has ever done the things I used to; for I read in a paper once an account of a thing I often did, and the writer said 'twas incredible. Ha! ha! incredible to the Frascuelos and Mazzantinis and the rest, who can kill bulls and are called *espadas*. Oh, yes! bulls so tired out they can't lift their heads. You didn't guess when you were telling me about Frascuelo and Mazzantini that I knew them. I knew all about both of them before you told me. I know their work, though I've not been within sight of a ring for more than thirty years. . . . Well, I'll tell you my story: I'll tell you my story—if I can."

The old man said the last words, as if to himself, in a low voice, then sank back in the armchair, and for a time was silent.

Let me say a word or two about myself and the circumstances which led me to seek out Montes.

I had been in Spain off and on a good deal, and from the first had taken a great liking to the people and country; and no one can love Spain and the Spaniards without becoming interested in the bull ring—the sport is so characteristic of the people, and in itself so enthralling. I set myself to study it in earnest, and when I came to know the best bullfighters, Frascuelo, Mazzantini, and Lagartijo, and heard them talk of their trade, I began to understand what skill and courage, what qualities of eye and hand and heart, this game demands. Through my love of the sport, I came to hear of Montes. He had left so great a name that thirty years after he had disappeared from the scene of his triumphs, he was still spoken of not infrequently. He would perhaps have been better remembered, had the feats attributed to him been less astounding. It was Frascuelo who told me that Montes was still alive:

"Montes," he cried out in answer to me; "I can tell you about Montes. You mean the old *espada* who, they say, used to kill the bull in its first rush into the ring—as if anyone could do that! I can tell you about him. He must have been clever; for an old *aficionado* I know, swears no one of us is fit to be in his *caudrilla*. Those old fellows are all like that, and I don't believe half they tell me about Montes. I dare say he was good enough in his day, but there are just as good men now as ever there were. When I was in Ronda, four years ago, I went to see Montes. He lives out of the town in a nice, little house all alone, with one woman to attend to him, a niece of his, they say. You know he was born in Ronda; but he would not talk to me; he only looked at me and laughed—the little, lame, conceited one!"

"You don't believe then, in spite of what they say, that he was better than Lagartijo or Mazzantini?" I asked.

"No, I don't," Frascuelo replied. "Of course, he may have known more than they do; that wouldn't be difficult, for neither of them knows much. Mazzantini is a good *matador* because he's very tall and strong—that's his advantage. For that, too, the women like him, and when he makes a mistake and has to try again, he gets forgiven. It wasn't so when I began. There were *aficionados* then, and if you made a mistake they began to jeer, and you were soon pelted out of the ring. Now the crowd knows nothing and is no longer content to follow those who do know. Lagartijo? Oh, he's very quick and daring, and the women and boys like that too. But he's ignorant: he knows nothing about a bull. Why, he's been wounded oftener in his five years than I in my twenty. And that's a pretty good test. Montes must have been clever; for he's very small, and I shouldn't think he was ever very strong, and then he was lame almost from the beginning, I've heard. I've no doubt he could teach the business to Mazzantini or Lagartijo, but that's not saying much. . . . He must have made a lot of money, too, to be able to live on it ever since. And they didn't pay as high then or even when I began as they do now."

So much I knew about Montes when, in the spring of 188–, I rode from Seville to Ronda, fell in love with the place at first sight, and resolved to stop at Polos' inn for some time. Ronda is built, so to speak, upon an island tableland high above the sea level, and is ringed about by still higher mountain ranges. It is one of the most peculiar and picturesque places in the world. A river runs almost all around it; and the sheer cliffs fall in many places three or four hundred feet, from the tableland to the water, like a wall. No wonder that the Moors held Ronda after they had lost every other foot of ground in Spain. Taking Ronda as my headquarters I made almost daily excursions, chiefly on foot, into the surrounding mountains. On one of these I heard again of Montes. A peasant with whom I had been talking and who was showing me a short cut back to the town, suddenly stopped and said, pointing to a little hut perched on the mountain shoulder in front of us, "From that house you can see Ronda. That's the house where Montes, the great *matador*, was born," he added, evidently with some pride. Then and there the conversation with Frascuelo came back to my memory, and I made up my mind to find Montes out and have a talk with him. I went to his house, which lay just outside the town, next day with the *alcalde*, who introduced me to him and then left us. The first sight of the man interested me. He was short—about five feet three or four, I should think—of well-knit, muscular frame. He seemed to me to have Moorish blood in him. His complexion was very dark and tanned; the features clean-cut; the nose sharp and inquisitive; the nostrils astonishingly mobile, the chin and jaws square, bony—resolute. His hair and thick moustache were snow white, and this, together with the deep wrinkles on the forehead and round the eyes and mouth, gave him an appearance of great age. He seemed to move, too, with extreme difficulty, his lameness, as he afterwards told me, being complicated with rheumatism. But when one looked at his eyes, the appearance of age vanished. They were large and brown, usually inexpressive, or rather impenetrable, brooding wells of unknown depths. But when anything excited him, the eyes would suddenly flash to life and become intensely luminous. The effect was startling. It seemed as if all the vast vitality of the man had been transmuted into those wonderful gleaming orbs: they radiated courage, energy, intellect. Then as his mood changed, the light would die out of the eyes; and the old, wizened wrinkled face would settle down into its ordinary ill-tempered, wearied expression. There was evidently so much in the man—courage, melancholy, keen intelligence—that in spite of an anything but flattering reception I returned again and again to the house. One day his niece told me that Montes was in bed, and from her description I inferred that he was suffering from an attack of malarial fever. The doctor who attended him, and whom I knew, confirmed this. Naturally enough, I did what I could for the sufferer, and so it came about that after his recovery he received me with kindness, and at last made up his mind to tell me the story of his life.

"I may as well begin at the beginning," Montes went on. "I was born near here about sixty years ago. You thought I was older. Don't deny it. I saw the surprise in your face. But it's true: in fact, I am not yet, I think, quite sixty. My father was a peasant with a few acres of land of his own and a cottage."

"I know it," I said. "I saw it the other day."

"Then you may have seen on the further side of the hill the pasture-ground for cattle which was my father's chief possession. It was good pasture; very good. . . . My mother was of a better class than my father; she was the daughter of the chemist in Ronda; she could read and write, and she did read, I remember, whenever she could get the chance, which wasn't often, with her four children to take care of—three girls and a boy—and the house to look after. We all loved her, she was so gentle besides, she told us wonderful stories; but I think I was her favorite. You see I was the youngest and a boy, and women are like that. My father was hard—at least, I thought him so, and feared rather than loved him; but the girls got on better with him. He never talked to me as he did to them. My mother wanted me to go to school and become a priest; she had taught me to read and write by the time I was six. But my father would not hear of it. 'If you had had three boys and one girl,' I remember him saying to her once, 'you could have done what you liked with this one. But as there is only one boy, he must work and help me.' So by the time I was nine I used to go off down to the pasture and watch the bulls all day long. For though the herd was a small one—only about twenty head—it required to be constantly watched. The cows were attended to in an enclosure close to the house. It was my task to mind the bulls in the lower pasture. Of course I had a pony, for such bulls in Spain are seldom approached, and cannot be driven by a man on foot. I see you don't understand. But it's simple enough. My father's bulls were of good stock, savage and strong; they were always taken for the ring, and he got high prices for them. He generally managed to sell three *novillos* and two bulls of four years old each year. And there was no bargaining, no trouble; the money was always ready for that class of animals. All day long I sat on my pony, or stood near it, minding the bulls. If any of them strayed too far, I had to go and get him back again. But in the heat of the day they never moved about much, and that time I turned to use by learning the lessons my mother gave me. So a couple of years passed. Of course in that time I got to know our bulls pretty well; but it was a remark of my father's which first taught me that each bull had an individual character and first set me to watch them closely. I must have been then about twelve years old; and in that summer I learned more than in the two previous years. My father, though he said nothing to me, must have noticed that I had gained confidence in dealing with the bulls; for one night, when I was in bed, I heard him say to my mother—'The little fellow is as good as a man now.' I was proud of his praise, and from that time on, I set to work to learn everything I could about the bulls.

"By degrees I came to know every one of them—better far than I ever got to know men or women later. Bulls, I found, were just like men, only simpler and kinder; some were good-tempered and honest, others were sulky and cunning. There was a black one which was wild and hot-tempered, but at bottom, good, while there was one almost as black, with light horns and flanks, which I never trusted. The other bulls didn't like him. I could see they didn't; they were all afraid of him. He was cunning and suspicious, and never made friends with any of them; he would always eat by himself far away from the others—but he had courage, too; I knew that as well as they did. He was sold that very summer with the black one for the ring in Ronda. One Sunday night, when my father and eldest sister (my mother would never go to *los toros*) came back from seeing the game in Ronda, they were wild with excitement, and began to tell the mother how one of our bulls had caught the *matador* and tossed him, and how the *chulos* could scarcely get the *matador* away. Then I cried out—'I know; 'twas Judas' (so I had christened him), and as I saw my father's look of surprise I went on confusedly, 'the bull with the white horns I mean. Juan, the black one, wouldn't have been clever enough.' My father only said, 'The boy's right'; but my mother drew me to her and kissed me, as if she were afraid. . . . Poor mother! I think even then she knew or divined something of what came to pass later. . . .

"It was the next summer, I think, that my father first found out how much I knew about the bulls. It happened in this way. There hadn't been much rain in the spring; the pasture, therefore, was thin, and that, of course, made the bulls restless. In the summer the weather was unsettled—spells of heat and then thunderstorms—till the animals became very excitable. One day, there was thunder in the air, I remember, they gave me a great deal of trouble and that annoyed me, for I wanted to read. I had got to a very interesting tale in the storybook my mother had given me on the day our bulls were sold. The story was about Cervantes—ah, you know who I mean, the great writer. Well, he was a great man, too. The story told how he escaped from the prison over there in Algiers and got back to Cadiz, and how a widow came to him to find out if he knew her son, who was also a slave of the Moors. And when she heard that Cervantes had seen her son working in chains, she bemoaned her wretchedness and ill-fortune, till the heart of the great man melted with pity, and he said to her, 'Come, mother, be hopeful, in one month your son shall be here with you.' And then the book told how Cervantes went back to slavery, and how glad the Bey was to get him again, for he was very clever; and how he asked the Bey, as he had returned of his free will, to send the widow's son home in his stead; and the Bey consented. That Cervantes was a man! . . . Well, I was reading the story, and I believed every word of it, as I do still, for no ordinary person could invent that sort of tale; and I grew very much excited and wanted to know all about Cervantes. But as I could only read slowly and with difficulty, I was afraid the sun would go down before I could get to the end. While I was reading as hard as ever I could, my father came down on foot and caught me. He hated to see me reading–I don't know why; and he was angry and struck at me. As I avoided the blow and got away from him, he pulled up the picket line, and got on my pony to drive one of the bulls back to the herd. I have thought since, he must have been very much annoyed before he came down and caught me. For though he knew a good deal about bulls, he didn't show it then. My pony was too weak to carry him easily, yet he acted as if he had been well mounted. For as I said, the bulls were hungry and excited, and my father should have seen this and driven the bull back quietly and with great patience. But no; he wouldn't let him feed even for a moment. At last the bull turned on him. My father held the goad fairly against his neck, but the bull came on just the same, and the pony could scarcely get out of the way in time. In a moment the bull turned and prepared to rush at him again. My father sat still on the little pony, and held the goad; but I knew that was no use; he knew it, too; but he was angry and wouldn't give in. At once I ran in between him and the bull, and then called to the bull, and went slowly up to him where he was shaking his head and pawing the ground. He was very angry, but he knew the difference between us quite well, and he let me come close to him without rushing at me, and then just shook his head to show me he was still angry, and soon began to feed quietly. In a moment or two I left him and went back to my father. He had got off the pony and was white and trembling, and he said:

"'Are you hurt?'

"And I said laughing, 'No: he didn't want to hurt me. He was only showing off his temper.'

"And my father said, 'There's not a man in all Spain that could have done that! You know more than I do—more than anybody.'

"After that he let me do as I liked, and the next two years were very happy ones. First came the marriage of my second sister, then the eldest one was married, and they were both good matches. And the bulls were sold well, and my father had less to do, as I could attend to the whole herd by myself. Those were two good years. My mother seemed to love me more and more every day, or I suppose I noticed it more, and she praised me for doing the lessons she gave me; and I had more and more time to study as the herd got to know me better and better.

"My only trouble was that I had never seen the bulls in the ring. But when I found my father was willing to take me, and 'twas mother who wanted me not to go, I put up with that, too, and said nothing, for I loved her greatly. Then of a sudden came the sorrow. It was in the late winter, just before my fifteenth birthday. I was born in March, I think. In January my mother caught cold, and as she grew worse my father fetched the doctor, and then her father and mother came to see her, but nothing did any good. In April she died. I wanted to die, too.

"After her death my father took to grumbling about the food and house and everything. Nothing my sister could do was right. I believe she only married in the summer because she couldn't stand his constant blame. At any rate she married badly, a good-for-nothing who had twice her years, and who ill-treated her continually. A month or two later my father, who must have been fifty, married again, a young woman, a laborer's daughter without a *duro*. He told me he was going to do it, for the house needed a woman. I suppose he was right. But I was too young then to take such things into consideration, and I had loved my mother. When I saw his new wife I did not like her, and we did not get on well together.

"Before this, however, early in the summer that followed the death of my mother, I went for the first time to see a bullfight. My father wanted me to go, and my sister, too; so I went. I shall never forget that day. The *chulos* made me laugh, they skipped about so and took such extra good care of themselves; but the *banderilleros* interested me. Their work required skill and courage, that I saw at once; but after they had planted the *banderillas* twice, I knew how it was done, and felt I could do it just as well or better. For the third or fourth *banderillero* made a mistake! He didn't even know with which horn the bull was going to strike; so he got frightened, and did not plant the *banderillas* fairly—in fact, one was on the side of the shoulder and the other didn't even stick in. As for the *picadores,* they didn't interest me at all. There was no skill or knowledge in their work. It was for the crowd, who liked to see blood and who understand nothing. Then came the turn of the *espada.* Ah! that seemed splendid to me. He knew his work I thought at first, and his work evidently required knowledge, skill, courage, strength—everything. I was intensely excited, and when the bull, struck to the heart, fell prone on his knees, and the blood gushed from his nose and mouth, I cheered and cheered till I was hoarse. But before the games were over, that very first day, I saw more than one *matador* make a mistake. At first I thought I must be wrong, but soon the event showed I was right. For the *matador* hadn't even got the bull to stand square when he tried his stroke and failed. You don't know what that means—'to stand square.'"

"I do partly," I replied, "but I don't see the reason of it. Will you explain?"

"It's very simple," Montes answered. "So long as the bull's standing with one hoof in front of the other, his shoulder blades almost meet, just as when you throw your arms back and your chest out; they don't meet, of course, but the space between them is not as regular, and, therefore, not as large as it is when their front hooves are square. The space between the shoulder blades is none too large at any time, for you have to strike with force to drive the sword through the inch-thick hide, and through a foot of muscle, sinew, and flesh besides, to the heart. Nor is the stroke a straight one. Then, too, there's always the backbone to avoid. And the space between the backbone and the nearest thick gristle of the shoulder blade is never more than an inch and a half. So if you narrow this space by even half an inch you increase your difficulty immensely. And that's not your object. Well, all this I've been telling you, I divined at once. Therefore, when I saw the bull wasn't standing quite square I knew the *matador* was either a bungler or else very clever and strong indeed. In a moment he proved himself to be a bungler, for his sword turned on the shoulder blade, and the bull, throwing up his head, almost caught him on his horns. Then I hissed and cried, 'Shame!' And the people stared at me. That butcher tried five times before he killed the bull, and at last even the most ignorant of the spectators knew I had been right in hissing him. He was one of your Mazzantinis, I suppose."

"Oh, no!" I replied, "I've seen Mazzantini try twice, but never five times. That's too much!"

"Well," Montes continued quietly, "the man who tries once and fails ought never to be allowed in a ring again. But to go on. That first day taught me I could be an *espada*. The only doubt in my mind was in regard to the nature of the bulls. Should I be able to understand new bulls—bulls, too, from different herds and of different race, as well as I understood our bulls? Going home that evening I tried to talk to my father, but he thought the sport had been very good, and when I wanted to show him the mistakes the *matadores* had made, he laughed at me, and, taking hold of my arm, he said, 'Here's where you need the gristle before you could kill a bull with a sword, even if he were tied for you.' My father was very proud of his size and strength, but what he said had reason in it, and made me doubt myself. Then he talked about the gains of the *matadores*. A fortune, he said, was given for a single day's work. Even the pay of the *chulos* seemed to me to be extravagant, and a *banderillero* got enough to make one rich for life. That night I thought over all I had seen and heard, and fell asleep and dreamt I was an *espada*, the best in Spain and rich, and married to a lovely girl with golden hair—as boys do dream.

"Next day I set myself to practice with our bulls. First I teased one till he grew angry and rushed at me; then, as a *chulo*, I stepped aside. And after I had practiced this several times, I began to try to move aside as late as possible and only just as far as was needful; for I soon found out the play of horn of every bull we had. The older the bull the heavier his neck and shoulders become, and, therefore, the sweep of horns in an old bull is much smaller than a young one's. Before the first morning's sport was over I knew that with our bulls at any rate I could beat any *chulo* I had seen the day before. Then I set myself to quiet the bulls, which was a little difficult, and after I had succeeded I went back to my pony to read and dream. Next day I played at being a *banderillero*, and found out at once that my knowledge of the animal was all important. For I knew always on which side to move to avoid the bull's rush. I knew how he meant to strike by the way he put his head down. To plant the *banderillas* perfectly would have been child's play to me, at least with our bulls. The *matador*'s work was harder to practice. I had no sword; besides, the bull I wished to pretend to kill, was not tired and wouldn't keep quiet. Yet I went on trying. The game had a fascination to me. A few days later, provided with a makeshift red *capa*, I got a bull far away from the others. Then I played with him till he was tired out. First I played as a *chulo*, and avoided his rushes by an inch or two only; then, as *banderillero*, I escaped his stroke, and, as I did so, struck his neck with two sticks. When he was tired I approached him with the *capa* and found I could make him do what I pleased, stand crooked or square in a moment, just as I liked. For I learned at once that as a rule the bull rushes at the *capa* and not at the man who holds it. Some bulls, however, are clever enough to charge the man. For weeks I kept up this game, till one day my father expressed his surprise at the thin and wretched appearance of the bulls. No wonder! The pasture ground had been a ring to them and me for many a week.

"After this I had to play *matador*—the only part which had any interest for me—without first tiring them. Then came a long series of new experiences, which in time made me what I was, a real *espada*, but which I can scarcely describe to you.

"For power over wild animals comes to a man, as it were, by leaps and bounds. Of a sudden one finds he can make a bull do something which the day before he could not make him do. It is all a matter of intimate knowledge of the nature of the animal. Just as the shepherd, as I've been told, knows the face of each sheep in a flock of a thousand, though I can see no difference between the faces of sheep, which are all alike stupid to me, so I came to know bulls, with a complete understanding of the nature and temper of each one. It's just because I can't tell you how I acquired this part of my knowledge that I was so long-winded in explaining to you my first steps. That I knew more than I have told you, will appear as I go on with my story, and that you must believe or disbelieve as you think best."

"Oh," I cried, "you've explained everything so clearly, and thrown light on so many things I didn't understand, that I shall believe whatever you tell me."

Old Montes went on as if he hadn't heard my protestation:

"The next three years were intolerable to me: my stepmother repaid my dislike with interest and found a hundred ways of making me uncomfortable, without doing anything I could complain of and get altered. In the spring of my nineteenth year I told my father I intended to go to Madrid and become an *espada*. When he found he couldn't induce me to stay, he said I might go. We parted, and I walked to Seville; there I did odd jobs for a few weeks in connection with the bull ring, such as feeding the bulls, helping to separate them, and so forth; and there I made an acquaintance who was afterwards a friend. Juan Valdera was one of the *cuadrilla* of Girvalda, a *matador* of the ordinary type. Juan was from Estramadura, and we could scarcely understand each other at first; but he was kindly and careless and I took a great liking to him. He was a fine man; tall, strong and handsome, with short, dark, wavy hair and dark moustache, and great black eyes. He liked me, I suppose, because I admired him and because I never wearied of hearing him tell of his conquests among women and even great ladies. Of course I told him I wished to enter the ring, and he promised to help me to get a place in Madrid where he knew many of the officials. 'You may do well with the *capa*,' I remember he said condescendingly, 'or even as a *banderillero*, but you'll never go further. You see, to be an *espada*, as I intend to be, you must have height and strength,' and he stretched his fine figure as he spoke. I acquiesced humbly enough. I felt that perhaps he and my father were right, and I didn't know whether I should even have strength enough for the task of an *espada*. To be brief, I saved a little money, and managed to get to Madrid late in the year, too late for the bull ring. Thinking over the matter I resolved to get work in a blacksmith's shop, and at length succeeded. As I had thought, the labor strengthened me greatly, and in the spring of my twentieth year, by Juan's help, I got employed on trial one Sunday as a *chulo*.

"I suppose," Montes went on, after a pause, "I ought to have been excited and nervous on that first Sunday—but I wasn't; I was only eager to do well in order to get engaged for the season. The blacksmith, Antonio, whom I had worked with, had advanced me the money for my costume, and Juan had taken me to a tailor and got the things made, and what I owed Antonio and the tailor weighed on me. Well, on that Sunday I was a failure at first. I went in the procession with the rest, then with the others I fluttered my *capa*; but when the bull rushed at me, instead of running away, like the rest, I wrapped my *capa* about me and, just as his horns were touching me, moved aside—not half a pace. The spectators cheered me, it is true, and I thought I had done very well, until Juan came over to me and said:

"'You mustn't show off like that. First of all, you'll get killed if you play that game; and then you fellows with the *capa* are there to make the bull run about to tire him out so that we *matadores* may kill him.'

"That was my first lesson in professional jealousy. After that I ran about like the rest, but without much heart in the sport. It seemed to me stupid. Besides, from Juan's anger and contempt, I felt sure I shouldn't get a permanent engagement. Bit by bit, however, my spirits rose again with the exercise, and when the fifth or sixth bull came in, I resolved to make him run. It was a good, honest bull; I saw that at once; he stood in the middle of the ring, excited, but not angry, in spite of the waving of the *capas* all around him. As soon as my turn came, I ran forward, nearer to him than the others had considered safe, and waved the challenge with my *capa*. At once he rushed at it, and I gave him a long run, half around the circle and ended it by stopping and letting him toss the *capa* which I held not quite at arm's length from my body. As I did this I didn't turn round to face him. I knew he'd toss the *capa* and not me, but the crowd rose and cheered as if the thing were extraordinary. Then I felt sure I should be engaged, and I was perfectly happy. Only Juan said to me a few minutes later:

"'You'll be killed, my boy, one of these fine days if you try those games. Your life will be a short one if you begin by trusting a bull.'

"But I didn't mind what he said. I thought he meant it as a friendly warning, and I was anxious only to get permanently engaged. And sure enough, as soon as the games were over, I was sent for by the director. He was kind to me, and asked me where I had played before. I told him that was my first trial.

"'Ah!' he said, turning to a gentleman who was with him, 'I knew it, Señor Duque; such courage always comes from—want of experience, let me call it.'

"'No,' replied the gentleman, whom I afterwards knew as the Duke of Medina Celi, the best *aficionado,* and one of the noblest men in Spain; 'I'm not so sure of that. Why,' he went on, speaking now to me, 'did you keep your back turned to the bull?'

"'Señor,' I answered, "twas an honest bull, and not angry, and I knew he'd toss the *capa* without paying any attention to me.'

"'Well,' said the Duke, 'if you know that much, and aren't afraid to risk your life on your knowledge, you'll go far. I must have a talk with you someday, when I've more time; you can come and see me. Send in your name; I shall remember,' And as he said this, he nodded to me and waved his hand to the director, and went away.

"Then and there the director made me sign an engagement for the season, and gave me one hundred *duros* as earnest money in advance of my pay. What an evening we had after that! Juan, the tailor, Antonio, the blacksmith, and I. How glad and proud I was to be able to pay my debts and still have sixty *duros* in my pocket after entertaining my friends. If Juan had not hurt me every now and then by the way he talked of my foolhardiness, I should have told them all I knew; but I didn't. I only said I was engaged at a salary of a hundred *duros* a month.

"'What!' said Juan. 'Come, tell the truth; make it fifty.'

"'No,' I said; 'it was a hundred,' and I pulled out the money.

"'Well,' he said, 'that only shows what it is to be small and young and foolhardy! Here am I, after six years' experience, second, too, in the *cuadrilla* of Girvalda, and I'm not getting much more than that.'

"Still, in spite of such little drawbacks, in spite, too, of the fact that Juan had to go away early, to meet 'a lovely creature,' as he said, that evening was one of the happiest I ever spent.

"All that summer through I worked every Sunday, and grew in favor with the Madrileñas, though not with these in Juan's way. I was timid and young; besides, I had a picture of a woman in my mind, and I saw no one like it. So I went on studying the bulls, learning all I could about the different breeds, and watching them in the ring. Then I sent money to my sister and to my father, and was happy.

"In the winter I was a good deal with Antonio; every day I did a spell of work in his shop to strengthen myself, and he, I think, got to know that I intended to become an *espada*. At any rate, after my first performance with the *capa*, he believed I could do whatever I wished. He used often to say God had given him strength and me brains, and he only wished he could exchange some of his muscle for some of my wits. Antonio was not very bright, but he was good-tempered, kind, and hardworking, the only friend I ever had. May Our Lady give his soul rest!

"Next spring when the director sent for me, I said that I wanted to work as a *banderillero*. He seemed to be surprised, told me I was a favorite with the *capa*, and had better stick to that for another season at least. But I was firm. Then he asked me whether I had ever used the *banderillas* and where? The director always believed I had been employed in some other ring before I came to Madrid. I told him I was confident I could do the work. 'Besides,' I added, 'I want more pay,' which was an untruth; but the argument seemed to him decisive, and he engaged me at two hundred *duros* a month, under the condition that, if the spectators wished it, I should work now and then with the *capa* as well. It didn't take me long to show the *aficionados* in Madrid that I was as good with the *banderillas* as I was with the *capa*. I could plant them when and where I liked. For in this season I found I could make the bull do almost anything. You know how the *banderillero* has to excite the bull to charge him before he can plant the darts. He does that to make the bull lower his head well, and he runs toward the bull partly so that the bull may not know when to toss his head up, partly because he can throw himself aside more easily when he's running fairly fast. Well, again and again I made the bull lower his head and then walked to him, planted the *banderillas,* and as he struck upwards swayed aside just enough to avoid the blow. That was an infinitely more difficult feat than anything I had ever done with the *capa,* and it gave me reputation among the *aficionados* and also with the *espadas*; but the ignorant herd of spectators preferred my trick with the *capa.* So the season came and went. I had many a carouse with Juan, and gave him money from time to time, because women always made him spend more than he got. From that time, too, I gave my sister fifty *duros* a month, and my father fifty. For before the season was half over my pay was raised to four hundred *duros* a month, and my name was always put on the bills. In fact I was rich and a favorite of the public.

"So time went on, and my third season in Madrid began, and with it came the beginning of the end. Never was anyone more absolutely content than I when we were told *los toros* would begin in a fortnight. On the first Sunday I was walking carelessly in the procession beside Juan, though I could have been next to the *espadas,* had I wished, when he suddenly nudged me, saying:

"'Look up! there on the second tier; there's a face for you.'

"I looked up, and saw a girl with the face of my dreams, only much more beautiful. I suppose I must have stopped, for Juan pulled me by the arm crying: 'You're moonstruck, man; come on!' and on I went—lovestruck in heart and body. What a face it was! The golden hair framed it like a picture, but the great eyes were hazel, and the lips scarlet, and she wore the *mantilla* like a queen. I moved forward like a man in a dream, conscious of nothing that went on round me, till I heard Juan say:

"'She's looking at us. She knows we've noticed her. All right, pretty one! We'll make friends afterwards.'

"'But how?' I asked, stupidly.

"'How!' he replied, mockingly. 'I'll just send someone to find out who she is, and then you can send her a box for next Sunday, and pray for her acquaintance, and the thing's done. I suppose that's her mother sitting behind her,' he went on. 'I wonder if the other girl next to her is her sister. She's as good-looking as the fair-haired one, and easier to win, I'd bet. Strange how all the timid ones take to me.' And again he looked up.

"I said nothing; nor did I look up at the place where she was sitting; but I worked that day as I had never worked before. Then, for the first time, I did something that has never been done since by anyone. The first bull was honest and kindly: I knew the sort. So, when the people began to call for *El Pequeño* (the little fellow)–that was the nickname they had given me–I took up a *capa*, and, when the bull chased me, I stopped suddenly, faced him, and threw the *capa* round me. He was within ten paces of me before he saw I had stopped, and he began to stop; but before he came to a standstill his horns were within a foot of me. He tossed his head once or twice as if he would strike me, and then went off. The people cheered and cheered as if they would never cease. Then I looked up at her. She must have been watching me, for she took the red rose from her hair and threw it into the ring toward me, crying, 'Bien! Muy bien! El Pequeño!"

"As I picked up the rose, pressed it to my lips, and hid it in my breast, I realized all that life holds of triumphant joy! . . . Then I made up my mind to show what I could do, and everything I did that day seemed to delight the public. At last, as I planted the *banderillas,* standing in front of the bull, and he tried twice in a quick succession to strike me and failed, the crowed cheered and cheered and cheered, so that, even when I went away, after bowing and stood among my fellows, ten minutes passed before they would let the game go on. I didn't look up again. No! I wanted to keep the memory of what she looked like when she threw me the rose.

"After the games were over, I met her, that same evening. Juan had brought it about, and he talked easily enough to the mother and daughter and niece, while I listened. We all went, I remember, to a restaurant in the Puerta del Sol, and ate and drank together. I said little or nothing the whole evening. The mother told us they had just come from the north: Alvareda was the family name; her daughter was Clemencia, the niece, Liberata. I heard everything in a sort of fever of hot pulses and cold fits of humility, while Juan told them all about himself, and what he meant to do and be. While Clemencia listened to him, I took my fill of gazing at her. At last Juan invited them all to *los toros* on the following Sunday, and promised them the best *palco* in the ring. He found out, too, where they lived, in a little street running parallel to the Alcala, and assured them of our visit within the week. Then they left, and as they went out of the door Liberta looked at Juan, while Clemencia chatted with him and teased him.

"'That's all right,' said Juan, turning to me when they were gone, 'and I don't know which is the more taking, the niece or Clemencia. Perhaps the niece; she looks at one so appealingly; and those who talk so with their eyes are always the best. I wonder have they any money? One might do worse than either with a good portion.'

"'Is that your real opinion?' I asked hesitatingly.

"'Yes,' he answered; 'why?'

"'Because, in that case leave Clemencia to me. Of course you could win her if you wanted to. But it makes no difference to you, and to me all the difference. If I cannot marry her, I shall never marry.'

"'Jesu!' he cried, 'how fast you go, but I'd do more than that for you, Montes; and besides, the niece really pleases me better.'

"So the matter was settled between us.

"Now, if I could tell you all that happened, I would. But much escaped me at the time that I afterwards remembered, and many things that then seemed to me to be as sure as a straight stroke, have since grown confused. I only know that Juan and I met them often, and that Juan paid court to the niece, while I from time to time talked timidly to Clemencia.

"One Sunday after another came and went, and we grew to know each other well. Clemencia did not chatter like other women: I liked her the better for it, and when I came to know she was very proud, I liked that, too. She charmed me; why? I can scarcely tell. I saw her faults gradually, but even her faults appeared to me fascinating. Her pride was insensate. I remember one Sunday afternoon after the games, I happened to go into a restaurant, and found her sitting there with her mother. I was in costume and carried in my hand a great nosegay of roses that a lady had thrown me in the ring. Of course as soon as I saw

Clemencia I went over to her and—you know it is the privilege of the *matadores* in Spain, even if they do not know the lady—taking a rose from the bunch I presented it to her as the fairest of the fair. Coming from the cold North, she didn't know the custom and scarcely seemed pleased. When I explained it to her, she exclaimed that it was monstrous; she'd never allow a mere *matador* to take such a liberty unless she knew and liked him. Juan expostulated with her laughingly; I said nothing; I knew what qualities our work required, and didn't think it needed any defense. I believed in that first season, I came to see that her name Clemencia wasn't very appropriate. At any rate she had courage and pride, that was certain. Very early in our friendship she wanted to know why I didn't become an *espada*.

"'A man without ambition,' she said, 'is like a woman without beauty.'

"I laughed at this and told her my ambition was to do my work well, and advancement was sure to follow in due course. Love of her seemed to have killed ambition in me. But no. She wouldn't rest content in spite of Juan's telling her my position already was more brilliant than that of most of the *espadas*.

"'He does things with the *capa* and the *banderillas* which no *espada* in all Spain would care to imitate. And that's position enough. Besides, to be an *espada* requires height and strength.'

"As he said this she seemed to be convinced, but it annoyed me a little, and afterwards as we walked together, I said to her,

"'If you want to see me work as an *espada,* you shall.'

"'Oh, no!' she answered half carelessly; 'if you can't do it, as Juan says, why should you try? To fail is worse than to lack ambition.'

"'Well,' I answered, 'you shall see.'

"And then I took my courage in both hands and went on:

"'If you cared for me I should be the first *espada* in the world next season.'

"She turned and looked at me curiously and said,

"'Of course I'd wish it if you could do it.'

"And I said, 'See, I love you as the priest loves the Virgin; tell me to be an *espada* and I shall be one for the sake of your love.'

"'That's what all men say, but love doesn't make a man tall and strong.'

"'No; nor do size and strength take the place of heart and head. Do you love me? That's the question.'

"'I like you, yes. But love—love, they say, comes after marriage.'

"'Will you marry me?'

"'Become an *espada* and then ask me again,' she answered coquettishly.

"The very next day I went to see the Duke of Medina Celi; the servants would scarcely let me pass till they heard my name and that the Duke had asked me to come. He received me kindly. I told him what I wanted.

"'Have you ever used the sword?' he asked in surprise. 'Can you do it? You see we don't want to lose the best man with *capa* and *banderillas* ever known, to get another second-class *espada*.'

"'Señor Duque, I have done better with the *banderillas* than I could with the *capa*. I shall do better with the *espada* than with the *banderillas*.'

"'You little fiend!' he laughed, 'I believe you will, though it is unheard-of to become an *espada* without training; but now for the means. All the *espadas* are engaged; it'll be difficult. Let me see. . . . The Queen has asked me to superintend the sports early in July, and then I shall give you your chance. Will that do? In the meantime, astonish us all with *capa* and *banderillas,* so that men may not think me mad when I put your name first on the bill.'

"I thanked him from my heart, as was his due, and after a little more talk I went away to tell Clemencia the news. She only said:

"'I'm glad. Now you'll get Juan to help you.'

"I stared at her.

"'Yes!' she went on, a little impatiently; 'he has been taught the work; he's sure to be able to show you a great deal.'

"I said not a word. She was sincere, I saw, but then she came from the North and knew nothing. I said to myself, 'That's how women are!'

"She continued, 'Of course you're clever with the *capa* and *banderillas,* and now you must do more than ever, as the Duke said, to deserve your chance.' And then she asked carelessly, 'Couldn't you bring the Duke and introduce him to us some time or other? I should like to thank him.'

"And I, thinking it meant our betrothal, was glad, and promised. And

I remember I did bring him once to the box and he was kind in a way, but not cordial as he always was when alone with me, and he told Clemencia that I'd go very far, and that any woman would be lucky to get me for a husband, and so on. After a little while he went away. But Clemencia was angry with him and said he put on airs; and, indeed, I had never seen him so cold and reserved; I could say little or nothing in his defense.

"Well, all that May I worked as I had never done. The director told me he knew I was to use the *espada* on the first Sunday in July, and he seemed to be glad; and one or two of the best *espadas* came to me and said they'd heard the news and should be glad to welcome me among them. All this excited me, and I did better and better. I used to pick out the old prints of Goya, the great painter—you know his works are in the Prado—and do everything the old *matadores* did, and invent new things. But nothing 'took' like my trick with the *capa*. One Sunday, I remember, I had done it with six bulls, one after another, and the people cheered and cheered. But the seventh was a bad bull, and, of course I didn't do it. And afterwards Clemencia asked me why I didn't, and I told her. For you see I didn't know then that women rate high what they don't understand. Mystery is everything to them. As if the explanation of such a thing makes it any easier! A man wins great battles by seizing the right moment and using it— the explanation is simple. One must be great in order to know the moment, that's all. But women don't see that it is only small men who exaggerate the difficulties of their work. Great men find their work easy and say so, and, therefore, you'll find that women underrate great men and overpraise small ones. Clemencia really thought I ought to learn the *espada*'s work from Juan. Ah! women are strange creatures. . . . Well, after that Sunday she was always bothering me to do the *capa* trick with every bull.

"'If you don't,' she used to say, 'you won't get the chance of being an *espada*.' And when she saw I laughed and paid no attention to her talk, she became more and more obstinate.

"If the people get to know you can only do it with some bulls, they

won't think much of you. Do it with every bull, then they can't say anything.'

"And I said 'No! and I shouldn't be able to say anything either.'

"'If you love me you will do as I say!'

"And when I didn't do as she wished—it was madness—she grew cold
to me, and sneered at me, and then urged me again, till I half yielded.
Really, by that time I hardly knew what I couldn't do, for each day I
seemed to get greater power over the bulls. At length a Sunday came, the
first, I think in June, or the last in May. Clemencia sat with her mother
and cousin in the best *palco*; I had got it from the director, who now refused me nothing. I had done my *capa* trick with three bulls, one after
the other, then the fourth came in. As soon as I saw him, I knew he was
bad, cunning I mean, and with black rage in the heart of him. The other
men stood aside to let me do the trick, but I wouldn't. I ran away like the
rest, and let him toss the *capa*. The people liked me, and so they cheered
just the same, thinking I was tired; but suddenly Clemencia called out:
'The *capa* round the shoulders; the *capa* trick!' and I looked up at her;
and she leaned over the front of the *palco*, and called out the words again.

"Then rage came into me, rage at her folly and cold heart; I took off
my cap to her, and turned and challenged the bull with the *capa,* and, as
he put down his head and rushed, I threw the *capa* round me and stood
still. I did not even look at him. I knew it was no use. He struck me here
in the thigh, and I went up into the air. The shock took away my senses.
As I came to myself they were carrying me out of the ring, and the people were all standing up; but, as I looked toward the *palco,* I saw she
wasn't standing up; she had a handkerchief before her face. At first I
thought she was crying, and I felt well, and longed to say to her, 'It
doesn't matter, I'm content'; then she put down the handkerchief and I
saw she wasn't crying; there wasn't a tear in her eyes. She seemed surprised merely, and shocked. I suppose she thought I could work miracles,
or rather she didn't care much whether I was hurt or not. That turned me
faint again. I came to myself in my bed, where I spent the next month.
The doctor told the Duke of Medina Celi—he had come to see me the
same afternoon—that the shock hadn't injured me, but I should be lame

always, as the bull's horn had torn the muscle of my thigh from the bone. 'How he didn't bleed to death,' he said, 'is a wonder; now he'll pull through, but no more play with the bulls for him.' I knew better than the doctor, but I said nothing to him, only to the Duke I said:

"'Señor, a promise is a promise; I shall use the *espada* in your show in July.'

"And he said, 'Yes, my poor boy, if you wish it, and are able to; but how came you to make such a mistake?"

"'I made no mistake, Señor.'

"'You knew you'd be struck?'

"I nodded. He looked at me for a moment, and then held out his hand. He understood everything, I'm sure; but he said nothing to me then.

"Juan came to see me in the evening, and next day Clemencia and her mother. Clemencia was sorry, that I could see, and wanted me to forgive her. As if I had anything to forgive when she stood there so lithe and straight, with her flower-like face and the appealing eyes. Then came days of pain while the doctors forced the muscles back into their places. Soon I was able to get up, with a crutch, and limp about. As I grew better, Clemencia came seldomer, and when she came, her mother never left the room. I knew what that meant. She had told her mother not to go away; for, though the mother thought no one good enough for her daughter, yet she pitied me, and would have left us alone—sometimes. She had a woman's heart. But no, not once. Then I set myself to get well soon. I would show them all, I said to myself, that a lame Montes was worth more than other men. And I got better, so the doctor said, with surprising speed. . . . One day, toward the end of June, I said to the servant of the Duke—he sent a servant every day to me with fruit and flowers—that I wished greatly to see his master. And the Duke came to see me, the very same day.

"I thanked him first for his kindness to me, and then asked:

"'Señor, have you put my name on the bills as *espada*?'

"'No,' he replied; 'you must get well first, and, indeed, if I were in your place, I should not try anything more till next season.'

"And I said, 'Señor Duque, it presses. Believe me, weak as I am, I can use the sword.'

"And he answered my very thought: 'Ah! She thinks you can't. And you want to prove the contrary. I shouldn't take the trouble, if I were you; but there! Don't deceive yourself or me; there is time yet for three or four days: I'll come again to see you, and if you wish to have your chance you shall. I give you my word.' As he left the room I had tears in my eyes; but I was glad, too, and confident: I'd teach the false friends a lesson. Save Antonio, the blacksmith, and some strangers, and the Duke's servant, no one had come near me for more than a week. Three days afterwards I wrote to the Duke asking him to fulfil his promise, and the very next day Juan, Clemencia, and her mother all came to see me together. They all wanted to know what it meant. My name as *espada* for the next Sunday, they said, was first on the bills placarded all over Madrid, and the Duke had put underneath it—'By special request of H.M. the Queen.' I said nothing but that I was going to work; and I noticed that Clemencia couldn't meet my eyes.

"What a day that was! That Sunday I mean. The Queen was in her box with the Duke beside her as our procession saluted them, and the great ring was crowded tier on tier, and she was in the best box I could get. But I tried not to think about her. My heart seemed to be frozen. Still I know now that I worked for her even then. When the first bull came in and the *capa* men played him, the people began to shout for me—'El Pequeño! El Pequeño! El Pequeño'—and wouldn't let the games go on. So I limped forward in my *espada*'s dress and took a *capa* from a man and challenged the bull, and he rushed at me—the honest one; I caught his look and knew it was all right, so I threw the *capa* round me and turned my back upon him. In one flash I saw the people rise in their places, and the Duke lean over the front of the *palco*; then, as the bull hesitated and stopped, and they began to cheer, I handed back the *capa*, and, after bowing, went again among the *espadas*. Then the people christened me afresh—'El Cojo' (The Cripple!)—and I had to come forward and bow again and again, the Queen threw me a gold cigarette case. I have it still. There it is. . . . I never looked up at Clemencia, though I could see her always. She threw no rose to me that day. . . . Then the time came when I should kill the bull. I took the *muleta* in my left hand and went toward him with the sword uncovered in my right. I needed no trick. I held him with my will, and he looked up at me. 'Poor brute,' I thought, 'you are happier than I am.' And he bowed his head with the great, wondering, kindly eyes, and I struck straight to the heart. On his knees he fell at my feet, and rolled over dead, almost without a quiver. As I hid my sword in the *muleta* and turned away, the people found their voices, 'Well done, The Cripple! Well done!' When I left the ring that day I left it as the first *espada* in Spain. So the Duke said, and he knew—none better. After one more Sunday the sports were over for the year, but that second Sunday I did better than the first, and I was engaged for the next season as first *espada*, with fifty thousand *duros* salary. Forty thousand I invested as the Duke advised—I have lived in the interest ever since—the other ten thousand I kept by me.

"I had resolved never to go near Clemencia again, and I kept my resolve for weeks. One day Juan came and told me Clemencia was suffering because of my absence. He said:

"'She's proud, you know, proud as the devil, and she won't come and see you or send to you, but she loves you. There's no doubt of that: she loves you. I know them, and I never saw a girl so gone on a man. Besides they're poor now, she and her mother; they've eaten up nearly all they had, and you're rich and could help them.'

"That made me think. I felt sure she didn't love me. That was plain enough. She hadn't even a good heart, or she would have come and cheered me up when I lay wounded—because of her obstinate folly. No! It wasn't worthwhile suffering any more on her account. That was clear. But if she needed me, if she were really poor? Oh, that I couldn't stand. I'd go to her. 'Are you sure?' I asked Juan, and when he said he was, I said:

"'Then I'll visit them tomorrow.'

"And on the next day I went. Clemencia received me, as usual; she was too proud to notice my long absence, but the mother wanted to know why I had kept away from them so long. From that time on the mother seemed to like me greatly. I told her I was still sore—which was the truth—and I had had much to do.

"'Some lady fallen in love with you, I suppose,' said Clemencia half-scoffingly—so that I could hardly believe she had wanted to see me.

"'No,' I answered, looking at her, 'one doesn't get love without seeking for it, sometimes not even then—when one's small and lame as I am.'

"Gradually the old relations established themselves again. But I had grown wiser, and watched her now with keen eyes as I had never done formerly. I found she had changed—in some subtle way had become different. She seemed kinder to me, but at the same time her character appeared to be even stronger than it had been. I remember noticing one peculiarity in her I had not remarked before. Her admiration of the physique of men was now keen and outspoken. When we went to the theatre (as we often did) I saw that the better-looking and more finely formed actors had a great attraction for her. I had never noticed this in her before. In fact, she had seemed to me to know nothing about virile beauty, beyond a girl's vague liking for men who were tall and strong. But now she looked at men critically. She had changed; that was certain. What was the cause? . . . I could not divine. Poor fool that I was! I didn't know then that good women seldom or never care much for mere bodily qualities in a man; the women who do are generally worthless. Now, too, she spoke well of the men of Southern Spain; when I first met her she professed to admire the women of the South, but to think little of the men. Now she admired the men, too; they were warmer-hearted, she said; had more love and passion in them, and were gentler with women than those of the North. Somehow I hoped that she referred to me, that her heart was beginning to plead for me, and I was very glad and proud, though it all seemed too good to be true.

"One day in October, when I called with Juan, we found them packing their things. They had to leave, they said, and take cheaper lodgings. Juan looked at me, and some way or other I got him to take Clemencia into another room. Then I spoke to the mother: Clemencia, I hoped would soon be my wife; in any case I couldn't allow her to want for anything; I would bring a thousand *duros* the next day, and they must not think of leaving their comfortable apartments. The mother cried and said, I was good: 'God makes few such men,' and so forth. The next day

I gave her the money, and it was arranged between us without saying any-thing to Clemencia. I remember about this time, in the early winter of that year, I began to see her faults more clear, and I noticed that she had altered in many ways. Her temper had changed. It used to be equable though passionate. It had become uncertain and irritable. She had changed greatly. For now, she would let me kiss her without remon-strance, and sometimes almost as if she didn't notice the kiss, whereas before it used always to be a matter of importance. And when I asked her when she would marry me, she would answer half-carelessly, 'Some time, I suppose,' as she used to do, but her manner was quite different. She even sighed once as she spoke. Certainly she had changed. What was the cause? I couldn't make it out, therefore I watched, not suspiciously but she had grown a little strange to me—a sort of puzzle, since she had been so unkind when I lay wounded. And partly from this feeling, partly from my great love for her, I noticed everything. Still I urged her to marry me. I thought as soon as we were married, and she had a child to take care of and to love, it would be all right with both of us. Fool that I was!

"In April, which was fine, I remember, that year in Madrid—you know how cold it is away up there, and how keen the wind is; as the Madrileños say, ''twon't blow out a candle, but it'll kill a man'—Clemencia began to grow pale and nervous. I couldn't make her out; and so, more than ever, pity strengthening love in me, I urged her to tell me when she would marry me; and one day she turned to me, and I saw she was quite white as she said:

"'After the season, perhaps.'

"Then I was happy, and ceased to press her. Early in May the games began—my golden time. I had grown quite strong again, and was surer of myself than ever. Besides, I wanted to do something to deserve my great happiness. Therefore, on one of the first days when the Queen and the Duke and Clemencia were looking on, I killed the bull with the sword immediately after he entered the ring, and before he had been tired at all. From that day on the people seemed crazy about me. I couldn't walk in the streets without being cheered; a crowd followed me wherever I went; great nobles asked me to their houses, and their ladies made much of me. But I didn't care, for all the time Clemencia was kind, and so I was happy.

"One day suddenly she asked me why I didn't make Juan an *espada*. I told her I had offered him the first place in my *caudrilla*; but he wouldn't accept it. She declared that it was natural of him to refuse when I had passed him in the race; but why didn't I go to the Duke and get him made an *espada?* I replied laughingly that the Duke didn't make men *espadas*, but God or their parents. Then her brows drew down, and she said she hadn't thought to find such mean jealousy in me. So I answered her seriously that I didn't believe Juan would succeed as an *espada*, or else I should do what I could to get him appointed. At once she came and put her arms on my shoulders, and said 'twas like me, and she would tell Juan; and after that I could do nothing but kiss her. A little later I asked Juan about it, and he told me he thought he could do the work at least as well as Girvalda, and if I got him the place, he would never forget my kindness. So I went to the director and told him what I wished. At first he refused, saying Juan had no talent, he would only get killed. When I pressed him he said all the *espadas* were engaged, and made other such excuses. So at last I said I'd work no more unless he gave Juan a chance. Then he yielded after grumbling a great deal.

"Two Sundays later Juan entered the ring for the first time as an *espada*. He looked the part to perfection. Never was there a more splendid figure of a man, and he was radiant in silver and blue. His mother was in the box that day with Clemencia and her mother. Just before we all parted as the sports were about to begin, Clemencia drew me on one side, and said, 'You'll see that he succeeds, won't you?' And I replied, 'Yes, of course, I will. Trust me; it'll be all right.' And it was, though I don't think it would have been, if she hadn't spoken. I remembered my promise to her, and when I saw that the bull which Juan ought to kill was vicious, I told another *espada* to kill him, and so got Juan an easy bull, which I took care to have tired out before I told him the moment had come. Juan wasn't a coward—no! but he hadn't the peculiar nerve needed for the business. The *matador's* spirit should rise to the danger, and Juan's didn't rise. He was white, but determined to do his best. That I could see.

So I said to him, 'Go on, man! Don't lose time, or he'll get his wind again. You're all right; I shall be near you as one of your *cuadrilla.*' And so I was, and if I hadn't been, Juan would have come to grief. Yes, he'd have come to grief that very first day.

"Naturally enough we spent the evening together. It was a real *tertulia,* Señora Alvareda said; but Clemencia sat silent with the great, dark eyes turned in upon her thoughts, and the niece and myself were nearly as quiet, while Juan talked for every one, not forgetting himself. As he had been depressed before the trial so now he was unduly exultant, forgetting altogether, as it seemed to me, not only his nervousness but also that it had taken him two strokes to kill the bull. His first attempt was a failure, and the second one, though it brought the bull to his knees, never reached his heart. But Juan was delighted and seemed never to weary of describing the bull and how he had struck him, his mother listening to him the while adoringly. It was past midnight when we parted from our friends; and Juan, as we returned to my rooms, would talk of nothing but the salary he expected to get. I was out of sorts; he had bragged so incessantly I had scarcely got a word with Clemencia, who could hardly find time to tell me she had a bad headache. Juan would come up with me; he wanted to know whether I'd go on the morrow to the director to get him a permanent engagement. I got rid of him, at last, by saying I was tired to death, and it would look better to let the director come and ask for his services. So at length we parted. After he left me I sat for some time wondering at Clemencia's paleness. She was growing thin too! And what thoughts had induced that rapt expression of face?

"Next morning I awoke late and had so much to do that I resolved to put off my visit to Clemencia till the afternoon, but in the meantime the director spoke to me of Juan as rather a bungler, and when I defended him, agreed at last to engage him for the next four Sundays. This was a better result than I had expected, so as soon as I was free I made off to tell Juan the good news. I met his mother at the street door where she was talking with some women; she followed me into the *patio* saying Juan was not at home.

"'Never mind,' I replied carelessly, 'I have good news for him, so I'll go upstairs to his room and wait.'

"'Oh!' she said, 'you can't do that; you mustn't; Juan wouldn't like it.'

"Then I laughed outright. Juan wouldn't like it—oh no! It was amusing to say that when we had lived together like brothers for years, and had had no secrets from one another. But she persisted and grew strangely hot and excited. Then I thought to myself—there you are again; these women understand nothing. So I went away, telling her to send Juan to me as soon as he came in. At this she seemed hugely relieved and became voluble in excuses. In fact her manner altered so entirely that before I had gone fifty yards down the street, it forced me to wonder. Suddenly my wonder changed to suspicion. Juan wasn't out! Who was with him I mustn't see?

"As I stopped involuntarily, I saw a man on the other side of the street who bowed to me. I went across and said:

"'Friend, I am Montes, the matador. Do you own this house?'

"He answered that he did, and that every one in Madrid knew me.

"So I said, 'Lend me a room on your first floor for an hour; *cosa de mujer* (A lady's in the case); you understand.'

"At once he led me upstairs and showed me a room from the windows of which I could see the entrance to Juan's lodging. I thanked him, and when he left me I stood near the window and smoked and thought. What could it all mean? . . . Had Clemencia anything to do with Juan? She made me get him his trial as *espada;* charged me to take care of him. He was from the South, too, and she had grown to like Southern men; 'they were passionate and gentle with women.' Curses on her! Her paleness occurred to me, her fits of abstraction. As I thought, every memory fitted into its place, and what had been mysterious grew plain to me; but I wouldn't accept the evidence of reason. No! I'd wait and see. Then at once I grew quiet. But again the thoughts came—like the flies that plague the cattle in summertime—and again I brushed them aside, and again they returned.

"Suddenly I saw Juan's mother come into the street wearing altogether too careless an expression. She looked about at haphazard as if she expected someone. After a moment or two of this she slipped back into the *patio* with mystery in her sudden decision and haste. Then out came a form I knew well, and, with stately, even step, looking neither to the right hand nor the left, walked down the street. It was Clemencia, as my heart had told me it would be. I should have known her anywhere even had she not—just below the window where I was watching—put back her *mantilla* with a certain proud grace of movement which I had admired a hundred times. As she moved her head to feel that the *mantilla* draped her properly I saw her face; it was drawn and set like one fighting against pain. That made me smile with pleasure.

"Five minutes later Juan swung out of the doorway in the full costume of an *espada*—he seemed to sleep in it now—with a cigarette between his teeth. Then I grew sad and pitiful. We had been such friends. I had meant only good to him always. And he was such a fool! I understand it all now; knew, as if I had been told, that the intimacy between them dated from the time when I lay suffering in bed. Thinking me useless and never having had any real affection for me, Clemencia had then followed her inclination and tried to win Juan. She had succeeded easily enough, no doubt, but not in getting him to marry her. Later, she induced me to make Juan an *espada*, hoping against hope that he'd marry her when his new position had made him rich. On the other hand he had set himself to cheat me because of the money I had given her mother, which relieved him from the necessity of helping them; and secondly, because it was only through my influence that he could hope to become an *espada*. Ignoble beasts! And then jealousy seized me as I thought of her admiration of handsome men, and at once I saw her in his arms. Forthwith pity, and sadness and anger left me, and, as I thought of him swaggering past the window, I laughed aloud. Poor weak fools! I, too, could cheat.

"He had passed out of the street. I went downstairs and thanked the landlord for his kindness to me. 'For your good-nature,' I said, 'you must come and see me work from a box next Sunday. Ask for me, I won't forget.' And he thanked me with many words and said he had never missed a Sunday since he had first seen me play with the *capa* three years before.

I laughed and nodded to him and went my way homewards, whither I knew Juan had gone before me.

"As I entered my room, he rose to meet me with a shadow as of doubt or fear upon him. But I laughed cheerfully, gaily enough to deceive even so finished an actor as he was, and told him the good news. 'Engaged,' I cried, slapping him on the shoulder. 'The director engages you for four Sundays certain.' And that word 'certain' made me laugh louder still—jubilantly. Then afraid of overdoing my part, I sat quietly for some time and listened to his expressions of fatuous self-satisfaction. As he left me to go and trumpet the news from *café* to *café*, I had to choke down my contempt for him by recalling that picture, by forcing myself to see them in each other's arms. Then I grew quiet again and went to call upon my betrothed.

"She was at home and received me as usual, but with more kindness than was her wont. 'She feels a little remorse at deceiving me,' I said to myself, reading her now as if her soul were an open book. I told her of Juan's engagement and she let slip 'I wish I had known that sooner!' But I did not appear to notice anything. It amused me now to see how shallow she was and how blind I had been. And then I played with her as she had often, doubtless, played with me. 'He will go far, will Juan,' I said, 'now that he has begun—very far, in a short time.' And within me I laughed at the double meaning as she turned startled eyes upon me. And then, 'His old loves will mourn for the distance which must soon separate him from them. Oh, yes, Juan will go far and leave them behind.' I saw a shade come upon her face, and, therefore, added: 'But no one will grudge him his success. He's so good-looking and good-tempered, and kind and true.' And then, she burst into tears, and I went to her and asked as if suspicious, 'Why, what's the matter, Clemencia?' Amid her sobs, she told me she didn't know, but she felt upset, out of sorts, nervous; she had a headache. 'Heartache,' I laughed to myself, and bade her go and lie down; rest would do her good; I'd come again on the morrow. As I turned to leave the room she called me back and put her arms round my neck and asked me to be patient with her; she was foolish, but she'd make it up to me yet. . . . And I comforted her, the poor, shallow fool, and went away.

"In some such fashion as this the days passed; each hour—now my eyes were opened—bringing me some fresh entertainment; for, in spite of their acting, I saw that none of them were happy. I knew everything. I guessed that Juan, loving his liberty, was advising Clemencia to make up to me, and I saw how badly she played her part. And all this had escaped me a few days before; I laughed at myself more contemptuously than at them. It interested me, too, to see that Liberata had grown suspicious. She no longer trusted Juan's protestations implicitly. Every now and then, with feminine bitterness, she thrust the knife of her own doubt and fear into Clemencia's wound. 'Don't you think, Montes, Clemencia is getting pale and thin?' she'd ask; 'it is for love of you, you know. She should marry soon.' And all the while she cursed me in her heart for a fool, while I laughed to myself. The comedy was infinitely amusing to me, for now I held the cords in my hand, and knew I could drop the curtain and cut short the acting just when I liked. Clemencia's mother, too, would some-times set to work to amuse me as she went about with eyes troubled, as if anxious for the future, and yet stomach-satisfied with the comforts of the present. She, too, thought it worthwhile, now and then, to befool me, when fear came upon her—between meals. That did not please me! When she tried to play with me, the inconceivable stupidity of my for-mer blind trust became a torture to me. Juan's mother I saw but little of; yet I liked her. She was honest at least, and deceit was difficult to her. Juan was her idol; all he did was right in her eyes; it was not her fault that she couldn't see he was like a poisoned well. All these days Juan was friendly to me as usual, with scarcely a shade of the old condescension in his manner. He no longer showed envy by remarking upon my luck. Since he himself had been tested, he seemed to give me as much respect as his self-love could spare. Nor did he now boast, as he used to do, of his height and strength. Once, however, on the Friday evening, I think it was, he congratulated Clemencia on my love for her, and joked about our marriage. The time had come to drop the curtain and make an end.

"On the Saturday I went to the ring and ordered my *palco* to be filled with flowers. From there I went to the Duke of Medina Celi. He received me as always, with kindness, thought I looked ill, and asked me whether I felt the old wound still. 'No,' I replied, 'no Señor Duque, and if I come to you now it is only to thank you once more for all your goodness to me.'

"And he said after a pause—I remember each word; for he meant well:

"'Montes, there's something very wrong.' And then, 'Montes, one should never adore a woman; they all want a master. My hairs have grown gray in learning that. . . . A woman, you see, may look well and yet be cold-hearted and—not good. But a man would be a fool to refuse nuts because one that looked all right was hollow.'

"'You are wise,' I said 'Señor Duque! and I have been foolish. I hope it may be well with you always; but wisdom and folly come to the same end at last.'

"After I left him I went to Antonio and thanked him, and gave him a letter to be opened in a week. There were three enclosures in it—one for himself, one for the mother of Juan, and one for the mother of Clemencia, and each held three thousand *duros*. As they had cheated me for money, money they should have—with my contempt. Then I went back to the ring, and as I looked up to my *palco* and saw that the front of it was one bed of white and scarlet blossoms, I smiled. 'White for purity,' I said, 'and scarlet for blood—a fit show!' And I went home and slept like a child.

"Next day in the ring I killed two bulls, one on his first rush, and the other after the usual play. Then another *espada* worked, and then came the turn of Juan. As the bull stood panting I looked up at the *palco*. There they all were, Clemencia with hands clasped on the flowers and fixed, dilated eyes, her mother half asleep behind her. Next to Clemencia, the niece with flushed cheeks, and leaning on her shoulder his mother. Juan was much more nervous then he had been on the previous Sunday. As his bull came into the ring he asked me hurriedly: 'Do you think it's an easy one?' I told him carelessly that all bulls were easy and he seemed to grow more and more nervous. When the bull was ready for him he turned to me, passing his tongue feverishly over his dry lips.

"'You'll stand by me, won't you, Montes?'

"And I asked with a smile:

"'Shall I stand by you as you've stood by me?'

"'Yes, of course, we've always been friends.'

"'I shall be as true to you as you have been to me!' I said. And I moved to his right hand and looked at the bull. It was a good one; I couldn't have picked a better. In his eyes I saw courage that would never yield and hate that would strike in the death throe, and I exulted and held his eyes with mine, and promised him revenge. While he bowed his horns to the *muleta,* he still looked at me and I at him; and as I felt that Juan had leveled his sword and was on the point of striking, I raised my head with a sweep to the side, as if I had been the bull; and as I swung, so the brave bull swung too. And then—then all the ring swam round with me, and yet I had heard the shouting and seen the spectators spring to their feet. . . .

"I was in the street close to the Alvaredas'. The mother met me at the door; she was crying and the tears were running down her fat, greasy cheeks. She told me Clemencia had fainted and had been carried home, and Juan was dead—ripped open—and his mother distracted, and 'twas a pity, for he was so handsome and kind and good-natured, and her best dress was ruined, and *los toros* shouldn't be allowed, and—as I brushed past her in disgust—that Clemencia was in her room crying.

"I went upstairs and entered the room. There she sat with her elbows on the table and her hair all around her face and down her back, and her fixed eyes stared at me. As I closed the door and folded my arms and looked at her, she rose, and her stare grew wild with surprise and horror, and then, almost without moving her lips, she said:

"'Holy Virgin! You did it! I see it in your face!'

"And my heart jumped against my arms for joy, and I said in the same slow whisper, imitating her:

"'Yes, I did it.'

"As I spoke she sprang forward with hate in her face, and poured out a stream of loathing and contempt on me. She vomited abuse as from her very soul: I was low and base and cowardly; I was—God knows what all. And he was handsome and kind, with a face like a king. . . . And I had thought she could love me, me, the ugly, little, lame cur, while he was there. And she laughed. She'd never have let my lips touch her if it hadn't been that her mother liked me and to please him. And now I had killed him, the best friend I had. Oh, 'twas horrible. Then she struck her head with her fists and asked how God, God, God, could allow me to kill a man whose finger was worth a thousand lives such as mine!

"Then I laughed and said:

"'You mistake. You killed him. You made him an *espada*—you!'

"As I spoke her eyes grew fixed and her mouth opened, and she seemed to struggle to speak, but she only groaned—and fell face forward on the floor.

"I turned and left the room as her mother entered it." After a long pause Montes went on:

"I heard afterwards that she died next morning in premature childbirth. I left Madrid that night and came here, where I have lived ever since, if this can be called living. . . . Yet at times, now fairly content, save for one thing—'Remorse?' Yes!"—and the old man rose to his feet, while his great eyes blazing with passion held me. "Remorse! That I let the bull kill him. I should have torn his throat out with my own hands."

The sport of table tennis, or Ping-Pong, is one that has been enjoyed by nearly everyone. But it is rare indeed to see it pop up as the subject of a short story. Adding spice to this story is that it is also a murder mystery with some clever twists and turns. Author George Allan England (1877–1936) wrote several books, including Darkness and Dawn *(1914)*, The Golden Blight *(1916), and* Vikings of the Ice *(1924).*

George Allan England

PING-PONG (1918)

THE CORONER'S INQUEST SEEMED hardly more than a matter of routine. So obvious was the fact that Douglas Powell, the eccentric retired cotton broker, had fallen to his death from one of his library windows on the third floor of his house on West Heights Boulevard that Coroner Drummond would undoubtedly have omitted even the formality of a finding in the matter, had not the law rendered it mandatory.

Assembled in the back room of McCabe's Undertaking Parlors, whither the body had been removed—for Mr. Powell was without relatives and Drummond had so ordered—the little gathering spoke in tones as subdued as the dim light from the frosted bulb overhead. The presence of death, weighing upon them all, muted and constrained the spirit of life.

"It seems quite obvious," judged Drummond, joining the tips of his thin fingers and squinting through his glasses, "that the deceased came to his death through accidental means. His library window was open. The fragment of woollen cloth caught on the blind cord corresponds to the fabric of the coat he wore last night. His body, as you have heard from Mr. Shannigan, the milkman, and from Mrs. Estill, the housekeeper, was discovered at 6:15 this morning lying in the soft earth of the flower bed under the window. Mulvey, here," and he gestured at the officer who, helmet in hand, stood very ill at ease beside the chair in which the coroner was seated, "has given us a very lucid statement of the manner in which Mrs. Estill summoned him, and of how he let the body remain where it was until my arrival. The evidence is self-explanatory and conclusive. If no further facts are forthcoming, I shall render a verdict of accidental death."

For a moment nobody moved or spoke. Drummond's eyes sought the witnesses, one by one—the housekeeper, pale, tight-lipped, and wary; Shannigan, who knew not where to put his hands and feet; the self-sufficient Mulvey; Dr. Edwin Graun, Powell's long-time friend and physician; and last of all Dr. Jamison Herrick, the police surgeon.

"Well, gentlemen," said he, "are there any further remarks to be made? If not, I will render my verdict."

The little pause that followed seemed to indicate unanimity of opinion. But before Drummond could take this fountain pen from his pocket, Dr. Herrick spoke up.

"Just a minute," said he, passing a hand over his bald head, as he sat there across the table from the coroner. "Before you make out the certificate, we should be positive of all the factors involved in this matter. I am still not quite satisfied that Mr. Powell's death was caused by the cranial fracture obviously due to his head striking that whitewashed boulder at the edge of the flower bed."

"You mean there may have been a fracture of the cervical vertebrae, as well?" inquired Graun. "If so, a little further examination will establish that fact. That, or the shock, may have killed him. This, however, is immaterial. The mere details do not matter. Whatever they may be, the prime factor remains that it was the fall which produced death. Am I not right?"

His full-fleshed, rubicund face assumed an inquiring expression. He twirled the little gold cigar cutter at the end of his watch chain, and looked from face to face. All met his gaze save Mrs. Estill. Her eyes, lowered and blinking, seemed studying the carpet as if mightily interested in the dull, obscure pattern there.

"Well, am I right, gentlemen, or not?" repeated he.

"I hardly know," answered the police surgeon. "What strikes me as peculiar is that the scalp wound shows no sign of bleeding, or at least none commensurate with the injury involved. In fact, the appearance of the wound—if I didn't feel so positive, myself, that the fall caused his death—would suggest to me the idea that Mr. Powell had already been dead for some time before having fallen from the window."

"What's that?" demanded Dr. Graun. "I don't quite follow you. How could he have been dead *before* he fell?"

"That is the puzzling factor in the case," replied Dr. Herrick. "Until we get it cleared up, I think we ought not to go ahead with the verdict."

Dr. Graun's eyes blinked with a thoughtful expression. For a moment he ceased spinning his cigar cutter. Then, while Drummond peered inquiringly at him, and Mrs. Estill's lips moved as if she were mechanically counting the number of pattern repetitions in the carpet, he said:—

"In view of the fact that I spent the evening with Mr. Powell last night, and that I left him at 11:30, in his usual health and spirits, I confess I'm at a loss to understand just how it all happened. Mrs. Estill heard us talking and playing ping-pong—his favorite game, gentlemen, barring chess—up to the time I left. She herself let me out, and chained and locked the front door after me, as she has just now testified. After that, she claims she went directly to bed, although of course there can be no witness to that fact.

"Mr. Powell was alive at 11:30. That much we know. The house shows no signs of having been entered. There are no traces of murder. Death must have been caused by the fall. That much we can be sure of by a process of elimination. No other hypothesis will fit the facts. Do any of you gentlemen see any other explanation?"

"I don't for one," answered the police surgeon, frowning. "That's what puzzles me so. Because even that won't hold water. If the fall caused Mr. Powell's death, how the devil does it happen that he didn't bleed freely from the wound on the head?"

For a moment Graun pondered. Then, looking up, he answered:—

"There's just one possible hypothesis that may fit the facts."

"And what is that?" demanded Herrick.

"Powell may have suffered an attack of heart failure while leaning out the window—"

"In which case there would undoubtedly have been more bleeding."

"Not necessarily," put in the coroner. "Circulation would have already stopped. I think, on the whole, that's the best explanation we can give. In the circumstances, I'll change my finding to death from natural causes or accident."

He reached for his pen, opened the death certificate on the table before him, and was about to begin filling it in when Herrick stayed his hand with the remark:—

"Hold on a minute, please, if you don't mind. Mrs. Estill, after Dr. Graun left, did you hear any sound that might have been caused by anybody entering Mr. Powell's library or bedroom? Did anything happen that in any way suggested trouble or violence of any kind?"

"No, sir," the housekeeper answered with an oblique and nervous look, bobbing her little jet-trimmed bonnet. "Not a thing, sir."

"Hear any footsteps, or anything of that kind?"

"In the library, sir? Nothing. That thick carpet deafens everything. It's extra thick, sir."

Frowning, the police surgeon fixed critical eyes on her.

"Now see here," he said. "Tell me just what you did hear last night, if anything."

"Well, sir, all I heard was the doctor, here, and Mr. Powell playing their game and talking, until about half-past eleven. First he'd say something and then the doctor would answer. I could hear the little ping-pong ball go *tack-tack-tack* on the library table. And then maybe it would fall to the floor."

"How did you know that, Mrs. Estill?"

"Why—there'd come a little pause in the game, and then it would go on again. Mr. Powell was wonderful fond of that game, God rest him! The kindest man and the best that ever—"

"What else did you hear?" interrupted the surgeon, dryly, while the coroner and Dr. Graun studied the woman with close attention. The housekeeper dabbed at her eyes with a moist handkerchief, gave a shrewd look at her inquisitor, and continued:—

"At half-past eleven I heard them say good-night, and the doctor went away. After that, everything was quiet, same as usual."

"Did you enter the library, or see Mr. Powell alive, after that time?"

"No, sir. He was always very particular about not being disturbed at night. That was his reading time. He was the best man in the world, sir, and always treated me like a lady, though he was odd in his ways. And I shall miss him—"

"That will do," interrupted Herrick, in no mood to listen to discursions regarding the character of the deceased. He bent his gaze on the coroner, seeming to peer through him at vacancy beyond. "This is most peculiar. Direct testimony exists, from two witnesses, that Mr. Powell was alive at 11:30, and yet the condition of the body certainly points to the fact that he was dead at that time. Dr. Graun, will you kindly give us a few additional details of your call on him, last night?"

"Certainly, with the greatest pleasure," answered Graun, still whirling his cigar cutter. "In fact, I'll go over the whole matter again. I arrived about nine—one of my weekly routine calls, such as I've been making for the past eight or ten months. I found him in his usual state of health, barring a noticeable increase in the mitral insufficiency that had been gaining on him, little by little, since last summer; nothing serious, however—nothing that would warrant me in the belief that he was going to be stricken with heart failure so soon."

"It's odd about heart cases, that way," put in Herrick. "You think a man—say with a leaky valve, or whatnot—might live for a year or two, or five; and he drops dead almost at once. Another man you wouldn't give a week to live—everything all shot to pieces—and he survives to bury you. During your call last night, Dr. Graun, did you make a stethoscopic examination?"

"I did, as usual," Graun answered, nodding. "Mr. Powell, of course, was something of a hypochondriac. If it were not for the old rule of *De mortuis nil nisi bonum*—nothing but good about the dead—I suppose I'd have to call him a particularly fussy crank. For the last three years he has never eaten a bite that he hasn't weighed in a little pair of scales. Half his time and attention have been given to proteids, calories, enzymes, Bulgarian milk cultures and all that sort of thing. Nobody but a crank would be so interested in a childish game like ping-pong at his age. Every time I called he insisted on playing a game. A good patient; I couldn't refuse—though Lord! how it bored me! You know the type, Herrick, don't you?"

"Yes, I know; but never mind about that, now. You say his condition wasn't such last night as to warrant any presumption of immediate danger?"

"Not that I could see," answered Graun, while Drummond listened with close attention and the others watched him anxiously—all save Mrs. Estill, who had once more gone back to counting the patterns in the carpet, as if to keep from hearing all those interrogatory questions.

"The only supposition that seems to meet the case is that, after I left him, he must have opened the window to get a breath of fresh air. We'd both been smoking, and the air was somewhat vitiated. He probably took several long breaths, had a syncope—as sometimes happens when an excess of oxygen suddenly enters the blood—fell forward and slid over the sill. That's the only hypothesis I can think of that fits all the known facts."

A little silence followed, during which the police surgeon rose, clasped his hands behind his back, and began slowly to pace up and down the dim-lit room. Graun continued to whirl the trinket on his watch chain. Suddenly Drummond, the coroner, spoke again.

"Mrs. Estill," he asked, "how did you know it was 11:30 when the doctor left?"

"The hall clock struck the half-hour, sir, just after I heard the street door close."

"Did you hear the library window open, at any time during the evening?"

The housekeeper pondered a moment, then nodded affirmation.

"Yes, sir, I did."

"At what time, please?"

"I can't just say, sir, but I think it was while they were playing their game."

"Did you hear it shut again?"

"No, sir."

"Are you sure this was during the course of the game?"

"No, sir, not just exactly sure, but I think so. Still, it may have been afterwards. I don't remember."

"Surely, it must have been afterwards," put in Dr. Graun. "I recall very distinctly that the air was close and smoky—recall thinking in a casual way that it would be a good thing to have a little fresh air, but didn't suggest it. That was while we were talking, before we'd started the routine game—the game, I'll confess, that my willingness to play helped me to retain Mr. Powell as a patient. Then something else diverted my mind. To my personal knowledge, the window was not opened during my call."

The coroner pondered a moment, while Herrick stopped his pacing, then put his pen to the certificate of death.

"I think, gentlemen," said he, "that we have heard enough. The case is conclusive and self-evident. Any further investigation would be a needless waste of time and energy. I shall give a finding of death by natural causes or accidental means."

While the others watched him with mute interest, a little inflated by the instinctive sense of dignity we all feel when taking part in official proceedings, Drummond filled in the blank, dried it with a blotter and put it in his pocket. He reached for his hat, on the table before him, and stood up.

"Thank you, gentlemen," said he. "I'm glad the case is so obvious—glad there are no painful or embarrassing complications. Thank you, Mrs. Estill. Good day."

Dr. Herrick likewise took his hat. The coroner, the surgeon, and the policeman departed with Shannigan, the milkman, leaving Dr. Graun with the housekeeper and McCabe, to talk over some further details. Out on the pavement, in the cheerful March sunshine once more, the little group broke up, Herrick touched his hat, gave the coroner a brief good-day and, turning on his heel, departed with his hands thrust far into his overcoat pockets and his deep eyes smouldering.

"A wound that didn't bleed," he murmured, "and a doubt concerning the time of a window being opened. H—m!"

Downtown walked Dr. Herrick, with the air of a man sunk in deep abstraction. Arriving at the Arcade Building, he took the elevator to the eleventh floor, and entered an office, the door of which bore the name:—

T. H. ASHLEY
INVESTIGATIONS

Then, giving his hand to the sharp-faced man who rose to greet him, he asked:—

"What's the news, Tom? Busy?"

Ashley was, and said so. Herrick continued:—

"I've got a case for you. Something urgent. It's a sticker with beautiful possibilities. If you can unravel it I'll get you a berth in the secret service. Here's a chance for you to win your spurs."

"What's the idea?" demanded Ashley. "Sit down, and let's have the facts."

Herrick told him all he knew. Ashley listened with close attention, especially when Herrick gave the housekeeper's testimony that the ping-pong game had lasted up to the time of Dr. Graun's departure.

"That lets Graun out," said he. "In other circumstances, since he was the last man to see Powell alive, some suspicion might attach to him."

"It certainly would," assented Herrick. "But his testimony absolutely coincides with hers. He goes clear. If nobody else entered that house, later, we have only two hypotheses—either the housekeeper murdered Powell, or he died a natural death. You must find out whether or not she would have any motive. Have a look at her and at the premises, and see what you make of it. I rather think the old lady hasn't told all she knows. She was a bit uncertain about the time of that window being opened. Another thing, when I first saw her at the house, and she gave her version of being notified of the accident by Shannigan, the milkman, I thought her grief was just a shade exaggerated. Now you know the principal facts. It's up to you. Get busy."

Ashley put a few questions to the doctor, squinting with narrowed eyes as he tilted back in his chair, hands deep in trouser pockets. Then, nodding, he answered:—

"All right, I'm on. Where shall I see you?"

"Headquarters, all morning."

"Good! I'm not promising anything, of course, but if there's any thread to pick up, I'll do my best to find it."

Within half an hour he was examining Powell's library, while Mrs. Estill, anxious and pale, stood with hands tightly clasped and nervously watched his investigation.

First he took a general survey of the room, then peered down from the window out of which Powell had fallen. With a large magnifying glass he examined the sill. At different angles he studied the thick-piled carpet from the table to the window.

Next he drew down the window blinds, switched on the electric light of the table, and inspected the table itself—a large oak table, still cleared of books and papers as it had been for the game. Finally he asked for the ping-pong set.

Silently Mrs. Estill brought it. A certain unwillingness was now manifest in her attitude; an uneasy suspicion of this abrupt, laconic individual intruding on the privacy of the house of death.

"Here's the things, sir," said she, putting the box on the table. "Everything's just as it was left last night."

"Did Mr. Powell always put the bats and balls in the box, this way, after playing?" demanded Ashley.

"Why—not always."

"Did he ever put them back?'

"Sometimes."

"What share of this property is coming to you now? This house and land?"

The woman's face twitched slightly.

"I—I don't know, sir. How can I know, till the will is read?"

"Ah, of course you can't," said Ashley. "Pardon my asking. I needn't detain you any longer. Please be good enough to leave."

Troubled, she obeyed him. When she was gone, Ashley took from his vest pocket a jeweler's *loupe,* screwed it into his eye, and carrying the two little ping-pong bats over to the window, raised the blinds.

By the clear light of the winter's day he spent several minutes closely studying the handles of the bats. From time to time he grunted, but what the significance of those grunts might be was betrayed by no remark.

This observation finished, he replaced the bats in the box, removed the *loupe* from his eye, and began pacing the heavily carpeted floor. As he walked, he keenly studied the carpet. He moved the table to one side, so that the light from the incandescents should fall unimpeded over the whole expanse of carpeting.

For a minute or two he seemed to discover nothing; but suddenly he stopped, peered down with close attention, and then, kneeling, began to poke with an inquisitive forefinger at the thick velvet-like fabric.

Carefully he extracted something from its tufts, looked at it a moment as he held it between his fingers, then laid it in his palm and once more put the magnifying glass to his eye. With the greatest minuteness he studied the object, through his lens. It was a tiny, curved fragment of thin glass.

"Glass!" he said, frowning. "H—m! Glass!"

He took from another pocket a small pasteboard box which, when opened, proved to be full of cotton wool. Into the cotton wool he dropped the shard of glass; he closed the box with care, and pocketed it again. Then he got down on his knees by the place where the table had stood, and with his reading glass meticulously examined the place where he had found the shard.

"More glass—powdered! This looks interesting!"

For about five minutes he studied the place. Then, his investigation seemingly at an end, he got up and summoned Mrs. Estill.

"Tell me," he asked, "how long ago was an electric-light bulb broken here?"

"Broken, sir? Why—I don't know. I don't remember that one was ever broken in this room. There was one in the hall last week, but—"

"You're quite positive no bulb was ever smashed in the library?"

"Yes, sir. Why?"

"All right, Mrs. Estill. Thank you very much indeed for your kindness. Good day!"

Leaving her very pale and anxious, he took his departure, with the box containing the ping-pong set. By the grim smile on his lips, one might have suspected that his errand at the house of Powell had not been entirely in vain.

Straight back to his office he proceeded, entered his little laboratory which led out of it, and spent about twenty minutes there. Then he rang up Dr. Herrick at police headquarters.

"Doctor," said he, "I have a little fresh evidence in the case that will require some expert medical testimony."

"Fine!" answered Herrick. "Come along down!"

"All right. But I think I'll need more than a single opinion on the matter. Please have Dr. Graun there, too. He knows so much about Mr. Powell's habits that he can give us a great deal of valuable information."

"O.K. I'll have him here by the time you arrive. Got some evidence, have you?"

"I don't know. That depends on what you and Graun say about the indications."

Dr. Graun was already in Herrick's office when Ashley arrived. Graun shook hands with the investigator, and then–sitting down beside the desk–inquired with a smile:–

"Well, Mr. Ashley, have you any further light to shed on the mystery?"

"That depends," answered Ashley, opening the ping-pong box. He laid the box on the desk, took out the bats and–while Graun and Herrick watched him with interest–held them up to view.

"First," said he, "I have discovered the curious fact that both of these handles show the same type of fingerprints. Perspiring fingers, of course, leave very definite marks."

"What?" asked Dr. Graun, scowling a little. "What has that got to do with the case?"

"The hands of one and the same individual were last in contact with both these bats," Ashley explained. "The texture of the skin as shown by the prints on both is unmistakably the same. In other words for some reason or other, after the game was finished, either Mr. Powell or you, Doctor, must have held both bats for some time."

"Very likely," answered Graun, nodding. "If I remember rightly, I believe I myself put both bats back in the box. But what bearing can that possibly have on the manner in which Mr. Powell met his death?'

"The hand prints do not indicate a hasty or casual touch," said Ashley. "In fact, both bats seem to have been held for some considerable time by the same person. This is certainly very puzzling. Can you explain it?"

Graun pondered a moment, then shook his head in negation.

"Well, no," he answered. "Perhaps you are mistaken."

Ashley smiled noncommittally, laid the bats down, and produced the little box of cotton wool. This he also opened. From it he shook out a piece of broken glass upon the desk, and pointing to it said:–

"Here, gentlemen, is a bit of very thin, curved glass, which I discovered on the carpet near the table."

"Glass, eh?" queried Herrick. "Well, where does that fit in?"

"There were also signs that a little powdered glass had been brushed up from the thick carpet," Ashley continued, as he stood by the desk and looked at both the other men seated. "The carpet had certainly been brushed. My inference is that somebody stepped on some pieces of thin glass there, and then brushed them up, but was unable to get all the powder up and also overlooked this little piece here."

"What possible bearing can that have?" put in Graun, puzzled.

"I don't know yet. Mrs. Estill informed me that she broke an electric-light bulb in the library, two or three days ago. Probably this glass, here, is a fragment of that bulb."

"Undoubtedly so," assented Graun. He picked up the bit of glass and carefully examined it. "The curve and the thinness strongly suggest such an explanation. Yes, that's what this must have been—part of a bulb. As such, it can't have any possible significance in this case."

Casually he tossed it in his palm, two or three times, then dropped it into the wastebasket. Ashley picked it out again, without comment, and once more deposited it carefully in the cotton wool.

"Mrs. Estill," said he, "showed some signs of perturbation when I showed it to her. I also asked her whether Mr. Powell ever used perfume of any kind. She rather evaded the question. Perfume, of course, often comes in thin vials. This glass, instead of being part of a bulb, may have been part of a vial."

"Yes, that's so, too," put in Graun, while the police surgeon, looking from one to the other, and obviously understanding little of what was forward, drummed on the polished surface of the desk with his nails.

"Well, what about all this, anyhow?" demanded he. "I don't see that we're getting anywhere, Ashley, or that your 'new evidence' is worth the powder to blow it."

Ashley smiled dryly as he made answer.

"The one fact that destroys both possibilities of an incandescent light or a vial of perfume is that my laboratory tests give conclusive evidence that this glass has been in contact with a very highly poisonous substance."

"What's that you say?' demanded Herrick, sharply, while Graun stared in astonishment. "What kind of substance? Some liquid?"

"No, a gas. I tested it carefully, before coming here, and discovered that it had been exposed to CO_2 gas. Carbon dioxide, you know."

"Carbon dioxide?" repeated Herrick. "Are you sure?"

"Positive! As both you gentlemen know, it is a violent and fatal poison. When inhaled in any quantity, as, for example, from a vial, it produces a spasm of the glottis and immediate death."

Dr. Graun peered from beneath wrinkled brows at Ashley. Some understanding of the matter now seemed to have dawned on him.

"Extraordinary!" murmured he. "This gives the case a new and decidedly sinister appearance. As things are shaping now, a good working hypothesis might be formed that after my departure last night somebody—under the pretense of having Mr. Powell smell a vial said to contain some pleasing odor—caused him to inhale CO_2. This, of course, would be premeditated murder. Murder in the first degree."

There came a little silence in the office, for perhaps the space of half a dozen heartbeats. Then, asked Herrick:—

"Would Mrs. Estill have had any motive?"

"Gentlemen," answered Graun, reluctantly, but with the air of a man doing his duty, "there is one fact which I assume you have not been aware of, but which it is imperative for you to know. Do not misunderstand me as bringing any accusation, but merely take the fact for what it is worth, in connection with the others."

"What fact, Doctor?" asked Herrick anxiously.

"This: that as a friend of some years' standing, Mr. Powell several times informed me that he intended to recompense the housekeeper for many years of faithful service by leaving her a half interest in the estate—a matter, probably, of some sixty thousand dollars."

"Ah, indeed," said the police surgeon. "This is getting interesting. I wish we'd had these facts at the inquest. Now we *are* coming on. Lord, what a wonderful proposition science is! So then, you say the old lady was to get half the estate?"

"Correct," answered Graun, nodding.

"And the other half was to go to—"

"That I don't know. He never told me."

"All right," said Herrick. "It looks as if Mrs. Estill was guilty, doesn't it? Now then, assuming that she really did do this murder, where the devil could she have got the knowledge or the means to carry it out? Would you judge that her intelligence was sufficient for such an undertaking?"

"Why, as for that," put in Ashley, "from even the little conversation I had with her, I analyzed her as a shrewd, canny woman. The matter seems to be clarifying itself, doesn't it?"

"I should say so!" ejaculated Herrick, while Dr. Graun sat pondering, with half-closed eyes. Suddenly Graun spoke.

"With even these few data in hand," said he, "I think we can make a beginning towards a reconstruction of the crime."

"More than a beginning," supplemented Ashley. From the ping-pong box he took out the bats again, and with them the little celluloid balls. Taking a bat in each hand, he stood there looking at the police surgeon.

"You are familiar with this game, Dr. Herrick?" asked he.

"Well, yes," Herrick answered. "I played it a few times, years ago, when it was all the rage."

"Very good! Now please close your eyes and listen."

Puzzled, Herrick obeyed. Ashley dropped a ball onto the hard surface of the desk. As it bounded, he struck it lightly with his righthand bat. At the next rebound he hit it back again with the left. To and fro he bounced it, varying the rhythm of the strokes a little.

Tick-tack, tick-tack, tick-tack went the ball.

"Tell me, Dr. Herrick," said Ashley, "as you sit there, without seeing what I am doing, could you by any possibility determine that one man is playing this game, and not two? Listen acutely and let me have your judgment."

Herrick gave the problem his acute attention, while Graun bent forward with obvious interest and wonderingly observed the little bouncing sphere of celluloid.

"Well?" questioned Ashley. "What do you say?"

Herrick opened his eyes and looked up questioningly at the investigator, who now stopped batting the ball and replaced it, with both bats, in the box.

"Bless my soul, but that's a curious deception!" he commented. "I could have sworn two men were playing!"

"So far, so good," smiled Ashley. "Remember, Doctor, the fingerprints on the bats indicate that they were both held for some time by one and the same individual."

"I don't see just what you're driving at," interpolated Graun, not seeming to understand at all.

"Ah, but you will in a minute," Ashley assured him. "Suppose we reconstruct the case, something like this. Follow me closely. Suppose that some person as yet unidentified, somebody with an interest in Mr. Powell's death, gave him a vial of CO_2 last night to smell. Mr. Powell died immediately, dropping the vial from his hand.

"His fall was undoubtedly eased to the floor by the person who murdered him, this person having, of course, been on the watch for just such a contingency. Then the murderer evidently brushed up the bits of broken and powdered glass, but couldn't quite get up all the powder, and also overlooked one tiny bit of glass—the one fragment which I now have in my box of cotton wool."

"Very ingenious," said the police surgeon, "but would any such bizarre explanation hold water?"

"Wait till I have done," answered the investigator, smiling again. "The murderer proceeded to continue the ping-pong game and to carry on a pretense of conversation, altering his voice to imitate Mr. Powell's. At some time, not determinable, he dragged the body to the window. The marks on the carpet amply prove the fact. He opened the window, slid the body over the sill, and let it drop into the soft earth of the flower bed.

"All these suppositions, joined to the fact that Mr. Powell's wound did not bleed and that the body gave some evidence that death had occurred previous to 11:30 last night, open up the way to some very entertaining speculations, do they not?"

Questioningly his eyes sought those of Dr. Graun, who sat there looking at him with the same studious gaze as from the beginning of the conference. Herrick's eyes, too, drawn by a strange and dawning wonder, fixed themselves on Graun.

"Doctor," asked he in a tense voice, "what have you got to say about all this?"

"Pardon me," answered Graun, "but I think I'll just light a cigar." Speaking, he drew from his waistcoat pocket a thin black Havana.

"Please excuse me for not offering you gentlemen a smoke also," said he with perfect calm, "but this is the only one I happen to have. It's rather choice, too—something I have cured according to my own particular formula."

He struck a match, lit the cigar and took three or four long pulls at it, each of which he inhaled deeply into his lungs and then blew forth into thin vapor.

"Very choice indeed," he remarked. "Highly valuable as an aid in answering difficult questions."

His mouth sagged a little as he spoke, and a peculiar, glassy look came into his narrowed eyes.

"Just one or two things more, gentlemen," said he. "The will left by Mr. Powell names a certain Frank Blaisdell as the joint heir with Mrs. Estill. Mr. Blaisdell was to turn over seventy-five per cent of the proceeds to me. He is in no way involved—a mere dummy I assure you. I state this to protect a weak, though an innocent man."

"Good God! What are you saying?" ejaculated Herrick, starting up. Graun raised a quivering hand.

"Sit down," he commanded, speaking thickly now and swaying a little in his chair. "Silence, and listen to me! I have a wife and two children. They deserve your consideration. Don't forget that!"

Over his face a grayish hue was drawing, like a mask. The muscles of his lips were twitching, but he controlled them with a supreme effort.

"Let—let the verdict for Powell stand," said Graun in a strange voice. "And write the same for me—heart failure. Then Katherine and the children need never know. This cigar—wonderful, isn't it? The name of the drug in it is—but never mind . . ."

The last words came in hardly more than a whisper. Suddenly Graun slumped forward; his head dropped on his breast. He shuddered slightly and was still.

"For God's sake!" whispered Herrick, his voice tense as a wire. He shook Graun by the shoulder. The doctor's arm fell limp and dangled horribly.

Silence fell in the office.

All at once, turning to Ashley, the police surgeon gulped:—

"What—what are we going to do? You've solved the case—you've won your spurs. If—"

"Spurs be damned!" retorted Ashley. "Think I'd worry about spurs *now*, with that wife and those children to be saved? Heart failure it is in both cases. Just let it go at that."

Sir Pelham Grenville Wodehouse (1881–1975) is by far the most successful writer of short stories on golf. This polished gem is one of his best, featuring a lovesick duffer who has managed to alienate the father of his heart's desire and plots to get on his right side to win his daughter's hand. The Oldest Member of the club is available as usual to dispense his sage advice. The unfolding of the humorous plot, if a bit predictable, is vintage Wodehouse. He authored ninety-two books, countless stories, and lyrics for Broadway musicals during his amazing career as both a British and an American citizen. Among his widely read books are My Man Jeeves *(1919),* Ukridge *(1924),* The Code of the Woosters *(1938),* The Butler Did It *(1957), and* The Girl in Blue *(1971).*

P. G. Wodehouse

THE LETTER OF
THE LAW (1924)

"**F**O–O–O–RE!"

The cry, in certain of its essentials not unlike the wail of a soul in torment, rolled out over the valley, and the young man on the seventh tee, from whose lips it had proceeded, observing that the little troupe of spavined octogenarians doddering along the fairway paid no attention whatever, gave his driver a twitch as if he was about to substitute action for words. Then he lowered the club and joined his companion on the bench.

"Better not, I suppose," he said, moodily.

The Oldest Member, who often infested the seventh tee on a fine afternoon, nodded.

"I think you are wise," he agreed. "Driving into people is a thing one always regrets. I have driven into people in my golfing days, and I was always sorry later. There is something about the reproachful eye of the victim as you meet it subsequently in the bar of the club-house which cannot fail to jar the man of sensibility. Like a wounded oyster. Wait till they are out of distance, says the good book. The only man I ever knew who derived solid profit from driving into somebody who was not out of distance was young Wilmot Byng. . . ."

The two young men started.

"Are you going to tell us a story?'

"I am."

"But—"

"I knew you would be pleased," said the Oldest Member.

Wilmot Byng at the time of which I speak (the sage proceeded) was an engaging young fellow with a clear-cut face and a drive almost as long as the Pro's. Strangers, watching him at his best, would express surprise that he had never taken a couple of days off and won the Open Championship, and you could have knocked them down with a putter when you informed them that his handicap was six. For Wilmot's game had a fatal defect. He was impatient. If held up during a round, he tended to press. Except for that, however, he had a sterling nature and frank blue eyes which won all hearts.

It was the fact that for some days past I had observed in these eyes a sort of cloud that led me to think that the lad had something on his mind. And when we were lunching together in the club-house one afternoon and he listlessly refused a most admirable steak and kidney pudding I shot at him a glance so significant that, blushing profusely, he told me all.

He loved, it seemed, and the partner he had selected for life's medal round was a charming girl named Gwendoline Poskitt.

I knew the girl well. Her father was one of my best friends. We had been at the University together. As an undergraduate, he had made a name as a hammer thrower. More recently, he had taken up golf, and being somewhat short-sighted and completely muscle-bound, had speedily won for himself in our little community the affectionate sobriquet of the First Grave Digger.

"Indeed?" I said. "So you love Gwendoline Poskitt, do you? Very sensible. Were I a younger man, I would do it myself. But she scorns your suit?"

"She doesn't scorn any such dashed thing," rejoined Wilmot with some heat. "She is all for my suit."

"You mean she returns your love?"

"She does."

"Then why refuse steak and kidney pudding?"

"Because her father will never consent to her becoming my wife. And it's no good saying Why not elope? because I suggested that and she would have none of it. She loves me dearly, she says—as a matter of fact, she admitted in so many words that I was the tree on which the fruit of her life hung—but she can't bring herself to forgo the big church wedding, with full choral effects and the Bishop doing his stuff and photographs in the illustrated weekly papers. As she quite rightly pointed out, were we to sneak off and get married at the registrar's, bim would go the Bishop and phut the photographs. I can't shake her."

"You ought not to want to shake her."

"Move her, I mean. Alter her resolution. So I've got to get her father's consent. And how can I, when he has it in for me the way he has?"

He gave a groan and began to crumble my bread. I took another piece and put it on the opposite side of my plate.

"Has it in for you?"

"Yes. It's like this. You know the Wrecking Crew?"

He was alluding to the quartet of golfing cripples of which Joseph Poskitt was a regular member. The others were Old Father Time, The Man With The Hoe, and Consul, the Almost Human.

"You know the way they dodder along and won't let anyone through. There have been ugly mutterings about it in the Club for months, and it came even harder on me than on most of the crowd, for, as you know, I like to play quick. Well, the other day I cracked under the strain. I could endure it no longer. I–"

"Drove into them?"

"Drove into them. Using my brassie for the shot. I took a nice easy stance, came back slow, keeping my head well down, and let fly–firing into the brown, as it were, and just trusting to luck which of them I hit. The man who drew the short straw was old Poskitt. I got him on the right leg. Did you tell me he got his blue at Oxford for throwing the hammer?"

"Throwing the hammer, yes."

"Not the high jump?'

"No."

"Odd. I should have said–"

I was deeply concerned. To drive into the father of the girl you love, no matter what the provocation, seemed to me an act of the most criminal folly and so I told him.

He quivered and broke a tumbler.

"Now there," he said, "you have touched on another cause for complaint. At the time, I had no notion that he was the father of the girl I loved. As a matter of fact, he wasn't, because I had not met Gwendoline then. She blew in later, having been on one of those round-the-world cruises. I must say I think that old buffers who hold people up and won't let them through ought to wear some sort of label indicating that they have pretty daughters who will be arriving shortly. Then one would know where one was and act accordingly. Still, there it is. I gave old Poskitt this juicy one, as described, and from what he said to me later in the changing room I am convinced that any suggestions on my part that I become his son-in-law will not be cordially received."

I ate cheese gravely. I could see that the situation was a difficult one.

"Well, the only thing I can advise," I said, "is that you cultivate him assiduously. Waylay him and give him cigars. Ask after his slice. Tell him it's a fine day. He has a dog named Edward. Seek Edward out and pat him. Many a young man has won over the father of the girl he loves by such tactics, so why not you?"

He agreed to do so, and in the days which followed Poskitt could not show his face in the club-house without having Wilmot spring out at him with perfectos. The dog Edward began to lose hair off his ribs through incessant patting. And gradually, as I had hoped, the breach healed. Came a morning when Wilmot, inquiring after my old friend's slice, was answered not with the usual malevolent grunt but with a reasonably cordial statement that it now showed signs of becoming a hook.

"Ah?" said Wilmot. "A cigar?"

"Thanks," said Poskitt.

"Nice doggie," said Wilmot, pursuing his advantage by administering a hearty buffet to Edward's aching torso before the shrinking animal could side-step.

"Ah," said Poskitt.

That afternoon, for the first time for weeks, Wilmot Byng took twice of steak and kidney pudding at lunch and followed it up with treacle tart and a spot of Stilton.

And so matters stood when the day arrived for the annual contest for the President's Cup.

The President's Cup, for all its high-sounding name, was one of the lowliest and most humble trophies offered for competition to the members of our club, ranking in the eyes of good judges somewhere between the Grandmothers' Umbrella and the Children's All-Day Sucker (open to boys and girls not yet having celebrated their seventh birthday). It has been instituted by a kindly committee for the benefit of the canaille of our little golfing world, those retired military, naval and business men who withdraw to the country and take up golf in their fifties. The contest was decided by medal play, if you could call it that, and no exponent with a handicap of under twenty-four was allowed to compete.

Nevertheless, there was no event on the fixture list which aroused among those involved a tenser enthusiasm. Centenarians sprang from their bathchairs to try their skill, and I have seen men with waist lines of sixty doing bending and stretching exercises for weeks in advance in order to limber themselves up for the big day. Form was eagerly discussed in the smoking room, and this year opinion wavered between two men:

Joseph Poskitt, the First Grave Digger, and Wadsworth Hemmingway, better known in sporting circles as Palsied Percy.

The betting, as I say, hovered uncertainly between these two, but there was no question as to which was the people's choice. Everybody was fond of Poskitt. You might wince as you saw his iron plough through the turf, but you could not help liking him, whereas Hemmingway was definitely unpopular. He was a retired solicitor, one of those dark, subtle, sinister men who carry the book of rules in their bag, and make it their best club. He was a confirmed hole-claimer, and such are never greatly esteemed by the more easy-going. He had, moreover, a way of suddenly clearing his throat on the greens which alone would have been sufficient to ensure dislike.

The President's Cup was an event which I always made a point of watching, if I could, considering it a spectacle that purged the soul with pity and terror: but on this occasion business in London unfortunately claimed me and I was compelled to deprive myself of my annual treat. I had a few words with Wilmot before leaving to catch my train. I was pleased with the lad.

"You've done splendidly, my boy," I said. "I notice distinct signs of softening on our friend's part."

"Me too," agreed Wilmot jubilantly. "He thanks me now when I give him a cigar."

"So I observed. Well, continue to spare no effort. Did you wish him success for this afternoon?"

"Yes. He seemed pleased."

"It might be a good idea if you were to offer to caddie for him. He would appreciate your skilled advice."

"I thought of that, but I'm playing myself."

"Today?"

I was surprised, for President's Cup day is usually looked on as a sort of Walpurgis Night, when fearful things are abroad and the prudent golfer stays at home.

"I promised a fellow a game, and I can't get out of it."

"You will be held up a good deal, I am afraid."

"I suppose so."

"Well, don't go forgetting yourself and driving into Poskitt."

"I should say not, ha, ha! Not likely, ho, ho! One doesn't do that sort of thing twice, does one? But excuse me now, if you don't mind, I have an appointment to wander in the woods with Gwendoline."

It was late in the evening when I returned home. I was about to ring up Poskitt to ask how the contest had come out, when the telephone rang and I was surprised to hear Hemmingway's voice.

"Hullo," said Hemmingway. "Are you doing anything tomorrow morning?"

"Nothing," I replied. "How did things come out this afternoon?"

"That is what I rang up about. Poskitt and I tied for a low score at a hundred and fifteen. I put the matter up to the Committee and they decided that there must be a play off—match play."

"You mean stroke play?"

"No, match play. It was my suggestion. I pointed out to Poskitt that by this method he would only have to play the first ten holes, thus saving wear and tear on his niblick."

"I see. But why was it necessary to refer the thing to the Committee?"

"Oh, there was some sort of foolish dispute. It turned on a question of rubs of the green. Well, if you aren't doing anything tomorrow, will you referee the play off?"

"Delighted."

"Thanks. I want somebody who knows the rules. Poskitt does not seem to realize that there are any."

"Why do you say that?"

"Well, he appears to think that when you're playing in a medal competition you can pick and choose which strokes you are going to count and which you aren't. Somebody drove into him when he was addressing his ball at the eleventh and he claims that that is what made him send it at right angles into a bush. As I told him, and the Committee supported me . . ."

A nameless fear caused the receiver to shake in my hand.

"Who drove into him?"

"I forget this name. Tall, good-looking young fellow with red hair—"

I had heard enough. Five minutes later, I was at Wilmot's door, beating upon it. As he opened it, I noticed that his face was flushed, his eye wild.

"Wilmot!" I cried.

"Yes, I know," he said impatiently, leading the way to the sitting-room. "I suppose you've been talking to Poskitt."

"To Hemmingway. He told me—"

"I know, I know. You were surprised?"

"I was shocked. Shocked to the core. I thought there was better stuff in you, young Byng. Why, when the desire to drive into people grips you, do you not fight against it and conquer it like a man? Have you no will power? Cannot you shake off this frightful craving?"

"It wasn't that at all."

"What wasn't what at all?"

"All that stuff about having no will power. I was in full possession of my faculties when I tickled up old Poskitt this afternoon. I acted by the light of pure reason. Seeing that I had nothing to lose—"

"Nothing to lose?"

"Not a thing. Gwendoline broke off the engagement this morning."

"What?"

"Yes. As you are aware, we went to wander in the woods. Well, you know how you feel when you are wandering in the woods with a girl you adore. The sunlight streamed through the overhanging branches, forming a golden pattern on the green below: the air was heavy with fragrant scents and murmurous with the drone of fleeting insects, and what with one thing and another I was led to remark that I loved her as no one had ever loved before. Upon which, she said that I did not love her as much as she loved me. I said yes, I did, because my love stood alone. She said no, it didn't, because hers did. I said it couldn't because mine did.

"Hot words ensued, and a few moments later she was saying that she never wanted to see or speak to me again, because I was an obstinate, fatheaded son of an Army mule. She then handed back my letters, which she was carrying in a bundle tied round with lilac ribbon somewhere in the interior of her costume, and left me. Naturally, then, when Poskitt and his accomplice held us up for five minutes on the eleventh, I saw no reason to hesitate. My life's happiness was wrecked, and I found a sort of melancholy consolation in letting him have it on the seat of the pants with a wristy spoon shot."

In the face of the profounder human tragedies there is little that one can say. I was pondering in gloomy silence on this ruin of two young lives, when the door bell rang. Wilmot went to answer it and came back carrying a letter in his hand. There was a look upon his face which I had not seen since the occasion when he missed the short putt on the eighteenth which would have given him the Spring medal.

"Listen," said Wilmot. "Cyanide. Do you happen to have any cyanide on you?"

"Cyanide?"

"Or arsenic would do. Read this. On second thoughts, I'll give you the gist. There is some rather fruity stuff in Para. One which I feel was intended for my eye alone. The nub is that Gwendoline says she's sorry and it's all on again."

The drama of the situation hit me like a stuffed eelskin.

"She loves you as of yore?"

Rather more than of yore, if anything, I gather."

"And you—"

"And I—"

"Have driven—"

"Have driven—"

"Into—"

"Into old Poskitt, catching him bending—"

"Causing him to lose a stroke and thereby tie for the President's Cup instead of winning it."

I had not thought that the young fellow's jaw could drop any farther, but at these words it fell another inch.

"You don't mean that?"

"Hemmingway rang me up just now to tell me that he and Poskitt turned in the same score and are playing it off tomorrow."

"Gosh!"

"Quite."

"What shall I do?"

I laid my hand upon his shoulder.

"Pray, my boy, that Poskitt will win tomorrow."

"But even then—"

"No. You have not studied the psychology of the long-handicap golfer as I have. It would not be possible for a twenty-four handicap man who had just won his first cup to continue to harbour resentment against his bitterest foe. In the hour of triumph Poskitt must inevitably melt. So pray, my boy."

A quick gleam lit up Wilmot Byng's blue eyes.

"You bet I'll pray," he said. "The way I'll pray will be nobody's business. Push off, and I'll start now."

At eleven o'clock the following morning I joined Poskitt and Hemmingway on the first tee, and a few minutes later the play off for the President's Cup had begun. From the very outset it was evident that this was to be a battle of styles. Two men of more sharply contrasted methods can seldom have come together on a golf course.

Poskitt, the d'Artagnan of the links, was a man who brought to the tee the tactics which in his youth had won him such fame as a hammer thrower. His plan was to clench his teeth, shut his eyes, whirl the club round his head and bring it down with sickening violence in the general direction of the sphere. Usually, the only result would be a ball topped along the ground or—as had been known to happen when he used his niblick—cut in half. But there would come times when by some mysterious dispensation of Providence he managed to connect, in which event the gallery would be stunned by the spectacle of a three-hundred-yarder down the middle. The whole thing, as he himself recognized, was a clean, sporting venture. He just let go and hoped for the best.

In direct antithesis to these methods were those of Wadsworth Hemmingway. It was his practice before playing a shot to stand over the ball for an appreciable time, shaking gently in every limb and eyeing it closely as if it were some difficult point of law. When eventually he began his back swing, it was with a slowness which reminded those who had travelled in Switzerland of moving glaciers. A cautious pause at the top, and the clubhead would descend to strike the ball squarely and dispatch it fifty yards down the course in a perfectly straight line.

The contest, in short, between a man who—on, say, the long fifteenth—oscillated between a three and a forty-two and one who on the same hole always got his twelve—never more, never less. The Salt of Golf, as you might say.

And yet, as I took my stand beside the first tee, I had no feeling of pleasurable anticipation. To ensure the enjoyment of the spectator of a golf match, one thing is essential. He must feel that the mimic warfare is being conducted in the gallant spirit of a medieval tourney, not in the mood of a Corsican vendetta. And today it was only too plain from the start that bitterness and hostility were rampant.

The dullest mind would have been convinced of this by the manner in which, when Hemmingway had spun a half-crown and won the honour, Poskitt picked up the coin and examined it on both sides with a hard stare. Reluctantly convinced by his inspection that there was no funny business afoot, he drew back and allowed his opponent to drive. And presently Hemmingway had completed his customary fifty-yarder, and it was Poskitt's turn to play.

A curious thing I have noticed about golf is that a festering grievance sometimes does wonders for a man's drive. It is as if pent-up emotion added zip to his swing. It was so on the present occasion. Assailing his ball with hideous violence, Poskitt sent it to within ten yards of the green, and a few moments later, despite the fact that Hemmingway cleared his throat both before and during the first, second and third putts, he was one up.

But this pent-up emotion is a thing that cuts both ways. It had helped Poskitt on the first. On the second, the short lake hole, it undid him. With all this generous wrath surging about inside him, he never looked like accomplishing the restrained mashie shot which would have left him by the pin. Outdriving the green by some hundred and seventy yards, he reached the woods that lay beyond it, and before he could extricate himself Hemmingway was on the green and he was obliged to concede. They went to the third all square.

Here Poskitt did one of his celebrated right-angle drives, and took seven to get out of the rough. Hemmingway, reaching the green with a steady eight, had six for it and won without difficulty.

The fourth is a dog-leg. Hemmingway drove short of the bunker. Poskitt followed with a stroke which I have never seen executed on the links before or since, a combination hook and slice. The ball, starting off as if impelled by dynamite, sailed well out to the left, then, after travelling one hundred and fifty yards, seemed to catch sight of the hole round the bend, paused in mid-air and, turning sharply to the right, soared on to the green.

All square once more, a ding-dong struggle brought them to the seventh, which Poskitt won. Hemmingway, recovering, secured the eighth.

The ninth brings you back to the water again, though to a narrower part of it, and when Poskitt, with another of his colossal drives, finished within fifty yards of the pin, it seemed as if the hole must be his. Allowing him four approach shots and three putts, he would be down in eight, a feat far beyond the scope of his opponent. He watched Hemmingway's drive just clear the water, and with a grunt of satisfaction started to leave the tee.

"One moment," said Hemmingway.

"Eh?"

"Are you not going to drive?"

"Don't you call that a drive?"

"I do not. A nice practice shot, but not a drive. You took the honour when it was not yours. I, if you recollect, won the last hole. I am afraid I must ask you to play again."

"What?"

"The rules are quite definite on this point," said Hemmingway, producing a well-thumbed volume.

There was an embarrassing silence.

"And what do the rules say about clearing your throat on the green when your opponent is putting?"

"There is no rule against that."

"Oh, no?"

"It is recognized that a tendency to bronchial catarrh is a misfortune for which the sufferer should be sympathized with rather than penalized."

"Oh yes?"

"Quite." Hemmingway glanced at his watch. "I noticed that three minutes have elapsed since I made my drive. I must point out to you that if you delay more than five minutes, you automatically lose the hole."

Poskitt returned to the tee and put down another ball. There was a splash.

"Playing three," said Hemmingway.

Poskitt drove again.

"Playing five," said Hemmingway.

"Must you recite?" said Poskitt.

"There is no rule against calling the score."

"I concede the hole," said Poskitt.

Wadsworth Hemmingway was one up at the turn.

There is nothing (said the Oldest Member) which, as a rule, I enjoy more than recounting stroke by stroke the course of a golf match. Indeed I have been told that I am sometimes almost too meticulous in my attention to detail. But there is one match which I have never been able to bring myself to report in this manner, and that is the play off for the President's Cup between Wadsworth Hemmingway and Joseph Poskitt.

The memory is too painful. As I said earlier, really bad golf is a thing which purges the soul, and a man becomes a better and broader man for watching it. But this contest, from the tenth hole—where Poskitt became all square—onwards, was so poisoned by the mental attitude of the principals that to recall it even today makes me shudder. It resolved itself into a struggle between a great-souled slosher, playing far above his form, and a subtle Machiavellian schemer who, outdriven on every hole, held his own by constant reference to the book of rules.

I need merely say that Poskitt, after a two hundred and sixty yard drive at the eleventh, lost the hole through dropping his club in a bunker, that, having accomplished an equally stupendous stroke at the twelfth, he became two down owing to a careless inquiry as to whether I did not think he could get on from there with a mashie ("seeking advice of one who was not his caddie') and that, when he had won the thirteenth, he became two down once more at the short fourteenth when a piece of well-timed throat-clearing on the part of his opponent caused him to miss the putt which should have given him a half.

But there was good stuff in Joseph Poskitt. He stuck to it manfully. The long fifteenth I had expected him to win, and he did, but I had not been prepared for his clever seven on the sixteenth. And when he obtained a half on the seventeenth by holing out from a bunker a hundred and fifty yards short of the green, I felt that all might yet be well. I could see that Hemmingway, confident that he would be dormy one, was a good deal shaken at coming to the eighteenth all square.

The eighteenth was one of those objectionable freak holes, which, in my opinion, deface a golf course. Ten yards from the tee the hill rose almost sheer to the tableland where the green had been constructed. I suppose that from tee to pin was a distance of not more than fifty yards. A certain three if you were on, anything if you were not.

It was essentially a hole unsuited to Poskitt's particular style. What Poskitt required, if he was to give of his best, was a great wide level prairie stretching out before him into the purple distance. Conditions like those of the eighteenth hole put him very much in the position of a house-painter who is suddenly called upon to execute a miniature. I could see that he was ill at ease as he teed his ball up, and I was saddened, but not surprised, when he topped it into the long grass at the foot of the hill.

But the unnerving experience of seeing his opponent hole out from bunkers had taken its toll of Hemmingway. He, too, was plainly not himself. He swung with his usual care, but must have swerved from the policy of a lifetime and lifted his head. He finished his stroke with a nice, workmanlike follow through, but this did him no good, for he had omitted to hit the ball. When he had disentangled himself, there it was, still standing up on its little mountain of sand.

"You missed it," said Poskitt.

"I am aware of the fact," said Hemmingway.

"What made you do that? Silly. You can't expect to get anywhere if you don't hit the ball."

"If you will kindly refrain from talking, I will play my second."

"Well, don't miss this one."

"Please."

"You'll never win at golf if you do things in this slipshod way. The very first thing is to hit the ball. If you don't you cannot make real progress. I should have thought you would have realized that."

Hemmingway appealed to me.

"Umpire, I should be glad if you would instruct my opponent to be quiet. Otherwise, I shall claim the hole and match."

"There is nothing in the rules," I said, "against the opponent offering genial sympathy and advice."

"Exactly," said Poskitt. "You don't want to miss it again, do you? Very well. All I'm doing is telling you not to."

I pursed my lips. I was apprehensive. I knew Hemmingway. Another man in his position might have been distracted by these cracks, but I could see that they had but solidified his determination to put his second up to the pin. I had seen wrath and resentment work a magic improvement in Poskitt's game, and I felt sure that they were about to do so in Wadsworth Hemmingway.

Nor was I mistaken. Concentration was written in every line of the man's face as he swung back. The next moment, the ball was soaring through the air, to fall three feet from the hole. And there was Poskitt faced with the task of playing two from the interior of a sort of jungle. Long grass twined itself about his ball, wild flowers draped it, a beetle was sitting on it. His caddie handed him a niblick, but I could not but feel that what was really required was a steam shovel. It was not a golf shot at all. The whole contract should have been handed to some capable excavation company.

But I had not realized to what lengths an ex-hammer-thrower can go, when armed with a niblick and really up against it. Just as film stars are happiest among their books, so was Joseph Poskitt happiest among the flowering shrubs with his niblick. His was a game into which the niblick had always entered very largely. It was the one club with which he really felt confident of expressing his personality. It removed all finicky science from the proceedings and put the issue squarely up to the bulging biceps and the will to win.

Even though the sight of his starting eyes and the knotted veins on his forehead had prepared me for an effort on the major scale, I gave an involuntary leap as the club came down. It was as if a shell had burst in my immediate neighbourhood. Nor were the effects so very dissimilar to those which a shell would have produced. A gaping chasm opened in the hillside. The air became full of a sort of macedoine of grass, dirt, flowers and beetles. And dimly, in the centre of this moving hash, one perceived the ball, travelling well. Accompanied by about a pound of mixed solids, it cleared the brow and vanished from our sight.

But when we had climbed the steep ascent and reached the green, my heart bled for Poskitt. He had made a gallant effort as ever man made and had reduced the lower slopes to what amounted to a devastated area, but he was lying a full ten feet from the hole and Hemmingway, an unerring putter over the short distance, was safe for three. Unless he could sink this ten-footer and secure a half, it seemed to me inevitable that my old friend must lose the match.

He did not sink it. He tried superbly, but when the ball stopped rolling three inches separated it from the hole.

One could see from Hemmingway's bearing as he poised his club that he had no doubts or qualms. A sinister smile curved his thin lips.

"This for it," he said, with sickening complacency.

He drew back the clubhead, paused for an instant, and brought it down.

And, as he did so, Poskitt coughed.

I have heard much coughing in my time. I am a regular theatre-goer, and I was once at a luncheon where an operatic basso got a crumb in his windpipe. But never have I heard a cough so stupendous as that which Joseph Poskitt emitted at this juncture. It was as if he had put a strong man's whole soul into the thing.

The effect on Wadsworth Hemmingway was disintegrating. Not even his cold self-control could stand up against it. A convulsive start passed through his whole frame. His club jerked forward, and the ball, leaping past the hole, skimmed across the green, took the edge in its stride and shot into the far bunker.

"Sorry," said Poskitt. "Swallowed a fly or something."

There was a moment when all Nature seemed to pause, breathless.

"Umpire," said Hemmingway.

"It's no good appealing to the umpire," said Poskitt. "I know the rules. They covered your bronchial catarrh, and they cover my fly or something. You had better concede the hole and match."

"I will not concede the hole and match."

"Well, then, hurry up and shoot," said Poskitt, looking at his watch, "because my wife's got a big luncheon party today, and I shall get hell if I'm late."

"Ah!" said Hemmingway.

"Well, snap into it," said Poskitt.

"I beg your pardon?"

"I said, 'Snap into it'."

"Why?"

"Because I want to go home."

Hemmingway pulled up the knees of his trousers and sat down.

"Your domestic arrangements have nothing to do with me," he said. "The rules allow me five minutes between strokes. I propose to take them."

I could see that Poskitt was shaken. He looked at his watch again.

"All right," he said. "I can manage another five minutes."

"You will have to manage a little more than that," said Hemmingway.

"With my next stroke I shall miss the ball. I shall then rest for another five minutes. I shall then miss the ball again. . . ."

"But we can't go on all day."

"Why not?"

"I must be at that lunch."

"Then what I would suggest is that you pick up and concede the hole and match."

"Caddie," said Poskitt.

"Sir?" said the caddie.

"Go to the club and get my house on the phone and tell my wife that I am unavoidably detained and shall not be able to attend that luncheon party."

He turned to me.

"Is this five minutes business really right?"

"Would you care to look at my book of the rules?" said Hemmingway. "I have it here in my bag."

"Five minutes," mused Poskitt.

"And as four and half have now elapsed," said Hemmingway, "I will now go and play my third."

He disappeared.

"Missed it," he said, returning and sitting down again. The caddie came back.

"Well?"

"The lady said, 'Oh, yeah?'"

"She said what?"

"'Oh, yeah?' I tell her what you tell me to tell her and she said 'Oh, yeah?'"

I saw Poskitt's face pale. Nor was I surprised. Any husband would pale if his wife, in response to his telephone message that he proposed to absent himself from her important luncheon party, replied "Oh, yeah?" And of all such husbands, Joseph Poskitt was the one who might be expected to pale most. Like so many of these big, muscle-bound men, he was a mere serf in the home. His wife ruled him with an unremitting firmness from the day they had stepped across the threshold of St. Peter's, Eaton Square.

He chewed his lower lip thoughtfully.

"You're sure it wasn't 'Oh, *yes*'—like that—without the mark of interrogation—as much as to say that she quite understood and that it would be perfectly all right?"

"She said, 'Oh, yeah?'"

"H'm," said Poskitt.

I walked away. I could not bear the spectacle of this old friend of mine in travail. What wives do to their husbands who at the eleventh hour edge out of important luncheon parties I am not able, as a bachelor, to say, but a mere glance was enough to tell me that in the Poskitt home, at least, it was something special. And yet to pick up and lose the first cup he had ever had a chance of winning. . . . No wonder Joseph Poskitt clutched his hair and rolled his eyes.

And so, as I say, I strolled off, and my wandering footsteps took me in the direction of the practice tee. Wilmot Byng was there, with an iron and a dozen balls.

He looked up, as I approached, with a pitiful eagerness.

"Is it over?"

"Not yet."

"They haven't holed out?"

"Not yet."

"But they must have done," said Wilmot, amazed. "I saw them both land on the green."

"Poskitt has played three and is lying dead."

"Well, where's Hemmingway?"

I peered round the bush which hides the eighteenth green from the practicing tee.

"Just about to play five from the far bunker."

"And Poskitt is dead in three?"

"Yes."

"Well, then . . ."

I explained the circumstances. Wilmot was aghast.

"But what's going to happen?"

I shook my head sadly.

"I fear that Poskitt has no alternative but to pick up. His wife, informed over the telephone that he would not be back to lunch, said 'Oh, yeah?'"

For a space Wilmot Byng stood brooding.

"You'd better be getting along," he advised. "From what you tell me, this seems to be one of those matches where an umpire on the spot is rather required."

I did so, for I could see that there was much in what he said. I found Poskitt pacing the green. Hemmingway climbed out of the bunker a moment later to announce that he had once more been unsuccessful in striking the ball.

He seemed disposed to conversation.

"A lot of wasps there are about this summer," he said. "One sang right past my ear just then."

"I wish it had bitten you," said Poskitt.

"Wasps," replied Hemmingway, who dabbled in Natural History, "do not bite. They sting. You are thinking of snakes."

"Your society would make anyone think of snakes."

"Gentlemen," I said. "Gentlemen!"

Saddened, I strolled away again. Golf to me is a sacred thing, and it pained me to see it played in this spirit. Moreover, I was beginning to want my lunch. It was partly the desire to converse with a rational human being and partly the reflection that he could pop into the clubhouse and bring me out a couple of ham sandwiches that led me to seek Wilmot Byng again. I made my way to the practice tee, and as I came in sight of it, I stopped dead.

Wilmot Byng, facing the bunker, was addressing a ball with his iron. And standing in the bunker, his club languidly raised for his sixth, or it may have been his seventh, was Wadsworth Hemmingway.

The next moment Wilmot had swung, and almost simultaneously a piercing cry of agony rang out over the countryside. A magnificent low, raking shot, with every ounce of wrist and weight behind it, had taken Hemmingway on the left leg.

Wilmot turned to me, and in his eyes there was the light which comes into the eyes of those who have set themselves a task and accomplished it.

"You'll have to disqualify that bird," he said. "He has dropped his club in a bunker."

Little (said the Oldest Member) remains to be told. When, accompanied by Wilmot, I returned to the green, I formally awarded the match and cup to Poskitt, at the same time condoling with his opponent on having had the bad luck to be in the line of flight of somebody's random practice drive. These things, I pointed out, were all in the game and must be accepted as rubs of the green. I added that Wilmot was prepared to apologize, and Wilmot said, Yes, fully prepared. Hemmingway was, however, none too well pleased, I fear, and shortly afterwards he left us, his last words being that he proposed to bring an action against Wilmot in the civil courts.

The young fellow appeared not to have heard the threat. He was gazing at Poskitt, pale but resolute.

"Mr. Poskitt," he said. "May I have a word with you?"

"A thousand," replied Poskitt, beaming on his benefactor, for whom it was plain that he had now taken a fancy amounting to adoration. "But later on, if you don't mind. I have to run like a . . ."

"Mr. Poskitt, I love your daughter."

"So do I," said Poskitt. "Very nice girl."

"I want to marry her."

"Well, why don't you?"

"You will give your consent?"

A kindly smile flickered over my old friend's face. He looked at his watch again, then patted Wilmot affectionately on the shoulder.

"I will do better than that, my boy," he said. "I will formally refuse my consent. I will forbid the match *in toto* and oppose it root and branch. That will fix everything nicely. When you have been married as long as I have, you will know that what these things require is tact and the proper handling."

And so it proved. Two minutes after Poskitt had announced that young Wilmot Byng wished to marry their daughter Gwendoline and that he, Poskitt, was resolved that this should be done only over his, Poskitt's, dead body, Mrs. Poskitt was sketching out the preliminary arrangements for the sacred ceremony. It took place a few weeks later at a fashionable church with full choral effects, and all were agreed that the Bishop had seldom been in finer voice. The bride, as one was able to see from the photographs in the illustrated weekly papers, looked charming.

A Chicago boxer drifting down South gets thrown in jail for trespassing on railroad property. The authorities, interested in boxing, let him out to fight in local matches. Not much of a life for the lad but the storytelling is superb. Originally presented in the Saturday Evening Post, *the story also appeared in* The Best American Short Stories 1965. *Author L. J. Amster worked as a writer and publicist for newspapers, radio, movies, and television in New York and Hollywood.*

L. J. Amster

CENTER OF GRAVITY (1964)

THE RAILROAD YARD BULL SQUINTED closely at the picture on the card that said I was licensed to box in Illinois.

"This you, boy?"

"Uh-huh."

The picture showed me when my nose was freshly broken and swollen across the hollow on each side, and the photographer, while setting up his camera, had warned me not to smile if I meant to use it on a license. That photographer was a champion. He was careful about the smiling but placed me in front of a flowery chintz drape, and when the picture was developed I looked as if I were wearing a large white flower behind my right ear.

"It does favor you some," the yard bull said. "Reckon it is you, awright."

"Usually I take a better picture."

"Well now," he said. "Funny you bein' a fighter. My name's Crumbaugh. I run the fights down to the opera house in Balmoral. Reckon you in shape to fight tomorrow evenin'?"

"Tomorrow? What about this?"

We were standing in the back room of a barbershop in a gritty railroad town where the barber served as the justice of the peace, and I was waiting to be tried for trespassing on railroad property.

Now the justice of the peace sat at a scarred, rolltop desk and wrote on a printed form. Under his close-cropped, iron-gray hair, the skin was speckled. He finished writing with a flourish that upset a soapy shaving brush on the desk. He wiped the desk with his sleeve and looked up.

"Well now, Andy," the justice of the peace said.

The yard bull said, "He's charged like that other boy."

The justice of the peace slapped the desk, and his metallic-looking head trembled. "Sergeant Crumbaugh, you know the law same's me. Now you charge this prisoner right and proper. Like he was arrested separate and by hisself."

"Awright, Judge. Awright. I charge this prisoner with trepassing. I arrested him off a gondola car on Train 119 on the bridge between here and Balmoral."

"Well now," the justice of the peace said. "That's the right way to do." He pointed the shaving brush at me. "How you pleading, boy?"

". . . ."

"Ten days." He became a barber again. "Now you all git. I got a customer waiting in the chair."

The barber went out, and Crumbaugh stepped in front of me. He pushed his long, pinched face forward. "Wait up, boy. About tomorrow evenin'. I got a boy coming over from Ridgeview Arsenal; reckon you and him weigh about the same."

"You know where I'll be."

"Well now," he said. "The sheriff and me are real good buddies. I reckon he'll let you out to fight."

He followed me to the door. "I'll call him while you on your way up there."

Outside, a van was waiting. A tall character, shaped like an elongated diamond, with narrow, muscular shoulders and a small, square face, leaned against the side of the van and picked absently at something in the palm of one hand. He wore a badge, a shoulder holster and gun, sunglasses and a baseball cap. I guessed he was a deputy sheriff.

When he saw us, the deputy pushed the cap back on his head and scratched his forehead. "Time you was inside, I thought you giving this boy a regular jury trial."

"Now, Dero," Crumbaugh said. His jaws, which were fastened far back on his head, loosened in a wide smile. "We wasn't no time at all." He caught my arm as I was climbing into the van. "I'll be up to see the sheriff myself. First thing tomorrow."

The deputy stood aside. "Come on, boy. We ain't got all day."

I entered the van. The Negro with whom I had shared the gondola in silence through the previous night sat on a bench on one side. He was a broad-shouldered, squat citizen and now he sat calmly, his large hands over his knees, looking like someone who was going to a job he didn't like but could do as well as anyone.

"We just missed having a crowd," I said.

"Umh. Those fellers in the cars near the end of the train was close to the other side of the bridge."

"Lucky us. We were in the middle."

"You tellin' me. We couldn't go nowheres. 'Less we had us a pair of wings. That bridge is eighty feet down. I know that bridge. I worked on it to build it."

"Your home around here?" I said it in a way he understood. Home was a point of departure.

"Not lately. Where's your home?"

"Home is where I hang my head."

"Yeah," he said. "Where you from mostly?"

"Chicago," I said. "Mostly Chicago."

I couldn't tell whether he was thinking about it, and soon he began to sing softly:

"Oh, you rob me of my silver,
You rob me of my gol'.
I'll be damn'
If you rob me
Of my soul . . .

"Love, o love, o careless love.
Love, o love, o careless love
Love, o love,
O careless love,
O you see
What love has done to me . . ."

He sang it all the way to the jail, and I settled back, my eyes closed, measuring the length of the ride by the number of verses and choruses. He sang clearly and with dignity, like a man who is often alone and his own judge, sounding the notes truly and sliding off into a minor tone that came up from a time and place long past and suggested something beyond the actual meaning of the words.

It must have been fourteen verses and choruses from the barbershop to the Onager County jail, a square structure of great rough-hewn stone blocks. Wind, weather and time had scored the surface of the stone and left flecks sticking out like barnacles.

The deputy ordered us inside the building. We entered the office, where an old man who limped crookedly received us. The old man was the turnkey. He had a growth on his face that made him look as if he carried a ball of tobacco in his mouth.

The deputy said, "They all yours, Bubber."

The turnkey nodded toward a narrow door behind him. "Sheriff's in the hopper, Dero," he said.

We heard the sound of a sudden rush of water. The narrow door was thrown open, and a character several inches taller than the tall deputy and wider in the hips came toward us. He was an older version of the deputy, and his small, square face hung protected between his shoulders.

The sheriff looked at me. "You the boy Crumbaugh was tellin' about?"

"Him and Crumbaugh appeared to be plottin' something," the deputy said. "Maybe a jailbreak."

The turnkey thought that was a funny notion and laughed, causing the growth on his face to jiggle loosely.

The sheriff said, "You best go on home now, Dero. Clarice is waitin' on you."

"Yah. Got to take her by the doctor's," the deputy said. He scratched his head through the baseball cap. "Be back after a while, I reckon." He turned to go out, ducking his head through a doorway.

The sheriff pointed to the Negro and told the turnkey, "Take him in, Bubber."

When we were alone, the sheriff settled himself deliberately in a swivel chair and stretched his long legs. He stared at his shoes.

"Tell me you a fighter," he said. He lifted his head and examined me. "How long you been fightin', boy?"

"About three years."

He was skeptical. "You ain't got the marks."

"I don't want 'em."

"When you fight last?"

"A week ago."

He raised one leg and dropped it over the other. But he didn't ask about the fight and it was just as well. That one wasn't a fight at all but another one of those things.

My opponent had been a local favorite, a young farmer with thick, plowman's shoulders and awkward, heavy legs. It was his seventh fight and he had won each time before. The matchmaker, his cousin, was very hopeful about the boy's prospects and spoke of taking him to New York sometime soon.

After the first round, I let him set the pace, but he was weary and moved slowly. He pawed tiredly at my face but didn't land a blow. I knew I had to work quickly. In the third round I moved in fast, caught a punch on my glove and fell to the floor, and he was too tired to show surprise. But it would look good in his record. I was a fighter from a big city.

Later, in the dressing room, the matchmaker gave me some money and waited till I counted it.

"That's right, ain't it?" he said. "Fifteen dollars."

"Tell you what. Give me another fin and you can have my stuff too." The ring clothes lay on a chair. "Five bucks. For the shoes, trunks, mouthpiece, jock, towel and bag." I held up the satiny blue trunks so he could see the white, six-pointed star stitched to the left leg. "I'll throw in the star too."

"What's that?"

"It's for good luck. The Star of David. A family heirloom."

"You said five dollars?"

He paid me and hurriedly pushed the clothes into the bag. His hurry was unnecessary. I wasn't going to change my mind.

That was a week ago.

The sheriff said, "Andy Crumbaugh says you wanna go down to Balmoral."

"He said you might let me go."

"I'm thinkin' about it," he said, and looked thoughtful. "If I do let you go, it ain't for good and all. You comin' back here to finish your time."

"It's only ten days, Sheriff. I can count ten days."

"Yah. You figure you in good shape to fight?"

"More or less."

"This boy Crumbaugh's fixin' for you to fight is mighty rough. Seen him fight a time or two. Corporal Valiant."

"It might be a good fight."

But the sheriff seemed worried. "What I'm thinkin' about is if you was to get hurt real bad. I'd be in trouble."

"Ummm . . ."

"Yah. You may be just a plain damn fool," the sheriff said. "Now you let me tell you somethin'. A while ago we had a boy here claimed to be a fighter. The old sheriff went and took this boy down to Roxburgh. Well, this boy got a bad knock on the head and he died. . . . Still," he said, "I sure'd like to take you down there."

"It's up to you, Sheriff."

"Well now, I got to make up my mind. I'll let you know in time."

"OK."

"Meanwhile," he said, "you rest up good. If you do go down there, I want you to put a good show for them folks."

He shifted in his chair and called out, "Say, Bubber!"

The barred door swung inward and the turnkey stood in the opening. "He ready?"

"Yah."

I entered a large, rectangular room with two rows of cells, one above the other, fitted into three walls. The far wall was given over to a pair of tall, barred windows. On the left, a stairway led to the catwalk halfway up the walls. At a table in the middle of the room, some men sat huddled and doing nothing. They looked up briefly and without recognition.

I said, "This is a pretty old building, eh?"

"It's old but it ain't pretty," the turnkey said. "More'n a hundred and seventy years, I reckon. Sign out front'll tell you all about it, time you leave here."

"A lot of history,"

"Yah. You take the end cell up there."

"What time do you feed in here?"

"Not till mornin' now."

"Can I get something from outside? I'll pay for it."

"Got to ask the sheriff, boy. You come down in a little bit."

I climbed the stairway and went along the catwalk to my cell, which was open like all the others. The door was a solid wooden slab, frozen against the wall, and its hinges were thick with rust. It looked like a lot of history, all right.

The only light in the cell came from a single bulb near the ceiling, which gave off a dull glow. There were two narrow cots, each with a thin mattress and a dark cotton blanket. The bedding smelled strongly of disinfectant. I didn't like the smell but it reassured me. No bug could hold out against anything that smelled like that.

I tried to move one of the cots away from the cold-sweating wall, but it was held in place by a metal band bolted to the floor. Scabs of rust covered the frame, and they broke under the pressure of my grip.

Then I heard footsteps on the catwalk behind me, and a shadow darkened the cell. I turned around. A citizen about my age stood in the doorway. He wore a bright yellow sweat shirt, and his long blond hair hung down over his forehead. His lips were turned out and he seemed to be laughing, but there was no humor in his face.

"What you fixin' to do?" he asked.

"Trying to rearrange the furniture. To make it more homey."

"Hah." He tossed his head, and the hair fell like a tassel.

"How long you gonna be here?"

"Ten days."

He pressed his lips together and seemed to be pouting.

"Of course, if I like it here I may stay longer," I said.

He blew out his breath. "Ten days. I could do that on my ear now," he said. "I been here eight months."

"Yeah?"

"Been a-waitin' on a trial."

"What for?"

"I done shot a feller." He said it calmly, but it didn't sound like an accident.

He inclined his head toward the cell next to mine and said, "This here's where I stay."

I looked in. His cell had more light. There was a pink-colored gooseneck lamp on a low table beside a framed picture of a flat-faced girl. A second picture of the girl hung on the wall over his bed, which was furnished with sheets and an encased pillow. I saw a bench, an electric grill and what looked like a box of canned foods.

"All the comforts," I said. "Is that your girl?"

"My wife. I made them pitchers. Hand-painted 'em."

"Ummm?"

"That's the line I follow—artist."

He told me his name was Harrington. He was a Virginian and until his arrest had worked in a factory where they made religious articles. It was a large place, Harrington told me, and employed more than 400 people. It was owned by a man named Koch. Harrington didn't mind being in jail so long as the sheriff let his wife come to see him every weekend. He believed his lawyer would get him out.

I said, "I've got to go down to see the turnkey."

"What's your name?"

"Benjamin. John Benjamin."

"What kind of name is that? What nationality?"

"Cafeterian," I said. "Like Jeff Davis's boy, Judah Benjamin."

"Huh?"

"It's history."

Going down the stairs, my shoes made a loud clatter, but none of the men at the table looked up. Each one sat as if apart, measuring his personal time by the pulsebeats in this temple. Their faces were leaden, like lids that covered some highly inflammable secret longing. They gazed at the barred door as though they expected it to open suddenly and leave them unguarded so they could rush out wildly to make a life or destroy one.

The Negro with whom I had been arrested stood alone at the side of the room, next to a radiator. When he saw me coming, his face opened in a broad grin that lighted up his dark skin.

"How you makin' it?" he asked.

"So far it's a draw. You hungry?"

"Well," he said, "I ain't hongry, rightly enough. But I could eat a little somethin' to keep from *gettin'* hongry."

"Good enough. I'm trying to ding the turnkey into buying me some food outside. He's got to ask the sheriff if it's OK. Go on up to my cell and wait, huh? It's the last one on this side."

I noticed that he was looking past me, and I turned. I saw a guy leaning against the wall beside the window, and he stared hard at me. His face tightened like a fist and he worked his mouth as if to spit.

"He looks unhappy," I said.

"That's one thing sure."

The other man twisted his face angrily. I waited, watching him. He wore tight-fitting denims, Western boots and a wide belt which was drawn through a heavy buckle. His fingers played with the buckle, and I looked at it. I saw the embossed steer's head and the word TEXAS.

"Let's go," I said to the Negro. "That character needs a lot of room for his misery."

"Yeah man," the Negro said. "He's gonna need all this world and the next one too."

As we walked together to the stairway, I whistled "The Eyes of Texas," but it went unnoticed. I went on to the barred door. On the other side, the turnkey sat at the desk and teased a mongrel dog with a bone. Each time the dog tried to get the bone, the turnkey slapped its muzzle sharply and the animal cringed, crawling backward under the desk. Then the turnkey made another attempt to lure the dog from its shelter.

"You speak to the sheriff?" I asked.

"Hold up, boy," the turnkey said. I didn't know whether he meant the order for me or the dog. Finally he dropped the bone, but the dog would not leave its safe place under the desk. The turnkey stood up and came toward me, carrying a parcel wrapped in a sheet of newspaper. He pressed the grease-stained package between the bars.

"Sheriff told me to give you this here couple-three sandwiches."

"Thanks."

"You lucky bein' here, boy," the turnkey said. "Sheriff Burden ain't a hard man like some."

"Tell him I appreciate it."

He went back to his chair, picked up the bone and resumed his game with the dog.

I tucked the parcel under my arm and headed for the stairway and went up. The Negro was waiting for me on the catwalk. I asked him to come in, and he followed but remained standing.

"Sit down," I said.

I opened the package and found four crudely made sandwiches, fatty lumps of meat between halves of cold biscuit.

"Ah, Southern cooking."

"Southern cooking ain't bad," the Negro said, "if you got the food to go with it."

"Compliments of Sheriff Burden." I tore the paper and divided the food. "He's a real good buddy," I said.

"He's a new one, I reckon. The other sheriff, he was a little bitty man, could sit on a dime and let his feet hang. A matchbox could hold his clothes."

The cold, gristly meat took some strenuous chewing. I looked down at the piece of newspaper near my hand and read an advertisement. It said that Onager County was 250 years old and would celebrate its anniversary at the annual fair. The advertiser, a company which manufactured surgical appliances, hoped that the coming anniversary would begin another 250 years of happy prosperity for everyone in the county.

I got the last bite of food down, swallowed convulsively and massaged my throat. "Need something to wash this down," I said.

"Yeah man. I'm dry as a wooden god."

We crossed the tier to the washroom and drank from one of the taps. Then we went back to my cell and sat down. He offered me his sack of tobacco.

"Roll one for me," I said.

He tapped some of the dry, brown grains into a paper trough and sealed it with a quick, rolling motion of thumb and forefinger. Then he held it up. "You wet the edge."

I ran the tip of my tongue along the edge of the paper and he pasted it down. He twisted the end of the paper and gave me the cigarette. Then he made another for himself and struck a match.

He drew on his cigarette and let thin wisps of smoke curl around his face. A vague smile of memory touched his mouth and went away. He moved his lips as if trying them before speaking. "Not to change the subject," he said. "I been to Chicago. Went up there one time just to see and be seen. Onliest time in my life I wasn't workin' or scufflin', one."

"You hit the number?"

"Nothing' like that. I stayed in Chicago with a real fine lady. But I reckon all that high livin' got too rich for my blood. I was bound to do something devilish." He waited for the full memory to return. "We was out walking one evening and she meet a lady friend name of Bella. This Bella shake my hand and say, 'Mister Cicero! Oh yeah. I heard a lot about you.' Right then I knowed it was gonna be a mess."

"Careless love."

"I'm tellin' you in front. That's the truth." He hummed the melody, warming it for a moment. Then his mouth opened and he sang:

"Oh, when you wear yo' apron high,
Oh, when you wear yo' apron high,
Oh, when you wear
Yo' apron high,
I can see
That love ain't passed you by. . . ."

I listened, thinking that he sang like a man who had been sick beyond hope and was getting well. Suddenly the light overhead flickered and stopped burning altogether. We went out to the catwalk and looked around. All the cells were dark. But there was a light burning in the washroom and two more in the high ceiling above the cell block.

"Must mean it's bedtime," he said. "Reckon ol' Bones got to go down and get some winks."

"Take it easy, Cicero."

"I got to take it easy. This bein' a ten-day detour and all."

"Good night."

"You be good to yourself, now."

I went into the cell and undressed and made a pillow of my clothes. But the smell of disinfectant was like a steel probe in my nostrils and I blinked wakefully.

A ten-day detour, Cicero had said. All on the same ticket, at no extra cost. Well, I've got it to do. And when it's done it'll be all done. Ten days I could account for. If I could do as much for the rest of my time.

I lay back, thinking of sleep, but it would not come. The reason was plain. A body in motion tends to remain so. It was someone's law. And I had been in motion, moving like someone in flight, and gathering momentum. Now it was piled up inside me, making a quiet turmoil like a bunch of feathers in an electrically charged cylinder.

I thought of sleep again, lying motionless, and finally it came. But the movement of something on my legs stirred me a little and I heard a thin, harsh, sniffling sound. I raised up and awakened instantly and completely.

A large rat stood on the bed, facing me casually and unafraid, like a familiar and docile pet. I went rigid. The rat tensed and braced itself, and I pulled up my knees. The rat scrabbled to retain its footing, and I bent over the side of the cot and picked up a shoe. The rat leaped as I threw the shoe and struck the soft body, turning it in midair. It twisted and dropped to the floor and fled from the cell. It nearly overran the catwalk, scrambled to a stop and dodged away to the left toward the wall. I jumped down and ran after it, but the rat had disappeared.

I spent some minutes trying to shut the thick, wooden door to the cell, but the rust-packed hinges held firm. I was entirely awake and decided to go down and ask the turnkey about moving to another cell. I went along the catwalk, thinking about the rat. He certainly was a big bastard. Probably full of a lot of history too.

The sheriff's office was dimly lighted and empty. I shook the barred door, hoping to bring the turnkey, but there was no response. I turned away and started back to the stairway.

A grimy old citizen in tattered clothing rose from the bench next to the table in the middle of the floor and shouted something.

"What's on your mind?" I asked him, and went over the bench.

"I wanna tell you something."

"I already know something, pop."

"Now, wait a minute," he said. "You don't know what I know."

"It's possible."

"Ah, you admit it," he said. "I've studied it out. I know." He placed a finger against the side of his nose. "It's all a matter of leverage, son. With the right leverage you can move a mountain. Any mountain."

"I thought it was faith."

"Aw," he said, and shook his head. "Used to be a fatalist myself. But I learned different. Take a Chinee."

"Another time, pop."

"You got any tobacco?"

"No. Sorry."

"Well, don't forget what I told you. It's all leverage. Gotta shift the center of gravity. Got the idea?"

He fell back on the bench, covered his face with his hands and began to mumble.

This was some detour. A champion detour.

I climbed to the upper tier and went into the washroom. I found a lean, bony-faced citizen sitting on a campstool, reading a book where the light was best. He looked up and grinned, and the skin puckered slightly over his cheekbones. He wore a shirt and trousers of matching blue, and his feet were stuck into leather slippers.

"How're you?" he said. His voice had a soft, raspy quality, and he spoke out of the side of his mouth. "You're a new arrival."

"Uh-huh."

"I was asleep," he said. "Let me be the last to welcome you to the Onager County Park of Culture and Unrest." He closed the book, leaving a finger sandwiched between the pages, and held it so I could see it was Shakespeare's complete works.

I said, "You a prisoner?"

"Indeed I am. A model prisoner. What's your crime?"

"Trespassing on railroad property."

"Very damned serious."

"What about you?"

"Oh, I'm just making a retreat," he said. "And there's a small technical matter of some alimony."

"You live in Onager?"

"I'm practically a native son. I've lived here almost three years."

"What's the attraction?"

"Onager? It's the Athens of the eastern seaboard. The public library is open five days a week. And it has another big thing in its favor: This area has the only really temperate climate in the entire country. That means a lot to someone born and raised in Los Angeles." His nose twitched and he stood up. "Shall we move to the living room?"

We went out and stopped beside the tall windows. Outside, a row of evenly spaced trees cut the highway into neat sections, and the lights from passing traffic blinked on and off, going by.

"Nice view," he said. "On a clear day, you can see the two-dollar window at the track."

"That's at Balmoral?"

"Yeah. That's one of my lesser vices, betting on horses. That, and talking confidentially to strangers."

I gave him my hand and told him my name.

"Fred Grimm," he said. "Author of Grimm's Law. Which same is: Break up the family and save the home."

There was something familiar about him, standing there with the book in his hand.

I said, "You know Chicago?—the near North Side?"

He shook his head, and this too reminded me of one of my father's friends, a man he always referred to as "F. X. Cleary." They used to meet in the evenings at a place near where we lived. It was the blank side of an office building and they called it "the wailing wall."

"I said, "My father has Shakespeare's plays in Yiddish. He used the book on his job."

"Oh?"

"His job was to read to the cigar makers in a factory while they worked."

"Yeah? I'd like to hear what he thinks of *King Lear*. I'm on it now."

In the distance a smoky haze floated up as if from a faraway fire. I thought about going to bed. "What do you do about the rats in here?"

"Our little four-footed friends been bothering you?"

"The one I saw wasn't little. I hit him with a shoe."

"Good work, John. That'll teach it a human being can be dangerous when cornered."

"If he's got a shoe."

"Indeed."

"I ought to try to get some sleep," I said. "There's a chance I'll need to be in good shape later today."

I told him about my talks with the railroad cop, Crumbaugh, and with the sheriff.

"You're a boxer," he said. "What're you doing rattling around the countryside?"

I moved my head automatically to let the question pass over my shoulder. It was a big question, crowding me, and it seemed to leave little room for an answer. Still, there were some names of cities and people, and Grimm was welcome to these, to make an answer for himself.

"I guess I've been on my way back to Chicago," I said, "From Miami. By the scenic route."

I had gone to Miami with Mickey Lester, a boxing manager I knew from the Chicago gymnasium where I trained. Soon after we arrived in Florida, he made a match for me with a Cuban lightweight named Enrique de los Reyes. The bout was for ten rounds and promised to pay well.

At the end of the bout I was glad it was over. My ribs ached from the pounding on the outside by Enrique and on the inside from the beating of my heart. While I dressed, Lester went out for a while, and when he came back his face looked like he had just made a large donation to a blood bank.

"It's OK, kid," he said.

Of course, it wasn't OK, not by $1,500 worth. Which was the amount of money I would have had left after paying Mickey Lester. The way it was, none of the boxers got paid, because the man who promoted the show had taken all the receipts and flown to Cleveland, where he dropped every dollar in a crap game.

Two days later Mickey Lester came to see me and asked if I could wire Chicago for money to take me home.

"I'm light, kid," Lester said. "Got just enough to get me out to the Coast."

That night I packed a toothbrush and razor into the bag I used for carrying my boxing gear and walked out of the hotel where I was staying, pretending I was just going down to the gym for a workout, and kept walking.

So—there was an answer of a kind to Grimm's question, but he was sharp enough, I saw in his face, to know that I had left out almost everything.

"Guess I'd better hit the kip," I said. "Just in case the sheriff decides to let me go."

"I'd like to see you box, John. I might just go down to Balmoral myself."

"How? Can you get out of here?"

"I can get out easy enough. I'll get an advance from my boss and pay my back alimony."

"How long does this alimony deal go on?"

"Forever. Or until she remarries. Which is the same thing," Grimm said. "She's a paid-up member of the Sodality of Our Lady of Perpetual Emotion, a veritable vixen." He grinned with half his mouth. "Oh, it was an idyll. An actual idyll. I rescued her from a runaway horse. Just like in the movies. Or a bad dream."

He talked like a man who was breaking a long vow of silence, hurriedly, letting the words tumble out and lie where they fell. "The alimony wouldn't be a strain, ordinarily," Grimm said. "But I've got other interests. Conflicting interests. I like to buy books and records. Bach, for instance, has been keeping me broke. Bach and his galloping monasteries. And I like to make a regular contribution to the pari-mutuel machines. So every once in a while I get the shorts."

"Well, maybe I'll see you at the opera house in Balmoral, huh?"

"Yeah. I'll get the dough. You look for me, John. I'll wear a White Russian in my lapel."

"If the sheriff lets me go. He's a nervous type."

"That he is. Always running around hunched over like a dog trying to ride a football."

I turned away and went back to my cell, kicked off my shoes and lay down. I was very tired, and the last thing I remembered was a feeling about my own center of gravity. It seemed to be shifting about a great deal, as if a number of levers were at work under it. It got very complicated, and I was asleep before I could decide which lever was mine.

Bubber, the turnkey, woke me up. He stood over me, shaking his head, and the growth on his face seemed about to fall off. He spoke in a wheedling singsong: "I know you ain't got no worries on your mind, sleepin' like you do."

"What time is it?"

"Past two o'clock. Sheriff wants for you to come down. You got company."

"Anyone I know?"

"Sergeant Crumbaugh," the turnkey said.

I crossed the tier to the washroom, washed some of the sleep from my face and went down to the office. Crumbaugh pumped my hand like an old friend, but the sheriff was silent and looked worried.

"I told you," Crumbaugh said. "It's all fixed. You coming down to Balmoral this evening. Sheriff Burden says he'll carry you down there hisself."

"All I hope is I ain't makin' no mistake." the sheriff said. "You got to put up a good show, boy."

"Yah," Crumbaugh said. "You do that and I'll see you get a little somethin' for it."

"I've been meaning to ask," I said. "How much?"

"Now, boy," Crumbaugh said. "Don't you fret. I ain't one to go back on my honest word. The sheriff'll tell you."

The sheriff swung around in his chair. "Now, you sure you wanna go, boy?"

Crumbaugh answered for me, "Leroy, you talkin' to a boy's a professional fighter."

"This Valiant," I said. "How big is he?"

"You taller'n him," Crumbaugh said. "And you must have got a longer reach. It's a fair match, to my mind."

"I weigh one-thirty-five."

"Like I say," Crumbaugh said. "Valiant weighs about one-forty."

"You think he'll be too heavy for you?" the sheriff asked.

"It depends."

"Ain't hardly no difference at all between you boys," Crumbaugh said. "You got the reach on him."

"I'll need some clothes," I said. "Trunks and shoes."

"Haw! Reckon we can fix you up awright," Crumbaugh said. "One of the boys'll be glad to borrow you his clothes."

"I wear size eight shoes."

"Eighter from Decatur," Crumbaugh said. "I'll remember that, awright."

The sheriff said, "You gonna have a doctor down there this evenin', ain't you?"

"Yah. Ol' Doc Newhouse."

"Well now," the sheriff said. "Doc's awright. Don't you misunderstand me. But he's been actin' mighty moon-happy of late. Looks to me like he's trying to be the sole and only support of half the moonshiners in the county."

"Yet and still," Crumbaugh said. "Folks got a heap of confidence in the old buzzard. He's the best damn coroner the county ever did have."

"You right there, Andy."

"Sheriff Burden," I said, "what're the chances of my getting something to eat? I'll pay for it."

"Well now," the sheriff said, "ain't no need for you to go spendin' your money. Reckon we got somethin' in the kitchen. . . . Eh, Bubber?"

"They some pork chops," the turnkey said.

"You can give him an apple, too," the sheriff said. "They in the bowl."

Bubber went out, and Crumbaugh stood up. "Leroy, I'm much

obliged to you," he said, and shook hands with the sheriff. "You all come to the stage door about half past eight, hah? I'll be waitin' on you."

"Sure. Reckon it'll do to have my brother Dero be this boy's second," the sheriff said.

Crumbaugh frowned. "You tell Dero he don't need to tote his pistol into the ring, now."

The sheriff laughed. "County regulations says a deputy got to be armed long's he's with a prisoner on the outside. But I'll tell Dero to leave it off."

They walked together to the front door, and Crumbaugh went out. Then the turnkey came back from the kitchen, bringing a package wrapped in a page from the Onager newspaper. I took it from him and he motioned me inside the cell block.

"See you later," I said.

I stopped to look in Grimm's cell before going on to my own. He was sleeping soundly, with the blanket drawn up over his mouth, and his long nose stuck out like a fleshy pin. His book lay on the floor beside the cot. I left, thinking I would see him later.

I went into my cell and opened the package. There were three cold pork chops, an apple and four slices of grayish bread that looked half baked. I put aside the bread and ate the chops and the apple, meanwhile reading the newspaper page. The food wasn't much for taste, but it relieved my hunger. I took off my shoes and stretched out. I was reading a letter from a farmer, telling how he had operated a successful rabbit farm for twenty-eight years, when I fell asleep.

Hours later I woke up and stared at the sheet of newspaper stuck to the wall in front of me. Grimm had come in while I was asleep and had written a note on it and pasted it to the wall with a piece of bread.

"Happy boss sent dough to ex-mate," the note said. "I'm getting out. See you tonight. Best luck. Fred Grimm."

I put on my shoes and went out and glanced toward the windows. I saw it was evening. I went down to where Cicero was standing in a cloud of thin steam that floated up from the wet socks on the radiator. The hard-faced Texan was leaning against the wall nearby, and he followed my movements with his eyes.

Cicero seemed different, as though he were feeling strained. I thought it might be the Texan. "Has the cowboy been behaving himself?" I asked.

"Aw, he ain't nothing but face," Cicero said. Then he raised his head and looked over my shoulder. "Mister Step-and-a-half callin' you."

I turned around, and the turnkey beckoned me impatiently.

"Well," I said, "I got to be going."

"You leavin?" Cicero asked.

"I'll be back. Going out for a little while."

"You jivin' me, man."

"No. The sheriff is taking me down to the Balmoral opera house."

"What you gonna do—sing?"

"No. They've got a fight show. I'm supposed to represent the Onager County A.C."

"Well, man," Cicero said. "Take it slow."

The turnkey took me to meet the sheriff, who was waiting in his car at the rear of the building. I got in beside him, but he didn't say anything when I greeted him. He started the car, and I pretended to watch the passing countryside, which was flat and uninteresting. The sheriff seemed to be brooding and kept his eyes fixed on the road.

We approached a bridge, and to the right I saw the railroad bridge where I had been arrested the day before. Then we entered Balmoral, and the sheriff made a sharp turn to his left, passed a number of parked cars and stopped beside a fireplug. I began to get out, but the sheriff held me.

"You sure you in good shape, now?" he asked.

"The doctor'll tell you I'm OK."

The sheriff seemed to plead with me. "I don't aim to be worryin' you, boy. But they's gonna be a mess if anything does happen."

We got out of the car and went to the stage door. We went in and found Crumbaugh and Dero waiting for us. Crumbaugh grinned happily and began to tell the sheriff about the size of the crowd and about some of the people in it.

The opera house still managed to retain its former character, despite the boxing ring and the way the seats were set out. At one end was a curtained stage, standing between elaborately carved but flaking pillars of imitation marble.

In the ring, a bout was under way, and I slowed to watch the fighters, but Crumbaugh went on ahead and halted in front of a door and pushed it open. He beckoned me to come on, and I followed him into the dressing room.

"You go on in the final," he said. He tilted his head in the direction of my adversary of the evening. "That's Valiant."

Valiant was alone, and naked except for a khaki towel around his waist. He sat on a tilted chair, holding a comic book, and ignored me. His pockmarked face looked as though someone in heavy, hobnailed boots had walked on it, and gashes ran though it like trenches. His ears were lumps of child's clay, and his body looked like hard-packed, gray clay too. His arms were tattooed up to the shoulders and the colors were beginning to fade. One tattoo showed a serpent coiled around a wide-handled knife.

"Be back directly," Crumbaugh said, and went away. The sheriff and Dero remained outside.

I closed the door behind me, and Valiant put down the comic book and straightened his chair. He rose and shuffled toward me, moving his feet like a crab and carrying his head like a man going around a corner with an egg in a spoon.

"Ya t'ink yer pretty good, huh?" he asked. His puffed lips, scarred inside, muffled the words.

"I am pretty good," I said.

"I been fightin' twelve years. I fought some of the best."

"You ought to know better. By now."

"Huh?"

"You never won a fight in a dressing room, did you?"

"They said you was from Chicago."

"So?"

"I boxed there many's the times. At the Stadium."

"An outdoor man."

"I beat Eddie Snyder."

"Never heard of him."

"I busted his ribs," Valiant said. "They liked me in Chicago. I done awright there."

"You had a good paper route."

"I never went hungry in Chi, Mac. Not me. I lived like a king."

The king of Chicago. Some monarch.

"They like my action in this burg," Valiant said. "Last week they give me some kid from town. I belted him out in the third round."

"You look like someone who'd hit a kid," I said.

His head jerked around. Then his belligerence gave way and he said, "I know you from somewheres, don't I?"

"Maybe." I put out my hand and said, "My name's Corporal Valiant."

"Sure. Sure. I t'ought I seen you before." But then he got it and pulled his hand out of mine and swung vaguely. "G'wan, ya muzzler," he said. "*I'm* Corporal Valiant."

He shuffled away, spluttering angry and indistinct sounds. He picked up the comic book, threw it down and kicked at it. I watched him, expecting anything, but he didn't look at me.

The door was thrown back violently and Crumbaugh came in with the doctor, a short, bald man whose glasses fell forward on his nose. The doctor carried the usual small, black bag. He also brought in a strong smell of liquor.

"Har ya, boys," the doctor said. He went over to punch Valiant lightly on the arm. Valiant brought up his hands, and the doctor said, "You look pretty good to me, son."

Crumbaugh said, "This boy's Johnny Benjamin, Doc. He's from Chicago."

The doctor came toward me and extended a soft hand. "Glad to know you, Johnny."

"Hello."

"Fine, Fine. Har you feelin'?"

"OK."

"Never had no aches or pains or trouble with your heart?" the doctor asked.

"No."

"Fine. Reckon you boys'll give us a good show this evenin'. May the best one win." He turned to Crumbaugh. "Andy, I will certify that these boys are fit."

"Say, Doctor," I said. "Have you got any extra bandages and absorbent cotton?"

The doctor searched his bag and found several rolls of bandages, and I picked out two which were the right width for my hands. While he looked for the cotton, Dero came in with a pair of damp trunks, a pair of boxing shoes and a jockstrap.

Dero said, "Boy says for you to take care and not lose this stuff."

The doctor closed his bag and said, "Good luck, boys."

"Well now, Doc," Crumbaugh said. "How's about takin' a little snort?" He held the door for the doctor and followed him out.

Dero glanced at me and asked, "You gonna need anything more?"

"I'm all right."

He looked relieved and said, "I'll be out here if you think of anything." He pulled the door back, and Fred Grimm came in. The deputy hesitated, then shrugged and went out.

"Hello, John," Grimm said. "Is it OK for me to visit?"

He had changed his clothes and was freshly shaved. In his hand was the book he had been reading in the jail, the complete Shakespeare.

I said, "I see you made it."

Valiant was dressing, and he acted as though we were not in the same room. He pulled on a pair of purple trunks and slipped his arms through the sleeves of a worn, brown bathrobe. Then he covered his hands with a pair of smelly green-wool bandages, the kind boxers use in training. He seemed to know how to do the bandaging.

Grimm said, "I brought this book along, thinking maybe you'd like to have it."

"You sure?"

"I want you to have it, John."

Valiant stood up and shot his fists at the air, punching at an imaginary target and accompanying the motions with snorting breaths from his nose. Suddenly he stopped shadow boxing and went to the door and left the room without looking at us once.

"Who's he?" Grimm asked.

"My esteemed opponent, Corporal Valiant."

"God," he said. "He must think I'm pretty creepy, bring you a book."

"Well," I said, "it's not a comic book."

"That it ain't," he said.

I began to get ready, and Grimm drew up a chair and sat down. He put the book on a table.

Grimm watched me dress for the fight, observing my actions as though they were a strange ritual. I wound a bandage around my hand, doubled it back and forth over the knuckles and between my fingers, used my teeth to tear the end of the gauze, knotted the two ends to prevent them from parting down the middle, and held out my hand.

"You want me to tie it?" he said. I turned my wrist and held it out to him and he tied the knot.

"That's a square knot," Grimm said. "The only knot I remember from my brief but honorable career in the Navy. I lasted three months till the old man got me out because I was under age."

"Were you sorry?"

"Not at first. I was fourteen. I was a big kid for my age, but the old man could hit harder."

He helped me with the other bandage, and I said, "Too bad the sheriff wants his brother in my corner. You could be my second."

"I wouldn't know what to do."

"Neither will Dero. His job is to keep an eye on me in case I try to escape," I said. "I'll ask Crumbaugh to tell the sheriff I want you in my corner."

"Don't. I tell you I don't know a thing about this business. I've only seen one fight in my life. And I went to that because one of the guys was a guy I knew. It was his last fight."

"Huh?"

"All those semiskilled intellectuals, the sportswriters, were sure he took a dive. But he never regained consciousness."

Under the circumstances, his reminiscences were out of order. But I didn't know how to stop him without shouting at him.

"This guy was really built," he said. "They used him as a model for some damned trophy. That is, they used his body but another model's head. His head was no bigger than a baby's."

"Look," I said. "Let's talk about something else. The batting averages in the Texas League."

Grimm was startled by my tone and stood up. "I didn't mean to get off like that."

He looked uncomfortable, and I said, "You're OK. But on the way down here, I got a big load of worry from the sheriff. And then . . ." I wanted to tell him about Valiant. But I didn't. Valiant was something I'd have to do alone and for myself.

"You want me to leave?"

"OK. Thanks for the book."

"Yeah."

He went out and I was alone. The room was windowless and the door was closed, but I felt chilled. I rubbed some warmth into my arms and punched at the air.

Behind me the door was thrown back and banged against the wall, and the deputy sheriff said, "You ready, boy? It's time now."

"Where're the gloves?"

"They got 'em in the ring, I reckon," Dero said.

I went to the door, taking the book with me. Dero saw it. His mouth opened.

"I don't want to leave this here," I said. "I'll take it with me. And you keep an eye on it in the corner."

"What you sayin', boy?"

"Here, you carry the book. I don't want anybody to clout it." I handed him the book and he took it, looking a little bewildered.

"Let's go," I said. I started down the aisle leading to the ring, and Dero followed me.

Valiant was already in the ring, seated on a low, wooden stool and talking with a soldier who stood beside him. I crawled through the ropes near the vacant corner, and the soldier turned to look at me and turned away again. Dero stayed outside the ring, standing on the apron. My book lay face down on the canvas near his feet.

There was a pair of gloves on the stool. They were damp with sweat and bulged in the wrong places. While Dero tied the laces, I glanced over the crowd, looking for Grimm. But he wasn't in any of the seats close to the ring, and the rest of the auditorium was shrouded in a dense tobacco fog.

Behind me, in the row of seats at ringside, an overstuffed woman who wore a wide, red straw hat pointed to me and said in a loud voice, "I'm bettin' on that boy. He's real cute." The very fat, redfaced man who sat next to her slapped the woman sharply on the thigh, making her rise from her chair. They laughed together, drunkenly.

Waiting like this always produced the sensation of a nervous bladder. It was the adrenal gland pressing on my kidney. I had read about it. Excitement stimulates the adrenal gland, which sends out something to speed up the heart action. It was a hell of a spot to have such a gland, right over the kidney. A familiar sour taste filled my mouth. "Hyperchasidity," my father called it when he told me how a big, brutal guy had threatened to beat him, a small man armed with a thin book. Fear tightened my nerves, and tremors ran under my skin. It was always like this and I was impatient for the first shock of contact.

Crumbaugh climbed into the ring. Someone struck the bell, and the crowd became attentive. Crumbaugh announced: "Folks, this is the fight you all been waitin' on." He went on to introduce Corporal Bobby Valiant from the U.S. Army Arsenal at Ridgeview, and the crowd responded with cheers and whistling. Crumbaugh waited for the noise to subside and then introduced me: "Johnny Benjamin out of Chicago, Illinois." Some of the crowd cheered, perhaps as much for Chicago, Illinois, as for me.

"Neighbors," Crumbaugh said, "I reckon you all would appreciate knowin' that Benjamin is a special protégé of our good sheriff, Leroy Burden. Stand up, Leroy, and take a bow."

When the applause and laughter ended, another man, bald and min-isterial-looking, entered the ring. He wore light-tan trousers and a T-shirt decorated with a picture of an artillery shell surrounded by the words: U.S. ARMY RIDGEVIEW ARSENAL.

Crumbaugh said, "The referee for this bout will be none other than our old friend, Chaplain Downer."

The referee called Valiant and me to the center of the ring and recited the rules in an uncertain voice. He sounded like he was delivering a bene-diction, and it would not have surprised me if his speech had ended. "Go, and sin no more."

"By the way," I said. "I didn't hear anyone mention how many rounds we're supposed to box."

"Ten rounds, son," the referee said.

I went back to my corner, and the bell sounded. I shuffled out to meet Valiant and he came toward me, crouched low and moving crablike, as though he were straddling puddles in a wet street. His hands hung below his knees.

We circled each other, and I jabbed his face lightly and Valiant swung at the same time, aiming for my groin. I dropped my right glove and blocked his swing and Valiant stepped back. His face was unprotected and I pumped my left hand into it, landing solidly. Again, I stuck my left in his face and crossed with a right that pounded his nose. He began to bleed from his nose and he snorted, blowing a bloody spray that speck-led me with red dots. I aimed a jab for his head and he ducked, but I hit him with an uppercut. He crouched lower and swung wildly, and I stopped the blow with my forearm. He started another swing, from be-low his knees, and lunged at me. The punch landed on the side of my head, but there was no force in it. My fear went away. I snapped a jab into his face and hit him hard on the jaw with my right. His knees buck-led, but he didn't fall. I jabbed him again, smearing blood over his face, and he stood flat-footed weaving his head from side to side like a snake. Then he rushed, caught me in his arms and wrestled me to the ropes. I tried to twist free and he brought up his head and struck my chin a sharp blow. I felt the quick, smarting pain of the wound as he pressed forward and continued to maul me with his head and shoulders. Finally, I let myself go limp and sagged against the ropes, and his weight carried him with me. I got my knee between his legs and jerked it upward, and he let go and I hit him on the chin as the bell rang. He ignored the bell and threw a punch that went over my head. He spun around, off balance, and was saved from falling by the referee.

Dero, my second, waited for me in the corner, blocking the stool. He was grinning happily and slapped my back as I walked around him.

"Sit down, Benny," he said. "Sit down, boy. You doin' good."

"Who's Benny?"

"You, boy," Dero said. "Heah, have some water."

I brushed the bottle aside and looked down at the patches of wet blood on my chest, belly and arms. Dero took off his baseball cap and flapped it up and down in front of me.

"Don't do that," I said. "You got a towel?"

"Reckon you could use one," he said. But he didn't move.

"Some second!"

He straightened up and laughed softly. "I like to bust a gut seein' you hit that boy's nose every time."

"Why don't you go sit down somewhere?"

"Me? I got to stay right here with you, boy."

I saw the book and reached down with both gloves to pick it up. I gave it to him, and he took it without understanding.

"Read to me," I said.

He stared at me and then lowered his glance to look at the page. He tilted his head and his lips moved silently. He seemed baffled.

"Tell me you readin' this?"

"Yeah. It's in English."

Dero shut the book with a loud noise and tossed it to me. "Boy, I think you gettin' simple, more'n likely."

I laid the book on the canvas next to the ring post and turned around as the bell rang.

Valiant rushed from his corner and stopped abruptly in the center of the ring. He waited, as if daring me to cross an imaginary line. I walked directly up to him, feinted with my left and pounded my right hand into his face. His mouth guard flew out of his mouth and landed near the edge of the ring. Blood ran from his nose. He doubled over and charged at me, flailing with both hands. I was too slow and he landed a low punch that sent a spurt of pain through me. I stepped back, keeping my left hand poised, and waited till the pain stopped. Meanwhile, Valiant pawed at the air between us.

The crowd urged Valiant to hit me again, and he tried to do it. But now I felt stronger and avoided his rushes. I jabbed his face repeatedly and solidly, and landed with a right. Valiant stumbled, shook his head and cursed me.

After that, he made no effort to protect himself but came at me again and again, swinging wildly at my lower body and failing to connect. He was easier to hit now and stumbled oftener, but he replied to my hardest punches by shaking his head and repeating his curses.

Some of them, when they're like that, are hard to stop with anything less than a baseball bat. They're all disarranged inside and you hit them on the chin, getting all your weight into it, and they only snort and keep moving in.

Valiant swung a long, looping right and I stepped back. He slipped on the bloody canvas and sat down. He looked tired and confused sitting there. I went over to a neutral corner and the referee kneeled and began to count slowly, speaking the numbers into Valiant's ear.

There was no way of telling how much time remained till the end of the round, but it seemed the referee would use all of it to help Valiant. Then the bell rang and Valiant's second came out and escorted his fighter to the corner, where he dropped to the stool.

When I reached my corner, Dero was trying to get my stool into the ring. He had been drinking and managed the stool with difficulty. Eventually he got it through the ropes and set it down.

"Now, they-ah," he said.

"Thanks."

"You awright, boy? You want anything?"

I didn't answer but let my hands droop and breathed deeply.

"Reckon you got a cut on your chin, Benny-boy," Dero said. "Heah, lemme look at it."

"Leave it alone. It's nothing."

"Nothin'?"

I was restless and impatient for the bout to resume. I stood up, and my action brought a drunken shout from the overstuffed woman in the red straw hat.

Dero said, "Reckon you think I'm useless."

"You're giving yourself the best of it, boy."

"Yah," he said. "I figure you oughta take him in the next round."

"What round is it?"

He cocked his head and looked suspicious. "The third," he said.

"Right. You're smart."

Dero took a deep breath and faced me squarely. "You know what, Benny-boy? You can just go—" His speech was heard by the people at ringside, and he left the ring amid the sound of laughter and cheers. The bell rang, silencing the laughter.

Valiant shuffled from his corner, looking white-faced and wary. When I came near him, he gathered himself and launched a desperate swing. I saw him start it and stepped inside, and hit him hard on the jaw. He sank to the floor and sprawled there, conscious and muttering curses.

The referee waved me to the side of the ring and dropped to one knee and began to count. This time I could hear him.

". . . nine," the referee said.

Suddenly Valiant sprang to his feet and dashed toward his corner. He grabbed his towel and bathrobe and began to leave the ring. The referee ran after him and tried to hold him, but Valiant wrenched loose.

"To hell with that fink," Valiant shouted. He succeeded in freeing himself from the clutches of his second and jumped down to the floor. The crowd howled in protest and several men rose in his path, as if to prevent him from leaving.

Valiant lowered his head and charged, and the aisle opened for him. He seemed to be shouting in answer to the crowd, but his words were drowned out by the loud booing. He ran all the way to the dressing room and slammed the door behind him. But the booing persisted, even while the audience was leaving.

The referee came toward me. "You the winner, I reckon," he said, and raised my hand.

He paused, about to say something more, and changed his mind. I walked to my corner. My second had disappeared, but Grimm was waiting for me at the ringside. I saw that he had picked up the book and was holding it under his arm. He untied the laces and pulled the gloves off my hands. They were trembling a little and he noticed it.

"Lousy fight," I said.

"The manly art of self-defense," Grimm said, and smiled with half his mouth.

"You didn't like it, huh?"

"Well," Grimm said, "I'm glad you won."

Sheriff Burden came up, looking very pleased, and pounded my back. He said, "You awright, boy. Sure 'nough." He was half drunk, at least, and felt fine. His drawl was longer than usual. "Yah, yah, boy. You really put it on Valiant, awright." He turned to Grimm. "I got me a fine boy. Ain' 'at so?"

Grimm nodded seriously, and the sheriff said, "You damn right."

"How'd you like to go down to Roxburgh, boy?" the sheriff asked.

"Roxburgh?"

"Yah. They got a couple-three boys down there I'd like to match you up with."

"Your new manager," Grimm said.

"Yeah."

"Go on and get you clothes, boy," the sheriff said. "I got to see a feller a minute." He slapped my back and went away, laughing excitedly.

Grimm walked with me to the door of the dressing room. I looked in and saw that it was empty. I felt relieved.

"You don't have to go," I said to Grimm.

"I guess I can get a later bus."

"Sure."

We went in and I removed the bandages and used them to wipe the blood from my arms and chest. Grimm sat watching me, his face serious. I fingered the cut on my chin and it didn't feel like much.

Sometimes, like now, a dressing room served as a decompression chamber. As the pressure decreased, the fight appeared like a train of separate incidents almost detached from one another. I laughed at the memory of Valiant's face as he left the ring, clawing frantically at the trailing bathrobe.

I was smiling when Crumbaugh and the sheriff came in. The sheriff brought a bottle of liquor and unscrewed the cap, fumbled it drunkenly and dropped it. He kicked the fallen cap aside and held up the bottle.

"Hell's fire," the sheriff said. "Heah's to the evidence."

He pressed the bottle to his lips and drank. Then he passed the bottle to me and said, "Won't hurt you none."

I lifted the bottle and let some of the liquor into my mouth and swallowed. It traveled like a flame along a fuse and exploded in my stomach. I offered the bottle to Grimm. He waved it aside.

"Thanks," Grimm said. "I'll pass." He patted my arm. "Guess I'd better blow."

"Thanks again for the book," I said to his back.

"Andy," the sheriff said, "I'm fixin' to take this boy down to Roxburgh. He'd go good down there, huh?"

Crumbaugh took a long drink, gulped, and gave the bottle to the sheriff. "You going to Roxburgh," Crumbaugh said. "They got a colored boy down there I'd like to see get a beatin'."

"Nawsuh," the sheriff said. "I don't aim for my boy to be fightin' with a nigger. Nawsuh."

"Well," Crumbaugh said, "this boy I got in mind stands in need of a real good beatin'. Ain't no one done it yet."

"I don't know about that," the sheriff said. "We'll see when the time comes. Eh, boy?"

Crumbaugh reached into his pocket and drew out some money and made a fan of five-dollar bills. "This is for you, boy."

"All of it?"

"Yah. You put up a good show this evening." He took the bottle from

the sheriff and drank. When he lowered the bottle, Crumbaugh said, "You know one thing. This moon sure makes a man hongry. I reckon this boy could eat a little something too. What d'you say we drive over to Noreen's, eh, Leroy?"

"She runnin' again?"

"Don't you know that?"

"Well now," the sheriff said, "I got to think of this boy."

"We'll see he don't get to messin' around," Crumbaugh said. "You takin' him to Roxburgh, he's got to keep in training."

There was a burned-out taste in my mouth and my tongue felt like a piece of charred rope. When I wet my lips, the spittle clung to them like a dry ash. It was always like this after a fight.

The sheriff saw the book in my hand and his face wrinkled in puzzlement. "What you totin', boy?" he asked. His glance wandered drunkenly as he examined the cover. "Where you get it?"

"Grimm gave it to me."

"'At's a funny idear, sure enough," Crumbaugh said. "Bringin' a boy a book. A boy 'at's a prizefighter, I mean."

"I can read too."

"Aw now," Crumbaugh said. "I don't mean to say you ignorant, boy."

"How can you tell?" I said, and moved toward the door. But the sheriff stood in my way and raised the bottle to the light. "Reckon we oughta kill this before we go, Andy," he said.

"Be better'n leavin' it lame like it is."

They emptied the bottle without offering me a drink. Then we went out to the car, where the sheriff halted abruptly and searched his pockets for the key to the door, and the jerky motions lifted the bottom of his coat. I saw he was wearing a gun. When he faced around, his look wavered and settled on me. "You drive, boy?"

"Yes."

"Reckon you'll do the driving."

Crumbaugh crowded onto the front seat beside the sheriff. "It's just th' other side of the horse track," he said. "Straight out this road."

"And best you drive careful," the sheriff said. "Don't want no trouble with the laws." He laughed good-naturedly.

I shifted gears, gained speed and drove into the quiet night, listening to the soft sound of the tires on the smooth pavement and the persistent, tuneless whistle of the wind in the power lines overhead. The two men sounded as though they were in another room.

Crumbaugh said, "You ain't been by Noreen's in some while, hah? Been real busy, I reckon."

"Yah. Been busy rightly enough."

"Leroy, what you think about puttin' on a real big fight show durin' fair week? We could take and fill 'at ball park up at Onager and make us a fine piece of money."

"Well now," the sheriff said. "Reckon you'd have to get the county's approval on something such as that."

"Aw, you ought not to have no trouble on that account. Big as you are in the county."

"Big as I am," the sheriff said, "I can't get the money so's I can deputize another three-four men."

"Yet and still, you the high sheriff, Leroy. I ain't aimin' to blow smoke up your nose. Just statin' a fact is all."

"I appreciate you mean rightly," the sheriff said. "Tell you what, Andy. You come up and see me tomorrow, or call me on the phone, one."

"Be mighty glad."

We were coming to the Balmoral racetrack. In the distance, a horse neighed, probably in answer to the sound of the motor. The road curved in the shadow of the high, darkened grandstand and took us toward a huge, flashing electric sign which advertised NOREEN'S INN. Neon horses flickered around the outer edge of the sign.

The inn stood in a glen about a hundred yards back from the road, at the end of a pebbled driveway, and it looked like one of those ancient veterans of the Civil War, dressed and barbered for his last parade on earth. The hedge on each side of the entrance resembled a pair of dusty and ragged muttonchop whiskers, and the tall, fluted columns across the front of the house were like the meaningless military braid on an old soldier's coat.

But whatever anyone might think of its appearance, Noreen's Inn certainly was a popular place. The parking lot in the rear was full to capacity.

The sheriff pointed to a cluster of small cabins beyond the parking lot. "Reckon he can pull up 'side of them cabins, eh, Andy?"

I stopped beside the nearest cabin and began to get out of the car, and the sheriff said, "Wait up, boy. Best you come on out this side. Don't want you takin' a notion to go off by yourself, now."

"What about the book? Will it be safe here?"

"Hah. Never hear of anyone stealin' a book long's I been sheriff."

"I can believe that."

"Y'know somethin'?" Crumbaugh said. "My gran'pappy growed tobacco right here on the old McCobb place."

"Dif'nt times, dif'nt crops," the sheriff said.

"But now, you got to give ol' Noreen her fair credit. They'd be a whole lot more hongry folks in this county anytime she's forced to close down for good and all."

"Ain't likely," the sheriff said. "She got too many powerful friends in the state."

We came to the front door and went in, and it was like stepping unexpectedly into the frenzied atmosphere of a revival meeting. A confusion of excited voices, explosive shrieks and loud music that sounded like a hymn beat against my eardrums. Two large amplifiers brought the music from a jukebox somewhere in the room. It seemed that everyone, including the couples dancing in the center of the floor, was holding a drink of one kind or another.

Some of the crowd recognized the sheriff, but none of them showed any alarm, and a few men looked at him directly and laughed. The sheriff fidgeted and seemed anxious to escape the people who were staring at him.

Crumbaugh saw an empty booth near the bar on the far side of the room and led the way toward it. As we went along, we passed several booths occupied by men and women in close embrace. Crumbaugh enjoyed staring at the embracing couples, but they were oblivious of him.

We came to the empty booth, and Crumbaugh beckoned to a girl standing nearby. She was dressed in tight slacks and a white blouse decorated with pictures of prancing horses.

"Har ya, Lucille?" Crumbaugh said when the girl came to the table.

"Just fine, Andy. What are you all havin'?"

"You tell Noreen me and Sheriff Burden wanna see her, hah?"

"And bring us some hamburgs," the sheriff said.

The girl walked away, and Crumbaugh stared at her rear and wagged his head. "Man, 'at's a real feisty li'l ol' gal," he said.

The sheriff grunted and turned away to watch an old man stagger toward the bar, aiming for it with a fixed, drunken look. "Old Harvey," the sheriff said. "Drunk as a hundred dollars."

The old man reached the bar, but the other customers flattened themselves against it and refused to give him an opening. He sniffed, nodding his head as though it were too heavy. Then he spun around on bent knees and went away, and the people at the bar laughed.

"Hah," Crumbaugh said. "They really put it on old Harvey."

"Sure did," the sheriff said.

A squarely built woman who wore a costume like Lucille's approached the table, smiling broadly. Her very black hair looked as if it had been dyed quite recently.

"Noreen," Crumbaugh said.

"Har you all?" Noreen said. Her voice was deep, like a man's. "How you been keepin' yourself, Sheriff?"

Crumbaugh moved and Noreen sat opposite me. "Don't believe I know this boy," she said.

"Johnny Benjamin."

"You the boy whipped Bobby Valiant," Noreen said. "I am happy to know you."

"See the fight?"

"Naw. But I would've, had I knowed it was gonna happen. It sure did my heart good to hear about it."

"You don't like Valiant?"

"Boy, you ain't sayin' half. Not after what he done to Sissie the other night. Took her out back and like to killed her. He put a knot on her head big as your fist. Wait'll I tell her you here. She's gonna love you to death."

"Nawsuh," the sheriff said. "This boy's in training."

"Hell, Sheriff, I know about fighters," Noreen said. She put her hand on mine. "Don't I, honey?"

"Aw-aw," the sheriff said quickly. "I got to get him to bed real soon."

"You treatin' this boy like a common prisoner."

'It's all right," I said. "The sheriff is interested in my health."

"Yah," the sheriff said.

"Leroy and me fixin' to put on a big show up at the Onager, come fair week," Crumbaugh said.

"'At so?" Noreen asked. "Tell you what. You match him up with Corporal Valiant again and I'll close my place and bring everybody."

"Well now," Crumbaugh said, "that sound like a mighty good idea."

"I'll get me some seats right up by the ringside," Noreen said. "Every time you sock him me and Sissie'll whoop and holler."

"Yah," Crumbaugh said. "A rematch sound like a mighty fine idea, don't it, Leroy?"

"We'll have a drink on it," Noreen said. She stood up and shouted, "Flannagan! Come on out here and meet some folks. And bring a bottle, love. . . . You ain't met Flannagan, Sheriff. My new husband."

"I bet he's a good man," the sheriff said.

"You right there," Noreen said. "He got to be for this li'l ol' gal." She turned to the bar again. "Flannagan! Call Sissie and tell her to come down. . . . Lucky thing I put in that phone system," she said. "It like to saved Sissie's life. . . . Now I'll tell you somethin' you can celebrate, Sheriff. Mavis'll be back in a couple-three days."

"Sure 'nough?" the sheriff said.

Noreen smiled and winked an eye. "I know you'll be mighty glad to see her."

"Well now . . ."

"Ain't no use for you to deny it, Sheriff."

The sheriff turned and tried to hide his face with his hand. But Noreen enjoyed baiting him. "Don't I know it?" she said. "You lookin' a li'l peaked, if I do say so."

The sheriff grinned foolishly. "Mavis is a good li'l ol' gal," he said.

"And so romantic," Noreen said. "She didn't hardly know that boy she run off with. I tried to make her wait awhile and see how things peter out. But not Mavis. Nawsuh."

While Noreen talked, the sheriff became increasingly miserable. He compressed his lips and filled his cheeks with air and slouched in his seat. Then Lucille arrived with the hamburgers and provided a diversion, and the sheriff exhaled noisily in relief.

Noreen lifted the check from Lucille's tray and said, "They my guests, honey."

Lucille nodded silently and turned to go, and Crumbaugh's eyes followed her.

"Ooo-eee, Lucille," Crumbaugh said.

"You takin' that name in vain, Andy," Noreen said. "Lucille gonna get married next weekend."

"Yet and still," Crumbaugh began as a smiling, sandy-haired man in a bartender's jacket came to the table, carrying an unopened bottle of liquor and four glasses.

Noreen said, "Come and set, love. And shake hands with Sheriff Burden and Johnny Benjamin, the boy who whipped Corporal Valiant this evening."

Flannagan squeezed into the booth beside his wife. "That one's a terrible lad," he said with a soft Irish brogue. "When he gets too much of the liquor in him, he loses all his nobility."

It was a funny thing for anyone to say about Valiant.

Flannagan poured generous drinks into the four glasses, and Crumbaugh said, "We shy a glass."

"Noreen and I are drinking outa the one glass," Flannagan said, and his wife smiled warmly.

"To your very good health, gents. And more power to you, Johnny."

The sheriff drank and grunted appreciatively. "'At's right good drinkin' liquor. Whey you gettin it?"

"It's the leprechaun's own brew," Flannagan said. "Distilled and bottled by me own little people."

"Hah. You talking like I was a federal man," the sheriff said.

Flannagan ignored the sheriff's complaint and raised the bottle and shook it. Tiny crystals formed on the surface of the liquor. "We call this 'church whiskey,'" he said, "for you can see the beads on it." He removed the cap. "Have another."

Flannagan watched me drink. "You like it, eh?" he said.

"Uh-huh. One more drink and I'll be seeing my own little people, the leprecohens."

Flannagan filled our glasses and Crumbaugh began to tell him about the fight. It didn't sound like the one I'd been in, but Flannagan listened eagerly. His head bobbed, and twice he interrupted Crumbaugh to ask me, "Is that so, Johnny?"

When Crumbaugh spoke of making another match with Valiant, Flannagan stared at me with round eyes full of wonder. He filled my glass. "Bring on the leprecohens, me boy. It's their night to dance."

"Reckon this boy's had a-plenty," the sheriff said, and looked at his wristwatch. "Time we's making tracks for home."

"Naw," Noreen said. "Sissie'll be here in a minute. You got to wait."

"Sorry, Noreen," the sheriff said. "You coming with us, Andy?"

"Reckon I'll just stay on for a li'l bit," Crumbaugh said. "I'll be awright."

Just then a girl with pale, blond hair came around the end of the bar and walked toward us. The ends of her blouse were tied in a knot under her full bosom. She wore little makeup, and when she smiled the cleft of her chin widened.

Noreen went to meet the girl and brought her to the table. "You know Andy and the sheriff," Noreen said. "And this boy's Johnny Benjamin."

"Har ya, Johnny."

The sheriff remained in his seat, and she passed her hand in front of him. Flannagan gave up his place to the girl. "I'll be getting back to work now," he said.

Noreen said, "By all rights, you got to give Johnny a real big hug and a kiss, Sissie. He whipped that no-'count Valiant this evening up to the opera house."

"Sure enough?"

"That's what I said. This boy's your hero," Noreen said.

"Oh . . ." Sissie leaned across the table and put her arms around my neck. Her mouth found mine quickly.

I heard Noreen laugh and clap her hands. "'At's the way to do, gal. Now give him another 'cause he gonna whip Valiant again."

The sheriff moved out of the booth and stood beside the table. He looked stern. "You folks finished with your damn foolishness, we'd best be on our way."

There was nothing to do about it, and I slid along the seat and got up.

"Reckon you won't mind if we see you all to your car," Noreen said. "We'll go out the back."

Sissie put her hand in mine and we walked on, with the sheriff and Noreen following. It was the damnedest procession.

"Look like Sissie really likes that boy," Noreen said. "They sweet."

The sheriff answered by clearing his throat noisily. When we came to the car, Noreen said, "Now you take good care of him, Sheriff."

"Yah."

"You kiss Johnny good night, Sissie, and we'll go on back."

Sissie dropped my hand and turned and pressed the length of her body against mine while she held me tightly. When we separated, the sheriff said, "Get inna car, boy."

"Want me to drive?" I asked.

"Hell's fire! Not after all 'at smoochin' you doin', boy. You liable to drive us into a ditch."

The sheriff jerked open the door, muttering under his breath. His eyes were narrowed and downcast, and he started the motor with a roar that startled Noreen and Sissie. As the sheriff swung the car about, the two women waved. I waved my hand in return, and the car shot ahead rapidly, passed through the parking lot, careened around the side of the house and went on. A half-minute more and we were back on the highway, going like hell.

The sheriff curved his body over the wheel in a space too small for him and held his foot hard against the accelerator. He paid no attention to the signs that warned of crossroads or railroad tracks. Luckily there was no other traffic on the highway.

My body swayed from side to side as though my head were a balloon. I gave myself up to remembering Sissie's eyes, nose, mouth and the pressure of her body.

The car hit a bump and leaped forward jerkily. "Damn woman," the sheriff said.

"How about slowing down a little?"

"You ain't scared, boy? You s'posed to be a hero."

"Oh, Noreen was only kidding, Sheriff."

"Gimme 'at bottle out of the compartment."

I opened the glove compartment, found a bottle of liquor, uncapped it and handed it to him.

"You wanna drink?" he said.

"No. I'm not driving."

He tilted the bottle to one side and watched the road while he drank. It was a big drink, judging from the number of times he swallowed. He set the bottle between his thighs.

"Now I'm gonna show you somethin'," he said, and reached behind him and brought up his gun. "Watch, boy." Without slowing the car, he began to fire into the darkness on his left, and I heard the noise of shattering glass. He was shooting at the insulators on the power lines and hitting them.

"Pretty good," I said.

He thought so too. "Reckon I ain't much hand with women, but I sure can handle a firin' piece."

He put the gun away and took another long drink from the bottle. "You a good boy," he said. "I'm gonna he'p you. See you take care and train right. You gonna do your roadwork ever' mornin'."

"You gonna let me out to do it?"

"Umm." He shook his head. "Can' let you do 'at, rightly 'nough. You bein' a prisoner and all. But now, you take and run round that tier. Say, fifty times." He mumbled to himself, making some calculations. "Fifty times'd be near two miles."

"Running indoors isn't much good, Sheriff. I need to get a lot of air into my lungs. And I should box three or four rounds every day."

"Huh?"

"Another thing. We could rig up a heavy bag in one of the cells."

"Hells' fire, boy. You in plenty good shape right now." He raised the bottle and drank. "Ain't no need for you to fret so," he said. "You done beat Valiant one time, the shape you in."

"What if he doesn't want to fight me again? You'll have to find someone else."

"Boy' you sure frettin' more'n you oughta. Me and Andy Crumbaugh gonna see about everything."

"I guess you can always arrest Valiant and hold him till he agrees to fight, huh?"

The sheriff laughed loudly. "Hah. 'At's a funny i-dear, boy."

I decided to ask him about moving my cell. "Mine is a damned rat's rest," I said.

"I'll tell Bubber to let you move. You can have Grimm's old cell."

He stopped the car at the rear of the jail, I picked up my book, and we went in together and woke up the turnkey, who was asleep in a chair. Bubber woke slowly, yawning and stretching his thin arms.

"It's you," he said. "Har you feelin'?"

"OK." I was ready for a go at the shadowboxing championship of the world.

Bubber unlocked the door and I entered the cell block hoping to find Cicero. But the room was empty, and the snores of the men asleep in the cells made it seem desolate. I climbed the stairs and went into the cell where I had seen Fred Grimm sleeping. I took off my shoes, put the book under the mattress near my head and lay thinking of Sissie.

When sleep came, I dreamed an old dream. But this time the girl was Sissie.

We were swimming toward each other from opposite sides of a turbulent river, rising and falling with every wave, but drawing closer stroke by stroke. Then there was the final, terrifyingly near yet drawing-away wave, and we were together on the crest of it, holding on and exhausted of everything but tenderness.

I felt myself being shaken and heard the turnkey say, "Get up, boy. It's near ten o'clock."

I raised my head. It throbbed a little, and the cut on my chin felt stiff and raw. The turnkey gave me a cardboard box which held an orange, three egg sandwiches and a container of milk.

"Sheriff said to tell you about doin' your roadwork."

"Not today. I'm breaking training today. I'll start again tomorrow."

"I'm tellin' you like he told me to, boy."

The turnkey left me. I got the book out from under the mattress, propped it against the cardboard box and opened the pages to the play, *King Lear,* which Grimm had been reading. I ate slowly as I read, wanting to finish my breakfast and the play at the same time. But I had eaten the last of the sandwiches and drunk the last sip of milk by the time I arrived at the point in the play where King Lear tells his daughter Cordelia: "Come, let's away to prison. We two alone will sing like birds i' th' cage."

I closed the book and went out to the catwalk and looked down. Cicero was spreading a wet handkerchief on top of the radiator at the side of the room. The Texan with the fancy belt stood nearby, showing Cicero a hard face.

I dressed and went down, wanting to speak to Cicero. As I approached him, some of the prisoners standing near him stepped back, looking quickly at me. Cicero's smile seemed tight and forced.

"What's up?" I asked him, feeling the tension all around me.

"Whyn't yew ask me?" the Texan said, fingering the buckle on his belt.

"OK, I ask you."

I knew it was coming but I waited. It seemed a long time.

"Yew can't be so tough an' a Jew too," the Texan said.

He saw me coming and was ready with his belt. The buckle flashed through the air and I threw up my arm. The buckle struck my wrist, slicing the skin, and I punched him squarely in the face. He fell back, lifted his leg and kicked me in the chest. He swung the belt again, but I caught it and tore it loose from his hand. He was wild with a punch and it gave me time to recover. I slashed at his face and head again and again. He sprang at me and tried to grab the belt, and I hit him on the jaw with my fist. His head struck the radiator and he fell. I chopped at his head with the buckle as he lay on the floor. Then someone rushed in and pulled me away, and I saw it was the deputy, Dero. The sheriff was coming fast from the office.

Dero continued to hold me while the sheriff went over to examine the Texan. I saw the sheriff kneel. Then he raised his head and called two men from the group behind me.

"You carry this boy to my office," the sheriff said. "And the rest of you get in your cells." He asked me, "What you been fightin' about?"

Cicero said. "The man tried to cold-cock him with his damn belt buckle."

"He ain't talking to you," Dero said. "Get in your cell."

Cicero walked away slowly, looking back over his shoulder. The sheriff turned to me and put out his hand. "Gimme that belt, boy."

"I want to keep it. I won it."

He took it from me. "It don't belong to you," he said, and put his hand on my arm. "Now you go on back to your cell."

The sheriff and the deputy went out, and the room became very quiet. I walked to the stairway and climbed up and entered my cell. I felt listless, and when I tried to read, the words seemed foreign. I put down the book, shielded my eyes and fell asleep.

I was awakened by the sounds of commotion in the cell block. I swung off the bed and went out to the catwalk. Down below, the turnkey was herding a group of men, including Cicero, toward the door.

"Hey," I called out, and Cicero waved.

The turnkey said, "C'mon now, all you train riders. You gettin' out."

I saw Harrington, my former next-door neighbor, and asked him, "What's going on?"

"I hear they lettin' all you train riders go," he said. "To make room for some new prisoners—moonshiners. Appears the federal men put on a big raid last evenin'."

I hurried downstairs, and when the turnkey saw me he shook his head. "Not you, boy. You stayin' with us."

"What?"

"Sheriff's orders."

"Where is he?"

"He'll be back directly. You ask him." He let the last of the departing men out and closed the door behind him. I turned back to the stairway and ran up the steps and went along the catwalk to the windows in the far wall. I hoped to see Cicero and to call out to him. I did see someone on the highway who looked like Cicero in the fading light, and I searched along the window for a way to open it. But the window was sealed firmly. I felt frightened, the fear rising in me, causing the skin to tighten over my scalp.

I heard new sounds behind me in the cell block and turned. Dero and the turnkey stood in the midst of the new group of prisoners, directing them to various cells. I guessed that the sheriff had returned, and ran to his office to see.

Sheriff Burden swung around in his swivel chair when I entered his office. "Say, you put us both in bad trouble, boy."

"It's a damn swindle."

"Ummm." He shook his head. "Now I'm forced to hold you. You beat that boy Tex real bad."

Dero, the deputy, came in and leaned against the sheriff's desk and smiled, probably pleased by the way I looked.

"Folks been asking me questions," the sheriff said. "The County Prosecutor, for one. Now we got to wait and see what happens to that boy in the hospital."

I stepped back and turned around and shook the door to call the turnkey.

"You wait up, boy," the sheriff said. "You know I'm gonna he'p you all I can. You my boy."

The turnkey stood in my way, and the sheriff went on. "One more thing. We got to change your cell. Dero'll show you where you stay."

The deputy came up and grasped my arm above the elbow and guided me toward a cell in a corner of the lower tier.

"You go on in, now," Dero said.

"Now? Why?"

"Go on," he said. His hand moved toward his shoulder holster, but instead of pulling his gun he pushed me into the cell. I heard the door slam behind me and the sound of a lock and then there was a sudden silence.

And my fear, feeding on the silence, grew like a wild plant, filling the space around me, making me shrink inside myself. I was more frightened then I had ever been in a whole life of being afraid. And I could not now, as in the past, try to overcome the fear by embracing it, by doing the thing I was afraid to do. There wasn't anything to do.

I sat on the bed and repeated every bitter word I knew, hoping that one of them would give me an anodyne against the fear, but the words had long before been drained of all substance.

I didn't hear the turnkey at the door and was only distantly aware of him as he unlocked the bolt and came in.

"You awright, boy?" he asked. He carried a paper box in both hands. "Got you a present."

I showed no interest and he made a disapproving sound with his tongue. "That ain't the way to do," he said, and put the box on the bed beside me. I saw that the box had come from Noreen's Inn and had been opened.

"Fried chicken," the turnkey said. "And safe to eat. We didn't find no hacksaw blade in it." He laughed.

I wanted him to leave me, but he wasn't ready. "I'll be by in the mornin'," he said. "Long's you here, Sheriff Burden wants you to take care. And I'm to see that you do your roadwork every day now."

The books and stories of Dame Agatha Christie (1890–1976), the doyenne of British crime fiction, continue to fascinate readers throughout the world. In this story we renew acquaintance with her estimable Belgian detective, Hercule Poirot, as he exercises his "little grey cells" to resolve the puzzling question of the sudden death of a chess master who was apparently in good health. Could murder be afoot? Among Agatha Christie's great novels are Peril at End House (1932), Death on the Nile (1938), Blood Will Tell (1951), Murder on the Orient Express (1960), and Sleeping Murder (1976).

Agatha Christie

A CHESS PROBLEM
(1920)

POIROT AND I OFTEN DINED AT A small restaurant in Soho. We were there one evening, when we observed a friend at an adjacent table. It was Inspector Japp, and as there was room at our table, he came and joined us. It was some time since either of us had seen him.

"Never do you drop in to see us nowadays," declared Poirot reproachfully. "Not since the affair of the Yellow Jasmine have we met, and that is nearly a month ago."

"I've been up north—that's why. Take any interest in chess, Moosior Poirot?" Japp asked.

"I have played it, yes."

"Did you see that curious business yesterday? Match between two players of world-wide reputation, and one died during the game?"

"I saw a mention of it. Dr. Savaronoff, the Russian champion, was one of the players, and the other, who succumbed to heart failure, was the brilliant young American, Gilmour Wilson."

"Quite right. Savaronoff beat Rubinstein and became Russian champion some years ago. Wilson is said to be a second Capablanca."

"A very curious occurrence," mused Poirot. "If I mistake not, you have a particular interest in the matter?"

Japp gave a rather embarrassed laugh.

"You've hit it, Moosior Poirot. I'm puzzled. Wilson was sound as a bell—no trace of heart trouble. His death is quite inexplicable."

"You suspect Dr. Savaronoff of putting him out of the way?" I cried.

"Hardly that," said Japp dryly. "I don't think even a Russian would murder another man in order not to be beaten at chess—and anyway, from all I can make out, the boot was likely to be on the other leg. The doctor is supposed to be very hot stuff—second to Lasker they say he is."

Poirot nodded thoughtfully.

"Then what exactly is your little idea?" he asked. "Why should Wilson be poisoned? For, I assume, of course, that it is poison you suspect."

"Naturally. Heart failure means your heart stops beating—that's all there is to that. That's what a doctor says officially at the moment, but privately he tips us the wink that he's not satisfied."

"When it is the autopsy to take place?"

"To-night. Wilson's death was extraordinarily sudden. He seemed quite as usual and was actually moving one of the pieces when he suddenly fell forward—dead!"

"There are very few poisons would act in such a fashion," objected Poirot.

"I know. The autopsy will help us, I expect. But why should any one want Gilmour Wilson out of the way—that's what I'd like to know. Harmless unassuming young fellow. Just come over here from the States, and apparently hadn't an enemy in the world."

"It seems incredible," I mused.

"Not at all," said Poirot, smiling. "Japp has his theory, I can see."

"I have, Moosior Poirot. I don't believe the poison was meant for Wilson—it was meant for the other man."

"Savaronoff?"

"Yes. Savaronoff fell foul of the Bolsheviks at the outbreak of the Revolution. He was even reported killed. In reality he escaped, and for three years endured incredible hardships in the wilds of Siberia. His sufferings were so great that he is now a changed man. His friends and acquaintances declare they would hardly have recognized him. His hair is white, and his whole aspect that of a man terribly aged. He is a semi-invalid, and seldom goes out, living alone with a niece, Sonia Daviloff, and a Russian manservant in a flat down Westminster way. It is possible that he still considers himself a marked man. Certainly he was very unwilling to agree to this chess contest. He refused several times point blank, and it was only when the newspapers took it up and began making a fuss about the 'unsportsmanlike refusal' that he gave in. Gilmour Wilson had gone on challenging him with real Yankee pertinacity, and in the end he got his way. Now I ask you, Moosior Poirot, why wasn't he willing? Because he didn't want attention drawn to him. Didn't want somebody or other to get on his track. That's my solution—Gilmour Wilson got pipped by mistake."

"There is no one who has any private reason to gain by Savaronoff's death?"

"Well, his niece, I suppose. He's recently come into an immense fortune. Left him by Madame Gospoja whose husband was a sugar profiteer under the old regime. They had an affair together once, I believe, and she refused steadfastly to credit the reports of his death."

"Where did the match take place?"

"In Savaronoff's own flat. He's an invalid, as I told you."

"Many people there to watch it?"

"At least a dozen—probably more."

Poirot made an expressive grimace.

"My poor Japp, your task is not an easy one."

"Once I know definitely that Wilson was poisoned, I can get on."

"Has it occurred to you that, in the meantime, supposing your assumption that Savaronoff was the intended victim to be correct, the murderer may try again?"

"Of course it has. Two men are watching Savaronoff's flat."

"That will be very useful if any one should call with a bomb under his arm," said Poirot dryly.

"You're getting interested, Moosior Poirot," said Japp, with a twinkle. "Care to come round to the mortuary and see Wilson's body before the doctors start on it? Who knows, his tie pin may be askew, and that may give you a valuable clue that will solve the mystery."

"My dear Japp, all through dinner my fingers have been itching to rearrange your own tie pin. You permit, yes? Ah! that is much more pleasing to the eye. Yes, by all means, let us go to the mortuary."

I could see that Poirot's attention was completely captivated by this new problem. It was so long since he had shown any interest over any outside case that I was quite rejoiced to see him back in his old form.

For my own part, I felt a deep pity as I looked down upon the motionless form and convulsed face of the hapless young American who had come by his death in such a strange way. Poirot examined the body attentively. There was no mark on it anywhere, except a small scar on the left hand.

"And the doctor says that's a burn, not a cut," explained Japp.

Poirot's attention shifted to the contents of the dead man's pockets which a constable spread out for our inspection. There was nothing much—a handkerchief, keys, notecase filled with notes, and some unimportant letters. But one object standing by itself filled Poirot with interest.

"A chessman!" he explained. "A white bishop. Was that in his pocket?"

"No, clasped in his hand. We had quite a difficulty to get it out of his fingers. It must be returned to Dr. Savaronoff sometime. It's part of a very beautiful set of carved-ivory chessmen."

"Permit me to return it to him. It will make an excuse for my going there."

"Aha!" cried Japp. "So you want to come in on this case?"

"I admit it. So skillfully have you aroused my interest."

"That's fine. Got you away from your brooding. Captain Hastings is pleased, too, I can see."

"Quite right," I said, laughing.

Poirot turned back towards the body.

"No other little detail you can tell me about—him?" he asked.

"I don't think so."

"Not even—that he was left-handed?"

"You're a wizard, Moosior Poirot. How did you know that? He *was* left-handed. Not that it's anything to do with the case."

"Nothing whatever," agreed Poirot hastily, seeing that Japp was slightly ruffled. "My little joke—that was all. I like to play you the trick, you see."

We went out upon an amicable understanding.

The following morning saw us wending our way to Dr. Savaronoff's flat in Westminster.

"Sonia Daviloff," I mused. "It's a pretty name."

Poirot stopped, and threw me a look of despair.

"Always looking for romance! You are incorrigible."

The door of the flat was opened to us by a manservant with a peculiarly wooden face. It seemed impossible to believe that that impassive countenance could ever display emotion.

Poirot presented a card on which Japp had scribbled a few words of introduction, and we were shown into a low, long room furnished with rich hangings and curios. One or two wonderful ikons hung upon the walls, and exquisite Persian rugs lay upon the floor. A samovar stood upon a table.

I was examining one of the ikons which I judged to be of considerable value, and turned to see Poirot prone upon the floor. Beautiful as the rug was, it hardly seemed to me to necessitate such close attention.

"Is it such a very wonderful specimen?" I asked.

"Eh? Oh! the rug? But no, it was not the rug I was remarking. But it *is* a beautiful specimen, far too beautiful to have a large nail wantonly driven through the middle of it. No, Hastings," as I came forward, "the nail is not there now. But the hole remains."

A sudden sound behind us made me spin round, and Poirot spring nimbly to his feet. A girl was standing in the doorway. Her eyes, full upon us, were dark with suspicion. She was of medium height, with a beautiful, rather sullen face, dark-blue eyes, and very black hair which was cut short. Her voice, when she spoke, was rich and sonorous, and completely un-English.

"I fear my uncle will be unable to see you. He is a great invalid."

"That is a pity, but perhaps you will kindly help me instead. You are Mademoiselle Daviloff, are you not?"

"Yes, I am Sonia Daviloff. What is it you want to know?"

"I am making some inquiries about that sad affair the night before last—the death of M. Gilmour Wilson. What can you tell me about it?"

The girl's eyes opened wide.

"He died of heart failure—as he was playing chess."

"The police are not so sure that it was—heart failure, Mademoiselle."

The girl gave a terrified gesture.

"It was true then," she cried. "Ivan was right."

"Who is Ivan, and why do you say he was right?"

"It was Ivan who opened the door to you—and he has already said to me that in his opinion Gilmour Wilson did not die a natural death—that he was poisoned by mistake."

"By mistake?"

"Yes, the poison was meant for my uncle."

She had quite forgotten her first distrust now, and was speaking eagerly.

"Why do you say that, Mademoiselle? Who should wish to poison Dr. Savaronoff?"

She shook her head.

"I do not know. I am all in the dark. And my uncle, he will not trust me. It is natural, perhaps. You see, he hardly knows me. He saw me as a child, and not since till I came to live with him here in London. But this much I do know: he is in fear of something. We have many secret societies in Russia, and one day I overhead something which made me think it was of just such a society he went in fear."

"Mademoiselle, your uncle is still in danger. I must save him. Now recount to me exactly the events of that fatal evening. Show me the chessboard, the table, how the two men sat—everything."

She went to the side of the room and brought out a small table. The top of it was exquisite, inlaid with squares of silver and black to represent a chessboard.

"This was sent to my uncle a few weeks ago as a present, with the request that he use it in the next match he played. It was in the middle of the room—so."

Poirot examined the table with what seemed to me quite unnecessary attention. He was not conducting the inquiry at all as I would have done. Many of his questions seemed to me pointless, and upon really vital matters he seemed to have no questions to ask.

After a minute examination of the table and the exact position it had occupied, he asked to see the chessmen. Sonia Daviloff brought them to him in a box. He examined one or two of them in a perfunctory manner.

"An exquisite set," he murmured absent-mindedly.

Still not a question as to what refreshments there had been, or what people had been present.

I cleared my throat significantly.

"Don't you think, Poirot, that—"

He interrupted me peremptorily.

"Do not think, my friend. Leave all to me. Mademoiselle, is it quite impossible that I should see your uncle?"

A faint smile showed itself on her face.

"He will see you, yes. You understand, it is my part to interview all strangers first."

She disappeared. I heard a murmur of voices in the next room, and a minute later she came back and motioned us to pass into the adjoining room.

The man who lay there on a couch was an imposing figure. Tall, gaunt, with huge bushy eyebrows and white beard, and a face haggard as the result of starvation and hardships, Dr. Savaronoff was a distinct personality.

I noted the peculiar formation of his head, its unusual height. A great chess player must have a great brain, I knew. I could easily understand Dr. Savaronoff's being the second greatest player in the world.

Poirot bowed.

"*M. le Docteur,* may I speak to you alone?"

Savaronoff turned to his niece.

"Leave us, Sonia."

She disappeared obediently.

"Now, sir, what is it?"

"Dr. Savaronoff, you have recently come into an enormous fortune. If you should–die unexpectedly, who inherits it?"

"I have made a will leaving everything to my niece, Sonia Daviloff. You do not suggest–"

"I suggest nothing, but you have not seen your niece since she was a child. It would have been easy for any one to impersonate her."

Savaronoff seemed thunderstruck by the suggestion. Poirot went on easily.

"Enough as to that. I give you the word of warning, that is all. What I want you to do now is to describe to me the game of chess the other evening."

"How do you mean–describe it?"

"Well, I do not play the chess myself, but I understanding that there are various regular ways of beginning–the gambit, do they not call it?"

Dr. Savaronoff smiled a little.

"Ah! I comprehend you now. Wilson opened Ruy Lopez–one of the soundest openings there is, and one frequently adopted in tournaments and matches."

"And how long had you been playing when the tragedy happened?"

"It must have been about the third or fourth move when Wilson suddenly fell forward over the table, stone dead."

Poirot rose to depart. He flung out his last question as though it was of absolutely no importance, but I knew better.

"Had he had anything to eat or drink?"

"A whiskey-and-soda, I think."

"Thank you, Dr. Savaronoff. I will disturb you no longer."

Ivan was in the hall to show us out. Poirot lingered on the threshold. "The flat below this, do you know who lives there?"

"Sir Charles Kingwell, a member of Parliament, sir. It has been let furnished lately, though."

"Thank you."

We went out into the bright winter sunlight.

"Well, really, Poirot," I burst out. "I don't think you've distinguished yourself this time. Surely your questions were very inadequate."

"You think so, Hastings?" Poirot looked at me appealingly. "I was *bouleversé*, yes. What would you have asked?"

I considered the question carefully, and then outlined my scheme to Poirot. He listened with what seemed to be close interest. My monologue lasted until we had nearly reached home.

"Very excellent, very searching, Hastings," said Poirot, as he inserted his key in the door and preceded me up the stairs. "But quite unnecessary."

"Unnecessary!" I cried, amazed. "If the man was poisoned—"

"Aha," cried Poirot, pouncing upon a note which lay on the table. "From Japp. Just as I thought." He flung it over to me. It was brief and to the point. No traces of poison had been found, and there was nothing to show how the man came by his death.

"You see," said Poirot, "our questions would have been quite unnecessary."

"You guessed this beforehand?"

"'Forecast the probable result of the deal,'" quoted Poirot from a recent bridge problem on which I had spent much time. "*Mon ami*, when you do that successfully, you do not call it guessing."

"Don't let's split hairs," I said impatiently, "You foresaw this?"

"I did."

"Why?"

Poirot put his hand into his pockets and pulled out—a white bishop.

"Why," I cried, "you forgot to give it back to Dr. Savaronoff."

"You are in error, my friend. That bishop still reposes in my left-hand pocket. I took its fellow from the box of chessmen Mademoiselle Daviloff kindly permitted me to examine. The plural of one bishop is two bishops."

He sounded the final *s* with a great hiss. I was completely mystified.

"But why did you take it?"

"*Parbleu*, I wanted to see if they were exactly alike."

He stood them on the table side by side.

"Well, they are, of course," I said, "exactly alike."

Poirot looked at them with his head on one side.

"They seem so, I admit. But one should take no fact for granted until it is proved. Bring me, I pray you, my little scales."

With infinite care he weighted the two chessmen, then turned to me with a face alight with triumph.

"I was right. See you, I was right. Impossible to deceive Hercule Poirot!"

He rushed to the telephone—waited impatiently.

"Is that Japp? Ah! Japp, it is you. Hercule Poirot speaks. Watch the manservant, Ivan. On no account let him slip through your fingers. Yes, yes, it is as I say."

He dashed down the receiver and turned to me.

"You see it not, Hastings? I will explain. Wilson was not poisoned, he was electrocuted. A thin metal rod passes up the middle of one of those chessmen. The table was prepared beforehand and set upon a certain spot on the floor. When the bishop was placed upon one of the silver squares, the current passed through Wilson's body, killing him instantly. The only mark was the electric burn upon his hand—his left hand, because he was left-handed. The 'special table' was an extremely cunning piece of mechanism. The table I examined was a duplicate, perfectly innocent. It was substituted for the other immediately after the murder. The thing was worked from the flat below, which, if you remember, was let furnished. But one accomplice at least was in Savaronoff's flat. The girl is an agent of a Russian secret society, working to inherit Savaronoff's money."

"And Ivan?"

"I strongly suspect that Ivan is the girl's confederate."

"It's amazing," I said at last. "Everything fits in. Savaronoff had an inkling of the plot, and that's why he was so averse to playing the match."

Poirot looked at me without speaking. Then he turned abruptly away, and began pacing up and down.

"Have you a book on chess by any chance, *mon ami?*" he asked suddenly.

"I believe I have somewhere."

It took me some time to ferret it out, but I found it at last, and brought it to Poirot, who sank down in a chair and started reading it with the greatest attention.

In about a quarter of an hour the telephone rang. I answered it. It was Japp. Ivan had left the flat, carrying a large bundle. He had sprung into a waiting taxi, and the chase had begun. He was evidently trying to lose his pursuers. In the end he seemed to fancy that he had done so, and had then driven to a big empty house at Hampstead. The house was surrounded.

I recounted all this to Poirot. He merely stared at me as though he scarcely took in what I was saying. He held out the chess book.

"Listen to this, my friend. This is the Ruy Lopez opening. 1 P-K$_4$, P-K$_4$; 2 Kt-KB$_3$, Kt-QB$_3$; 3 B-Kt$_5$. Then there comes a question as to Black's best third move. He has the choice of various defences. It was White's third move that killed Gilmour Wilson, 3B-Kt$_5$. Only the third move—does that say nothing to you?"

I hadn't the least idea what he meant, and told him so.

"Suppose, Hastings, that while you were sitting in this chair, you heard the front door being opened and shut, what would you think?"

"I should think some one had gone out."

"Yes—but there are always two ways of looking at things. Some one gone out—some one come *in*—two totally different things, Hastings. But if you assumed the wrong one, presently some little discrepancy would creep in and show you that you were on the wrong track."

"What does all this mean, Poirot?"

Poirot sprang to his feet with sudden energy.

"It means that I have been a triple imbecile. Quick, quick, to the flat in Westminster. We may yet be in time."

We tore off in a taxi. Poirot returned no answer to my excited questions. We raced up the stairs. Repeated rings and knocks brought no reply, but listening closely I could distinguish a hollow groan coming from within.

The hall porter proved to have a master key, and after a few difficulties he consented to use it.

Poirot went straight to the inner room. A whiff of chloroform met us. On the floor was Sonia Daviloff, gagged and bound, with a great wad of saturated cotton wool over her nose and mouth. Poirot tore it off and began to take measures to restore her. Presently a doctor arrived, and Poirot handed her over to his charge and drew aside with me. There was no sign of Dr. Savaronoff.

"What does it all mean?" I asked, bewildered.

"It means that before two equal deductions I chose the wrong one. You heard me say that it would be easy for any one to impersonate Sonia Daviloff because her uncle had not seen her for so many years?"

"Yes?"

"Well, precisely the opposite held good also. It was equally easy for any one to *impersonate the uncle!*"

"What?"

"Savaronoff *did* die at the outbreak of the Revolution. The man who pretended to have escaped with such terrible hardships, the man so changed 'that his own friends could hardly recognize him,' the man who successfully laid claim to an enormous fortune—is an impostor. He guessed I should get on the right track in the end, so he sent off the honest Ivan on a tortuous wild-goose chase, chloroformed the girl, and got out, having by now doubtless realized most of the securities left by Madam Gospoja."

"But—but who tried to kill him?"

"Nobody tried to kill *him.* Wilson was the intended victim all along."

"But why?"

"My friend, the real Savaronoff was the second greatest chess player in the world. In all probability his impersonator did not even know the rudiments of the game. Certainly he could not sustain the fiction of a match. He tried all he knew to avoid the contest. When that failed, Wilson's doom was sealed. At all costs he must be prevented from discovering that the great Savaronoff did not even know how to play chess. Wilson was fond of the Ruy Lopez opening, and was certain to use it. The false Savaronoff arranged for death to come with the third move, before any complications of defence set in."

"But, my dear Poirot," I persisted, "are we dealing with a lunatic? I quite follow your reasoning, and admit that you must be right, but to kill a man just to sustain his rôle! Surely there were simpler ways out of the difficulty than that! He could have said that his doctor forbade the strain of a match."

Poirot wrinkled his forehead.

"*Certainement*, Hastings," he said, "there were other ways, but none so convincing. Besides, you are assuming that to kill a man is a thing to avoid, are you not? Our imposter's mind, it does not act that way. I put myself in his place, a thing impossible for you. I picture his thoughts. He enjoys himself as the professor at that match. I doubt not he has visited the chess tourneys to study his part. He sits and frowns in thought; he gives the impression that he is thinking great plans, and all the time he laughs in himself. He is aware that two moves are all that he knows—and all that he *need know*. Again, it would appeal to his mind to foresee the events and to make Wilson his own executioner. . . . Oh, yes, Hastings, I begin to understand our friend and his psychology."

I shrugged.

"Well, I suppose you're right, but I can't understand any one running a risk he could so easily avoid."

"Risk!" Poirot snorted. "Where then lay the risk? Would Japp have solved the problem? No; if the false Savaronoff had not made one small mistake he would have run no risk."

"And his mistake?" I asked, although I suspected the answer.

"*Mon ami*, he overlooked the little grey cells of Hercule Poirot."

Poirot has his virtues, but modesty is not one of them.

"Hog" is a big-time football coach at a Southern school. He's horribly over-weight and has heart problems, recruiting violations are looming, and his next opponent is the Alabama Crimson Tide. And we think we've got problems. This is a great story, though, told with panache and humor. First published in the Antioch Review, *it was included in* The Best American Short Stories 1980. *Gordon Weaver has had a distinguished literary career, winning a first in the 1979 O. Henry Prize Stories and achieving the St. Lawrence Award for fiction in 1973. He founded and edited the* Mississippi Review, *and was the editor of* Cedar Creek Press *and for the* Cimarron Review. *His books include* Give Him a Stone *(1975),* The Eight Corners of the World *(1988), and several collections of stories.*

Gordon Weaver

HOG'S HEART
(1980)

*Nor mouth had, no nor mind, expressed
What heart heard of, ghost guessed*

IT IS EVERYTHING AND IT IS NOTHING. Hog says, "Different times, it's different feeling. Sometimes I feel like that it might could just be a feeling."

"Goddammit, Hog," says Dr. Odie Anderson. Hog, perched on the edge of the examination table, feels ridiculous, feet suspended above the floor like a child's, wearing a paper hospital gown that, like a dress, barely covers his scarred knees. Though the air conditioning sighs incessantly, he exudes a light sweat, pasting the gown to his skin, thighs and buttocks cemented to the table's chill metal surface. "Is it chest pain?" the doctor says. "Is it pains in your arm or shoulder? Is it pain you feel in your neck or your jaw?"

Says Hog, "It might could be I just imagine it sometimes." Dr. Odie Anderson, team physician, sits in his swivel chair, shabby coat thrown open, crumpled collar unbuttoned, necktie askew, feet up and crossed on his littered desk. Hog sees the holes in the soles of the doctor's shoes. Odie Anderson's head lolls slightly. His eyes, bulging and glossy, like those of a man with arrested goiter, roll. His tongue probes his cheeks and teeth as if he seeks a particle of his breakfast. He licks his lips, moistens the rim of scraggly beard around his open mouth.

"Damn," says Dr. Anderson, "is it choking? Your breath hard to get? Sick to your stomach a lot?" Hog closes his eyes, wipes sweat from the lids with thumb and forefinger.

"All like that. Sometimes." Hog turns his head to the window before opening his eyes. The rectangle of searing morning light dizzies him. He grips the edge of the table with both hands, feels the trickle of sweat droplets course downward from the tonsure above his jug ears, from the folds of flesh at his throat, from the sausage rolls of fat at the back of his neck, from his armpits. He represses malarial shudders as the air conditioning blows on his bare back where the paper gown gaps.

"You-all want me to send you to Jackson to the hospital? You want all kind of tests, swallowing radioactivity so's they can take movies of your veins?" Almost touching the windowpane, the leaves of a magnolia tree shine in the brilliant light as if filmed with clear grease. One visible blossom appears molded of dull white wax, which will surely melt and run if the sun's rays reach it. A swath of campus lawn shimmers in the heat like green fire. The length of sidewalk Hog can see is empty. The cobbled street beyond is empty, stones buckled.

"Not now," Hog says. "I might could maybe go come spring if I can get off recruiting awhile."

"Well now," Dr. Anderson is saying, "you *are* fat as a damn house, Hog, and your blood pressure *is* high. You might could be a classic case, except you don't smoke and last I heard your old daddy's still kicking up there to Soso."

"Daddy's fine. He's a little bitty man, though. I come by my size favoring Mama's people." A pulpcutter's truck, stacked high as a hayrick with pine logs, passes on the street, headed north toward the Laurel Masonite plant.

"You just as leave get dressed, Hog," the doctor says. "I can't find nothing wrong in there. Hell, damn it to hell, you strong as stump whiskey and mean as a yard dog!" Hog focuses on buttoning his shirt, zipping his fly to evade Dr. Anderson's leering cackle.

Sometimes it is everything. It is the sticky, brittle feel of sweat drying on his skin, the drafty breath of the air conditioning that makes him shudder in spasms, raises goose bumps on his forearms. It is the late August morning's heat and humidity hovering like a cloud outside, waiting to drop on him, clutch him. It is baked streets and sidewalks, the withering campus and lawns, everyone in Hattiesburg driven indoors until dusk brings relief from the glaring sun of south Mississippi.

"Say hey for me to Marice and them big chaps," says Odie Anderson. It is his wife and four sons, the steaming campus of Mississippi Southern University, the athletic dormitory and stadium, the office where his senior assistants wait to review game films, the approach of the season opener at home against Alabama, this fourth year of his five-year contract, two-a-day workouts, and recruiting trips across the Deep South, and a pending NCAA investigation. It is all things now and up to now—his people up at Soso, paying his dues coaching high school and junior college, his professional career cut short by injury in Canada—all things seeming to have come together to shape his conviction of his imminent demise from heart failure.

"We going to whip up on 'Bama, Hog?"

"We die trying," says Hog. They laugh. It is nothing. Hog decides he is not dying, not about to, not subject to be dying. It is something that is probably nothing, and because he cannot define or express it, it is a terror there is no point in fearing.

Fraternity and sorority pep-club banners limply drape the stadium walls. *Beat Bama. Roll Back the Tide. Go Southern. We Back Hog's Boys.* The stadium throws heat into Hog's face like the coils of a kiln. The painted letters swim before his eyes, air pressing him like leaden mist. He consciously begins to reach, pull for each breath, fetid on his tongue. Awash with sweat, he lurches, into the shade of the stadium entrance to his office.

Inside, the dimness of the hall leaves him lightblind, air conditioning a clammy shock, his heaving echoing off the glossy tiles and paneling. Hog finds himself, eyes adjusting, before the Gallery of Greats, a wall-length display of photos and newspaper clippings, trophies and pennants, locked behind glass. This pantheon of Mississippi Southern's finest athletes, record setters, and semi-All Americans is a vanity he cannot resist.

His breathing slows and softens, sweat drying in his clothes as he steps closer. There he is, the great Hog Hammond in the prime of his prowess and renown.

Three pictures of Hog: a senior, nineteen years ago, posed in half-crouch, helmet off to show his bullet head, arms raised shoulder high, fingers curled like talons, vicious animal snarl on his glistening face; Hog, nineteen years ago, down in his three-point stance, right arm lifting to whip the shiver-pad into the throat of an imaginary offensive guard; Hog, snapped in action in the legendary Alabama game nineteen years ago, charging full-tilt, only steps away from brutally dumping the confused Alabama quarterback for a loss. The Alabama quarterback is static, doomed; Hog is motion, power, purpose.

The yellowed newspaper clippings are curled at the edges. *Southern Shocks Ole Miss. Southern Stalemates Mighty Tide. The Hog Signs for Canada Pros.*

Athletic Director Tub Moorman is upon him like an assassin with a garrote, the only warning the quick stink of the dead cigar he chews, laced with the candy odor of his talc and hair oil. Hog feels a catch in his throat, a twinge in his sternum, salivates.

"Best not live on old-timey laurels, Hog," says Athletic Director Tub Moorman. A column of nausea rises from the pit of Hog's belly to his chest, tip swaying into his gullet like a cottonmouth's head. He tenses to hold his windpipe open. "Best look to *this* season," Tub Moorman says.

Hog, pinned against the cool glass of the Gallery of Greats, gags, covers it with a cough.

"I'm directly this minute subject to review game films," he is able to say. Tub Moorman is a butterball, head round as a cookpot, dirty-gray hair slicked with reeking tonic, florid face gleaming with aftershave. He dresses like a New Orleans pimp, white shoes, chartreuse slacks, loud blazer, gaudy jewel in his wide tie, gold digital watch, oversize diamond on his fat pinky, glossy manicured nails. His sour, ashy breath cuts through the carnival of his lotions. He limps slightly from chronic gout.

"This year four," Tub Moorman says. "Year one we don't care much do you win, play what you find when you come on board. Year two, three, your business to scout the ridges and hollows for talent. Year four, we looking to see do you *pro*duce, see do we want to keep you-all in the family after year five. This year four. Root hog or die, hear?" The athletic director laughs without removing his unlit cigar from his mouth. Hog can see the slimy, chewed butt of the cigar, Tub Moorman's wet tongue and stained teeth.

Hog is able to say, "I'm feeling a touch puny today." before he must clamp his lips.

"You *know* we-all mighty high on you, Hog," Tub Moorman says, "you one of us and all." He flicks his lizard's eyes at the gallery's pictures and clippings. "You a great one. Withouten you got injured so soon in Canada, you might could of been *truly* famous as a professional."

"I'm subject to give it all I got," Hog gasps, bile in his mouth.

"It's subject to take it," says the athletic director, "and maybe then some. Fact, you got to beat Alabama or Ole Miss or Georgia Tech or Florida, somebody famous, or we got to be finding us the man will."

"I might could," Hog is able to say without opening his jaws, and, "I got me a nigger place kicker can be the difference."

Tub Moorman's laugh is a gurgling, like the flush of a sewer. "We-all ain't particular," says Tub Moorman, "but the NCAA is. Best not let no *in*vestigators find out your Cuba nigger got a forged transcript, son." Hog hurried to the nearest toilet, the athletic director's stench clinging to him, chest thick with sickness, throat charged with acid, head swimming.

Wretching into the closet commode, Hog blows and bellows like a teased bull, purges his nostrils of the residue of Tub Moorman's smell.

On the portable screen, Alabama routs Ole Miss before a record homecoming crowd at Oxford. Slivers of the sun penetrate the room at the edges of the blackout curtains, casting an eerie illumination on the ceiling. The projector chatters, the air conditioning chugs. Only Sonny McCartney, Hog's coordinator, takes notes, writing a crabbed hand into manila folders, calling for freeze-frames and reruns. Sonny McCartney reminds Hog frequently that national ranking is only a matter of planning, implementation of strategy, time.

Wally Everett, offensive assistant, mans the projector. Once a fleet wide receiver for the Tarheels of North Carolina, he wears a prim and superior expression on his patrician face. Because he wears a jacket and necktie in even the warmest weather, he is sometimes mistaken by students for a professor. Believing there is no excuse for vulgar or obscene language, on or off the playing field, he is a frequent speaker at Fellowship of Christian Athletes banquets. He sits up straight in his chair, one leg crossed over the other at the knee, like a woman, hands, when not operating the projector's levers and buttons, folded in his lap.

The defensive assistant, Gary Lee Stringer, slouches in a chair at the back of the room. He played a rugged noseguard for a small Baptist college in Oklahoma, looks like an aging ex-athlete should, unkempt, moody, unintellectual. He shifts his weight in his chair, stamps his feet often as Alabama's three-deep-at-every-position squad shreds the Rebels on the screen. He snorts, says, "I seen two county fairs and a train, but I ain't never seen nothing like them! Them sumbitches *good*, Hog!"

"The problem," says Sonny McCartney, "is to decide what we can do best against them."

"They execute to perfection," says Wally Everett.

Wally rewinds the film for one more showing. Sonny rereads his notes. Gary Lee Stringer spits a stream of juice from his Red Man cud into the nearby wastebasket. The room is darker with the projector bulb off, the air conditioning louder in the greater silence. Hog holds tightly to the arms of his chair, sensing the formation of an awful formlessness in his chest.

It feels to him as if, at the very center of his heart, a hole, a spot of nothingness, appears. He braces himself. The hole at the center of his heart doubles in size, doubles again; his vital, central substance is disappearing, vanishing without a trace left to rattle against his ribs. He tries to hear the movement of his blood, but there is only the perpetual churning of the air conditioning, the click and snap of the projector being readied.

"Hog," says Gary Lee Stringer, pausing to rise an inch off his chair, break wind with a hard vibrato, "Hog, they going to eat our lunch come opening day."

"Every offense has a defense," Sonny McCartney says.

"There is little argument with basic execution," Wally says.

It will grow, Hog believes, this void in his chest, until he remains, sitting, a hollow shell with useless arms, legs, head. At which point he will be dead. He waits in his chair to die.

"Alabama don't know we have Carabajal," Sonny says.

"Neither does the NC double-A. Yet," Wally says. "But they will if we permit just one person close enough to speak to him."

"Is that tutoring done learned him some English yet?" Gary Lee asks.

"Again?" says Wally, finger on the projector's start button.

"Ain't this a shame?" says Gary Lee. "Our best offense a nigger from Cuba don't talk hardly no English."

"*I* did not forge his transcript," Wally says.

"He *can* kick," says Sonny, and, "Hog?"

Hog, dying, rises from his chair. "You-all discuss this without me," he says and finds he can take a step toward the door. "I got to get me some fresh air, I am feeling puny, boys," says Hog, reaches the door, opens it, leaves, walking slowly, carefully, afraid to bump anything, afraid that he will break like a man made of blown glass, no core left to him at all, no heart.

There is no reason Hog should wake in the still-dark hours of early morning, no stomach upset or troubling dream. At first, he is merely awake, Marice beside him; then his eyes focus, show him the lighter darkness, false dawn at the bedroom windows; and then he sees the ceiling, walls, furniture, the glow of the nightlight from the master bedroom's full bath, the light blanket covering him and his wife, Marice in silhouette, the back of her head studded with curlers. He hears the gentle growl of her snoring. He hears the cooled air cycling through the house on which the mortgage runs past the year 2000.

He lies very still, in the king-size bed, shuts out what he can see and hear and the rich smell of Marice's Shalimar perfume, closes himself away, then knows what has awakened him, so totally, from a deep sleep. Now Hog listens, measures the rhythms, recognizes the subtle reduction in pace, tempo, intensity of his heartbeat. His heart is slowing, and this has awakened him, so that he can die knowing he is dying. There comes a minuscule hesitation, a near-catch, a stutter before the muffled thump of each beat. He lies very still, holds his breath, then inches his left hand free of the cover, moves it into position to press the declining pulse in his right wrist with his forefinger.

His heart will run down like a flywheel yielding up its motion to the darkness of the master bedroom. He is dying here and now, at the moment of false dawn that shows him the shafts of pine trunks in his yard, the wrinkled texture of his new lawn of Bermuda grass. He will die and be discovered by Marice when she wakes to the electric buzz of the alarm on her bedside table.

"Marice," Hog croaks. "Marice." His voice surprises him; how long can a man speak, live, on the momentum of his last heartbeats? "Marice." She groans, turns to him, eyes shut, groping. Her arm comes across his chest, takes hold of his shoulder. She nuzzles his jaw, kisses him clumsily in her half-sleep, presses her head into his throat, her curlers stabbing the soft flesh.

Hog says, "Marice, I do love you and thank you for marrying me, when my people is just redneck pulpcutters and you are from fine high-type people in Biloxi. It is always a wonder to me why you married me when I was just a football player, and now coach, and you was runnerup

Miss Gulf Coast and all. They is mortgage life insurance on the house, Marice, so's you will have the house all paid for."

"Big sweet thing," his wife mumbles into his collarbone.

"No, Marice," he says. "I love you and thank you for giving me our boys. I am dying, Marice, and it is just as good I do now, because we will not beat Alabama or Ole Miss nor nobody big-timey, and the NCAA will likely soon get me for giving a scholarship to a Cuba nigger has to have an interpreter to play football, and we would lose this house and all except I am dying and you will get it because of insurance."

"Lovey, you want me to be sweet for you?" Marice says, kisses his hairy chest, strokes his face, the slick bald crown of his head.

"No," Hog says. "Listen, Marice. Tell me can you hear my heart going." She mutters as he turns her head gently, places her ear against his breast, then resumes her light growling snore.

Dying. Hog lifts her to her side of the bed, throws back the cover, rises, pads out of the master bedroom. Dying, he walks down the hall to the bedrooms where his four sons sleep the perfect sleep of children.

He can stand at the end of the hall, look into both bedrooms, see them sleeping, two to each room, and he stands, looking upon the future of his name and line, stands thinking of his wife and sons, how he loves them, in his wonderful new home with a mortgage that runs beyond the year 2000. Hog thinks it cruel to die when he can see the future sleeping in the two bedrooms.

It is the coming of true dawn, flaring in the windows of his sons' bedrooms, that grants him a reprieve. True dawn comes, lights the trees and grass and the shrubbery outside, stirs a mockingbird to its first notes high in some pine tree, primes his flickering heart to fresh rhythm. He feels it kick into vigor like a refueled engine, then goes to the hall bathroom and sits, grateful and weeping, on the edge of the bathtub, staring at his blank-white toes and toenails and his lavender-tinged white feet, his heart resuming speed and strength for another day.

Marice and his sons are somewhere outside with Daddy and Brother-boy, seeing the new machinery shed or feeding Brother-boy's catfish. Hog's mama serves him a big square of cornbread with a glass of cold butter-milk.

The golden cornbread, straight from the oven, radiates heat like a small sun. Hog bites, chews, swallows, breaks into a film of sweat as he chills his mouth with buttermilk. Not hungry, he gives himself over to the duty of eating for her—bite, chew, swallow, drink—his mama's presence. He sweats more freely with the effort, feels a liquid warmth emerge in his belly, grow. Hog feigns gusto, moans, smacks his lips, slurps for her. A viscous heat squirts into his chest, warming it.

"No more," he says as she reaches toward the pan with a knife to cut him another helping. "Oh, please, Mama, no," says Hog. He tries to smile.

"I want to know what is the matter with my biggest boy," she says. "You say you are feeling some puny, but I know my boy, Euliss. I think you are troubled in your spirit, son."

"I have worries, Mama," he tells her. "We got to play Alabama."

"Is it you and Marice? Is it your family, Euliss, my grandbabies?"

"We all fine, Mama. Truly." He averts his eyes. She does not look right, not his old mama, in this modern kitchen, chrome and Formica and plastic-covered chairs, double oven set in the polished brick wall, blender built into the countertop, bronze-tone refrigerator large as two football lockers, automatic ice-cube maker, frostless, Masonite veneer on the cupboards. Hog remembers her cooking at an iron woodstove, chopping wood for it as skillfully as she took the head off a chicken, while he clung to her long skirts, sucking a sugar-tit. He remembers her buying fifty-pound blocks of ice from the nigger wagon driver from Laurel, taking his tongs and carrying it into the house herself (she wouldn't allow a nigger in her kitchen) until Hog was old enough to fetch and carry for her, his daddy out in the woods cutting pulp timber dawn to dusk.

Hog covers his eyes with his hand to hide the start of tears, hurt and joy mixing in him like a gumbo in a cauldron, that his mama had this fine kitchen in this fine new brick home built by his daddy and Brother-boy on a loan secured by Hog's signature and Hog's life insurance, that his mama is old and will not ever again be like he remembers her, that she will not live forever.

"I do believe my boy is troubled in his soul," Mama says.

"Not my soul, Mama." Hog favors his mama's people, comes by his size from her daddy, a pulpcutter who died before he was born. Hog remembers her telling how her daddy lacked four and one-half fingers from his two hands, cutting pulpwood for Masonite in Laurel all his life until a falling tree killed him. Hog looks at her fingers, at his own.

"Are you right with Jesus, Euliss?" she says. She leans across the table, hands clenched in prayer now. "I pray to Jesus," says his mama, "for my boy Euliss. I pray for him each day and at meeting particular." It is as if a dam bursts somewhere on the margins of Hog's interior, a deluge of tepidness rushing to drown his heart.

"We go to church regular in Hattiesburg, Mama," he is able to say before this spill deprives him of words and will, his heart now a remoteness, like the sound of children swimming in a far pond.

"Pray with me, Euliss," she says. "Oh, pray Jesus ease your trouble, drive doubt and Satan out! Oh, I am praying to You, Jesus, praying up my biggest boy to You!" Her locked hands shake as if she tries to lift a weight too great for her wiry arms, her eyes squeezed shut to see only Blessed Jesus, lips puckered as through she drew the Holy Spirit into her lungs. Hog cannot look.

It is his old mama, old now, who attends the Primitive Baptist Church of Soso, where she wrestles Satan until she falls, frothing, to the floor before the tiny congregation, where she washes the feet of elders, weeping. "Jesus, Jesus, speak to my boy Euliss," she prays in the fine, modern kitchen of the modern brick ranch built on land won by two generations' driving scrub cattle and cutting pulpwood.

Nose clogged with sobbing, Hog's heart moves like a wellhouse pump lifting a thick, hot sweetness into his mouth. This death is filling, filled with Mama's love, all he feels of his memories of her, Daddy, Brother-boy. "JesuspleaseJesusplease," she chants.

"Mama," says Hog, standing up, voice breaking on his lips like a bubble of honey, "I got to go find Daddy and Marice and Brother-boy and those chaps. Time flying, Mama." He flees, the waters of her love receding in his wake, her prayer echoing damply in his ears.

Hog and his daddy pause at the electrified strand of fencing to admire the glossy Angus at the salt lick, clustered in the narrow shade of the old mule-driven mill where Hog helped his daddy crush cane for syrup. Hog sees the Angus melded with the scrubby mavericks he ran in the woods with razorbacks for his daddy, hears the squeak and crunch of the mill turning, crackle of cane stalks. "Now see this, Euliss," says his daddy, a small man who has aged by shriveling, drying, hardening. "Don't it beat all for raising a shoat in a nigger-rigged crib?" his hardness glowing redly in the terrible sunshine, burnished with pride over the new cement floor of his pigpen. Hog, gasping, clucks appreciation for him. "Wait and see Brother-boy feed them fish!" his daddy says.

"Daddy," Hog says, "how is it Mama so much for churching and you never setting foot in it, even for revivals?" Hog's daddy expertly blows his nose between thumb and forefinger, flicks snot into the grass as they pass the row of humming beehives, their stark whiteness conjuring the weathered stumps and gums Hog helped rob in his youth, wreathed in smoke, veiled.

"I never held to it," his daddy says, and would go on toward the pond, stopped by Hog's heavy hand on his shoulder.

"You didn't never believe in God? Ain't you never been so scared of dying or even of living so's you wanted to pray like Mama?" His voice sounds muffled, as if cushioned by water.

"I never faulted her for it, Euliss," says his daddy. And, "And no man dast fault me for not. Son, a man don't get hardly no show in life, most of us. Now, not you, but me and Brother-boy and your mama. Life wearies a man. Them as needs Jesus-ing to die quiet in bed or wherever, I say fine, like for Mama. Me nor mine never got no show, excepting you, naturally, Euliss, a famous player and coach and all. I guess I can die withouten I screech to Jesus to please let me not have to."

"Daddy," says Hog. Blood fills his chest, a steady seeping, a rich lake about his heart, pooling in the pit of his belly, pressing his lungs. "Daddy, was I a good boy?"

"Now, Euliss!" His daddy embraces him there near the line of bee-hives, the spread fingers of his horny hands clasping Hog's heaving sides. "Euliss, don't you know I have bragged on you since you was a chap?"

"Are you proud of me still now I'm growed a man?" His daddy laughs, releases him.

"Oh, I recollect you then, son! You was a pistol for that football. I recollect you not ten years old going out to lift the new calf day by day to build muscles for football playing!"

"Daddy." He feels a pleasant cleft in his breast widen, a tide of blood.

"Recollect the time I *told* you not to be blocking yourself into the gallery post for football practice? I had to frail you with a stick to teach you not. Oh, son, you was a pure pistol for that footballing! Your daddy been bragging on you since, Euliss!"

"Find Brother-boy, see them fish," Hog chokes with his last breath, heart and lungs and belly a sweet sea of blood, this death almost desirable to him. He staggers away, suffocating in the fluids of his emotions.

"Brother," says Hog, "Brother-boy, are you resentful you stayed and lived your life here? Ain't you never wanted a wife and chaps of your own? Do you resent I went away to school for football and to Canada for my own life whiles you just stay working for Daddy?" Brother-boy looks like Hog remembers himself half-a-dozen years ago, less bald, less overweight. From a large cardboard drum, he scoops meal, sows it over the dark green surface of the artificial pond. The catfish swim to the top, thrash, feeding, rile the pond into bubbles and spray. "Was I a good brother to you? Is it enough I signed a note so's you can start a fish farm and all this cattle and stock of Daddy's?"

Brother-boy, sowing the meal in wide arcs over the pond, says, "I never grudged you all the fine things you got, Euliss. You was a special person, famous playing football in college and Canada, now a coach." His brother's voice dims, lost in the liquid whip of the pond's surface, the frenzied feeding of the catfish. "I am a happy enough man, Euliss," says Brother-boy. "Mama and Daddy need me. They getting old, Euliss. I don't need me no wife nor chaps, and I got a big brother was a famous player once and now a coach, and your sons is my nephews." Hog remembers Brother-boy, a baby wearing a shift, a chap following after him at chores, coming to see him play for Jones Agricultural Institute & Junior College in Laurel, for Mississippi Southern, once coming by train and bus all the way up to Calgary, there to see Hog's career end. Says his brother, "It is my way to accept what is."

Hog lurches away, seeking an anchor for his heart, tossed in a wave of sweet blood. He wishes he could wish to die here and now if he must die. But this wish is like a dry wind that evaporates the splash of love and memory within him, turning this nectar stale, then sour.

Seeking an overview of the last full drill in pads, Hog takes to a stubby knoll, shaded by a massive live oak tree. From here, the practice field falls into neat divisions of labor.

At the far end of the field, parallel to the highway running toward Laurel and Soso, chimeric behind the rising heat waves, Fulgencio Carabajal placekicks ball after ball through jerry-built wooden goalposts, the first-string center snapping, third-team quarterback holding, two redshirts to shag balls for the Cuban, who takes a break every dozen or two dozen balls to talk with his interpreter. Hog watches Fulgenico's soccer-style approach, hears the hollow strike of the side of his shoe on the ball, the pock of this sound like a counterpoint to the beating of Hog's heart. He tries to follow the ball up between the uprights, loses it in the face of the sun that washes out the green of the grass.

Closest to Hog's shady knoll, the first- and second-team quarterbacks alternate short spot passes with long, lazy bombs to a self-renewing line of receivers who wait their turns casually, hands on hips. Catching balls in long fly patterns, receivers trot up to the base of Hog's knoll, showboating for him. The slap of ball in hands comes as if deliberately timed to the throb of his heart, adding its emphasis to the twist of its constrictions.

At the field's center, Sonny McCartney coordinates, wears a gambler's green eyeshade, clipboard and ballpoint in hand. Sonny moves from offense to defense in the shimmer of the heat like a man wading against a current. Hog squints to find Gary Lee Stringer, on his knees to demonstrate firing off the snap to his noseguard, his jersey as sweated as any player's. Wally Everett, as immobile as Hog, stands among his offensive players, stopping the drill frequently with his whistle, calling them close for short lectures, as unperturbed by the temperature and humidity as if he chalked on a blackboard in an air-conditioned classroom.

Hog's heart picks up its pace, the intensity of each convulsion increasing to a thud, a bang. Now he cannot distinguish the echo of his accelerating heartbeat from the smack of pads down on the practice field, the slap of balls on sweaty palms, thumping of the tackling dummy, crash of shoulders against the blocking sled, squealing springs, hollow pock of Fulgencio Carabajal's kicking.

Hog closes his eyes to die, digs with his cleats for a firmer stance on the knoll, prepared to topple into the dusty grass. He tenses his flesh, wonders why this raucous slamming of his heart does not shake him, why he does not explode into shards of flesh and bone. And wonders why he is not yet dead, still holding against his chest's vibrations, when he hears Sonny McCartney blow the final whistle to end the drill. The blood's song in his ears fades like Sonny's whistle in the superheated air of late afternoon.

It is light. Light, falling upon Hog, his wife still sleeping as he rises. Special, harder and brighter light, Hog fixing himself a quick breakfast in the kitchen, chrome trim catching and displaying early morning's show of light to him while Marice is dressing, his sons stirring in their bedrooms. Light, the morning sky clear as creek water, climbing sun electric-white, overwhelming Hog's sense of trees, houses, streets, driving slowly through Hattiesburg to the stadium. And lighting his consciousness, pinning his attention in the gloom of the squad's locker room, his talk to his players before they emerge into the light of the stadium.

Hog tells them, "It is not just football. It is like life. It is mental toughness. I do not know if you are as good as Alabama. Newspapers and TV is saying not, saying they will whip our butts. If it is, they is nothing any of us or you-all can do. We-all have to face that. It is Alabama we are playing today. Maybe it is like that you-all have to go out and play them knowing you will not have any show. It might could be I am saying mental toughness is just having it in you to face up knowing they will whip your butt. I don't know no more to say." He leads them out into the light.

He see, hears, registers it all, but all is a dependency of this light. The game flows like impure motes in perfect light. The game is exact, concrete, but still only a function of this light. The opening game against Alabama is a play of small shadows within the mounting intensity of light.

At the edge of the chalked boundary, Hog notes the legendary figure of the opposing coach across the field, tall, chain-smoking cigarettes, houndstooth-checked hat, coatless in the dense heat Hog does not feel. This light has no temperature for Hog, a light beyond heat or cold.

"They eating our damn lunch, Hog!" Gary Lee Stringer screams in his ear when Alabama, starting on their twenty after Fulgencio Carabajal sends the kickoff into the end-zone bleachers, drives in classic ground-game fashion for the first touchdown. The kick for extra point is wide, the snap mishandled.

"I do declare we can run wide on them, Hog," says Wally Everett as Southern moves the ball in uneven spurts to the Crimson Tide thirty-seven, where, stalled by a broken play, Fulgencio Carabajal effortlessly kicks the three-pointer. "I have seen teams field-goaled to death," Wally says.

Late in the second quarter, Southern trails only 13–9 after Fulgencio splits the uprights from fifty-six yards out. "We *got* the momentum, Hog," says Sonny McCartney, earphones clamped on to maintain contact with the press-box spotters. "We can run wide and pray Fulgencio don't break his leg."

Gary Lee Stringer, dancing, hugging the necks of his tackles, spits, screams, "I seen a train and a fair, but I ain't never see *this* day before!"

"Notice the Bear's acting nervous over there?" Wally says, points to the excited assistants clustering in a quick conference around the houndstooth hat across the field.

Says Hog, "You can't never tell a thing about nothing how it's going to be."

His death comes as light, as clarity, comprehensive and pervasive. There is nothing Hog does not see, hear, know. Everything is here, in this light, and not here. It is a moment obliterating moments, time, place.

He knows a possible great legend is unfolding on the playing field, an astounding upset of Alabama's Crimson Tide. Hog knows he has come to this possible wonder by clear chronology, sequence of accident and design, peopled since the beginning with his many selves and those who have marked and made him who and what he is in this instant of his death. Light draws him in, draws everything together in him, Hog, the context of his death.

Dr. Odie Anderson sits on a campstool behind the players' bench, feet up on the bench, scratching his beard with both hands, rolling his bulged eyes at the scoreboard. Athletic Director Tub Moorman's face is wine-red with excitement, unlit cigar chewed to pulpy rags. Gary Lee Stringer drools tobacco juice when he shouts out encouragement to his stiffening defense. Wally Everett smirks as he counsels his quarterback. Sonny McCartney relays information from up in the press box, where Marice and the four sons of Hog watch the game through binoculars, drinking complimentary Coca-Colas. On the bench next to his chattering interpreter, Fulgencio Carabajal waits indifferently for his next field-goal attempt.

In the new modern kitchen in Soso, Mississippi, Hog's people, Mama, Daddy, Brother-boy, listen to the radio broadcast, proud and praying. Folded into Hog's memory like pecans in pralines are the many Hogs that make him Hog: a boy in Soso lifting new calves to build muscle, football find at Jones Agricultural Institute & Junior College, bona fide gridiron legendary Little All American on this field, sure-fire prospect with Calgary's Stampeders in the Canadian Football League, career cut short by knee and ankle injuries, high-school coach, defensive assistant, coordinator, Hog here and now, head coach in Mississippi Southern University–all these in the marvel of his death's light.

Dying, Hog looks into the glare of the sun, finds his death is not pain or sweetness but totality and transcendence, dies as they rush to where he lies on the turf, dying, accepting this light that is the heart of him joining all light, Hog and not-Hog, past knowing and feeling or need and desire to say it is only light. He dies hearing Fulgenico Carabajal say, "*Es muerte?*" gone into such light as makes light and darkness one.

The Russian Alexander Pushkin (1799–1837) is considered one of the great-est poets in history. His most famous works in verse are the luminous narrative poem Eugene Onegin and the play Boris Godunov. Tragically, Pushkin died young, killed in a duel with a rival over the affections of his wife. The following story concerns a gambling game called faro, in which players bet on cards drawn from a dealing box.

Alexander Pushkin

THE QUEEN OF SPADES (1834)

AT THE HOUSE OF Naroumov, a cavalry officer, the long winter night had been passed in gambling. At five in the morning breakfast was served to the weary players. The winners ate with relish; the losers, on the contrary, pushed back their plates and sat brooding gloomily. Under the influence of the good wine, however, the conversation then became general.

"Well, Sourine?" said the host inquiringly.

"Oh, I lost as usual. My luck is abominable. No matter how cool I keep, I never win."

"How is it, Herman, that you never touch a card?" remarked one of the men, addressing a young officer of the Engineering Corps. "Here you are with the rest of us at five o'clock in the morning, and you have neither played nor bet all night."

"Play interests me greatly," replied the person addressed, "but I hardly care to sacrifice the necessaries of life for uncertain superfluities."

"Herman is a German, therefore economical; that explains it," said Tomsky. "But the person I can't quite understand is my grandmother, the Countess Anna Fedorovna."

"Why?" inquired a chorus of voices.

"I can't understand why my grandmother never gambles."

"I don't see anything very striking in the fact that a woman of eighty refuses to gamble," objected Naroumov.

"Have you never heard her story?"

"No."

"Well, then, listen to it. To begin with, sixty years ago my grandmother went to Paris, where she was all the fashion. People crowded each other in the streets to get a chance to see the 'Muscovite Venus,' as she was called. All the great ladies played faro, then. On one occasion, while playing with the Duke of Orleans, she lost an enormous sum. She told her husband of the debt, but he refused outright to pay it. Nothing could induce him to change his mind on the subject, and grandmother was at her wits' ends. Finally, she remembered a friend of hers, Count Saint-Germain. You must have heard of him, as many wonderful stories have been told about him. He is said to have discovered the elixir of life, the philosopher's stone, and many other equally marvelous things. He had money at his disposal, and my grandmother knew it. She sent him a note asking him to come to see her. He obeyed her summons and found her in great distress. She painted the cruelty of her husband in the darkest colors, and ended by telling the Count that she depended upon his friendship and generosity.

"'I could lend you the money,' replied the Count, after a moment of thoughtfulness, 'but I know that you would not enjoy a moment's rest until you had returned it; it would only add to your embarrassment. There is another way of freeing yourself.'

"'But I have no money at all,' insisted my grandmother.

"'There is no need of money. Listen to me.'

"The Count then told her a secret which any of us would give a good deal to know."

The young gamesters were all attention. Tomsky lit his pipe, took a few whiffs, then continued:

"The next evening, grandmother appeared at Versailles at the Queen's gaming-table. The Duke of Orleans was the dealer. Grandmother made some excuse for not having brought any money, and began to punt. She chose three cards in succession, again and again, winning every time, and was soon out of debt."

"A fable," remarked Herman; "perhaps the cards were marked."

"I hardly think so," replied Tomsky, with an air of importance.

"So you have a grandmother who knows three winning cards, and you haven't found out the magic secret."

"I must say I have not. She had four sons, one of them being my father, all of whom are devoted to play; she never told the secret to one of them. But my uncle told me this much, on his word of honor. Tchaplitzky, who died in poverty after having squandered millions, lost at one time, at play, nearly three hundred thousand rubles. He was desperate and grandmother took pity on him. She told him the three cards, making him swear never to use them again. He returned to the game, staked fifty thousand rubles on each card, and came out ahead, after paying his debts."

As day was dawning the party now broke up, each one draining his glass and taking his leave.

The Countess Anna Fedorovna was seated before her mirror in her dressing-room. Three women were assisting at her toilet. The old Countess no longer made the slightest pretensions to beauty, but she still clung to all the habits of her youth, and spent as much time at her toilet as she had done sixty years before. At the window a young girl, her ward, sat at her needlework.

ALEXANDER PUSHKIN

"Good afternoon, grandmother," cried a young officer, who had just entered the room. "I have come to ask a favor of you."

"What, Pavel?"

"I want to be allowed to present one of my friends to you, and to take you to the ball on Tuesday night."

"Take me to the ball and present him to me there."

After a few more remarks the officer walked up to the window where Lisaveta Ivanovna sat.

"Whom do you wish to present?" asked the girl.

"Naroumov; do you know him?"

"No; is he a soldier?"

"Yes."

"An engineer?"

"No; why do you ask?"

The girl smiled and made no reply.

Pavel Tomsky took his leave, and, left to herself, Lisaveta glanced out of the window. Soon, a young officer appeared at the corner of the street; the girl blushed and bent her head low over her canvas.

This appearance of the officer had become a daily occurrence. The man was totally unknown to her, and as she was not accustomed to co-quetting with the soldiers she saw on the street, she hardly knew how to explain his presence. His persistence finally roused an interest entirely strange to her. One day, she even ventured to smile upon her admirer, for such he seemed to be.

The reader need hardly be told that the officer was no other than Her-man, the would-be gambler, whose imagination had been strongly ex-cited by the story told by Tomsky of the three magic cards.

"Ah," he thought, "if the old Countess would only reveal the secret to me. Why not try to win her good-will and appeal to her sympathy?"

With this idea in mind, he took up his daily station before the house, watching the pretty face at the window, and trusting to fate to bring about the desired acquaintance.

One day, as Lisaveta was standing on the pavement about to enter the carriage after the Countess, she felt herself jostled and a note was thrust into her hand. Turning, she saw the young officer at her elbow. As quick as thought, she put the note in her glove and entered the carriage. On her return from the drive, she hastened to her chamber to read the missive, in a state of excitement mingled with fear. It was a tender and respectful declaration of affection, copied word for word from a German novel. Of this fact, Lisa was, of course, ignorant.

The young girl was much impressed by the missive, but she felt that the writer must not be encouraged. She therefore wrote a few lines of explanation and, at the first opportunity, dropped it, with the letter, out of the window. The officer hastily crossed the street, picked up the papers and entered a shop to read them.

In no wise daunted by this rebuff, he found the opportunity to send her another note in a few days. He received no reply, but, evidently understanding the female heart, he persevered, begging for an interview. He was rewarded at last by the following:

"To-night we go to the ambassador's ball. We shall remain until two o'clock. I can arrange for a meeting in this way. After our departure, the servants will probably all go out, or go to sleep. At half-past eleven enter the vestibule boldly, and if you see any one, inquire for the Countess; if not, ascend the stairs, turn to the left and go on until you come to a door, which opens into her bedchamber. Enter this room and behind a screen you will find another door leading to a corridor; from this a spiral staircase leads to my sitting-room. I shall expect to find you there on my return."

Herman trembled like a leaf as the appointed hour drew near. He obeyed instructions fully, and, as he met no one, he reached the old lady's bedchamber without difficulty. Instead of going out of the small door behind the screen, however, he concealed himself in a closet to await the return of the old Countess.

The hours dragged slowly by; at last he heard the sound of wheels. Immediately lamps were lighted and servants began moving about. Finally the old woman tottered into the room, completely exhausted. Her women removed her wraps and proceeded to get her in readiness for the night. Herman watched the proceedings with a curiosity not unmingled with superstitious fear. When at last she was attired in cap and gown, the old woman looked less uncanny than when she wore her ball-dress of blue brocade.

She sat down in an easy chair beside a table, as she was in the habit of doing before retiring, and her women withdrew. As the old lady sat swaying to and fro, seemingly oblivious to her surroundings, Herman crept out of his hiding-place.

At the slight noise the old woman opened her eyes, and gazed at the intruder with a half-dazed expression.

"Have no fear, I beg of you," said Herman, in a calm voice. "I have not come to harm you, but to ask a favor of you instead."

The Countess looked at him in silence, seemingly without comprehending him. Herman thought she might be deaf, so he put his lips close to her ear and repeated his remark. The listener remained perfectly mute.

"You could make my fortune without its costing you anything," pleaded the young man; "only tell me the three cards which are sure to win, and—"

Herman paused as the old woman opened her lips as if about to speak.

"It was only a jest; I swear to you, it was only a jest," came from the withered lips.

"There was no jesting about it. Remember Tchaplitzky, who, thanks to you, was able to pay his debts."

An expression of interior agitation passed over the face of the old woman; then she relapsed into her former apathy.

"Will you tell me the names of the magic cards, or not?" asked Herman after a pause.

There was no reply.

The young man then drew a pistol from his pocket, exclaiming: "You old witch, I'll force you to tell me!"

At the sight of the weapon the Countess gave a second sign of life. She threw back her head and put out her hands as if to protect herself; then they dropped and she sat motionless.

Herman grasped her arm roughly, and was about to renew his threats, when he saw that she was dead!

Seated in her room, still in her ball-dress, Lisaveta gave herself up to her reflections. She had expected to find the young officer there, but she felt relieved to see that he was not.

Strangely enough, that very night at the ball, Tomsky had rallied her about her preference for the young officer, assuring her that he knew more than she supposed he did.

"Of whom are you speaking?" she had asked in alarm, fearing her adventure had been discovered.

"Of the remarkable man," was the reply. "His name is Herman."

Lisa made no reply.

"This Herman," continued Tomsky, "is a romantic character; he has the profile of a Napoleon and the heart of a Mephistopheles. It is said he has at least three crimes on his conscience. But how pale you are."

"It is only a slight headache. But why do you talk to me of this Herman?"

"Because I believe he has serious intentions concerning you."

"Where has he seen me?"

"At church, perhaps, or on the street."

The conversation was interrupted at this point, to the great regret of the young girl. The words of Tomsky made a deep impression upon her, and she realized how imprudently she had acted. She was thinking of all this and a great deal more when the door of her apartment suddenly opened, and Herman stood before her. She drew back at sight of him, trembling violently.

"Where have you been?" she asked in a frightened whisper.

"In the bedchamber of the Countess. She is dead," was the calm reply.

"My God! What are you saying?" cried the girl.

"Furthermore, I believe that I was the cause of her death."

The words of Tomsky flashed through Lisa's mind.

Herman sat down and told her all. She listened with a feeling of terror and disgust. So those passionate letters, that audacious pursuit were not the result of tenderness and love. It was money that he desired. The poor girl felt that she had in a sense been an accomplice in the death of her benefactress. She began to weep bitterly. Herman regarded her in silence.

"You are a monster!" exclaimed Lisa, drying her eyes.

"I didn't intend to kill her; the pistol was not even loaded."

"How are you going to get out of the house?" inquired Lisa. "It is nearly daylight. I intended to show you the way to a secret staircase, while the Countess was asleep, as we would have to cross her chamber. Now I am afraid to do so."

"Direct me, and I will find the way alone," replied Herman.

She gave him minute instructions and a key with which to open the street door. The young man pressed the cold, inert hand, then went out.

The death of the Countess had surprised no one, as it had long been expected. Her funeral was attended by every one of note in the vicinity. Herman mingled with the throng without attracting any especial attention. After all the friends had taken their last look at the dead face, the young man approached the bier. He prostrated himself on the cold floor, and remained motionless for a long time. He rose at last with a face almost as pale as that of the corpse itself, and went up the steps to look into the casket. As he looked down it seemed to him that the rigid face returned his glance mockingly, closing one eye. He turned abruptly away, made a false step, and fell to the floor. He was picked up, and at the same moment, Lisaveta was carried out in a faint.

Herman did not recover his usual composure during the entire day. He dined alone at an out-of-the-way restaurant, and drank a great deal, in the hope of stifling his emotion. The wine only served to stimulate his imagination. He returned home and threw himself down on his bed without undressing.

During the night he awoke with a start; the moon shone into his chamber, making everything plainly visible. Some one looked in at the window, then quickly disappeared. He paid no attention to this, but soon he heard the vestibule door open. He thought it was his orderly, returning late, drunk as usual. The step was an unfamiliar one, and he heard the shuffling sound of loose slippers.

The door of his room opened, and a woman in white entered. She came close to the bed, and the terrified man recognized the Countess.

"I have come to you against my will," she said abruptly; "but I was commanded to grant your request. The tray, seven, and ace in succession are the magic cards. Twenty-four hours must elapse between the use of each card, and after the three have been used you must never play again."

The phantom then turned and walked away. Herman heard the outside door close, and again saw the form pass the window.

He rose and went out into the hall, where his orderly lay asleep on the floor. The door was closed. Finding no trace of a visitor, he returned to his room, lit his candle, and wrote down what he had just heard.

Two fixed ideas cannot exist in the brain at the same time any more than two bodies can occupy the same point in space. The tray, seven, and ace soon chased away the thoughts of the dead woman, and all other thoughts from the brain of the young officer. All his ideas merged into a single one: how to turn to advantage the secret paid for so dearly. He even thought of resigning his commission and going to Paris to force a fortune from conquered fate. Chance rescued him from his embarrassment.

Tchekalinsky, a man who had passed his whole life at cards, opened a club at St. Petersburg. His long experience secured for him the confidence of his companions, and his hospitality and genial humor conciliated society.

The gilded youth flocked around him, neglecting society, preferring the charms of faro to those of their sweethearts. Naroumov invited Herman to accompany him to the club, and the young man accepted the invitation only too willingly.

The two officers found the apartments full. Generals and statesman played whist; young men lounged on sofas, eating ices or smoking. In the principal salon stood a long table, at which about twenty men sat playing faro, the host of the establishment being the banker.

He was a man of about sixty, gray-haired and respectable. His ruddy face shone with genial humor; his eyes sparkled and a constant smile hovered around his lips.

Naroumov presented Herman. The host gave him a cordial hand-shake, begged him not to stand upon ceremony, and returned to his dealing. More than thirty cards were already on the table. Tchekalinsky paused after each coup, to allow the punters time to recognize their gains or losses, politely answering all questions and constantly smiling.

After the deal was over, the cards were shuffled and the game began again.

"Permit me to choose a card," said Herman, stretching out his hand over the head of a portly gentleman, to reach a livret. The banker bowed without replying.

Herman chose a card, and wrote the amount of his stake upon it with a piece of chalk.

"How much is that?" asked the banker; "excuse me, sir, but I do not see well."

"Forty thousand rubles," said Herman coolly.

All eyes were instantly turned to the speaker.

"He has lost his wits," thought Naroumov.

"Allow me to observe," said Tchekalinsky, with his eternal smile, "that your stake is excessive."

"What of it?" replied Herman, nettled. "Do you accept it or not?"

The banker nodded in assent. "I have only to remind you that the cash will be necessary; of course your word is good, but to keep the confidence of my patrons, I prefer the ready money."

Herman took a bank-check from his pocket and handed it to his host. The latter examined it attentively, then laid it on the card chosen.

He began dealing; to the right, a nine; to the left, a tray.

"The tray wins," said Herman, showing the card he held—a tray.

A murmur ran through the crowd. Tchekalinsky frowned for a second only, then his smile returned. He took a roll of bank-bills from his pocket and counted out the required sum. Herman received it and at once left the table.

The next evening saw him at the place again. Every one eyed him curiously, and Tchekalinsky greeted him cordially.

He selected his card and placed upon it his fresh stake. The banker began dealing; to the right, a nine; to the left, a seven.

Herman then showed his card—a seven spot. The onlookers exclaimed, and the host was visibly disturbed. He counted out ninety-four-thousand rubles and passed them to Herman, who accepted them without showing the least surprise and at once withdrew.

The following evening he went again. His appearance was the signal for the cessation of all occupation, every one being eager to watch the development of events. He selected his card—an ace.

The dealing began: to the right, a queen; to the left, an ace.

"The ace wins," remarked Herman, turning up his card without glancing at it.

"Your queen is killed," remarked Tchekalinsky quietly.

Herman trembled; looking down, he saw, not the ace he had selected, but the queen of spades. He could scarcely believe his eyes. It seemed impossible that he could have made such a mistake. As he stared at the card it seemed to him that the queen winked one eye at him mockingly.

"The old woman!" he exclaimed involuntarily.

The croupier raked in the money while he looked on in stupid terror. When he left the table, all made way for him to pass; the cards were shuffled, and the gambling went on.

Herman became a lunatic. He was confined at the hospital at Oboukov, where he spoke to no one, but kept constantly murmuring in a monotonous tone: "The tray, seven, ace! The tray, seven, queen!"

This is a hockey story, not about the game itself but the search by boys for a suitable place to play during a winter thaw. There is nostalgia here as well as the optimism of youth. Author Peter LaSalle has written a novel, Strange Sunlight *(1984), and two story collections,* The Graves of Famous Writers *(1980) and* Hockey Sur Glace *(1996), the latter entirely about hockey. His hockey fiction is considered the best ever written on the subject. LaSalle's stories have also appeared in* The Paris Review, Best American Short Stories, *and* Prize Stories: The O. Henry Awards. *He is a graduate of Harvard and professor of English at the University of Texas, Austin.*

Peter LaSalle
VAN ARSDALE'S POND (1996)

THE BOYS SAID THEY DIDN'T CARE if the ice wasn't good on Whittaker's Pond, because there was the other pond they had heard about. No, they had never been there, but that didn't matter—they had heard.

Maybe the ice had come suddenly in December, before Christmas the way it sometimes could, altogether unexpected. Somebody's older brother inevitably had a tale about skating on Thanksgiving Day, when the cutout turkeys were still scotch-taped to the windows of Nausauket Elementary School, but nobody really believed that. Though by early December it might take only two or three truly cold nights of the red alcohol in the thermometer outside a frosted window cringing low in the clear, frigid darkness, and then lower. And to see Whittaker's Pond then was to come upon it the next afternoon after the last buzzing school bell had finally sounded at three, to hike the half-mile or so off the state two-lane and over the dun-colored knolls, then into the shadowy woods proper with the crunching leaves and the minty pines and the bunches of white birches, to finally spot it below, Whittaker's Pond. Before a snowfall, the ice might be glaringly black, not frozen much up by the end with the earthen dam that the Eagle Scouts had rebuilt who knows how many years before (had any kid actually *known* an Eagle Scout?), and surely more than the rule-of-thumb six inches thick down by the shallow end where the squat hoarfrosted bushes grew right through the surface and would at least give you something to grab onto if you were the first kid gingerly inching out to test if it was safe (one flimsy shoe or boot placed soft, like a floating dandelion puff, then the other). But it probably wasn't December, and the issue now was not really whether the ice was safe, but whether it was smooth enough and reasonably skatable after a midseason thaw. And, again, even if the ice wasn't good, they knew about the other pond.

One thing that was certain was that the boys' mothers, young, did what they always did on winter afternoons. They took time away from their sitting in front of a rattling Singer machine, or baking pies in the cramped kitchens heady with the aromas of shortening and cinnamon, and they got everything ready for the boys. One mother liked to place her son's long wool skating socks, the gray ones, on the radiator in the hallway; she would have them warmed when he came through the back storm door, in such a hurry because "There's ice, Mom!" and the others were waiting for him and he was already late. Another mother might simply gather together what she knew her son would need, have the scuffed skates and the taped stick ready, the puck on which she noticed what she had never noticed before: the boy had carved his initials into the hard black rubber, probably with a carpenter's nail, and how lovely was his attempt at scrolling the letters for the job that must have taken him hours, making each period after each letter an ornate asterisk.

A moment like that could render a mother, standing in her housewife's dress and apron, staring at the puck, very sad.

And the boys were not in the classroom any longer. They were not gazing at the clock above the coatroom, and they were not banging past each other in their crazed charge to flee through the big battered green doors and out of the place at last. At this point they had already been home, already enjoyed the snack of Hydrox cookies and milk that waited for them, let's say, on a chrome-trimmed kitchen table, and the pack of them, six all told, were trudging up a knoll, there beside the two-lane. They wore galoshes, heavy coats, and peaked leather caps or knit toques. They carried their skates by putting them onto the blade end of the stick, either slung by the loop of the tied-together dirty laces or the stick poked through the handy space below the sole on the skates' bottoms; they jutted the sticks over their shoulders, and the effect was that of what could be seen in old fairy-tale books, telling the story of any meandering tramp with his long pole and full sack of belongings toted that way, exactly the same for all of them.

One could watch them from a distance, going down the snow-covered slope of another knoll now; they were a moving line, a queue, each with the stick over the shoulder, the skates dangling. They appeared to be on a real journey, not just a long walk to a pond. The entered into the woods.

There was the sharp, clean smell of the snow itself that slapped your nostrils when you inhaled. A fat jay on a bare tree limb screeched away at them, then nearly detonated off in a swoosh of fluttering blue, the branch still shaking.

Of course, the boys talked:

"I wonder about it," a tall one for his age said, "and who knows what Whittaker's will be like after so much melting."

"You could be right." A rosy-cheeked boy said that, optimistic. "But I have a feeling it's going to be OK, and it will be good ice, I'm sure, even if we haven't had ice for a week."

"More than a week," the taller boy said.

"It warmed up over the weekend," one of the twins said.

"It did, you're right about that," the other one of the twins said. "It warmed up a lot over the weekend."

"But last night was cold, and that's all that counts," the rosy-cheeked boy told them.

"I suppose," one of the twins said.

"Yeah," the other said.

Because this wasn't like the first freeze of a season whatsoever. As already said, with a first freeze, be it the reputed Thanksgiving surprise or late ice, not coming until a week after New Year's, the situation was basically simple. First the fragile skin of a surface, then the huge extended star patterns in it when it turned solid, and finally the thick, lenslike covering, sturdier and sturdier, as hopefully the subsequent days brought nothing more in the sky than the welcome gray dimness, no sun and only cold. But once a surface had formed for the year, usually intact until March, any number of variations could occur.

If it stayed cold, there eventually came the snow, sometimes a howling blizzard, and the cover of accumulated white posed the source of the complication. In the most frigid of winters, when the weather lady on the one television station that came in clear in this part of the state sang of storms flopping down from Canada one after another, in that kind of cold the boys could shovel a rectangle for play. And while that surface could quickly be gouged to ruts from the wear of consecutive afternoons of games, and while there was always the nuisance of losing a puck into the downy dust of the pile when somebody missed a pass along the edge, that meant, nevertheless, they had ice, and ice didn't have to be perfect: nobody ever expected perfect ice after the first freeze of the year, that famous black ice. The boys sometimes talked of how they almost had it in them to rig up long plywood slabs with the stems of old broken hockey sticks for handles nailed to the boards, for the variety of ready plows that teenage guys on the high-school team heartily manned, four of them to a slab, pushing hard to clean a whole pond for practice sessions. But, understandably, these boys were too young and not that organized; just lugging a couple of heavy snow shovels through the woods and to Whittaker's Pond was work enough, a feat to challenge Hannibal with his bell-jangling elephants transporting war supplies across the towering Alps, as far as they were concerned. The real problems began with a midseason melt. The snow could turn to slush, refreezing when the next cold front arrived in uneven lumps like a cake that hadn't risen right, or, much worse, porous, crusted, and flimsy with no surface gloss to speak of, everywhere a pinto patterning of giant air bubbles each a few feet wide to be crunched into by blades, what their skates could barely stumble across, never mind glide over. In short, the boys had no idea what they would find at Whittaker's Pond after this midseason warming and the return to the cold. They could be lucky, certainly, and sometimes a melt was thorough enough to mean a flood of water atop the surface all over again, and then a fine glaze indeed with the subsequent refreezing.

They walked on through the woods. The twins bounced lines off one another like echoes, their talk never saying much of anything. The rosy-cheeked boy kept telling everybody that he knew the ice would be good, and the taller boy wasn't sure of that or much else lately, but he was willing to try to believe that all would prove OK. The group of them probably talked about the Providence Reds hockey team. They probably talked about how tough the cattle-drive master, Gil Favor, was on *Rawhide*, how funny the show with Dobie Gillis could be. They probably talked as well about the faraway territory called "girls," somebody claiming that in his classroom that very morning there was a prime example of a girl's bossiness, then playing up to the teacher, from a certain Cheryl Beaupre, a performance nobody would *believe*; then somebody else claiming that in his classroom that same afternoon he had managed to execute his old trick with the tawnily blond Diane Maloney yet another time—dropping his yellow pencil to the linoleum under his desk, pretending for a long while that he couldn't find it around the worn-shiny steel stem of that desk, and the whole time enjoying a leisurely ogle of Diane's panties, kelly green this particular day. But mostly they talked about the ice, what they might find at Whittaker's Pond. There was a measure of bullying, sad to say, from the boy who was noticeably wiry, gruff too; he picked on a boy with a soft voice who always found himself last in the queue.

"It could have melted a lot, it might not even be safe," the bullying boy said, and turning to the boy with the soft voice, he told him, "What if you fell through?"

The soft-voiced boy didn't answer him.

"You don't drown, you know, you just go into shock, like somebody plugged one of your fingers into a hungry hundred-and-twenty-volt socket. Freezing shock, worse than electric shock, and just like that."

He snapped his fingers, leered at the other boy. He was delighting in scaring him.

"Shut up," one of the twins told the bully.

"Yeah, shut up," the other one said.

At home the mothers maybe returned to the sewing machine, or started on what had to be done at the ironing board, the electric flat fragrant of heat and scorched cotton, and one of those dime-store plastic daisies stuck into the top of a soda bottle used for sprinkling water during the task. Maybe one of them walked to a window, put fingers to the cold pane, and whispered aloud but to nobody in particular: "My son is in the woods now, going to the pond. All I can do is hope that all is well and safe for him." And the fathers? The fathers worked jobs like that of auto mechanic or assistant records clerk somewhere in the steam-heated basement of the town hall, and occasionally one of them, weary at this stage in the long afternoon, would just sigh to think, "How, oh how, did I ever get this old?"

Until, as soon as the boys could see through the trees to the lopsided oval of Whittaker's Pond, they knew that the worst thing imaginable—the ultimate destruction of midseason ice—had happened. And any good luck with the days of melt producing a sizable water coating that in turn pristinely refroze, those hopes were gone when they saw what they saw: yes, there had been snow that melted to slush, but somewhere in the process, kids, probably not even in grade school, had committed the transgression of transgressions, stomping indiscriminately and savagely on the pond with their rubber boots in a maddened patterning of indented dance steps, which had eventually frozen solid and ruined any chance of decent skating, any chance of pond hockey completely.

The bullying boy seemed to take satisfaction in this disaster, saying: "Just as I figured, a total mess." He turned again to the boy he had been picking on, adding, "And now you won't even be able to freeze to death, or drown."

"It must have been real little kids," that other boy said blankly in reply, "kids who nobody ever told that you aren't supposed to ruin ice. They must have come from those new houses in the plat in back."

The boys stared in disbelief. (Years later the bullying boy, Jimmy Arsenault, was killed in a foreign war that nobody supported, as his valiantly attempting to save a wounded pal brought him close to an enemy sniper. The timid boy, Wayne Wright, might have gone on to a position of great success if the rule worked that the world eventually found a balance in such opposites, like the bullying boy becoming a selfless battle hero of sorts. But that didn't happen. The timid boy didn't turn out to be a known movie star, or even a mayor; he would never marry, would in time end up in a meaningless town office job himself, living alone with a tiger-striped cat in a local apartment house, where the neighbors considered him strange. Concerning what became of somebody in life, as with what kind of ice you might find, there often seemed little more than sheer chance.) Meanwhile, the twins were now starting to growl their disappointment.

"Shit," one said.

"Yeah," said the other, "shit."

(Who knew what became of them, because wasn't it true that nobody ever knew or heard what became of twins later on? It seemed that being twins in itself was a full-time justification, a defining task, in life; they were the Ericksons.)

"There's the other pond," the optimistic boy said. "The kids from over on Long Street were talking about it at school. They say it's better than Whittaker's, anyway, and with it sitting on a chicken farm like that, nobody much knows about it except for them and the farmer. Nobody will have wrecked that ice, and they're all probably out there already, those Long Street kids, they're probably playing and having a ball. Who cares about this?" He tipped his head toward the pond, Whittaker's, which all of them had been anticipating skating on since they had woken that morning, when they realized exactly how cold it had been during the night and that the thaw was finally over; they had been thinking about it the entire day in the blur of the several hours of school. "Who *cares*?"

But the twins announced they were tired. They didn't feel like tramping through the snow anymore, would just as well head home and watch late-afternoon TV cartoons in their basement rumpus room. And the bullying boy, possibly out of inherent perversity, argued that in his opinion you couldn't even get to Van Arsdale's chicken farm this way, through these woods, and the soft-voiced, bullied boy needed no more persuasion than that and completely agreed with him.

"But what about what we've been saying the whole way here," the rosy-cheeked boy said, "how we kept telling each other that if the ice is no good on Whittaker's, we can still go to the other pond, a *better* pond, I tell you."

"That was way back then," one of the twins said.

"Way back when," the other said, liking the rhyme of it, chuckling.

"That's funny," the first twin said.

"Yeah," the other said.

The entire contingent was about to abandon the plan of going on, but the boy who was tall for his age spoke up:

"I'll go with you," he said to the optimistic boy.

"Well, here's somebody who wants good ice," that boy replied to him.

The others were soon gone, and the two remaining boys crossed the pond's ruined ice, waded slow through the deep drifts along the other side, and headed on through the pillars of the tall trees. The day was still now, losing light. They walked for a half-hour.

"I think they might have been right," was the only thing the rosy-cheeked boy said.

And with that he pivoted, and also was gone.

So, the boy who was taller kept going without the rosy-cheeked boy. (Here there was predictability: the rosy-cheeked boy, cheerful by nature, eventually attended a good college, then worked to establish his own successful real estate agency; he would have a wonderful wife and five children. His name was Alan Lelaidier.) The taller boy marched through the trees, and he wondered why he was determined to go on, to be frank. Was it to prove a point? Or did he, in fact, expect to find good ice at the pond at Van Arsdale's chicken farm, a crew of boys playing hockey there and welcoming him into their game? He didn't know. To be frank again, he wasn't as much as sure if he had *actually* gone into the woods with skates and hockey stick along with the bunch of his pals that afternoon, or if this too were but another imagining, the way so much felt to him like but another imagining lately. And in the imagining, the insubstantiality of it, smoke wafted from chimneys in the frozen late afternoon of a forgotten Rhode Island town, where mothers kept so lovingly busy in warm, wooden bungalows, and fathers, weary, wrestled through jobs that seemed to matter little, to lead nowhere. The boy was cold, and when he got to the top of another knoll, into a clearing with some tumbledown snow-fencing, he could see that the sky had lifted; a band of the palest of blue was widening above the hills black with their blanketing of winter trees, and he could see the buttery wedge of a moon. Without the cloud cover, the night would be very, very cold.

His toes were numb in the galoshes, he flipped the fuzzy gray earflaps down on his peaked leather cap, which felt good. (But was this really him? Was this Larry Gaudette? Or was this the shadow of somebody he often suspected he was, alone, the way he would always be alone in the course of an early marriage that didn't work out, then separated from his children in later years with carpentry jobs in Connecticut and upstate New York, places that were continents away from who he was, where he was from—more alone than ever. He *was* almost watching a boy trudge along.) Still, he didn't care about the cold. He could picture the pond at Van Arsdale's. He could envision it protected in a little bowl of hills, the farmer's white clapboard house and the rickety red chicken sheds on a rise beyond that, the lights in the house's windows yellow at dusk.

He saw himself skating on a beautifully glassy surface, good ice, all right, dribbling a puck, telling himself how he had never liked anything in the world, loved anything, as much as to hear his blades cutting over the ice, to be skating.

He trudged on, suspecting that possibly it—*everything, always*—could turn out OK, even if somebody like the overoptimistic boy, who had left, ultimately saw folly in it. There *might* be good ice, and trying to think only of that, he, like so many of us, continued deeper and deeper into the woods.

A sports story collection wouldn't be complete without a piece from the master of baseball yarns, Ring Lardner. Like P. G. Wodehouse on golf, Lardner has written more humorous stories about the national pastime than anyone. "Harmony," first published in McClure's magazine, is about old-time ballplayers who form a barbershop quartet. Lardner has an ear for their colloquial jargon, plus a real feel for the game. He had a brilliant career as a sportswriter for newspapers in Chicago and New York. Books containing Lardner's stories are You Know Me, Al (1916), Round Up (1929), and the Collected Stories of Ring Lardner (1941).

Ring Lardner

HARMONY
(1915)

EVEN A BASEBALL WRITER MUST sometimes work. Regretfully I yielded my seat in the P. G., walked past the section where Art Graham, Bill Cole, Lefty Parks and young Waldron were giving expert tonsorial treatment to "Sweet Adeline," and flopped down beside Ryan, the manager.

"Well, Cap," I said, "we're due in Springfield in a little over an hour and I haven't written a line."

"Don't let me stop you," said Ryan.

"I want you to start me," I said.

"Lord!" said Ryan. "You oughtn't to have any trouble grinding out stuff these days, with the club in first place and young Waldron gone crazy. He's worth a story any day."

"That's the trouble," said I. "He's been worked so much that there's nothing more to say about him. Everybody in the country knows that he's hitting .420, that he's made nine home runs, twelve triples and twenty-some doubles, that he's stolen twenty-five bases, and that he can play the piano and sing like Car*us*'. They've run his picture oftener than Billy Sunday and Mary Pickford put together. Of course, you might come through with how you got him."

"Oh, that's the mystery," said Ryan.

"So I've heard you say," I retorted. "But it wouldn't be a mystery if you'd let me print it."

"Well," said Ryan, "if you're really hard up I suppose I might as well come through. Only there's really no mystery at all about it; it's just what I consider the most remarkable piece of scouting ever done. I've been making a mystery of it just to have a little fun with Dick Hodges. You know he's got the Jackson club and he's still so sore about my stealing Waldron he'll hardly speak to me.

"I'll give you the dope if you want it, though it's a boost for Art Graham, not me. There's lots of people think the reason I've kept the thing a secret is because I'm modest.

"They give me credit for having found Waldron myself. But Graham is the bird that deserves the credit and I'll admit that he almost had to get down on his knees to make me take his tip. Yes, sir, Art Graham was the scout, and now he's sitting on the bench and the boy he recommended has got his place."

"That sounds pretty good," I said. "And how did Graham get wise?"

"I'm going to tell you. You're in a hurry; so I'll make it snappy.

"You weren't with us last fall, were you? Well, we had a day off in Detroit, along late in the season. Graham's got relatives in Jackson; so he asked me if he could spend the day there. I told him he could and asked him to keep his eyes peeled for good young pitchers, if he happened to go to the ball game. So he went to Jackson and the next morning he came back all excited. I asked him if he'd found me a pitcher and he said he hadn't, but he'd seen the best natural hitter he'd ever looked at—a kid named Waldron.

"'Well,' I said, 'you're the last one that ought to be recommending out-fielders. If there's one good enough to hold a regular job, it might be your job he'd get.'

"But Art said that didn't make any difference to him—he was looking out for the good of the club. Well, I didn't see my way clear to asking the old man to dig up good money for an outfielder nobody'd ever heard of, when we were pretty well stocked with them, so I tried to stall Art; but he kept after me and kept after me till I agreed to stick in a draft for the kid just to keep Art quiet. So the draft went in and we got him. Then, as you know, Hodges tried to get him back, and that made me suspicious enough to hold on to him. Hodges finally came over to see me and wanted to know who'd tipped me to Waldron. That's where the mystery stuff started, because I saw that Hodges was all heated up and wanted to kid him along. So I told him we had some mighty good scouts working for us, and he said he knew our regular scouts and they couldn't tell a ball-player from a torn ligament. Then he offered me fifty bucks if I'd tell him the truth and I just laughed at him. I said: 'A fella happened to be in Jackson one day and saw him work. But I won't tell you who the fella was, because you're too anxious to know.' Then he insisted on knowing what day the scout had been in Jackson. I said I'd tell him that if he'd tell me why he was so blame curious. So he gave me his end of it.

"It seems his brother, up in Ludington, had seen this kid play ball on the lots and had signed him right up for Hodges and taken him to Jackson, and of course, Hodges knew he had a world beater the minute he saw him. But he also knew he wasn't going to be able to keep him in Jackson, and, naturally he began to figure how he could get the most money for him. It was already August when the boy landed in Jackson; so there wasn't much chance of getting a big price last season. He decided to teach the kid what he didn't know about baseball and to keep him under cover till this year. Then everybody would be touting him and there'd be plenty of competition. Hodges could sell to the highest bidder.

"He had Waldron out practising every day, but wouldn't let him play in a game, and every player on the Jackson club had promised to keep the secret till this year. So Hodges wanted to find out from me which one of his players had broken the promise.

"Then I asked him if he was perfectly sure that Waldron hadn't played in a game, and he said he had gone in to hit for somebody just once. I asked him what date that was and he told me. It was the day Art had been in Jackson. So I said:

"'There's your mystery solved. That's the day my scout saw him, and you'll have to give the scout a little credit for picking a star after seeing him make one base hit.'

"Then Hodges said:

"'That makes it all the more a mystery. Because, in the first place, he batted under a fake name. And, in the second place, he didn't make a base hit. He popped out.'

"That's about all there is to it. You can ask Art how he picked the kid out for a star from seeing him pop out once. I've asked him myself, and he's told me that he liked the way Waldron swung. Personally, I believe one of those Jackson boys got too gabby. But Art swears not."

"That *is* a story," I said gratefully. "An old outfielder who must know he's slipping recommends a busher after seeing him pop out once. And the busher jumps right in and gets his job."

I looked down the aisle toward the song birds. Art Graham, now a bench warmer, and young Waldron, whom he had touted and who was the cause of his being sent to the bench, were harmonizing at the tops of their strong and not too pleasant voices.

"And probably the strangest part of the story," I added, "is that Art doesn't seem to regret it. He and the kid appear to be the best of friends."

"Anybody who can sing is Art's friend," said Ryan.

I left him and went back to my seat to tear off my seven hundred words before we reached Springfield. I considered for a moment the advisability of asking Graham for an explanation of his wonderful bit of scouting, but decided to save that part of it for another day. I was in a hurry and, besides, Waldron was just teaching them a new "wallop," and it would have been folly for me to interrupt.

"It's on the word 'you,'" Waldron was saying. "I come down a tone; Lefty goes up a half tone, and Bill comes up two tones. Art just sings it like always. Now try her again," I heard him direct the song birds. They tried her again, making a worse noise than ever:

"I only know I love you;
Love me, and the world (the world) is mine (the world is mine)."

"No," said Waldron. "Lefty missed it. If you fellas knew music, I could teach it to you with the piano when we get to Boston. On the word 'love,' in the next to the last line, we hit a regular F chord. Bill's singing the low F in the bass and Lefty's hitting middle C in the baritone, and Art's on high F and I'm up to A. Then, on the word 'you,' I come down to G, and Art hits E, and Lefty goes up half a tone to C sharp, and Cole comes up from F to A in the bass. That makes a good wallop. It's a change from the F chord to the A chord. Now let's try her again," Waldron urged.

They tried her again:

"I only know I love you—"

"No, no!" said young Waldron. "Art and I were all right; but Bill came up too far, and Lefty never moved off that C. Half a tone up, Lefty. Now try her again."

We were an hour late into Springfield, and it was past six o'clock when we pulled out. I had filed my stuff, and when I came back in the car the concert was over for the time, and Art Graham was sitting alone.

"Where are your pals?" I asked.

"Gone to the diner," he replied.

"Aren't you going to eat?"

"No," he said, "I'm savin' up for the steamed clams." I took the seat beside him.

"I sent in a story about you," I said.

"Am I fired?" he asked.

"No, nothing like that."

"Well," he said, "you must be hard up when you can't find nothin' better to write about than a old has-been."

"Cap just told me who it was that found Waldron," said I.

"Oh, that," said Art. "I don't see no story in that."

"I thought it was quite a stunt," I said. "It isn't everybody that can pick out a second Cobb by just seeing him hit a fly ball."

Graham smiled.

"No," he replied, "they's few as smart as that."

"If you ever get through playing ball," I went on, "you oughtn't to have any trouble landing a job. Good scouts don't grow on trees."

"It looks like I'm pretty near through now," said Art, still smiling. "But you won't never catch me scoutin' for nobody. It's too lonesome a job."

I had passed up lunch to retain my seat in the card game; so I was hungry. Moreover, it was evident that Graham was not going to wax garrulous on the subject of his scouting ability. I left him and sought the diner. I found a vacant chair opposite Bill Cole.

"Try the minced ham," he advised, "but lay off'n the sparrow-grass. It's tougher'n a double-header in St. Louis."

"We're over an hour late," I said.

"You'll have to do a hurry-up on your story, won't you?" asked Bill. "Or did you write it already?"

"All written and on the way."

"Well, what did you tell 'em?" he inquired. "Did you tell 'em we had a pleasant trip, and Lenke lost his shirt in the poker game, and I'm goin' to pitch to-morrow, and the Boston club's heard about it and hope it'll rain?"

"No," I said. "I gave them a regular story to-night—about how Graham picked Waldron."

"Who give it to you?"

"Ryan," I told him.

"Then you didn't get the real story," said Cole, "Ryan himself don't know the best part of it, and he ain't goin' to know it for a w'ile. He'll maybe find it out after Art's got the can, but not before. And I hope nothin' like that'll happen for twenty years. When it does happen, I want to be sent along with Art, 'cause I and him's been roomies now since 1911, and I wouldn't hardly know how to act with him off'n the club. He's a nut all right on the singin' stuff, and if he was gone I might get a chanct to give my voice a rest. But he's a pretty good guy, even if he is crazy."

"I'd like to hear the real story," I said.

"Sure you would," he answered, "and I'd like to tell it to you. I will tell it to you if you'll give me your promise not to spill it till Art's gone. Art told it to I and Lefty in the club-house at Cleveland pretty near a month ago, and the three of us and Waldron is the only ones that knows it. I figure I've did pretty well to keep it to myself this long, but it seems like I got to tell somebody."

"You can depend on me," I assured him, "not to say a word about it till Art's in Minneapolis, or wherever they're going to send him."

"I guess I can trust you," said Cole. "But if you cross me, I'll shoot my fast one up there in the press coop some day and knock your teeth loose."

"Shoot," said I.

"Well," said Cole, "I s'pose Ryan told you that Art fell for the kid after just seein' him pop out."

"Yes, and Ryan said he considered it a remarkable piece of scouting."

"It was all o' that. It'd of been remarkable enough if Art'd saw the bird pop out and then recommended him. But he didn't even see him pop out."

"What are you giving me?"

"The fac's," said Bill Cole. "Art not only didn't see him pop out, but he didn't even see him with a ball suit on. He wasn't never inside the Jackson ball park in his life."

"Waldron?"

"No. Art I'm talkin' about."

"Then somebody tipped him off," I said, quickly.

"No, sir. Nobody tipped him off, neither. He went to Jackson and spent the ev'nin' at his uncle's house, and Waldron was there. Him and Art was together the whole ev'nin'. But Art didn't even ask him if he could slide feet first. And then he come back to Detroit and got Ryan to draft him. But to give you the whole story, I'll have to go back a ways. We ain't nowheres near Worcester yet, so they's no hurry, except that Art'll prob'ly be sendin' for me pretty quick to come in and learn Waldron's lost chord.

"You wasn't with this club when we had Mike McCann. But you must of heard of him; outside his pitchin', I mean. He was on the stage a couple o' winters, and he had the swellest tenor voice I ever heard. I never seen no grand opera, but I'll bet this here C'ruso or McCormack or Gadski or none o' them had nothin' on him for a pure tenor. Every note as clear as a bell. You couldn't hardly keep your eyes dry when he'd tear off 'Silver Threads' or 'The River Shannon.'

"Well, when Art was still with the Washin'ton club yet, I and Lefty and Mike used to pal around together and onct or twict we'd hit up some harmony. I couldn't support a fam'ly o' Mormons with my voice, but it was better in them days than it is now. I used to carry the lead, and Lefty'd hit the baritone and Mike the tenor. We didn't have no bass. But most o' the time we let Mike do the singin' alone, 'cause he had us outclassed, and the other boys kept tellin' us to shut up and give 'em a treat. First it'd be 'Silver Threads' and then 'Jerusalem' and then 'My Wild Irish Rose' and this and that, whatever the boys ast him for. Jake Martin used to say he couldn't help a short pair if Mike wasn't singin'.

"Finally Ryan pulled off the trade with Griffith, and Graham come on our club. Then they wasn't no more solo work. They made a bass out o' me, and Art sung the lead, and Mike and Lefty took care o' the tenor and baritone. Art didn't care what the other boys wanted to hear. They could holler their heads off for Mike to sing a solo, but no sooner'd Mike start singin' than Art'd chime in with him and pretty soon we'd all four be goin' it. Art's a nut on singin', but he don't care nothin' about list'nin', not even to a canary. He'd rather harmonize than hit one past the outfielders with two on.

"At first we done all our serenadin' on the train. Art'd get us out o' bed early so's we could be through breakfast and back in the car in time to tear off a few before we got to wherever we was goin'.

"It got so's Art wouldn't leave us alone in the different towns we played at. We couldn't go to no show or nothin.' We had to stick in the hotel and sing, up in our room or Mike's. And then he went so nuts over it that he got Mike to come and room in the same house with him at home, and I and Lefty was supposed to help keep the neighbors awake every night. O' course we had mornin' practice w'ile we was home, and Art used to have us come to the park early and get in a little harmony before we went on the field. But Ryan finally nailed that. He says that when he ordered mornin' practice he meant baseball and not no minstrel show.

"Then Lefty, who wasn't married, goes and gets himself a girl. I met her a couple o' times, and she looked all right. Lefty might of married her if Art'd of left him alone. But nothin' doin'. We was home all through June onct, and instead o' comin' round nights to sing with us, Lefty'd take this here doll to one o' the parks or somewheres. Well, sir, Art was pretty near wild. He scouted round till he'd found out why Lefty'd quit us and then he tried pretty near everybody else on the club to see if they wasn't someone who could hit the baritone. They wasn't nobody. So the next time we went on the road, Art give Lefty a earful about what a sucker a man was to get married, and looks wasn't everything and the girl was prob'ly after Lefty's money and he wasn't bein' a good fella to break up the quartette and spoil our good times, and so on, and kept pesterin' and teasin' Lefty till he give the girl up. I'd of saw Art in the Texas League before I'd of shook a girl to please him, but you know these left-handers.

"Art had it all framed that we was goin' on the stage, the four of us, and he seen a vaudeville man in New York and got us booked for eight hundred a week—I don't know if it was one week or two. But he sprung it on me in September and says we could get solid bookin' from October to March; so I ast him what he thought my Missus would say when I told her I couldn't get enough o' bein' away from home from March to October, so I was figurin' on travelin' the vaudeville circuit the other four or five months and makin' it unanimous? Art says I was tied to a woman's apron and all that stuff, but I give him the cold stare and he had to pass up that dandy little scheme.

"At that, I guess we could of got by on the stage all right, Mike was better than this here Waldron and I hadn't wore my voice out yet on the coachin' line, tellin' the boys to touch all the bases.

"They was about five or six songs that we could kill. 'Adeline' was our star piece. Remember where it comes in, 'Your fair face beams'? Mike used to go away up on 'fair.' Then they was 'The Old Millstream' and 'Put on Your Old Gray Bonnet.' I done some fancy work in that one. Then they was 'Down in Jungle Town' that we had pretty good. And then they was one that maybe you never heard. I don't know the name of it. It run somethin' like this."

Bill sottoed his voice so that I alone could hear the beautiful refrain:

"Years, years, I've waited years
Only to see you, just to call you 'dear.'
Come, come, I love but thee,
Come to your sweetheart's arms; come back to me.'

"That one had a lot o' wallops in it, and we didn't overlook none o' them. The boys used to make us sing it six or seven times a night. But 'Down in the Cornfield' was Art's favor-ight. They was a part in that where I sung the lead down low and the other three done a banjo stunt. Then they was 'Castle on the Nile' and 'Come Back to Erin' and a whole lot more.

"Well, the four of us wasn't hardly ever separated for three years. We was practisin' all the w'ile like as if we was goin' to play the big time, and we never made a nickel off'n it. The only audience we had was the ball players or the people travelin' on the same trains or stoppin' at the same hotels, and they got it all for nothin'. But we had a good time, 'specially Art.

"You know what a pitcher Mike was. He could go in there stone cold and stick ten out o' twelve over that old plate with somethin' on 'em. And he was the willin'est guy in the world. He pitched his own game every third or fourth day, and between them games he was warmin' up all the time to go in for somebody else. In 1911, when we was up in the race for aw'ile he pitched eight games out o' twenty, along in September, and win seven o' them, and besides that, he finished up five o' the twelve he didn't start. We didn't win the pennant, and I've always figured that them three weeks killed Mike.

"Anyway, he wasn't worth nothin' to the club the next year; but they carried him along, hopin' he'd come back and show somethin'. But he was pretty near through, and he knowed it. I knowed it, too, and so did everybody else on the club, only Graham. Art never got wise till the trainin' trip two years ago this last spring. Then he come to me one day.

"'Bill,' he says, 'I don't believe Mike's comin' back.'

"'Well,' I says, 'you're gettin's so's they can't nobody hide nothin' from you. Next thing you'll be findin' out that Sam Crawford can hit.'

"'Never mind the comical stuff,' he says. 'They ain't no joke about this!'

"'No,' I says, 'and I never said they was. They'll look a long w'ile before they find another pitcher like Mike.'

"'Pitcher my foot!' says Art. 'I don't care if they have to pitch the bat boy. But when Mike goes, where'll our quartette be?'

"'Well,' I says, 'do you get paid every first and fifteenth for singin' or for crownin' that old pill?'

"'If you couldn't talk about money, you'd be deaf and dumb,' says Art.

"'But you ain't playin' ball because it's fun, are you?'

"'No,' he says, 'they ain't no fun for me in playin' ball. They's no fun doin' nothin' but harmonizin', and if Mike goes, I won't even have that.'

"'I and you and Lefty can harmonize,' I says.

"'It'd be swell stuff harmonizin' without no tenor,' says Art. 'It'd be like swingin' without no bat.'

"Well, he ast me did I think the club'd carry Mike through another season, and I told him they'd already carried him a year without him bein' no good to them, and I figured if he didn't show somethin' his first time out, they'd ask for waivers. Art kept broodin' and broodin' about it till they wasn't hardly no livin' with him. If he ast me onct he ast me a thousand times if I didn't think they might maybe hold onto Mike another season on account of all he'd did for 'em. I kept tellin' him I didn't think so; but that didn't satisfy him and he finally went to Ryan and ast him point blank.

"'Are you goin' to keep McCann?' Art ast him.

"'If he's goin' to do us any good, I am,' says Ryan. "If he ain't, he'll have to look for another job.'

"After that, all through the trainin' trip, he was right on Mike's heels.

"'How does the old souper feel?' he'd ask him.

"'Great!' Mike'd say.

"Then Art'd watch him warm up, to see if he had anything on the ball.

"'He's comin' fine,' he'd tell me. 'His curve broke to-day just as good as I ever seen it.'

"But that didn't fool me, or it didn't fool Mike neither. He could throw about four hooks and then he was through. And he could of hit you in the head with his fast one and you'd of thought you had a rash.

"One night, just before the season opened up, we was singin' on the train, and when we got through, Mike says:

"'Well, boys, you better be lookin' for another C'ruso.'

"'What are you talkin' about?' says Art.

"'I'm talkin' about myself,' says Mike. 'I'll be up there in Minneapolis this summer, pitchin' onct a week and swappin' stories about the Civil War with Joe Cantillon.'

"'You're crazy,' says Art. 'Your arm's as good as I ever seen it.'

"'Then,' says Mike, 'you must of been playin' blindfolded all these years. This is just between us, 'cause Ryan'll find it out for himself; my arm's rotten, and I can't do nothin' to help it.'

"Then Art got sore as a boil.

"'You're a yellow, quittin' dog,' he says. 'Just because you come round a little slow, you talk about Minneapolis. Why don't you resign off'n the club?'

"'I might just as well,' Mike says, and left us.

"You'd of thought that Art would of gave up then, 'cause when a ball player admits he's slippin', you can bet your last nickel that he's through. Most o' them stalls along and tries to kid themself and everybody else long after they know they're gone. But Art kept talkin' like they was still some hope o' Mike comin' round, and when Ryan told us one night in St. Louis that he was goin' to give Mike his chanct, the next day, Art was as nervous as a bride goin' to get married. I wasn't nervous. I just felt sorry, 'cause I knowed the old boy was hopeless.

"Ryan had told him he was goin' to work if the weather suited him. Well, the day was perfect. So Mike went out to the park along about noon and took Jake with him to warm up. Jake told me afterwards that Mike was throwin', just easy like, from half-past twelve till the rest of us got there. He was tryin' to heat up the old souper and he couldn't of ast for a better break in the weather, but they wasn't enough sunshine in the world to make that old whip crack.

"Well, sir, you'd of thought to see Art that Mike was his son or his brother or somebody and just breakin' into the league. Art wasn't in the outfield practisin' more than two minutes. He come in and stood behind Mike w'ile he was warmin' up and kept tellin' how good he looked, but the only guy he was kiddin' was himself.

"Then the game starts and our club goes in and gets three runs.

"'Pretty soft for you now, Mike,' says Art, on the bench. 'They can't score three off'n you in three years.'

"Say, it's lucky he ever got the side out in the first innin'. Everybody that come up hit one on the pick, but our infield pulled two o' the greatest plays I ever seen and they didn't score. In the second, we got three more, and I thought maybe the old bird was goin' to be lucky enough to scrape through.

"For four or five innin's, he got the grandest support that was ever gave a pitcher; but I'll swear that what he throwed up there didn't have no more on it than September Morning. Every time Art come to the bench, he says to Mike, 'Keep it up, old boy. You got more than you ever had.'

"Well, in the seventh, Mike still had 'em shut out, and we was six runs to the good. Then a couple o' the St. Louis boys hit 'em where they couldn't nobody reach 'em and they was two on and two out. Then somebody got a hold o' one and sent it on a line to the left o' second base. I forgot who it was now; but whoever it was, he was supposed to be a right field hitter, and Art was layin' over the other way for him. Art started with the crack o' the bat, and I never seen a man make a better try for a ball. He had it judged perfect; but Cobb or Speaker or none o' them couldn't of catched it. Art just managed to touch it by stretchin' to the limit. It went on to the fence and everybody come in. They didn't score no more in that innin'.

"Then Art come in from the field and what do you think he tried to pull?

"'I don't know what was the matter with me on that fly ball,' he says. 'I ought to caught it in my pants pocket. But I didn't get started till it was right on top o' me.'

"'You misjudged, it, didn't you?' says Ryan.

"'I certainly did,' says Art without crackin'.

"'Well,' says Ryan, 'I wisht you'd misjudge all o' them that way. I never seen a better play on a ball.'

"So then Art knowed they wasn't no more use trying to alibi the old boy.

"Mike had a turn at bat and when he come back, Ryan ast him how he felt.

"'I guess I can get six more o' them out,' he says.

"Well, they didn't score in the eighth, and when the ninth come Ryan sent I and Lefty out to warm up. We throwed a few w'ile our club was battin'; but when it come St. Louis' last chanct, we was too much interested in the ball game to know if we was throwin' or bakin biscuits.

"The first guy hits a line drive, and somebody jumps a mile in the air and stabs it. The next fella fouled out, and they was only one more to get. And then what do you think come off? Whoever it was hittin' lifted a fly ball to centre field. Art didn't have to move out of his tracks. I've saw him catch a hundred just like it behind his back. But you know what he was thinkin'. He was sayin' to himself, 'If I nail this one, we're li'ble to keep our tenor singer a w'ile longer.' And he dropped it.

"Then they was five base hits that sounded like the fourth o' July, and they come so fast that Ryan didn't have time to send for I or Lefty. Anyway, I guess he thought he might as well leave Mike in there and take it.

"They wasn't no singin' in the clubhouse after that game. I and Lefty always let the others start it. Mike, o' course, didn't feel like no jubilee, and Art was so busy tryin' not to let nobody see him cry that he kept his head clear down in his socks. Finally he beat it for town all alone, and we didn't see nothin' of him till after supper. Then he got us together and we all went up to Mike's room.

"'I want to try this here "Old Girl o' Mine,"'" he says.

"'Better sing our old stuff,' says Mike. 'This looks like the last time.'

"Then Art choked up and it was ten minutes before he could get goin'. We sung everything we knowed, and it was two o'clock in the mornin' before Art had enough. Ryan come in after midnight and set a w'ile listenin', but he didn't chase us to bed. He knowed better'n any of us that it was a farewell. When I and Art was startin' for our room, Art turned to Mike and says:

"'Old boy, I'd of gave every nickel I ever owned to of caught that fly ball.'

"'I know you would,' Mike says, 'and I know what made you drop it. But don't worry about it, 'cause it was just a question o' time, and if I'd of got away with that game, they'd of murdered some o' the infielders next time I started.'

"Mike was sent home the next day, and we didn't see him again. He was shipped to Minneapolis before we got back. And the rest o' the season I might as well of lived in a cemetery w'ile we was on the road. Art was so bad that I thought onct or twict I'd have to change roomies. Onct in a w'ile he'd start hummin' and then he'd break off short and growl at me. He tried out two or three o' the other boys on the club to see if he couldn't find a new tenor singer, but nothin' doin'. One night he made Lefty try the tenor. Well, Lefty's voice is bad enough down low. When he gets up about so high, you think you're in the stockyards.

"And Art had a rotten year in baseball, too. The old boy's still pretty near as good on a fly ball as anybody in the league; but you ought to saw him before his legs begin to give out. He could cover as much ground as

Speaker and he was just as sure. But the year Mike left us, he missed pretty near half as many as he got. He told me one night, he says:

"'Do you know, Bill, I stand out there and pray that nobody'll hit one to me. Every time I see one comin' I think o' that one I dropped for Mike in St. Louis, and then I'm just as li'ble to have it come down on my bean as in my glove.'

"'You're crazy,' I says, 'to let a thing like that make a bum out o' you.'

"But he kept on droppin' fly balls till Ryan was talkin' about settin' him on the bench where it wouldn't hurt nothin' if his nerve give out. But Ryan didn't have nobody else to play out there, so Art held on.

"He come back the next spring—that's a year ago—feelin' more cheerful and like himself than I'd saw him for a long w'ile. And they was a kid named Burton tryin' out for second base that could sing pretty near as good as Mike. It didn't take Art more'n a day to find this out, and every mornin' and night for a few days the four of us would be together, hittin' her up. But the kid didn't have no more idea o' how to play the bag than Charley Chaplin. Art seen in a minute that he couldn't never beat Cragin out of his job, so what does he do but take him out and try and learn him to play the outfield. He wasn't no worse there than at second base; he couldn't of been. But before he'd practised out there three days they was bruises all over his head and shoulders where fly balls had hit him. Well, the kid wasn't with us long enough to see the first exhibition game, and after he'd went, Art was Old Man Grump again.

"'What's the matter with you?' I says to him. 'You was all smiles the day we reported and now you could easy pass for a undertaker.'

"'Well,' he says, 'I had a great winter, singin' all the w'ile. We got a good quartette down home and I never enjoyed myself as much in my life. And I kind o' had a hunch that I was goin' to be lucky and find somebody amongst the bushers that could hit up the old tenor.'

"'Your hunch was right,' I says. 'That Burton kid was as good a tenor as you'd want.'

"'Yes,' he says, 'and my hunch could of played ball just as good as him.'

"Well, sir, if you didn't never room with a corpse, you don't know what a whale of a time I had all last season. About the middle of August he was at his worst.

"'Bill,' he says, 'I'm goin' to leave this old baseball flat on its back if somethin' don't happen. I can't stand these here lonesome nights. I ain't like the rest o' the boys that can go and set all ev'nin' at a pitcher show or hang around them Dutch gardens. I got to be singin' or I am mis'rable.'

"'Go ahead and sing,' says I. 'I'll try and keep the cops back.'

"'No,' he says, 'I don't want to sing alone. I want to harmonize and we can't do that 'cause we ain't got no tenor.'

"I don't know if you'll believe me or not, but sure as we're settin' here he went to Ryan one day in Philly and tried to get him to make a trade for Harper.

"'What do I want him for?' says Ryan.

"'I hear he ain't satisfied,' says Art.

"'I ain't runnin' no ball players' benefit association,' says Ryan and Art had to give it up. But he didn't want Harper on the club for no other reason than because he's a tenor singer!

"And then come that Dee-troit trip, and Art got permission to go to Jackson. He says he intended to drop in at the ball park, but his uncle wanted to borry some money off'n him on a farm, so Art had to drive out and see the farm. Then, that night, this here Waldron was up to call on Art's cousin—a swell doll, Art tells me. And Waldron set down to the py-ana and begin to sing and play. Then it was all off; they wasn't no spoonin' in the parlor that night. Art wouldn't leave the kid get off'n the py-ana stool long enough to even find out if the girl was a blonde or a brunette.

"O' course Art knowed the boy was with the Jackson club as soon as they was interduced 'cause Art's uncle says somethin' about the both o' them bein' ball players, and so on. But Art swears he never thought o' recommendin' him till the kid got up to go home. Then he ast him what position did he play and found out all about him, only o' course Waldron didn't tell him how good he was 'cause he didn't know himself.

"So Art ast him would he like a trial in the big show, and the kid says he would. Then Art says maybe the kid would hear from him, and then Waldron left and Art went to bed, and he says he stayed awake all night plannin' the thing out and wonderin' would he have the nerve to pull it off. You see he thought that if Ryan fell for it, Waldron'd join us as soon as his season was over and then Ryan'd see he wasn't no good; but he'd prob'ly keep him till we was through for the year, and Art could alibi himself some way, say he'd got the wrong name or somethin'. All he wanted, he says, was to have the kid along the last month or six weeks, so's we could harmonize. A nut? I guess not.

"Well, as you know, Waldron got sick and didn't report, and when Art seen him on the train this spring he couldn't hardly believe his eyes. He thought surely the kid would of been canned durin' the winter without no trial.

"Here's another hot one. When we went out the first day for practice, Art takes the kid off in a corner and tries to learn him enough baseball so's he won't show himself up and get sent away somewheres before we had a little benefit from his singin'. Can you imagine that? Tryin' to learn this kid baseball, when he was born with a slidin' pad on.

"You know the rest of it. They wasn't never no question about Waldron makin' good. It's just like everybody says—he's the best natural ball player that's broke in since Cobb. They ain't nothin' he can't do. But it *is* a funny thing that Art's job should be the one he'd get. I spoke about that to Art when he give me the story.

"'Well,' he says, 'I can't expect everything to break right. I figure I'm lucky to of picked a guy that's good enough to hang on. I'm in stronger with Ryan right now, and with the old man, too, than when I was out there playin' every day. Besides, the bench is a pretty good place to watch the game from. And this club won't be shy a tenor singer for nine years.'

"'No,' I says, 'but they'll be shy a lead and a baritone and a bass before I and you and Lefty is much older.

"'What of it?' he says. 'We'll look up old Mike and all go somewhere and live together.'"

We were nearing Worcester. Bill Cole and I arose from our table and started back toward our car. In the first vestibule we encountered Buck, the trainer.

"Mr. Graham's been lookin' all over for you, Mr. Cole," he said.

"I've been rehearsin' my part," said Bill.

We found Art Graham, Lefty and young Waldron in Art's seat. The kid was talking.

"Lefty missed it again. If you fellas knew music, I could teach it to you on the piano when we get to Boston. Lefty, on the word 'love,' in the next to the last line, you're on middle C. Then, on the word 'you,' you slide up half a tone. That'd ought to be a snap, but you don't get it. I'm on high A and come down to G and Bill's on low F and comes up to A. Art just sings the regular two notes, F and E. It's a change from the F chord to the A chord. It makes a dandy wallop and it ought to be a —"

"Here's Bill now," interrupted Lefty, as he caught sight of Cole.

Art Graham treated his roommate to a cold stare.

"Where the h—l have you been?" he said angrily.

"Lookin' for the lost chord," said Bill.

"Set down here and learn this," growled Art. "We won't never get it if we don't work."

"Yes, let's tackle her again," said Waldron. "Bill comes up two full tones, from F to A. Lefty goes up half a tone, Art sings just like always, and I come down a tone. Now try her again."

Two years ago it was that Bill Cole told me that story. Two weeks ago Art Graham boarded the evening train on one of the many roads that lead to Minneapolis.

The day Art was let out, I cornered Ryan in the club-house after the others had dressed and gone home.

"Did you ever know," I asked, "that Art recommended Waldron without having seen him in a ball suit?"

"I told you long ago how Art picked Waldron," he said.

"Yes," said I, "but you didn't have the right story."

So I gave it to him.

"You newspaper fellas," he said when I had done, "are the biggest suckers in the world. Now I've never given you a bad steer in my life. But you don't believe what I tell you and you go and fall for one of Bill Cole's hop dreams. Don't you know that he was the biggest liar in baseball? He'd tell you that Walter Johnson was Jack's father if he thought he could get away with it. And that bunk he gave you about Waldron. Does it sound reasonable?"

"Just as reasonable," I replied, "as the stuff about Art's grabbing him after seeing him pop out."

"I don't claim he did," said Ryan. "That's what Art told me. One of those Jackson ball players could give you the real truth, only of course he wouldn't because if Hodges ever found it out he'd shoot him full of holes. Art Graham's no fool. He isn't touting ball players because they can sing tenor or alto or anything else."

Nevertheless, I believe Bill Cole; else I wouldn't print the story. And Ryan would believe, too, if he weren't in such a mood these days that he disagrees with everybody. For in spite of Waldron's wonderful work, and he is at his best right now, the club hasn't done nearly as well as when Art and Bill and Lefty were still with us.

There seems to be a lack of harmony.

The topic here involves father and son hunting ducks, but the theme deals more with family relationships and coping with tragedy. Paul Horgan (1903–1995) twice won the Pulitzer Prize, in 1955 for Great River, *a two-volume history of the Rio Grande, and in 1976 for* Lamy of Santa Fe, *a biography. Altogether, Horgan wrote 47 books, including 17 novels and four volumes of short stories. This story was originally published under the title "Terror at Daybreak" in the* Saturday Evening Post.

Paul Horgan

THE HUNTSMEN (1949)

EAST OF TOWN ABOUT A DOZEN miles ran the river. To a place near its edge before dawn on Saturday came Mr. Pollock and his younger son, Madison, accompanied by their dog, Punch. It was a cold morning in autumn. The boy was hardly awake yet. His father had to nudge him to climb out of the car when they stopped in a clump of rust-brown salt cedar at the end of the sandy road Mr. Pollock knew about. For years it had brought him from the paved highway and through the low dunes of sand and clay to his favorite spot for duck hunting.

Madison left the car, carrying his own new shotgun. Over his bony little shoulder was slung his canvas bag for shells. As they moved forward to walk beside the river to the blind, the father did not have to tell Madison to be as quiet as possible. He merely gave by example a lesson in the caution and delicacy of how to move when there were surely ducks out on the river. Punch, an elderly rat-tailed spaniel, went heavily but silently on the sand, pausing at intervals to be sure the others were following. As they came between two huge clumps of salt cedar that rattled in the faint cold wind before daylight, Mr. Pollock halted and held his freezing fist by his ear. The gesture said, "Listen!" Madison turned his head and held his breath.

Then, yes, how could his father ever have heard it, it was so faint, but now he could hear it too—the reedy, murmurous sound of ducks disturbed and talking over there, out of sight under the high carved clay banks of the red Pecos River earth.

The boy's heart began to pound. He loved his father for this experience. They stood shivering in the graying dark until there was no more sleepy music from the hidden water. Then they walked carefully up the river, keeping away from the bank until Mr. Pollock found the shallow dirt canyon which led to his favorite blind. The bank rose before them a little, making a small peninsula screened at the edge by a spare rank of young willows. Here was the place. They knelt down and allowed the day to come. It was now not far off.

Though nobody knew it, Mr. Pollock came for this as much as for anything else. In the spectacle of the natural world he found his poetry, his music, his art gallery. This was his culture, and what it meant to him he had no way to tell, except through example, for the benefit of his sons. All his feelings were buried, anyhow. He was a short, heavy man who walked leaning backward, to carry his weight evenly. He was a director of the local bank and the manager of a building and loan association. During business hours he was a leading citizen of Main Street. Many people felt about him as they would about a doctor, for he knew and helped with serious problems in their families which had to do with the possession and safety of their homes. His large light eyes saw everything and betrayed nothing. His mouth was small in his big face, and he said little, but when he spoke, he was believed.

Wherever the town showed its mind or strength, you'd see a Pollock. If Mr. Pollock would sit on platforms as a silent endorsement of civic desires or ambitions, his wife was likely to be one of the speakers. Her voice was loud and harsh, somehow inappropriate to her small size; but everyone was always impressed as she struggled to bend the public will to her personal belief. She governed her family in much the same way, overwhelming them with her anxious vitality, which was a happy joke among them all until in some issue she yielded to the tears that always seemed to lie in waiting behind her pinch-nose eyeglasses. But she was as apt to weep for happiness and her good fortune in such a kind, sober husband and in two such wonderful boys, as she was out of "nerves."

The parents embraced so completely their station in middle life that it was hard to imagine either of them as ever having been boy and girl. Especially was this impossible for their sons to do. It was as though Mr. and Mrs. Pollock had ceded to their sons all graces of person and fiber, and were content to lose those beauties which had once served their mindless purpose in the founding of the family.

Edwin was eighteen, his brother Madison twelve. Both were already taller than their parents, and far more communicative than the father. Give either of the boys something to take part in, and, according to their ages, they would fling themselves into it, and pretty soon end up in charge of it. Edwin was a great local athlete. He was also an honor man in high-school studies. Boys and girls alike admired him as a terrible cynic, and the yearbook in his senior year said that if you ever wanted a shock, just ask Edwin Pollock for his honest opinion of anything. But it added that he always grinned when he gave it, which accounted for all the "broken hearts" he left scattered around him. So tribute was already paid in pathetic and heartfelt ways to Edwin's powers of comeliness, strength and warmth in life. He was a junior public figure in the small city, and was loved most of all because he never seemed to know it.

Now, before going to college, he was taking a year to learn the value of a dollar—his father's favorite words—by selling farm-implement machinery up and down the Pecos valley, which lay fertile and prosperous in the wilderness of dry plains all around, graced by the far-distant lift and loom of the southernmost Rocky Mountains.

Madison Pollock at twelve had the energy and the laughable daring of a half-grown cat. Of all the Pollocks, he was the funniest and the most high-spirited. He loved to show off, knowing exactly how to make people delight in his antics. He, too, was a good student, and he had a few pygmy enemies because he seemed to have been born with all the books in his head, for he never studied, or said he didn't. He probably didn't. He was the only blond Pollock. His eyes were dark blue, his cheeks a furious dusky pink, and his whole self, no matter what he did, seemed always to look dry and clean.

The last member of the Pollock family was Punch, the spaniel, who was an actual character because they had all put their characters into him ever since his puppydom. Now, in his privileged later life, Punch was a leading citizen of the alleys of town, and with his mornings to himself, he made his daily tour of inspection and gluttony along the backyards of countless friends. They would hear him coming, with his collar chain and tags tinkling, and would know that this day, like all the others, would pursue its reassuring course, under the great sky whose light, beating upon houses, and streets, and plains, and the long river, could show everything except what the future would bring.

Waiting for daylight by the river, Mr. Pollock and Madison shivered companionably. Behind them rose the river's eastern bluffs in cold shadow. But they could see the edge of the skyline now, outlined by a faint lift of pearly light. As still as the rest of the river world, they waited. But they waited in growing excitement, for over and about them proceeded the immense arrival of day. The light gained behind them, and turned to the color of embers, and in the dome of the sky came a smoky blue, and then the western sky showed a pale rose against which the curved shadow of the sleeping earth swept a dying image. Little clouds that were lost in the dark now came to show like wisps of flame in the east. What was that now, on the endless western horizon? The rosy light came down, dispelling the blue earth shadow, and struck the tips of the mountains which so remotely faced the coming sun.

It suddenly seemed colder. Madison hugged himself around his gun. The grand vision before them arose in their spirits, too, and their faces were open with the wonder and promise of this splendor. All this was what Mr. Pollock meant and said nothing about. His greatest moment was still to come, and nothing must destroy it.

Down the distant mountains crept the growing light, until soon there was a blade of golden light cutting across the whole plain at the mountain base, and behind the escarpment to the east blazed visible rays of glory as the sun showed itself at last, tearing the long quiet horizon clouds into silken rags of fire.

Just then the air was filled from everywhere with sound as startling as the vision which grew and grew and spilled over the world. Up from the black lazy water rose the birds in salute to the sunrise. Their calls made a chorus that veered and varied like the wind. They wheeled and shuttered, stirring like a strike of life itself, and went off to taste the sky.

Madison was half standing in the big commotion of all nature. His empty gun was raised. His father reached up and pulled him down again. "They'll come back and settle down," he said in his mild, grainy voice, "if we keep still."

Madison subsided. He swallowed. As thoughtlessly as a duck, he himself had saluted the day, out of an excitement older than memory, and a recognition of glory as near as his impassive father.

The light was now drawing eastward across the plans. Farmhouses began to show, little cubicles poured with gold. Trees stood plain. Green fields of winter wheat looked out of the receding twilight. In a few moments there would be no mystery, no startling grandeur, but only daytime, and a forgotten sun climbing overhead showing, common, the red rocks of the cliffs, the endless sweep of the plains, the smoke-defined town, and the mountains with their faint hovering clouds.

The ducks returned. Madison saw them before he heard them, little twinkling specks of black that moved together against the dove-wing colors of the northern sky. Then came their sound again, from everywhere, as though a cloud could be heard.

Mr. Pollock nodded and silently thrust two shells into his gun and then closed it. Madison copied him, watching his father now, instead of the flight. Punch quivered, his nose lifted to the sky.

Mr. Pollock gave Madison a half look and raised his gun in a trial sight. Then he indicated that if the birds flew over them and started to settle on the river beyond the willows, they would shoot.

Here they came, growing specks along the silver reflection of the gun barrels. The air drummed. All sound vanished and only sight was left, tense, as the guns made their arcs with the circle and swift descent of the ducks. Then, by a common power of agreement, they both fired. The shots broke the whole adventure in stunning strike, and dawn, and boy, and father, and sky life, and river world blazed into an instant of ringing silence.

The flight struck upward again and were gone beyond speed. But two fell, and they saw them, and they knew where.

Madison jumped to his feet. He was charged with love for the birds he had helped to kill. All huntsmen from before his own small lifetime stirred in him. His teeth chattered with mindless power and memory. But his father showed him in silent example how to break his gun and lay it for safety's sake on the ground, and lovingly, because of its exciting oily smell, its sweet smooth wood, its power of compressed dominion over living things. With a hand on Punch, Mr. Pollock led the way through the willows to the shallow water and beyond, where their game lay on the long mudbank in midstream.

Madison's belly felt full to bursting with joy. He wished his brother Edwin could see him now. He wanted to be like Edwin in every way—his body, his style, his mind and his famous cynicism. He felt like Edwin right now, and as he walked he spread his legs somewhat as Edwin did, and made a rather hard-boiled expression on his face. This was more like it. None of that childish excitement. Madison did his best to seem offhand; the master of his gun, and of his power to kill, and provide.

Later they moved downstream. They had chances to shoot three more times before Mr. Pollock said that they'd better think about getting back, as he intended to be at his office by ten o'clock, where there was other quarry to size up and bring to terms. He had his canvas pouch pockets full of birds, whose inert weight bumped against his stride with the majestic bother of all trophies.

Madison carried three ducks by hand. There was still enough baby in him to want to hold them forever, just as they were, just as he had made them, with their tiny head and neck feathering of green and blue fire, their stripes of white, black and brown, their leathery bills, their dear death. Punch was allowed to carry one bird in his important jaws. He almost pranced in slow dignity as they returned down the river to the hidden car. All three of them felt the same feelings.

Mr. Pollock unlocked the car and opened the back door on the left side. The back seat was covered by heavy brown wrapping paper—Mrs. Pollock's contribution to the good sense and economy of the expedition. There they put down their bleeding ducks.

This was about nine o'clock. There were no mysteries left in the day. True, it was running a little colder, for low gray clouds were unfolding from the east. But everything stood clear and simple, so far just like another day.

"Mad, you take the guns and put them in the car," said Mr. Pollock. "I counted one more duck that we knocked down last time. I'll take Punch and go back and find him. You wait here."

Madison hadn't seen another duck fall. But one thing that was never done was to question the father—aloud anyhow. He took Mr. Pollock's gun, which was left open at the break, and empty of shells. He saw the man and the dog trudge off. He went around the car to the other side and opened the front door. There he hurriedly put the two shotguns on the seat, side by side, making the same angle with their open chambers and barrels, muzzles outward. He shut the door on them with a vague feeling of forgetting something, but it seemed more desirable at the moment to get around to the other side of the car in a hurry, in order to watch Mr. Pollock and Punch as they rattled and cracked through the tall reeds up the river. There were a few pauses, while the father would halt and reconstruct the angles of flight, sight, fire and fall. Then the search would continue. Finally Punch gave out his wheezing bark, at the very instant Madison was saying to himself, *They'll never find it, because there isn't one.*

As the retrievers walked patiently back toward the car, Punch carried in his proudly lifted jaws one more dead duck.

Well, sure enough.

But Mr. Pollock was short about his triumph. He had a good eye, a faithful sense of numbers, and a lifelong principle of collecting what was due to him. He simply trusted these faculties. Impervious to compliments, he took the duck from Punch, and leaning somewhat backward, walked heavily around the car to the right side and opened the front door to see where the shotguns were.

So it was that everybody else came to find out where Madison had put the guns, and how. Madison's gun was released by the opening of the car door, and slid along the mohair covering of the seat toward the floor of the car. It struck with force. The breech closed as the butt thumped on the floor, and what Madison had half forgotten then took effect. He had not removed the shells from his gun. The impact of the gunstock on the floor jarred the gun sharply. One barrel fired.

Madison was right there, for he had come around the car to watch, and finally to take his place on the front seat.

That flash of color and sound—what did it do—go off?

The duck fell from Mr. Pollock's hand. It trailed a trifle of slimy blood on the dried mud earth. Mr. Pollock bent forward and made a long agonized sound of groan on the word, "Oh-h-h," and fell down, bleeding, too, slowly, until he was humped leaning against the car with his arms around his middle, his head forced back and his eyes closing from the lower lids up, slowly, shutting out the light of the sky and the mind, both.

He was alone with his younger son and his weight of authority now passed to the boy. Madison, as if he were being watched by a host of

416

people, pursed his lips and pinched them with his fingers, and said, nearly aloud, "Now let's see."

But his heart was banging with sick hurry in him, and choking him in the throat. He wanted to talk to his father, but his father was gone, for the time being—he could see that—and he was afraid to reach him, for he knew whose fault it was that Mr. Pollock lay there like something else.

He knelt down and put his arms under Mr. Pollock's shoulders, thinking to lift him into the car. He could not budge him.

Plans occurred to him. Perhaps if he waited a little while, Mr. Pollock would wake up refreshed, and they would get into the car and go back to town, and he and Edwin would clean the ducks in the backyard, and Mom would cook them, with an apple and an onion inside each one. Or perhaps Dr. Dave Sessions would come by here duck hunting, and operate at once, with the heroic assistance of young Madison Pollock.

Or perhaps he, too, would simply die. He closed his eyes to feel how this would be. When he opened them again, he was crying and fully aware of what he had done.

As reality returned to him, he saw what he must do. He managed inch by inch to move his father down to earth from the side of the car. Mr. Pollock was breathing wetly. He seemed to shake his head blindly at Madison as the boy moved him. Now the car was free.

Madison put Punch on guard. The dog looked hungrily after the boy, but stayed where he was meant to be, beside his still master. Madison got into the car, and remembered the few times he had stolen rides alone in it, against every law of the household: no boy of twelve should be allowed to drive, think what could happen—and all the rest of Mrs. Pollock's timeless obedience to the whimpering gods of worry.

He pinched his lips and again said, "Now let's see," as he rehearsed the technique of driving. He started the engine, put the gear into reverse and let the clutch go, but too suddenly. The car leaped backward and then stopped, the engine stalled with too much gas. He started over again, this time swinging in a wide arc to turn around and head for the highway over the dunes. Just before he drove forward, Madison glanced back fearfully to see if perhaps his father would sharply call to him, asking, "Where do you think you're going with that car? You know you are not supposed to drive it."

But there was no such threat, and he whined along in second gear, swaying with the lift and boggle of the car over the uneven road. On the back seat, the inert necks and heads of the dead ducks rolled from side to side in little arcs. Mrs. Pollock's brown paper was moist and stained in places.

When he reached the highway, he stopped the car just off the paving on the shoulder of the road. He sat there, numb, for a little while, as three or four cars went flashing by.

What would he have to say if he stopped someone? How could he ever say it? He hoped nobody would stop.

He looked both ways. The highway was now empty as far as he could see. His heart fell with pity and relief, even as he licked his dry mouth in a panic of disgust over his great betrayal.

But here came a car, way up at the crest of the cliff, where, in a deep cut, the highway took its course across the great wilderness which led to West Texas and beyond. The car came fast down the long slope toward the bridge.

Inviting his own doom, Madison got out and stepped into the near lane. Long before he could see the driver he began to wave his arms. He ended by leaping off the ground a few times.

The driver began to slacken his speed, and when he saw that this was a boy, he slammed on the brakes. Something told him before he stopped that here was bad trouble, which spoke so powerfully through that young, jumping figure alone in that big spread of country. The boy did not come to him, so he left his own car and walked back to find young Madison Pollock, with his teeth chattering and his right arm pointing off up the river and trying to tell.

"What's it, son?" asked the driver. He was Tim Motherwell, of the Soil Conservation Service. He squatted down before Madison and began to chew on a match, not looking at him, but musing in his presence as though they were two men with all the time in the world to decide or exchange something important. He had noticed blood on the boy's field jacket. What might have put it there he was already imagining, when Madison managed to tell him what lay up the sandy road by the river.

Tim nodded mildly, but he lost no time. He pulled his weathered green government pickup truck well off the highway and returned to Mr. Pollock's car. He drove Madison back up the river.

As they went, Madison tried to tell him how it had happened. "I did it," he kept repeating.

"We'll see," Tim replied, and wondered, like so many people in the next few days, what could ever reclaim this boy from this morning.

Madison was awry in every possible way. His thick yellow hair was tangled and upright. His face was white, but square patches of dusky-peach red tried to show on his cheekbones. His eyes were wild. He kept trying to put his hands on his round young thighs in composure, but they would not stay there, and would spring up in the air as though moved by counterweights.

In a moment they came to a halt and got out of the car. Punch was there, trembling with fear and strangeness, and stood up to greet them with a high, stifled yawp, but did not leave his post. They came forward and Tim bent down. Almost at once he saw that the father was dead.

They got to town as soon as they could manage, and in ten minutes the news was everywhere.

If people did not say it aloud, they spoke plainly with their eyes. "Oh, that poor boy! He will never get over this!"

In everybody's face, Madison read, "That is the boy who killed his father," and somehow in those who looked at him or talked about him, awe was mingled with pity, and guilt with forgiveness.

After the three days—the rest of Saturday, all day Sunday, until Monday afternoon, when the funeral was held—Madison Pollock was in danger. Edwin knew it. The boy's teeth would chatter suddenly. By turns he longed to be with his mother, and could not bear facing her. "My baby," she would sob, smothering him with crushing sympathy. And then again she would have hours during which she would exile him in silent grief and widowhood. He was afraid most of all that Edwin would not like him anymore. He spent hours awake at night breaking his will on terrible schemes to make everything up to everybody. But an imp of maturity abided in him, and told him how useless were these waking dreams. He must shrink even from them.

Tuesday morning he did not want to go back to school, giving as his reason that someone had let the air out of his bicycle tires. Edwin went to see, and it was true. The brothers looked at each other, both knowing who had done it. They did not discuss it. Instead, Edwin drove Madison over to school in the car, but he could not make him get out of the car and fall in with the tumbling boys who played touch football on the play-field.

"One of these days, you know, Mad," said Edwin, meaning that he'd have to start school again sooner or later.

Madison shook his head. "Never. I can't."

"Why not?"

Madison shrugged. He didn't know.

"How about trying, say just the first period?" asked Edwin. "I'll promise to be here when the bell rings after the first period, and if you still want to then, I'll let you out of it."

Madison shook his head.

"Well, then, what do you want to do?"

"Nothing."

The brothers sat in silence, staring straight ahead through the windshield while Edwin played a little jazzy tune on his teeth with his thumbnail. A couple of boys spotted the car and ran over to get Madison, calling his name. Madison crouched down and said hoarsely, "Come on, come on. Let's go, let's go."

Edwin drove off.

Without further discussion, Edwin simply let Maddy stay with him that day as he went on his business calls down the valley. This made an idle and drowsy day for Madison, and when it was over, and they were home for supper, he was ready to go to bed early.

It was barely half past seven when someone drifted with heavily shod steps up on the wooden porch and knocked once or twice on the beveled plate-glass pane of the front door. Edwin put on the porch light and could see through the white net curtain inside the glass that a familiar figure stood there, slowly spinning his fawn-colored felt hat on his forefinger. It was Tim Motherwell, offhand and mild.

He came in and shook hands, saying that he just happened to be driving up this street, and thought of looking in for a second, to see if there was anything he could do, and to tell Mrs. Pollock that he certainly felt for her. At this, she raised her head with a hazy social smile, as though to say that people like her should not inflict their misfortunes upon others, but the imposture lasted only a moment before her little face with its passionately trembling eye lenses appeared to dissolve like molten glass, and she lay back in her chair, subject to the grief that pounded upon her from without.

Edwin asked Tim to sit down, which he declined to do. In a minute or two, Mrs. Pollock recovered enough to ask Edwin to show Tim the messages of sympathy they had received, and the long list of those who had sent flowers. Tim examined these gravely, while the widow watched him hungrily for signs of dolorous pride in the tribute paid to the stricken family. Tim read what people said about Mr. Pollock, and gave the papers back to Edwin without a word, but with a black sparkling look in his eyes which was like thought itself made manifest. Mrs. Pollock covered her face and wept again. Edwin felt ashamed of her, and then, for feeling so, ashamed of himself.

Well, he had to be going, said Tim. Edwin went out to the pickup truck with him, and the real purpose of the call became clear. They talked for about fifteen minutes, Tim at the wheel, Edwin leaning his chin on his fists on the open windowsill of the car. Their conversation was muted and serious. Tim felt younger, Edwin felt older, and both felt like good men, assembled in honor of what needed to be done for someone—in this case, Madison Pollock.

Edwin said, yes, his brother was in a bad way, and said something had to be worked out. Tim said he suspected as much, and with modesty and diffidence told what he would do about it if it were his kid brother.

When the essential matter was finished, there was a long terminal pause, after which Tim, where he sat, jumped comically, as though he felt an electric shock, and said, "I'd better get a move on or my little woman won't act so little, time I get there. See you, Ed."

"See you, Tim. Sure do thank you."

Tim switched on his car lights and drove off. Edwin watched him round the next corner. The red taillight on the truck spoke for Tim as long as Edwin could see it, admire it and covet the goodly strength it stood for.

The next morning, Mrs. Pollock, in the name of what Dad would have wanted, declared that this time Madison must go to school, and ordered Edwin to drive him there again.

Madison turned white. "No, I can't."

"Yes, you can. Oh, what have I done to deserve— You know how your father slaved to give you boys a good education, and now, here you sit, and won't—" Her brokenhearted righteousness welled up in her, more powerful than grief itself, and she crushed the boys with the very same love which had given them being.

Madison left the table and went to the backyard. There he was violently sick at his stomach. Edwin found him there, shuddering on the back steps like a starving cat.

"Come on, Maddy," he said, and practically dragged the boy to the car. They drove off, heading south toward the school. Madison set his jaws and braced his feet against the floorboards the closer they came to the red brick school building, but Edwin, without a glance, drove right on past and continued on south and out of town down the valley.

"I'd gain his confidence," Tim had said. "I wouldn't hurry."

So once again—this time defying the suffering authority at home— Edwin took his brother with him, and did the same all the rest of the week. They visited farms in the broad flat valley, and while Edwin talked business, Madison was let alone just to fool around. They spent one afternoon tinkering with an ailing tractor. One evening they lingered with a little crowd of itinerant cotton pickers who had a bonfire going under some cottonwoods by an irrigation ditch; and to guitar music, clapped hands and country song, the illimitable twilight came down like forgiveness over Madison and everyone in the world. Sometimes Edwin took him along to have a glass of beer, though Mad drank only soda. Another time they called on a girl Edwin knew in the little town of Dexter, and the conversation, full of evocative memories and half-suggested plans, brought Madison a wondering sense of more trouble, sweeter than his awful kind.

And then on Saturday—one week after Madison's first time out hunting—Edwin, having made a few preparations in private, got up at four in the morning and went in his shivering nakedness to Maddy's sleeping porch and woke him up. "Come on, get up," he said.

Madison was stunned with sleep. "What for?"

"Never mind what for. I've got your clothes. We can dress in the living room, where it's warm. Be quiet. Don't wake Mom."

The boy followed his brother. In the front room they got dressed stealthily. It was exciting. "Where're we going?"

"Never you mind. Come on. We'll get breakfast downtown."

Edwin was dressed first. Waiting for Maddy, he sat down at the dining-room table, and wrote a note which Mrs. Pollock told everybody later she would keep forever.

"Dear Mom," it said, "don't worry. Mad and I have gone off on a job. Back during the day. Taking Punch along for the buggy ride. Be a good girl and don't worry. Love and kisses, E."

He propped it up against the crystal fruit bowl in the center of the table, where she would easily find it. He knew that when she came to his fond, impudent advice to be a good girl, she, in whom there remained no degree of girl whatever, would weep over it with famished pride, to see that the power of the family had passed to him, the firstborn, now escaped into his own life. It was not cruel to make her weep. It was almost a kindness, for in these days it gave her solace to feel anything but the main dream of her shocking loss.

The boys went gently out the front door, and around to the backyard to Punch's house, which they had built together so long ago. He knew them now as they approached, and mildly banged his ugly rattail on the floor of his residence.

"Come on, Punch, old boy," said Edwin softly. The self-important old dog got up slowly and stretched himself, first fore and then aft. And then with a prankish lunge he assumed the gaiety of a puppy, but could not sustain it, and soberly followed his masters to their car, which was parked in the alley. Edwin unlocked it, they all got in, and Edwin drove off. The night was black and empty in the cold streets of town.

They had coffee, canned orange juice and ham and eggs in Charlie the Greek's, without conversation, though not without communication, for Edwin could feel Maddy throbbing beside him with doubtful wonder. Edwin once turned on his swivel stool to face Madison and cuff him near the ear—an action which said that he was not to worry, or be afraid, or in doubt, for this was still the family, doing its best for him, no matter how things might look.

It was still pitch dark when they drove off again and headed out toward the east, where the road forked to go either down the valley or out to the river. Madison looked sidewise to question his brother. Edwin, though he felt the look, did not acknowledge it, but merely drove on in general confidence and repose.

At the crossroads they were slowed down by a traffic light which blinked all night long. Madison looked to the right, along the highway which would take them on one of their familiar days of salesmanship at the valley farms. But Edwin, resuming high gear, drove straight ahead on the other highway, which led to the river. Maddy's teeth began to chatter.

The first pale strips of day now showed ahead of them in the east. Suddenly, it was there. With it came a colder feeling. Edwin speeded up as though to race the dawn.

Where were they going? Maddy put his hand on the door handle beside him with an unformed motion that he might open the door and, speed or no speed, get out right now. Why not? Edwin caught this out of the corner of his eye in the half-light of the instrument panel. He began to whistle a little tune inside his teeth, leaned over and snapped the door handle up to a locked position.

By the time they saw the river, its slow sparse waters were reflecting the faint early light in the midst of heavy shade over the earth. Maddy, in terror, both did and did not believe it when the family car slowed down at the far end of the Pecos River bridge and took the sandy turnoff of the road that ran over the dunes, in the same darkness, by the same willows, in the same cold, to the same screen of salt cedars as a week ago this morning.

Edwin stopped the car and got out. He opened the rear door for Punch, who scrambled forth with his head lifted amid the marshy smells on the faintly stirring air. At the luggage compartment, Edwin unlocked the handle and flung open the lid. He took out two shotguns, a canvas bag full of shells, and two pairs of rubber boots.

"Come on, Mad!" he called.

The front door opened and Madison stepped out, against his wish.

Edwin threw Maddy's boots to him. "Put them on."

"What for?"

"Put them on."

Maddy was overwhelmed. He was numb, inside and out. He put the boots on.

Edwin handed him his own gun.

"No."

"Take it. Go on. We're going to get some ducks."

Madison took it. He could hardly feel it in his grasp.

Edwin led the way up the river to the blind where, long ago, he too, had first come with his father. The day was nearing. Again, sky, mountain, plain and earth's own curve evolved toward the moment of glory and revelation.

Once again not only all light but all sound and all space beat upon the senses when the sun rose. The ducks were there again. They fled the shadows and streaked noisily into the lofty light. Like his father, Edwin stayed their fire at the dawn flight. The birds would return. To be ready—

"Load," said Edwin.

Madison fumbled with his gun. He could not handle it. Edwin took it from him and loaded it, closed it, which cocked it, and handed it back. "You take the first one, Mad."

They waited. The older brother set his jaws. He knew what he was doing, and the pain he was causing.

Presently the birds were coming over again. Edwin pointed. Madison
saw only a dazzle of flying black specks in the yellowing day.

"Now," whispered Edwin.

Madison raised his gun and tried to sight, leading the flight, which
seemed everywhere. He was shaking. He fired alone. Nothing fell. He
brought down his gun. His head was ringing. He looked at Edwin.

"Tough," said Edwin.

Madison thrust his gun at Edwin for him to take. "Let me go," he said
in pitiful modesty.

Edwin shook his head and pushed the gun back in his brother's grasp.
"You'll do better next time."

"I will?"

"Sure."

Edwin, whistling silently, turned his gaze over the sky.

What? thought Madison. And this was astounding: powerfully like a
wind, free and lofting, the idea blew through him, and he thought, *Of
course I will.*

He looked at Edwin to find an explanation of the excitement which
spread so fast in his being. But Edwin was immovable, watching the
lower reaches of the sky.

"I will get some next time," whispered Madison. "I got three last Saturday, and I'll get more today."

Edwin nodded briefly. His heart began to thump with relief. He could
never have said so, but Edwin knew they had come here to put death in
its place, and were going to succeed.

Sherwood Anderson (1876–1941) began his writing career after serving in the Spanish-American War and working as a copywriter. He is famous for Winesburg, Ohio *(1919)*, a collection of tales about small-town America. Anderson also wrote poetry, essays, and novels, including A Storyteller's Story *(1924)*, Dark Laughter *(1925)*, and Tar, A Midwest Childhood *(1926)*. *"I'm a Fool"* is a masterpiece of short fiction, in which a dramatic monologue about horse racing scenes reveals the character of the narrator.

Sherwood Anderson

I'M A FOOL (1923)

IT WAS A HARD JOLT TO ME, one of the most bitterest I ever had to face. And it all came about through my own foolishness, too. Even yet, sometimes, when I think of it I want to cry or swear or kick myself. Perhaps, even now, after all this time, there will be a kind of satisfaction in making myself look cheap by telling of it.

It began at three o'clock one October afternoon as I sat in the grandstand at the fall trotting and pacing meet at Sandusky, Ohio.

To tell the truth, I felt a little foolish that I should be sitting in the grandstand at all. During the summer before, I had left my home town with Harry Whitehead and, with a nigger named Burt, had taken a job as swipe with one of the two horses Harry was campaigning through the fall race meets that year. Mother cried and my sister Mildred, who wanted to get a job as a schoolteacher in our town that fall, stormed and scolded about the house all during the week before I left. They both thought it something disgraceful that one of our family should take a place as a swipe with race horses. I've an idea Mildred thought my taking the place would stand in the way of her getting the job she'd been working so long for.

But after all, I had to work, and there was no other work to be got. A big lumbering fellow of nineteen couldn't just hang around the house and I had got too big to mow people's lawns and sell newspapers. Little chaps who could get next to people's sympathies by their sizes were always getting jobs away from me. There was one fellow who kept saying to everyone who wanted a lawn mowed or a cistern cleaned that he was saving money to work his way through college, and I used to lay awake nights thinking up ways to injure him without being found out. I kept thinking of wagons running over him and bricks falling on his head as he walked along the street. But never mind him.

I got the place with Harry and I liked Burt fine. We got along splendid together. He was a big nigger with a lazy sprawling body and soft, kind eyes, and when it came to a fight he could hit like Jack Johnson. He had Bucephalus, a big black pacing stallion that could do 2:09 or 2:10, if he had to, and I had a little gelding named Doctor Fritz that never lost a race all fall when Harry wanted him to win.

We set out from home late in July in a boxcar with the two horses and after that, until late November, we kept moving along to the race meets and the fairs. It was a peachy time for me, I'll say that. Sometimes now I think that boys who are raised regular in houses, and never had a fine nigger like Burt for best friend, and go to high schools and college, and never steal anything, or get drunk a little, or learn to swear from fellows who know how, or come walking up in front of a grandstand in their shirt sleeves and with dirty horsey pants on when the races are going on and the grandstand is full of people all dressed up— What's the use of talking about it? Such fellows don't know nothing at all. They've never had no opportunity.

But I did. Burt taught me how to rub down a horse and put the bandages on after a race and steam a horse out and a lot of valuable things for any man to know. He could wrap a bandage on a horse's leg so smooth that if it had been the same color you would think it was his skin, and I guess he'd have been a big driver, too, and to the top like Murphy and Walter Cox and the others, if he hadn't been black.

Gee whizz, it was fun. You got to a county seat town, maybe say on Saturday or Sunday, and the fair began the next Tuesday and lasted until Friday afternoon. Doctor Fritz would be, say, in the 2:25 trot on Tuesday afternoon and on Thursday afternoon Bucephalus would knock 'em cold in the free-for-all pace. It left you a lot of time to hang around and listen to horse talk, and see Burt knock some yap cold that got too gay, and you'd find out about horses and men and pick up a lot of stuff you could use all the rest of your life, if you had some sense and salted down what you heard and felt and saw.

And then at the end of the week when the race meet was over, and Harry had run home to tend up to his livery stable business, you and Burt hitched the two horses to carts and drove slow and steady across country, to the place for the next meeting, so as to not overheat the horses, etc., etc., you know.

Gee whizz, Gosh amighty, the nice hickory nut and beechnut and oaks and other kinds of trees along the roads, all brown and red, and the good smells, and Burt singing a song that was called "Deep River," and the country girls at the windows of houses and everything. You can stick your colleges up your nose for all me. I guess I know where I got my education.

Why, one of those little burgs of towns you come to on the way, say now on a Saturday afternoon, and Burt says, "Let's lay up here." And you did.

And you took the horses to a livery stable and fed them, and you got your good clothes out of a box and put them on.

And the town was full of farmers gaping, because they could see you were race horse people, and the kids maybe never see a nigger before and was afraid and run away when the two of us walked down their main street.

And that was before Prohibition, and all that foolishness, and so you went into a saloon, the two of you, and all of the yaps come and stood around, and there was always someone pretended he was horsey and knew things and spoke up and began asking questions, and all you did was to lie and lie all you could about what horses you had, and I said I owned them, and then some fellow said, "Will you have a drink of whisky?" and Burt knocked his eye out the way he could say, off-hand like, "Oh, well, all right, I'm agreeable to a little nip. I'll split a quart with you." Gee whizz.

But that isn't what I want to tell my story about. We got home late in November and I promised Mother I'd quit the race horses for good. There's a lot of things you've got to promise a mother, because she don't know any better.

And so, there not being any work in our town any more than when I left there to go to the races, I went off to Sandusky and got a pretty good place taking care of horses for a man who owned a teaming and delivery and storage and coal and real estate business there. It was a pretty good place with good eats, and a day off each week, and sleeping on a cot in a big barn, and mostly just shoveling in hay and oats to a lot of big good-enough skates of horses, that couldn't have trotted a race with a toad. I wasn't dissatisfied and I could send money home.

And then, as I started to tell you, the fall races come to Sandusky and I got the day off and I went. I left the job at noon and had on my good clothes and my new brown derby hat I'd just bought the Saturday before, and a stand-up collar.

First of all I went downtown and walked about with the dudes. I've always thought to myself, Put up a good front, and so I did it. I had forty dollars in my pocket and so I went into the West House, a big hotel, and walked up to the cigar stand. "Give me three twenty-five-cent cigars," I said. There was a lot of horsemen and strangers and dressed-up people from other towns standing around in the lobby and in the bar, and I mingled amongst them. In the bar there was a fellow with a cane and a Windsor tie on, that it made me sick to look at him. I like a man to be a man and dress up, but not to go put on that kind of airs. So I pushed him aside, kind of rough, and had me a drink of whisky. And then he looked at me as though he thought maybe he'd get gay, but he changed his mind and didn't say anything. And then I had another drink of whisky, just to show him something, and went out and had a hack out to the races, all to myself, and when I got there I bought myself the best seat I could get up in the grandstand, but didn't go in for any of these boxes. That's putting on too many airs.

And so there I was, sitting up in the grandstand as gay as you please and looking down on the swipes coming out with their horses, and with their dirty horsey pants on and the horse blankets swung over their shoulders, same as I had been doing all the year before. I liked one thing about the same as the other, sitting up there and feeling grand and being down there and looking up at the yaps and feeling grander and more important, too. One thing's about as good as another, if you take it just right. I've often said that.

Well, right in front of me, in the grandstand that day, there was a fellow with a couple of girls and they was about my age. The young fellow was a nice guy all right. He was the kind maybe that goes to college and then comes to be a lawyer or maybe a newspaper editor or something like that, but he wasn't stuck on himself. There are some of that kind are all right and he was one of the ones.

He had his sister with him and another girl, and the sister looked around over his shoulder, accidental at first, not intending to start anything—she wasn't that kind—and her eyes and mine happened to meet.

You know how it is. Gee, she was a peach! She had on a soft dress, kind of a blue stuff and it looked carelessly made, but was well sewed and made and everything. I knew that much. I blushed when she looked right at me and so did she. She was the nicest girl I've ever seen in my life. She wasn't stuck on herself and she could talk proper grammar without being like a schoolteacher or something like that. What I mean is, she was

O.K. I think maybe her father was well-to-do, but not rich to make her chesty because she was his daughter, as some are. Maybe he owned a drugstore or a drygoods store in their home town, or something like that. She never told me and I never asked.

My own people are all O.K. too, when you come to that. My grandfather was Welsh and over in the old country, in Wales, he was— But never mind that.

The first heat of the first race came off and the young fellow setting there with the two girls left them and went down to make a bet. I knew what he was up to, but he didn't talk big and noisy and let everyone around know he was a sport, as some do. He wasn't that kind. Well, he come back and I heard him tell the two girls what horse he'd bet on, and when the heat was trotted they all half got to their feet and acted in the excited, sweaty way people do when they've got money down on a race, and the horse they bet on is up there pretty close at the end, and they think maybe he'll come on with a rush, but he never does because he hasn't got the old juice in him, come right down to it.

And then, pretty soon, the horses came out for the 2:18 pace and there was a horse in it I knew. He was a horse Bob French had in his string but Bob didn't own him. He was a horse owned by a Mr. Mathers down at Marietta, Ohio.

This Mr. Mathers had a lot of money and owned some coal mines or something, and he had a swell place out in the country, and he was stuck on race horses, but was a Presbyterian or something, and I think more than likely his wife was one, too, maybe a stiffer one than himself. So he never raced his horses hisself, and the story round the Ohio race tracks was that when one of his horses got ready to go to the races he turned him over to Bob French and pretended to his wife he was sold.

So Bob had the horses and he did pretty much as he pleased, and you can't blame Bob, at least I never did. Sometimes he was out to win and sometimes he wasn't. I never cared much about that when I was swiping a horse. What I did want to know was that my horse had the speed and could go out in front, if you wanted him to.

And, as I'm telling you, there was Bob in this race with one of Mr. Mathers' horses, was named "About Ben Ahem" or something like that, and was fast as a streak. He was a gelding and had a mark of 2:21, but could step in :08 or :09.

Because when Burt and I were out, as I've told you, the year before, there was a nigger Burt knew, worked for Mr. Mathers, and we went out there one day when we didn't have no race on at the Marietta Fair and our boss Harry was gone home.

And so everyone was gone to the fair but just this one nigger and he took us all through Mr. Mathers' swell house and he and Burt tapped a bottle of wine Mr. Mathers had hid in his bedroom, back in a closet, without his wife knowing, and he showed us this Ahem horse. Burt was always stuck on being a driver but didn't have much chance to get to the top, being a nigger, and he and the other nigger gulped that whole bottle of wine and Burt got a little lit up.

So the nigger let Burt take this About Ben Ahem and step him a mile in a track Mr. Mathers had all to himself, right there on the farm. And Mr. Mathers had one child, a daughter, kinda sick and not very good-looking, and she came home and we had to hustle and get About Ben Ahem stuck back in the barn.

I'm only telling you to get everything straight. At Sandusky, that afternoon I was at the fair, this young fellow with the two girls was fussed, being with the girls and losing his bet. You know how a fellow is that way. One of them was his girl and the other his sister. I had figured that out.

"Gee whizz," I says to myself, "I'm going to give him the dope."

He was mighty nice when I touched him on the shoulder. He and the girls were nice to me right from the start and clear to the end. I'm not blaming them.

And so he leaned back and I give him the dope on About Ben Ahem. "Don't bet a cent on his first heat because he'll go like an oxen hitched to a plow, but when the first heat is over go right down and lay on your pile." That's what I told him.

Well, I never saw a fellow treat anyone sweller. There was a fat man sit-

ting beside the little girl, that had looked at me twice by this time, and I
at her, and both blushing, and what did he do but have the nerve to turn
and ask the fat man to get up and change places with me so I could set
with this crowd.

Gee whizz, craps amighty. There I was. What a chump I was to go and
get gay up there in the West House bar, and just because that dude was
standing there with a cane and that kind of a necktie on, to go and get
all balled up and drink that whisky, just to show off.

Of course she would know, me setting right beside her and letting her
smell of my breath. I could have kicked myself right down out of that
grandstand and all around that race track and made a faster record than
most of the skates of horses they had there that year.

Because that girl wasn't any mutt of a girl. What wouldn't I have give
right then for a stick of chewing gum to chew, or a lozenger, or some
liquorice, or most anything. I was glad I had those twenty-five-cent cigars in my pocket and right away I give that fellow one and lit one myself.
Then that fat man got up and we changed places and there I was, plunked
right down beside her.

They introduced themselves and the fellow's best girl, he had with
him, was named Miss Elinor Woodbury, and her father was a manufac-
turer of barrels from a place called Tiffin, Ohio. And the fellow himself
was named Wilbur Wessen and his sister was Miss Lucy Wessen.

I suppose it was their having such swell names got me off my trolley.
A fellow, just because he has been a swipe with a race horse, and works
taking care of horses for a man in the teaming, delivery and storage business, isn't any better or worse than anyone else. I've often thought that,
and said it too.

But you know how a fellow is. There's something in that kind of nice
clothes, and the kind of nice eyes she had, and the way she had looked
at me, awhile before, over her brother's shoulder, and me looking back
at her, and both of us blushing.

I couldn't show her up for a boob, could I?

I made a fool of myself, that's what I did. I said my name was Walter
Mathers from Marietta, Ohio, and then I told all three of them the

smashingest lie you ever heard. What I said was that my father owned the horse About Ben Ahem and that he had let him out to this Bob French for racing purposes, because of our family was proud and had never gone into racing that way, in our own name, I mean. Then I had got started and they were all leaning over and listening, and Miss Lucy Wessen's eyes were shining, and I went the whole hog.

I told about our place down at Marietta, and about the big stables and the grand brick house we had on a hill, up above the Ohio River, but I knew enough not to do it in no bragging way. What I did was to start things and then let them drag the rest out of me. I acted just as reluctant to tell as I could. Our family hasn't got any barrel factory, and since I've known us, we've always been pretty poor, but not asking anything of any one at that, and my grandfather, over in Wales—but never mind that.

We set there talking like we had known each other for years and years, and I went and told them that my father had been expecting maybe this Bob French wasn't on the square, and had sent me up to Sandusky on the sly to find out what I could.

And I bluffed it through I had found out all about the 2:18 pace, in which About Ben Ahem was to start.

I said he would lose the first heat by pacing like a lame cow and then he would come back and skin 'em alive after that. And to back up what I said I took thirty dollars out of my pocket and handed it to Mr. Wilbur Wessen and asked him, would he mind, after the first heat, to go down and place it on About Ben Ahem for whatever odds he could get. What I said was that I didn't want Bob French to see me and none of the swipes.

Sure enough the first heat come off and About Ben Ahem went off his stride, up the back stretch, and looked like a wooden horse or a sick one, and come in to be last. Then this Wilbur Wessen went down to the betting place under the grandstand and there I was with the two girls, and when that Miss Woodbury was looking the other way once, Lucy Wessen kinda, with her shoulder you know, kinda touched me. Not just tucking down, I don't mean. You know how a woman can do. They get close, but not getting gay either. You know what they do. Gee whizz.

And then they give me a jolt. What they had done, when I didn't know, was to get together, and they had decided Wilbur Wessen would bet fifty dollars, and the two girls had gone and put in ten dollars each, of their own money, too. I was sick then, but I was sicker later.

About the gelding, About Ben Ahem, and their winning their money, I wasn't worried a lot about that. It come out O.K. Ahem stepped the next three heats like a bushel of spoiled eggs going to market before they could be found out, and Wilbur Wessen had got nine to two for the money. There was something else eating at me.

Because Wilbur come back, after he had bet the money, and after that he spent most of his time talking to that Miss Woodbury, and Lucy Wessen and I was left alone together like on a desert island. Gee, if I'd only been on the square or if there had been any way of getting myself on the square. There ain't any Walter Mathers, like I said to her and them, and there hasn't ever been one, but if there was, I bet I'd go to Marietta, Ohio, and shoot him tomorrow.

There I was, big boob that I am. Pretty soon the race was over, and Wilbur had gone down and collected our money, and we had a hack downtown, and he stood us a swell supper at the West House, and a bottle of champagne beside.

And I was with that girl and she wasn't saying much, and I wasn't saying much either. One thing I know. She wasn't stuck on me because of the lie about my father being rich and all that. There's a way you know. . . . Craps amighty. There's a kind of girl, you see just once in your life, and if you don't get busy and make hay, then you're gone for good and all, and might as well go jump off a bridge. They give you a look from inside of them somewhere, and it ain't no vamping, and what it means is—you want that girl to be your wife, and you want nice things around her like flowers and swell clothes, and you want her to have the kids you're going to have, and you want good music played and no ragtime. Gee whizz.

There's a place over near Sandusky, across a kind of bay, and it's called Cedar Point. And after we had supper we went over to it in a launch, all by ourselves. Wilbur and Miss Lucy and that Miss Woodbury had to catch a ten-o'clock train back to Tiffin, Ohio, because, when you're out with girls like that you can't get careless and miss any trains and stay out all night, like you can with some kinds of Janes.

And Wilbur blowed himself to the launch and it cost him fifteen cold plunks, but I wouldn't never have knew if I hadn't listened. He wasn't no tinhorn kind of a sport.

Over at the Cedar Point place, we didn't stay around where there was a gang of common kind of cattle at all.

There was big dance halls and dining places for yaps, and there was a beach you could walk along and get where it was dark, and we went there.

She didn't talk hardly at all and neither did I, and I was thinking how glad I was my mother was all right, and always made us kids learn to eat with a fork at table, and not swill soup, and not be noisy and rough like a gang you see around a race track that way.

Then Wilbur and his girl went away up the beach and Lucy and I sat down in a dark place, where there was some roots of old trees, the water had washed up, and after that time, till we had to go back in the launch and they had to catch their trains, wasn't nothing at all. It went like winking your eye.

Here's how it was. The place we were setting in was dark, like I said, and there was the roots from that old stump sticking up like arms, and there was a watery smell, and the night was like—as if you could put your hand out and feel it—so warm and soft and dark and sweet like an orange.

I most cried and I most swore and I most jumped up and danced, I was so mad and happy and sad.

When Wilbur come back from being alone with his girl, and she saw him coming, Lucy she says, "We got to go to the train now," and she was most crying too, but she never knew nothing I knew, and she couldn't be so all busted up. And then, before Wilbur and Miss Woodbury got up to where we was, she put her face up and kissed me quick and put her head up against me and she was all quivering and— Gee whizz.

Sometimes I hope I have cancer and die. I guess you know what I mean. We went in the launch across the bay to the train like that, and it was dark, too. She whispered and said it was like she and I could get out of the boat and walk on the water, and it sounded foolish, but I knew what she meant.

And then quick we were right at the depot, and there was a big gang of yaps, the kind that goes to the fairs, and crowded and milling around like cattle, and how could I tell her? "It won't be long because you'll write and I'll write to you." That's all she said.

I got a chance like a hay barn afire. A swell chance I got.

And maybe she would write me, down at Marietta that way, and the letter would come back, and stamped on the front of it by the U.S.A. "there ain't any such guy," or something like that, whatever they stamp on a letter that way.

And me trying to pass myself off for a bigbug and a swell—to her, as decent a little body as God ever made. Craps amighty—a swell chance I got!

And then the train come in, and she got on it, and Wilbur Wessen he come and shook hands with me, and that Miss Woodbury was nice too and bowed to me, and I at her, and the train went and I busted out and cried like a kid.

Gee, I could have run after that train and made Dan Patch look like a freight train after a wreck but, socks amighty, what was the use? Did you ever see such a fool?

I'll bet you what—if I had an arm broke right now or a train had run over my foot—I wouldn't go to no doctor at all. I'd go set down and let her hurt and hurt—that's what I'd do.

I'll bet you what—if I hadn't a drunk that booze I'd a never been such a boob as to go tell such a lie—that couldn't never be made straight to a lady like her.

I wish I had that fellow right here that had on a Windsor tie and carried a cane. I'd smash him for fair. Gosh darn his eyes. He's a big fool—that's what he is.

And if I'm not another, you just go find me one and I'll quit working and be a bum and give him my job. I don't care nothing for working, and earning money, and saving it for no such boob as myself.

PERMISSIONS ACKNOWLEDGMENTS

Irwin Shaw, "Mixed Doubles," originally published in *The New Yorker*, August 9, 1947. Reprinted with permission. © Irwin Shaw. All rights reserved.

Rudyard Kipling, "The Maltese Cat," originally published in 1895 and reprinted in *The Day's Work* by Rudyard Kipling.

Richard Ford, "Winterkill," originally published in *Esquire*, November 1983. From *Rock Springs: Stories*, © 1987 by Richard Ford. Used by permission of Grove/Atlantic, Inc.

James Buechler, "John Sobieski Runs," originally published in *Saturday Evening Post*, October 10, 1964.

Frank Harris, "Montes: The Matador," originally published in 1891. From *The Short Stories of Frank Harris*, 1975.

George Allan England, "Ping-Pong," originally published in *All-Story Weekly*, September, 28, 1918.

P. G. Wodehouse, "The Letter of the Law," originally published in 1924.

L. J. Amster, "Center of Gravity," originally published in *Saturday Evening Post*, 1964.

Agatha Christie, "A Chess Problem," from *The Big Four*, 1927, Dodd, Mead and Co., publisher.

Gordon Weaver, "Hog's Heart." Copyright © 1979 by the Antioch Review, Inc. First appeared in the *Antioch Review*, Vol. 37, No. 1. Reprinted with permission of the editors.

Alexander Pushkin, "The Queen of Spades." Copyright 1901 by the Current Literature Publishing Company, translation by H. Twitchell.

Peter LaSalle, "Van Arsdale's Pond," from Peter LaSalle, *Hockey sur Glace*, 1996. Reprinted by permission of Breakaway Books, Halcottsville, New York. (800) 548-4348, *www.breakawaybooks.com*.

Ring Lardner, "Harmony," from *Round Up*, Charles Scribner's Sons, 1924.

Paul Horgan, "The Huntsmen," originally published in 1949 as "Terror at Daybreak," in *Saturday Evening Post*. From *The Peach Stone: Stories from Four Decades*, by Paul Horgan. Copyright © 1967 by Paul Horgan. Copyright renewed 1995 by Thomas B. Catron III. Reprinted by permission of Farrar, Straus and Giroux, LLC.

Sherwood Anderson, "I'm a Fool," from Sherwood Anderson, *Horses and Men*, 1922, and reprinted in *Sherwood Anderson: Short Stories*, 1962.